# ACCLAIM FOR BILLY COFFEY

"In the first line of the book, Coffey's hillbilly narrator invites his accidental guest (that would be us, the readers) to 'come on out of that sun' and set a spell. The spell is immediate. We are altogether bewitched by the teller, by his lyrical telling, and by the tale itself, whose darkness is infernal . . . Everything is at stake in this battle between good and evil—including the identity of the narrator, revealed at last. To Christians and non-Christians alike, this roaring tale will leave a powerful mark."

—*BOOKPAGE* ON *THE CURSE OF CROW HOLLOW*

"Coffey spins a wicked tale . . . [*The Curse of Crow Hollow*] blends folklore, superstition, and subconscious dread in the vein of Shirley Jackson's 'The Lottery.'"

—*KIRKUS REVIEWS*

"An edge-of-your-seat, don't-read-in-the-dark book with amazing characters . . . Coffey takes readers on a wild roller-coaster ride without ever going over the top."

—*RT BOOK REVIEWS*, 4 ½ STARS, TOP PICK! ON *THE CURSE OF CROW HOLLOW*

"Conjures a sense of genteel Southern charm . . . this creepy tale will delight enthusiasts of Tosca Lee's *Demon* and other horror stories."

—*LIBRARY JOURNAL* ON *THE CURSE OF CROW HOLLOW*

"With lyrical writing and a rich narrative voice, Billy Coffey effortlessly weaves a coming-of-age story into a suspenseful, page-turning novel. *In the Heart of the Dark Wood* is a beautiful journey that takes the reader down a road filled with Southern gothic characters and settings; perfectly balanced with redemption and triumph of the human spirit. Allie is a courageous character that is sure to capture any reader's heart. *In the Heart of the Dark Wood* is not to be missed."

—MICHAEL MORRIS, AUTHOR OF *SLOW WAY HOME* AND *MAN IN THE BLUE MOON*

"Coffey pens a coming-of-age story about the tribulations of the heart that is profoundly believable. The dialogues between characters are intensely rewarding to follow, and readers will anticipate the danger ahead; they will not pull away from the novel until it is finished. Suspense and mysteries of spirit make for a winning combination for any reader."

—*RT BOOK REVIEWS*, 4 1/2 STARS, ON *IN THE HEART OF THE DARK WOOD*

"*The Devil Walks in Mattingly* . . . recalls Flannery O'Conner with its glimpses of the grotesque and supernatural."

—*BOOKPAGE*

"[*The Devil Walks in Mattingly* is] a story that will hold your attention until the last page."

—JESSICA STRINGER, *SOUTHERN LIVING*

"Billy Coffey is one of the most lyrical writers of our time. His latest work, *The Devil Walks in Mattingly*, is not a page-turner to be devoured in a one-night frenzy. Instead, it should be valued as a literary delicacy, with each savory syllable sipped slowly. By allowing ourselves to steep in this story, readers are treated to a delightful sensory escape one delicious word at a time. Even then, we leave his imaginary world hungry for more, eager for another serving of Coffey's tremendous talent."

—JULIE CANTRELL, *NEW YORK TIMES* AND *USA TODAY* BESTSELLING AUTHOR OF *INTO THE FREE* AND *WHEN MOUNTAINS MOVE*

"Coffey (*When Mockingbirds Sing*) has a profound sense of Southern spirituality. His narrative moves the reader from Jake and Kate's false heaven to a terrible hell, then back again to a glorious grace."

—PUBLISHERS WEEKLY ON THE DEVIL WALKS IN MATTINGLY

"[A]n inspirational and atmospheric tale."

—LIBRARY JOURNAL, STARRED REVIEW OF WHEN MOCKINGBIRDS SING

"This intriguing read challenges mainstream religious ideas of how God might be revealed to both the devout and the doubtful."

—PUBLISHERS WEEKLY REVIEW OF WHEN MOCKINGBIRDS SING

"Readers will appreciate how slim the line is between belief and unbelief, faith and fiction, and love and hate as supplied through this telling story of the human heart always in need of rescue."

—CBA RETAILERS + RESOURCES REVIEW
OF WHEN MOCKINGBIRDS SING

"Billy Coffey is a minstrel who writes with intense depth of feeling and vibrant, rich description. The characters who live in this book face challenges that stretch the deepest fabric of their beings. You will remember *When Mockingbirds Sing* long after you finish it."

—ROBERT WHITLOW, BESTSELLING AUTHOR OF THE CHOICE

"*When Mockingbirds Sing* by Billy Coffey made me realize how often we think we know how God works, when in reality we don't have a clue. God's ways are so much more mysterious than we can imagine. Billy Coffey is an author we're going to be hearing more about. I'll be looking for his next book!"

—COLLEEN COBLE, USA TODAY BESTSELLING AUTHOR OF
THE INN AT OCEAN'S EDGE AND THE HOPE BEACH SERIES

# THERE
# WILL BE
# STARS

# OTHER NOVELS BY BILLY COFFEY

# THERE
# WILL BE
# STARS

\* \* \*

Billy Coffey

THOMAS NELSON
Since 1798

Published in Nashville, Tennessee, by Thomas Nelson. Thomas Nelson is a registered trademark of HarperCollins Christian Publishing, Inc.

Published in association with Books & Such Literary Management, 52 Mission Circle, Suite 122, PMB 170, Santa Rosa, California, 95409–5370, www.booksandsuch.com.

Thomas Nelson titles may be purchased in bulk for educational, business, fund-raising, or sales promotional use. For information, please e-mail SpecialMarkets@ThomasNelson.com.

Scripture quotations are taken from the King James Version and the New American Standard Bible®. Copyright © 1960, 1962, 1963, 1968, 1971, 1972, 1973, 1975, 1977, 1995 by The Lockman Foundation. Used by permission. (www.Lockman.org)

Publisher's Note: This novel is a work of fiction. Names, characters, places, and incidents are either products of the author's imagination or used fictitiously. All characters are fictional, and any similarity to people living or dead is purely coincidental.

### Library of Congress Cataloging-in-Publication Data

Names: Coffey, Billy, author.
Title: There will be stars / Billy Coffey.
Description: Nashville: Thomas Nelson, 2016.
Identifiers: LCCN 2015044775 | ISBN 9780718026820 (paperback)
Subjects: LCSH: Future life--Fiction. | Death--Fiction. | GSAFD: Christian
   fiction.
Classification: LCC PS3603.O3165 T48 2016 | DDC 813/.6--dc23 LC record
   available at http://lccn.loc.gov/2015044775

*Printed in the United States of America*

16 17 18 19 20 RRD 5 4 3 2 1

For Mom

# Publisher's Note

Billy Coffey's novels are all set in Mattingly, Virginia, and can be read in any order. If you've read previous Mattingly books, you may be interested in knowing that *There Will Be Stars* takes place a few years after *In the Heart of the Dark Wood*, in which Zach and Allie were lost in the woods.

Enjoy!

*In the world it is called Tolerance, but in hell it is called Despair . . . the sin that believes in nothing, cares for nothing, seeks to know nothing, interferes with nothing, enjoys nothing, hates nothing, finds purpose in nothing, lives for nothing, and remains alive because there is nothing for which it will die.*

—Dorothy Sayers

# Part I

# Heaven

## -1-

Sometimes, if he was not so drunk or the twins so loud, Bobby Barnes would consider how those rides to the mountain had become an echo of his life. Night would fill the gaps between the trees with a black so thick and hard the world itself seemed to end beyond the headlights' reach. No future. No past. Only the illusion of this single moment, stretched taut and endless. He loved the lonely feeling, the nothingness, even if the road upon which he sought escape from town was the very road that would return him to it. All living was a circle. Something of Bobby had come to understand that, though its truth remained a mystery too deep for his heart to plumb. Life was a circle and the road a loop, and both flowed but seldom forward. They instead wound back upon themselves, the past leaching into the present and the present shrouding the future, reminding him that all could flee from their troubles, but only toward and never away.

One of the boys said something. Matthew or Mark, Bobby couldn't tell. The pale orange light off the radio made the twins appear even more identical, just as the music made them sound even more the same. Carbon copies, those boys. When they'd been born—back when Carla still wore her wedding ring and the only future she and Bobby envisioned was one they would face together—Bobby had joked they would have to write the boys' names on the bottoms of their feet to tell them apart. Now Matthew and Mark were eight. Still the same, but only on the outside.

The other boy joined in, something about a movie or a cartoon, Bobby couldn't hear. The deejay had put on "Highway to Hell" and Mark asked Bobby to turn that up, he liked it, though not enough to keep from fighting with his brother. He felt the seat move as one twin shouldered the other, heard the sharp battle cry of "Stupid!" Bobby pursed his lips and said nothing. Being a good father involved knowing when to step in and when to let things ride. He relaxed his grip on the wheel and gulped the beer in his hand.

Night whisked by as the truck climbed the high road above town, the engine purring. No vehicle in Mattingly ran so fine as Bobby Barnes's old Dodge. Let the town speak what lies they wished, no one could deny that truth. He eased his foot down on the gas, felt the growl beneath him and the smile creeping over his face. His ears popped, followed by the come-and-gone sound of a lone cricket. The headlights caught flashes of reds and yellows on the October trees and the glowing eyes of deer along the road, standing like silent monsters in the dark.

"Tell'm, Daddy," Matthew said beside him. "He's so stupid."

"Am not," Mark yelled. "*You're* stupid. You're *double* stupid."

Another shove, maybe a slap, Bobby couldn't know. He

did know if things got out of hand and one of those boys spilled his beer, he'd have to get the belt out when they got home.

"Ain't nobody stupid," he said. "Matthew, you got what you think, Mark's got what he does. Don't mean either one's right or wrong. That's called an opinion. Y'all know what opinions are like?"

"Butts," Mark said.

"'Cause everybody's got one," said Matthew.

Both snickered. Bobby toasted his parental wisdom with another swallow. He finished the can and tossed it through the open slot in the window behind them, where it rattled against the other empties in the bed. The sound echoed back and mixed with the boys' laughter and the guitar solo over the radio, Angus Young hammering on the ax as Bobby's eyes widened against a heaviness that fell over him, a chill that formed a straight line from the middle of his forehead to his nonexistent gut, settling in the bottoms of his feet. It was as if he had been struck by some pale lightning, pulled apart and pieced back together in the same breath.

"Whatsa matter, Daddy?" Matthew asked.

Bobby reached for the last of the six-pack on the dash. "Dunno," he said. "Think a rabbit run over my grave. Like you get a funny feeling? Like you done before what you're doing now."

"That's 'cause we take a ride every night," Matthew said.

"Ain't that. *Know* that. 'Member this morning when we was going out to Timmy's and we seen Laura Beth sashaying like she always does down the walk? 'Member I whistled to her and said I knew she'd be there?"

Mark said, "You always whistle at Laura Beth."

"I'll have you know I ain't never whistled to Laura Beth Gowdy before in my life, boy. Why'd I ever wanna do such a thing? Little Miss Priss. Been that way since high school."

3

He took a sip. "Didn't whistle 'cause she's comely, I whistled because I *knew*. Felt that rabbit and I *knew*. Like Jake? I knew he'd be at Timmy's, too, wanting one a his words. And that woman preacher."

"You said you bet she'd be outside the church," Mark said, "but she weren't."

"No, but I said Andy would be pushing a broom when we went to get gas."

"Mr. Sommerville *always* pushing a broom," Matthew said.

"But Junior ain't always been there. And I *knew* he would be. Remember? And your mom called this afternoon."

Mark rolled down the window and let his hand play with the cool mountain air. "Momma's way finer than Laura Beth Gowdy. Daddy? Laura Beth paints her hair. Momma's looks like that on purpose."

That sense (Bobby couldn't name it, something besides a rabbit, French or what he sometimes called Hi-talian) had left the soles of his feet. The worse feeling of his son's stare took its place. He kept his eyes to the road. He'd never say so out loud and risk hurting Mark's feelings, but sometimes the boy got to him. Mark could nudge his daddy in directions best not traveled.

"Your momma found somebody else to love on her, for what grief that cost us all and what good that does her now. Pondering Carla's fineness does me no good service."

For a while there were only the sounds of the big tires and the songs crackling over the radio, the classic rock station out of Stanley. Bobby felt the truck drift past the center line and corrected. Matthew leaned his head against his daddy's shoulder, drifting to sleep. Mark hummed along with Axl Rose about patience. Bobby fell into old thoughts of things lost that could never be gained again.

"Maybe we should get up here and go Camden way," he said. "All these rabbits could mean Lady Luck's on my side. Could go up to that 7-and-Eleven, get us a scratcher. What y'all say?"

Mark looked Bobby's way. "You won't."

\* \* \*

Ahead loomed a T in the road, a marker that read 237 and an arrow pointing right and left just ahead of the stop sign. Bobby intended to roll right through—few traveled those mountaintops in the night, which was why he chose that road to ride with his sons—but then he felt his foot pressing harder on the brake. A chill rushed through him again. The truck stopped along a line of newer pavement and the cracked asphalt of what everyone in Mattingly called the Ridge Road.

He looked down and saw the left blinker winking. Left, on through the mountains and then down again, back to the valley and the shop.

His hands, though, gripped the wheel as if to turn right for Camden.

Matthew's head was still pressed against Bobby's shoulder. "'Nother rabbit get you, Daddy?"

Bobby reached for a beer not there. "Guess it did."

Mark stuck a skinny arm through his window and pointed. "Let's go this-a-way," he said. "Daddy? Let's get us a scratcher."

Bobby opened his mouth to say sure and heard himself say, "Guess we won't. Can't be wasting money on fanciful wishes. Ain't like old Laura Beth Gowdy's husband is calling up saying he's gotta build onto the bank 'cause of all the money I got there. We'll just take our ride."

Mark's finger still pointed. "You said that last time."

Bobby chuckled—he always did when he didn't understand a word Mark said—and turned left. Farther into the mountains, higher, higher, because up here it was the three of them and no one else, no one to call Bobby "pervert" and "drunk" and "rooned." Because up here in the dark of road and forest, Bobby Barnes possessed all the world he needed.

He turned left as Mark's pallid face kept toward the empty stretch of road to Camden and brake lights flashed far ahead. Bobby leaned forward, wondering if those were from a car or from the six-pack he'd drunk since leaving the shop.

"Ain't nobody should be up here."

Matthew yawned. "We up here, Daddy."

The radio popped and hissed and then went clear as the truck crested the ridge. Barren trees let in a view of the valleys below—Mattingly's few lights on one side, Stanley's crowded ones on the other.

"I love this song," Matthew said. "Crank it, Daddy."

Bobby didn't. A war had broken out inside him, one part sloshing from the beer and the other bearing up under that heavy feeling once more. Two parts becoming a whole. He fixed his eyes ahead, where that flicker of lights had been, and wondered who that could be and why he felt like him and the boys were no longer on a ride. He let off the gas and fumbled with the radio dial.

Matthew began to sing, a pale imitation of John Fogerty's voice, a bad moon a-rising and trouble on the way.

The car ahead. Brake lights disappearing around the sharp S in the road. Matthew singing, his voice high, almost warning that they shouldn't go around tonight because it's bound to take their lives, that bad moon on the rise. Mark saying something Bobby couldn't hear.

The truck thundered forward as though pulled by an

unseen force toward the curve in the road, and now that feeling again, that French word Bobby couldn't remember, seizing him. He took the middle part of the S and found empty road on the other side. Matthew strummed at a guitar that existed only in his mind. The moon shone down over the broken outline of the trees. Shadows danced through dying leaves. Bobby looked at Mark and smiled. He winked even if he thought Mark couldn't see, because Mark Barnes might be too smart for his own good but he was Bobby's boy and so was Matthew, and Bobby would be nothing without them.

The truck took the bottom part of the curve. Bobby opened his mouth. "It's—" was all that came out. The rest became swallowed by the terror on Mark's face.

Matthew screamed.

Bobby turned to headlights in front of them. He stood up on the brake, mashing it to the floor, but time was all that slowed. The truck continued on. He heard the sharp screech of tires locking and felt the waving motion of the back end loosing. One arm shot out for Matthew's chest, but Bobby had nothing to hold Mark in place. His youngest (youngest by thirty seconds) doubled in on himself. Mark flew in a soundless gasp: one leg pinwheeling out of the open window, a bit of thick brown hair standing on end, the fingers of a tiny hand. And those headlights, blinding him and blinding Matthew, glimmering off the unbuckled seat belt none of them ever used.

Metal scraped metal, a crunching that folded the truck's hood like a wave. Matthew floated toward the windshield. Bobby felt himself thrown forward. He lamented that of all the things he needed to say, his last word had been so meaningless. And in his last moment, Bobby understood that he had been in this place times beyond counting and would be here again uncountable times still. He heard glass shatter and felt the steering wheel press into his chest. He heard himself scream and scream again. There was pain and loss and a fear beyond all he had ever known, and as blackness deep and unending took him, a single thought slipped through his life's final breath:

*There will be stars.*

# -2-

Even as a child, Bobby greeted the day in pieces. One sense would rouse enough to nudge the next and that one another, brittle links forming a chain of sound and smell and touch and taste and sight, pulling him back to a life he no longer wanted. Yet that morning arrived unlike all those before. The plink of water dripping from the gutter above; the sour smell of garbage; his throat, sore from screaming; gravel needling the back of his bare head; the sticky, bitter taste on his tongue. These came to Bobby not separate but as one, a chain thick and heavy that lashed him with a power more suited to raise from deep death than drunken sleep.

Something scurried over his palm. Bobby jerked the hand away and forced a deep breath that caught midway in his chest, where it bloomed into a stab of pain. He barked a cough and opened his eyes. Shadows rose in narrowing lines. And there—*there* were the stars, winking in a jagged sky of black night and blue morning. Dozens of them, hundreds, and how had he known there would be stars?

He rose to his elbows, looking for Matthew and Mark. All Bobby saw was his cap and a pink tail that disappeared into the mound of white trash bags against the far wall. His boots scattered the beer cans lying close; red, white, and blue pinwheels tumbling on into the alley. On either side, bricked back walls of the shops lining this part of downtown lay bare but for a thin layer of brown grime. The line ended at the turn-in off Second Street, where a puddle of muddy water flashed yellow against the blinker.

It was not the first time Bobby had woken in a strange place with no memory of how or when he'd gotten there. This time, at least, he woke close to home. He eased to his feet, fighting against the pain in his chest and the swaying alley, plucking his cap from the ground. The wood door into the shop stood four feet away; eight steps reached it. As Bobby turned the handle, that same deep sense struck him once more. A sense of heaviness buckled his legs. For one wheezing breath, Bobby's mind quickened to a single impenetrable truth—he had done this before. Been here before.

"Déjà vu."

*A rabbit running over your grave* is how he'd learned it as a boy. That felt right. Bobby had the gooseflesh on his arms and the back of his neck to prove it, yet the feeling passed through and was gone as the door shut behind him. The air carried thick smells of oil and grease, and Bobby knew he was safe. He was home.

"Matthew? Mark?" he called. His throat seized from dryness, making him wince. "Where y'all at?"

A single yellow bulb buzzed over the workbench against the far wall, its surface clean but for black dust packed into the scratches. Much of the light ended near the front of the second bay door, where sat Bea Campbell's little rust bucket of a car. Outside, day lightened with soft bars that slanted through three Plexiglas windows. The glow settled onto the giant rolling toolbox against the wall, stickers that read PENNZOIL and

QUAKER STATE and MARY SHOULD HAVE ABORTED JESUS. Bobby yawned and staggered. His right boot skirted the edge of the service pit dug out of the concrete. He lifted his cap and bent over, peering inside.

No one there.

He pushed on a bathroom door with EMPLOYEE ONLY written in black Sharpie across a peeling strip of duct tape. The loud click of the switch on the inside wall brought a light that made Bobby wince. He moaned and felt his way to the toilet, mumbling those two words again—"Déjà vu." By the time he emptied himself, Bobby decided that hadn't been what he'd felt at all. He remembered a story, Stephen King or maybe Neil Gaiman, about a man who got hold of a tainted batch of beer that turned him into a monster. Maybe that was what happened. Carla had warned him it would, before she'd left and after. Maybe Timmy had sold him some bad beer and it had gotten into Bobby's brain. He rubbed the spot in his chest and decided he'd look that story up. It was a good one.

Beyond the door, the clock tower in town tolled six.

Cold water from the tap. He washed his neck and face, rubbing the soap in hard. One brush went through a mop of hair, which was then hidden by the cap, another brush went over yellowing teeth. Only then did Bobby ponder his reflection in the filthy mirror above the sink.

What stared back was too little for ego to inflate: one grimy cap pulled low to hide the gray on his head, one patchy beard and gaunt face, two bony shoulders attached to skinny arms. One blue work shirt, wrinkled but unsoiled. The eyes last. Bobby never relished looking there. The beard and body could be owed to time and a scrappy nature, but his eyes held hard truths not ably bent. Only the faintest hint of the blue that had once filled them remained, a color of deep ice that as a child offered an illusion of current. Those eyes now looked the color of ash. Their shimmer had departed long before that Saturday morning in the little bathroom off his shop. Before Carla and before the boys, before those two town kids went missing. What life once lay there had leaked away. Or perhaps that life had gone nowhere and instead lay stagnant and rotting. As he stared, Bobby found that prospect troubled him more. What leaked away could perhaps be found again, but what was dead was lost forever.

Just below a swatch of red spider webs that marched across his right cheek lay another mark, this one dark and swollen, as though something had hit him. Bobby leaned close to the glass and touched the spot, wincing as he did. He tried to remember how the mark had gotten there but couldn't. The monster, he supposed. Whatever all that beer had made him do.

He walked from the bathroom toward a dawn breaking in yellows and oranges over downtown. Past racks of carburetor cleaner and motor oil, containers of Gojo for greasy hands that had known no grease in a long while. Past rows of windshield wipers and belts hanging from the pegboard wall and into the small waiting room, where he lifted the blinds. On the counter, a coffee maker set to a timer gurgled beside an empty cash register. Bobby reached under the counter for a mug and the half bottle of bourbon that would be his breakfast. He drank, coughing as the liquid scorched his parched throat, then swallowed again. The coffee remained untouched.

The window looked out on the bit of Main that bordered the shop, Bobby's last foothold in the world. At the edge of the lot sat his truck, right where it should be. No windows had been broken and no tires slashed, nor could Bobby see fresh graffiti on the outside walls. Sheriff Barnett was nowhere in sight. Good. Whatever had happened the night before, he'd gotten the Dodge back safe, had broken no laws, and no one had bothered him. He toasted that bit of good fortune with another gulp from the bottle.

A Tom Franklin novel lay between the seat and armrest of the recliner in the middle of the room. Bobby sat and placed the book atop the leaning stack of others between the chair and a small table. Already a smattering of people passed, some on foot and others in their trucks and cars, collars and windows open to a day that would feel more like early April than late October. None glanced Bobby's way. The liquor in him was enough to turn their forgetfulness from the blessing it usually was to the hurt it sometimes became.

✶ ✶ ✶

The alley door opened and banged shut. Bobby sat up and cocked his ear, then relaxed when he heard a boy's laugh. The sound of four light feet echoing across the shop floor, Matthew trotting in first, Mark just behind. Both wore faded jeans and sneakers, though Matthew had opted for an Iron Man shirt and Mark a Captain America. If there was consternation to Bobby's voice, neither child minded. They crowded into the chair and planted two kisses so soft against Bobby's grizzled cheeks that they went unfelt.

"Where y'all been?"

"Playin'," Matthew said.

"Little early, don't y'all think?"

Mark shrugged.

Bobby rubbed his eyes and yawned. "Y'all remember what we got into last night? Seems I've lost the memory."

"We watch cartoons, Daddy?" Matthew asked. "It's Saturday."

"I suppose. Just let me get caught up on all the bad first."

He kicked the footrest down, making the boys giggle as the rocker moved them forward and back, and found the remote to the small Zenith atop the Pepsi machine. The day's news sounded as sour as Bobby felt: an outbreak of a disease he couldn't pronounce; children murdered at a school in some faraway country that didn't matter to him at all; a woman found dead on an old service road between Mattingly and Stanley; the World Series; a man hoisting a sign with a crowd of others, screaming that if the ragheads wanted a fight, then we should damn well give them one.

He found the cartoons and put the remote away, poured a cup of coffee. A splash of Irish whiskey would offer a much better taste than the expired milk he settled for. Bobby wished he'd kept back some of that bourbon. Still, the hot liquid made his throat feel some better and the look of the day did its best to lift his spirits. He thought maybe he'd just sit with the boys awhile, watch some Bugs Bunny or whatever passed for cartoons these days—shoot, he had all the time in the world—but before reaching the recliner, his eyes settled on the phone against the wall.

The cord on the receiver had been tugged and wound about Bobby's finger so many times that it sagged near the floor, and that sense—that French word he'd remembered earlier but had forgotten again now—brushed against him like a memory. He cocked his head to the side. The boys laughed at the TV and the oil heater in the shop kicked on and the world beyond passed on the same as always, but Bobby heard little of that and saw even less. He saw only the phone and that dangly cord, and how both grew larger as the wall behind it seemed to melt away. No, not larger. *Closer.* Bobby was moving toward the phone, and when had he started that, and why was his right hand moving out?

The phone rang with more a scream than a trill. Bobby let out a sharp "Ooh" and stumbled backward, clipping the edge of the recliner. Coffee shot in a hot stream that barely missed Mark's face and made Matthew laugh. Books scattered across the floor, the table, and Bobby himself. He rolled to his stomach, scrambling as the phone screamed again. In his periphery Bobby spotted a boy in long pants and a baseball cap watching from the sidewalk. The boy pointed through the window and said something to the woman with him, who tugged him on.

He jerked the phone from the wall and hollered a frantic "Bobby?" that came out as a whisper against his aching throat. "Bobby's Service."

A voice on the other end said, "Bobby? That you?"

"Bea?" He turned and slumped against the wall, letting gravity ease him to the floor. Mark watched with some concern and did not move from his place. Matthew went back to his cartoon. "What you doin', callin' this early? You liked to scare me to death."

"Sun's up, ain't it? Whatsa matter with your voice?"

Bobby coughed into his forearm. "Woke up
(*from screaming, I screamed and the boys screamed too*)
with a scratch."

"You tie one on?" Bea asked. "That what you been doing 'stead a fixin' my car, Bobby Barnes?"

"Your . . ." Bobby leaned his head into the shop. Bea's car hadn't moved from its spot. He'd meant to at least pop the hood the day before but hadn't gotten around to it. "I ain't tied one on, Bea."

"And I'm the Queen of England. I can hear it in your speakin'. Here ain't even breakfast, and you're sauced."

Bobby rolled his eyes, making the kids laugh. "Well, Your Highness, I'll have you know I got your car all tore down yesterday. Got stuff everywhere, matter of fact, and I know how it all goes back. Just gonna need some time."

"Ain't got *time*," Bea said. "Had to get the sheriff to drive me to the so-curity office in Stanley yesterday. Now I got to get to Camden to pay the cable, else they take Maury off the TV from me."

Bobby didn't know anything about a Maury.

"Thought you said it was just a belt need changin'," Bea said. "I done paid you for it already."

"Well now, that's true enough, Bea, but a belt was only my initial impression. Things changed once I got under the hood." Bobby thought things over, trying to decide how far he could push things. He cupped a hand around his mouth and the receiver so Mark couldn't hear. "It's your transmission."

"Transmission? Bobby, I ain't ever had no transmission trouble."

"Car's near as old as I am, Bea. Got near two hundred K on it." He winked at the boys. Matthew winked back. Mark didn't. "Things is gonna go bad eventually. 'Specially on a Ford."

"How much we talkin'?"

Bobby wound the cord around his finger. Wasn't a few days earlier he'd come across Bea Campbell standing in her drive with her hose sagging down off her two swollen knees, kicking her little Escort's front tire with her walker as the engine screeched and whined. Somehow Bobby had been sober enough to talk her into letting him take the car to his shop. Wouldn't cost hardly a thing, he'd said, probably a belt was all. Now here they were, three days and a hundred dollars later, mired in a conversation Bobby took less as haggling and more as a hostage situation.

He spoke in the grave tone of someone calling to say a loved one had passed: "New tranny can get expensive, Bea. Maybe four thousand. Labor counted in, 'course."

She screamed so hard Bobby moved the phone from his ear. "Four *thousand*?"

"Now, Bea, transmission's a highly skilled procedure—"

"You know what everybody tole me when they seen you takin' away my car, Bobby Barnes? 'You a fool of an old woman,' that's what they said. 'Give your old car over to that preevert.' Now look at me, out all the money I got in the world."

Bobby cupped his hand to the receiver again. "I ain't no *pervert*, Bea Campbell. You hear me? Them kids came *home*. They got caught up and lost in the woods and they weren't nowhere 'round me and you *know* that."

"Maybe I oughta call Sheriff. Huh? Tell Jake to come on down there and have a word, see what you doin' to my *car*. I'm tryin' to do the Christian thing here, Bobby. Do a good deed for a man don't nobody got respect for. A no-good, selfish scum of a man. And here's what I get. Lord gonna give me money for a new transmission? You think I can go down to the bank and get Charlie Gowdy to float me a loan?"

Not really asking, Bobby thought, more pleading for an answer he wasn't about to give.

"But you know what?" Bea said. "Ain't no good deed gonna turn you 'round to the good. You done give up. You just plumb give up on everything."

"You blame me?" Bobby shouted. "Everybody in town thinking in their heads what you just said with your lips." The line clicked off. Matthew and Mark shrank as far as they could into the recliner, as though the backrest somehow gave them harbor from their daddy's words. "Think I'm gonna fix up that heap a bolts you drive now? How 'bout I drop it all in your driveway instead? Serve you right, Bea Campbell."

He threw the receiver as hard and as far as he could, aiming for the far wall but forgetting the cord plugged into its bottom. The phone stretched midway past the recliner and the dozen books littering the floor, then whipped back in a straight line for Bobby's nose. He ducked at the last moment and left the receiver hanging like a noose.

"You okay, Daddy?" Matthew asked.

He whispered, "Right as the rain, bud."

"How's Miz Campbell?" Mark asked.

"Oh, she's fine. Passes along her best."

He eased himself up, holding the wall to keep himself steady and his breakfast firmly in place. Bobby walked for another beer first and into the shop, not bothering to flip the sign from Closed to Open. Hanging from a nail in the concrete wall was an old radio that he kept tuned to the classic rock station out of Stanley—Tesla and Skid Row and Guns N' Roses, the soundtrack of his youth. He flipped the switch. Guitar song filled the shop.

"Good one," he shouted back through the door. "This your song here, Matthew. Got that bad moon risin'."

He sat on the car's hood, singing and drinking, his boots propped on the bumper. Matthew and Mark slipped into the shop, wanting to be near their daddy but not too near, not yet. *Wary of the monster*, Bobby thought. He sang his song and thought about that story of the man who drank too much and who had written it, because it was a good one. Then Bobby decided it didn't matter much in the end. By then, nothing much mattered at all.

## -3-

For as much as the shop's thick walls provided a sense of protection, there were times Bobby felt them a prison. Most of his days were spent watching from the window those he had once considered neighbors and friends while the boys played in the pit or the alley. Reading his books as the television droned. Keeping the world at arm's length. For Bobby's own good, and the good of all.

Yet there were times when going out became a necessity. The boys refused to let an evening pass without a trip to the mountains, and even Bobby agreed those rides offered a bit of peace to buttress him against what hell awaited him at next dawn. And hell it would be, one form or another. Things were predictable inside the shop. But outside, in the world? Why, anybody could accuse you of anything. He'd learned that back a ways, with the Granderson girl.

After debating with Matthew and Mark (mostly Mark) over what to do, Bobby came to the realization that if Bea Campbell needed a belt put on her little deathtrap of a car, a belt it would be. Not because it was the honest thing (Mark again), but because Bea was just the sort of person to run crying to the sheriff. Bobby had no interest in crossing Jake Barnett's radar, their past a shaky one at best. Besides, he'd already drunk the money Bea'd paid him.

Fixing the car soon presented another problem—there wasn't enough beer to get to the next day. Bobby would need that. Beer was what made him a good mechanic. He knew it, the boys knew it, everyone in Mattingly knew it, even if they called him a drunk in the process. To work otherwise, he told the twins, "is like doctoring without your gloves on."

Stacked neatly inside the refrigerator that morning were

twenty-two cans that took up most of the three narrow shelves, saving room only for the quart of spoiled milk he'd splashed in his coffee.

"And that ain't enough," he told Matthew, and Matthew alone. Bobby had learned not to involve Mark in any drinking-related discussions. *You don't need any*, Mark would say, just as Carla once said. "I'll burn through that before I get this old heap up and running again. And then what? Nothing for after lunch or before supper. Nothing for the ride. What's a ride without comfort? Can't do no good work if I'm all shaky."

Matthew nodded his agreement, brown hair jiggling before settling back in place, the part on the side straight and clean. "Guess we better go get some then, Daddy."

Bobby tapped his boy on the shoulder. "Guess we should do just that. Tell your brother get his shoes on. We got errands."

\* \* \*

They piled into the truck—Matthew in the middle and Mark on the end. Bobby took four beers along and pulled onto the street without looking, clipping the curb before pointing the hood toward the Texaco at the edge of town. He tried to keep the truck in the middle of the lane and what beer he didn't drink inside the can and told the boys how it hadn't been too long ago he could go most anywhere for a nip so long as it was in some old farmer's barn or somebody's woods. Hollis Devereaux had crafted the best. Had a still called Jenny that brewed the best moonshine you'd ever swallow. But then Hollis near got killed by that girl who run off and Hollis up and quit, took Jenny apart and buried her in the ground. Now only place to get your courage was up to Timmy's Texaco, and that was only beer in a can, though every once in a while Timmy would get some special like the bourbon Bobby had taken for breakfast.

"Asked Hollis to brew me up some a couple months back. That man looked at me like I was the devil."

"You believe in the devil, Daddy?" Mark asked.

"I do."

"You believe in God?"

"Two's near the same as one," Bobby said, and then he kept talking before Mark dragged him to a place he'd rather not go. Mark was like that. "So that's why we got to go to Timmy's. We get there, y'all can come in. But mind yourselfs, okay?"

"God ain't the same as the devil," Mark said. "One's like day and one's like night. Light and dark ain't the same."

"Opposites," Matthew said.

Mark thanked his brother. "You go on in that church up there, Daddy. Ask the preacher. He'll tell you."

The church being the big Methodist one coming up on the left, and the preacher no man but a woman. Bobby was not so drunk that he divulged this information (which Mark would surely use in his childlike but not unwise way to convince Bobby he should not only pop in and say hello, but offer to be re-dunked in the river). He'd forgotten the preacher's name. Something literary, though Bobby couldn't remember for the heaviness shuddering through him again. As they neared the church, a flash more picture than thought overcame him: the preacher—*Jane? Jean?*—standing out front in a pair of jeans and a blue shirt, pushing her hair back as she studied the flower beds.

This time the feeling did not go away. It did not pass through. It grew instead like a storm as the truck neared the lot and the big Mattingly Methodist Church sign out front. A chill passed through Bobby, raising the hairs on his arms.

"Rabbit." He chuckled, though he felt little humor in that word. "Biggest one ever," he said to the kids, and Bobby couldn't understand their strange looks, as though neither boy understood. Hadn't he told them? Bobby could swear he had that memory.

Then he saw her, the woman preacher, standing in front of the flowers where Bobby knew she'd be. She was neither tall nor short, nor did her appearance bear anything worthy of remembrance. Yet he saw in her a strange sort of beauty nonetheless, as though the parts of her were forgettable but the whole of her was not, those parts bound by something more enduring than flesh and bone. Her skin carried the earthy tone of fall, white tinged with the color of coffee. Her hair lay in tight black coils that tumbled down over her shoulders, giving her an air of the exotic. And there—*There!* he nearly yelled—brushing away a bit of her curls. The only difference Bobby could see between the picture in his mind and the one in his eyes was the preacher wore not a blue shirt but a pink one.

Matthew's face twisted into an expression of worry and fear that looked more at home on his brother's. "Daddy, whatsa matter?"

"Nothing. Got flustered for a minute. I just . . . *seen* it. In my head. Like . . . something heavy. Felt it this morning when I woke up, too. And right before Bea called. Y'all seen that, right? I reached for that phone 'fore it even rang."

"She wasn't there yesterday," Mark said. "That preacher."

What Bobby wanted to say was they hadn't been out that way at all the day before. He'd stayed in the shop reading Tom Franklin and the boys had played and watched TV and then the three of them had built a fort out of an old tarp and a couple dirty towels, and all they'd done after that was . . . what?

He couldn't remember.

Shouldn't he remember?

He wrenched his neck to see the preacher behind and the others around him, errand runners and loafers milling about the shops that filled the four square blocks of Mattingly's downtown. That feeling settled upon him again. Not a wave, more a steady rain that tingled Bobby's head and face. He scanned the line of cars in front and the few people crossing the street, saw the doors of the sewing shop and the florist open to the day's first customers. What he said next seemed to rise from a place unknown and mysterious, some part of his mind that held the memory not of things gone but of things not yet.

"I'm gonna see Laura Beth. Laura Beth Gowdy gonna come right down that sidewalk on the other side of the street, and she's gonna be wearing a yellow dress with blue polka dots and sunglasses."

"Miz Gowdy paints her hair," Mark said. He offered the words as though the truth of them constituted a secret beheld by only the highest and most powerful. "You havin' more a that didja poop, Daddy?"

"Déjà vu," Bobby said. He looked at Mark. "How you know about that? I didn't tell you that."

"Look!" Matthew screamed.

He pointed a stubby finger. Rounding the corner from the pharmacy came none other than Laura Beth, as long-legged and firm as Bobby had ever seen her. Blond hair hung to the middle of her tanned back. Not a yellow dress but a blue skirt and white shirt that accentuated every curve and inch of bare skin. She held her purse close to her breasts, wobbling as she dodged and weaved around those who greeted her good morning, returning neither salutations nor so much as a smile through her perfect white teeth. She addressed the world through a pair of dark sunglasses that hid her eyes and most of the area between her nose and forehead.

Bobby slowed the truck to a near crawl. The line of vehicles behind him grew. Laura Beth's chin turned toward him. What he felt next was neither wave nor rain, but an impulse to stick his head out of the truck's window and catcall Laura Beth right there in front of everyone. He went so far as to pucker his lips and switch hands on the steering wheel before Mark told him no. The whistle died in his mouth.

And just as the two of them crossed each other, Laura Beth stopped. She stared across the street, peering through the few cars that moved between her and him. He saw her mouth drop open and the very tips of her eyebrows inch up over those big sunglasses. His foot touched the brake, nearly stopping the truck in the middle of the street. A horn bellowed. Bobby heard a voice telling the drunk to get out of the way and vaguely recognized the drunk as himself. Neither of the twins said to move. Even Mark fell silent, following his brother's gaze to where Laura Beth stood. Her expression was one of growing shock.

*No*, Bobby thought. *Not that. She's scared.*

Laura Beth's purse dropped. It would have spilled onto the sidewalk had the tips of her fingers not held on to the leather strap, dangling the purse like a hung man inches from the pavement. She stepped off the sidewalk and into the street. Her eyes (or at least what Bobby imagined to be her eyes) bored into his own. Laura Beth acted either unaware of or unconcerned with the traffic, did not so much as flinch when the car approaching skidded to a stop mere feet from her. Everyone within sight paused to stare. She came forward, lips moving to speak a question Bobby knew he could not bear to hear. He mashed the accelerator and woke the big truck's engine.

The boys' heads slammed into the back of the seat. Bobby worked the steering wheel to get them away and safe, though safe from what, he did not know. He chanced a look in the rearview as Main Street faded behind them. The line of vehicles had shrunk to the size of one of Matthew's toys. Laura Beth remained in the middle of the street. She stared motionless, as though seeing Bobby for the first time.

Matthew turned around in his seat. "What's that about, Daddy?"

"I don't know. Something ain't right." Bobby took off his cap. His breaths were deep and shuddering. The spot in his chest throbbed again. "We're gonna get to Timmy's, fill up, and get my beer. Maybe some food. But that's it, okay? After that, we get home and stay. No more goin' out. Maybe not even tonight."

Matthew's face dropped. "But I like our rides."

"No."

Bobby looked everywhere—through the windshield and out both windows, in the mirrors. He looked at his son last. Whatever protest Matthew may have had a mind to give faded as soon as he met his father's eyes.

"She ain't never done that," Mark said. His head bobbed as the truck crossed the bridge. "Miz Gowdy paints her hair and keeps on walking and she don't turn 'round even when you whistle."

Bobby shot him a look. "How you know I was gonna whistle?"

Mark went quiet.

"Son? How you know that? You feeling it, too?"

Matthew touched Bobby's arm. "You scared, Daddy?"

"No. Just wanna get back home." He looked at Mark, who had shrunk down in the seat. "We get to Timmy's, I want y'all to stay in the truck. Don't get out, no matter what."

This time he received no argument.

## -4-

Away from town, traffic eased to passing farmers and boys playing chicken on their bikes. Each would glance only long enough to recognize Bobby's truck before finding something else of interest. A cloud, a funny-looking tree, whatever was close that they could stare at until he'd passed and gone. No one looked at Bobby anymore but to sneer or whisper. None but Laura Beth, he supposed, and that was what had frightened him most.

Yet by the time the Texaco appeared in the distance, Bobby had nearly convinced both himself and the boys the entire episode had never happened. Laura Beth hadn't seen him at all, and he had most certainly not been the reason she'd stepped out in the middle of all that traffic. Probably one of the storefronts she'd been staring at, some sale on dresses or a fancy necklace sparkling in the morning light. That woman always enjoyed spending her husband's bank money.

"Might as well head on to Andy's," Mark said.

Bobby turned his head. "Son, Andy's is clear back 'cross town. Don't need his gas when Timmy's right here. Timmy's got beer."

"Might as well head there anyway. It'll save time."

"Goin' on's what'll save us time."

He thought different as they pulled into the lot and the heaviness swept over him once more. He stopped the truck short of the pumps and let it idle. Matthew asked what was wrong. Bobby didn't reply, though he suspected Mark could give that answer. How that was so—how Mark could know what was happening or at least be sharing some of what Bobby felt—remained a mystery.

"Sheriff's in there," Bobby said.

Matthew looked ahead. "Don't see his truck."

"Don't need to see it. Jake's standing in that store right now with that stupid hat a his on, talking to Timmy." He shook his head. "I know it. Mark? I *know*. Do you?"

Mark leaned up in the seat. He asked, "How you know that, Daddy?"

Bobby wanted to turn back almost more than he wanted anything in the world. He pulled the gearshift down to drive and crept on, wanting his beer just a little more. He stopped at the nearest pump and said, "Y'all stay put."

It was a slow walk to the door, steady and mostly straight, trying to keep from wobbling. Bobby put a hand to his mouth and smelled his breath. Sheriff Barnett stood where Bobby had known he would be. Their eyes met only for a moment before Bobby lowered his head and took a left for the drink coolers. He wanted

(*needed*)

two cases but settled for only one. The cooler door thundered shut, making him wince. No use waiting for Jake to leave. Sheriff wouldn't, not until he could flex his muscle and have one of his words.

Bobby walked to the register and set the beer on the counter. Timmy Griffith, owner and operator of Timmy's Texaco, brother-in-law to Jake and an all-around idiot so far as Bobby was concerned, started punching buttons.

"Bobby," he said.

"Say, Timmy. This and thirty on the pump. Get it on my way out."

Bobby looked up, meeting Timmy's stare. He was a big man with arms that looked the size of Bobby's legs and close-cropped hair that showed the slightest gray at the temples. Mean looking, until he smiled. Timmy didn't.

Jake asked, "Brings you out this early, Bobby?"

"Ain't early for a working man. Got errands and a job to do."

"So I heard. Bea Campbell called me a little while ago. Said you had her car in the shop and wouldn't fix it."

Bobby slapped the counter. "Now that ain't true, Jake. Told Bea I'd get it fixed and I will, soon as everybody stops getting on my case about it."

"Take it easy, Bobby." Fiddling with that ugly cowboy hat of his. "Just asking is all."

"Sure, Jake. Just asking." He stared at Timmy. "You gonna ring me up or not?"

"Need a word first," Jake said.

"Heaven's sake, Sheriff. Can't you leave me alone for onced?"

"Not with you coming in here drunk before breakfast. I take you outside right now and tell you walk a line, how many steps will it take before you fall off?"

"Many as you want, 'cause I ain't drunk."

"Sure acting like it," Timmy said. "I bet Jake a five you'd stumble before you even made it in here."

Bobby showed his teeth. "Shows what you know. Didn't stumble at all."

"I won't let Timmy sell you beer, Bobby," Jake said. "You had enough. Why don't you get on back home and sober up, try again Monday? And don't you be sauced working on Bea's car either. I'll call her back and have a talk, tell her you'll

27

make good on what you're supposed to. As it is, I expect you best get on."

"You telling me my business, Jake?"

The sheriff didn't move. "I'm suggesting your best course of action. I'm more like to peel what's left of you up off the road one day. Trying to keep that from happening."

Bobby grinned again. "Well, ain't that sweet."

He left the beer on the counter and walked to the door. Head up, wanting to hide his shame and the anger that shame kindled. Matthew and Mark watched from the truck. Bobby pushed on the door and stopped.

"Don't see your Blazer out here, Jake."

"Got Kate's truck around the side. Blazer's over in Camden."

"What for?"

Jake wouldn't say. Bobby didn't budge and didn't turn. He'd have the truth. Sheriff might've taken his pride, but he wouldn't get everything.

"Got up early this morning for my rounds," Jake said. "Had trouble sleeping. Noticed brakes were a little mushy. Went back home, got me some coffee until the shop in Camden opened."

"Don't think I coulda put those brakes on for you?"

"Didn't know if I'd catch you sober."

"You talk to Bea, ask what she called me. You do that, Jake."

"I will."

Bobby pushed the door open. Behind him, Timmy said, "Still sell you that gas, Bobby."

"Keep it," Bobby said. "I don't want nothing you got."

He made it halfway to the truck before he did stumble, catching the toe of his boot on the curb where one of the pumps sat. The long string of cusswords Bobby yelled were directed inside the store—to Timmy and to Jake especially—though both of the twins heard plain. They shrank into the seat as Bobby climbed inside. He slammed the door and gunned the engine, though the truck didn't move. Bobby could feel the stares from the store, every word that passed:

*He's drunk, yeah he's always drunk, been like that years now Carla and the boys and what all he saw down in Orleans, all those dead after Katrina can't really blame him I guess, no you can't, must be tough, been tough on us all, maybe I should go have another word.*

That last thought moved Bobby's hand. He eased the gear to drive and pulled away, keeping the bill of his cap between him and whatever of him Jake could see. Neither twin said a word. Matthew didn't ask why Bobby hadn't gotten any beer and Mark didn't mention where they'd have to go now. Bobby knew they were afraid. He'd taken pains to keep a level head whenever the boys were with him. The alcohol helped—the alcohol was downright necessary—but sometimes it wasn't enough. Boys didn't understand. They had no idea how hard it was to wake up each day knowing the only good that could happen was to lay your head down again that night. Life to Matthew and Mark was play. The world lay wide for them and held neither fear nor danger. They knew nothing of what it felt to fail and have those things they most cherished stolen away, and that was how Bobby wanted things kept. Still, that didn't stop him from mashing down on the gas as he pulled out of the lot. That didn't stop Bobby from hoisting his middle finger, to the Texaco and Jake Barnett, to the town itself. He opened up the engine and disappeared.

# -5-

Mark didn't have to bring up the needle on the tank; Bobby knew they couldn't go back to the shop without a little go juice. They had plenty for one night but not enough for two, and the next day was Sunday. Couldn't get gas on the Sabbath; whole blamed town shut down for Jesus. That meant a trip back from where they'd come, to the only other gas station around.

Laura Beth had gotten away to wherever she'd been going. At least Bobby had that to ease his mind. The boys came around, talking more the farther they got from the Texaco. Matthew focused on the needle. Mark focused on his father.

"You still got that thing, Daddy? That thing you feel?"

No. Yes. Bobby didn't know. The world still felt off somehow, different. They passed the church again. He saw no preacher and felt no crashing heaviness, only the soft buzzing under his skin that meant the liquor and beer had done their job.

Ahead lay another bridge, this one older and in poorer shape than its twin on the other side of town, the field and the railroad tracks and a smattering of homes. Some miles past stood the tiny white BP station owned by Andy Sommerville. Andy's truck sat alone to the left of the store. To the right, Bobby spotted another truck he knew well. A sawed-off shotgun rested in the rack at the back window.

"That's Junior Hewitt. Junior's in there."

He knew this by his eyes alone. No sense of repetition preceded that knowledge, and none followed. Bobby parked in front of the pump and got out, telling the kids once more to remain inside. This time he pumped the gas first, then pulled the truck around to where Junior had parked. When Mark asked why, Bobby only said he needed to ask Andy something.

He crossed the lot and spotted Junior's big body through the window, squatting at the leftmost of Andy's three coolers. The weight again, a breeze this time, there long enough to tell Bobby the big man was there for night crawlers before the feeling passed through and was gone. Junior was on his way to Rankin's Creek that Saturday morning. Gonna do some fishing. He heard a whisper deep in his mind—*Best spot in this town to catch your supper, but don't tell nobody.*

Andy stood in the first aisle with a broom in his hands. Bobby swung on the door, ringing the bell above.

(*Morning Bobby he'll say. Morning Bobby*)

"Morning, Bobby."

Junior stood up. The container of worms he held filled only a small part of his right hand. For a moment Bobby thought that plastic bowl was a baseball Junior was winding to throw the same as he had way back at Mattingly High and in the minors after. Junior Hewitt was not Mattingly's most famous person but the most famous person still in town, and to the town's great shame.

Bobby stared at the container. That feeling again, mixed with a spark of fear as he realized Junior was looking at him funny.

"Get some gas out there?" Andy asked. He'd already propped the broom against a rack of soda and walked partway around the counter.

Bobby looked away from Junior, who seemed to have frozen himself in place by the coolers. "Yeah. Got thirty."

Andy punched buttons on the register as Bobby dug into his pocket, wondering what to say.

31

"Anything else for you, Bobby?"

"Nope."

Junior watched. The container of worms had all but disappeared in his hand, swallowed by the five fingers shut into a fist around it.

Bobby handed the money over. He dipped his voice but didn't know why: "Say, Andy, there is one thing."

"Shoot."

"Everything around here, you know . . . all right?"

"All right?"

"Yeah, you know. Everything. I don't know. The same?"

Andy chuckled. "You know how it is here, Bobby. Don't *nothing* change."

"I know, but"—lowering his voice more—"things don't feel right. It's like—"

"Say, Bobby." Junior had snuck up from the coolers and now stood so close that Bobby could smell the stink off his body. He had to tilt his head nearly all the way back to see the man's eyes. "Goin' on up here?"

"Nothing," Bobby said. "Just talking is all. Nothing big."

But Bobby guessed his talk must be big indeed, or else Junior's eyes wouldn't be so wide and flickering and his breaths wouldn't come like quick whistles through his nose. His Bib-Alls, stretched to the point of snapping, looked like a faded blue wall. Bobby thought the man was probably just high is all, Junior most times was, got his weed from Hersey Childress's place out past Boone's Pond.

Junior looked away long enough to say, "Need these night crawlers, Andy. You ring me up?"

"Sure, Junior. Gonna dip a line this morning?"

His eyes went back to Bobby. "Goin' to Rankin's Crick. That's—"

"Best spot in town," Bobby said. "Best spot in this town to catch your supper, but don't tell nobody."

Junior's face went white. "What's at?"

"That'll be five and a quarter, Junior," Andy said.

Junior didn't hear. He dropped the can of worms and pressed down hard on Bobby's shoulders, buckling his knees. Bobby grimaced at the pressure.

"How you know what I was gonna say?" He spoke deep and slow the way he always did, like words passed through molasses. "Bobby? How you know?"

The register drawer snapped open, catching Andy in his side. He jumped back as if his mind had tricked him into thinking Junior had reached across the counter. Wasn't a body in all of Mattingly who didn't shy from Junior Hewitt. Even Matthew and Mark had been warned to watch that man's temper.

"How you know that, Bobby?" Screaming it this time. Spittle flew from Junior's mouth. "It ain't supposed to happen this way. It ain't *ever* happened this way."

Bobby tried answering that he didn't know and didn't understand at all, but the vise of flesh and bone clamped to his shoulders moved to his throat. He gagged as Junior's paw squeezed. What little air he possessed flew out in a wet cough. Andy moved from the register and rounded the counter, screaming for Junior to turn Bobby loose, saying he was going to call Jake. Bobby didn't have breath enough to tell him to call over to the Texaco, that's where Jake was.

Junior left his worms on the counter and dragged Bobby by the neck, pushing on the door so hard it strained the hinges. He forced Bobby toward the side of the store where he'd parked. Andy followed as far as the door. That's where he drew Junior's gaze. The big man turned around and said,

"Get on inside, Andy. I got another hand ain't doin' nothing. It'd just as soon find your neck."

Bobby pawed at Junior's hand, trying to pry it off. The grip came harder. Things turned gray at the edges. Somewhere far away, Bobby heard Matthew and Mark screaming. Junior got as far as his rusted truck before he pulled Bobby to himself and then pushed him away in one powerful motion. Bobby drew a halting breath, a moment of sheer ecstasy that ended in pain as he met the concrete.

Junior loomed over him, casting Bobby's entire body in shadow. Bobby's fists were balled, ready to fight however he could if only to preserve his honor with his sons, and yet the voice he heard speak sounded not booming and angry, but small and confused:

"You tell me what's going on, Bobby."

"I don't *know*."

Junior hefted him again, this time by the shoulders. Bobby's boots dangled above the ground. Matthew and Mark began beating on the back window. Junior didn't hear. His lips trembled. Fear. Like Laura Beth. Junior was afraid, and that only scared Bobby more.

"I don't know what's happening, Junior, I swear. Please don't hurt me." Whimpering, the words sprayed through his spit. "I woke up is all. Woke up and then things started happening that I *knew* would happen like the same things over and over and I cain't turn it off, Junior. I cain't make it *stop* and I think I'm going crazy."

Junior held him there. His arms did not tremble with Bobby's weight, nor did his stare lessen. "You knew what was gonna happen?"

"I knew Bea would call. And Jake? I *knew* he'd be at Timmy's before I ever got in there. I knew you was goin' fishing, too. It feels heavy. So *heavy*. Carla's gonna call the shop later. She gonna *call* me, Junior. I know it like it's already happened and Carla ain't called in months. I'm scared. Please don't hurt me."

But Junior did. His grip hardened to the point that Bobby could feel his bones beginning to crack. The twins had given up and now looked on helpless as Junior's mouth twisted into a scowl.

"Ha!" he shouted. He shook Bobby quick like a rag doll and then set him down. "Ain't gotta go fishin' today. Caught *you*, Bobby Barnes. Ha!"

Bobby swayed on his feet. "You ain't gonna kill me?"

"Ain't gotta." He laughed again. "Come on, get in your truck. We got somebody to visit."

"Who?"

"Somebody to help." He moved toward Bobby's truck, sending the twins scurrying to the middle. "Come on now, we got to get. Andy's got Jake on the way. I don't want to have to do this all over again."

"Do what again?"

Junior shook his head. "Have this talk."

## -6-

As she often did in the early morning, Dorothea Cash paused in the kitchen of her yellow Victorian and shut her eyes to the blessings granted her. She did so not out of ignorance (never that), but so those blessings could feel more genuine. The eyes played tricks. That truth had taken Dorothea longer to learn than she bothered to fret over. The eyes fooled you into seeing too much. They were windows through which you gazed upon all but yourself.

She breathed in, letting her other senses take hold. The slight sweetness of the roast in the oven. Corn pudding and Tommy's mashed potatoes. Pies cooling on the windowsill, apple for Juliet and George's blueberry. The dull pain in her fingers, something that vexed but never bothered. Then the sounds. Those were always Dorothea's favorite. She raised a finger and held it, counting in her mind. At three, she pointed at the nearest kitchen window as a mockingbird sang from the bushes outside. Another finger at the count of four, meeting a dog's bark. Two hands now, raised high over her head, swooping down in a slow arc as the clock tower struck noon and a car's horn bellowed somewhere in town. She smiled. Many in the former life possessed talent enough to lead a symphony of instruments. Only the Lord and Dorothea Cash could conduct a symphony of the world.

It was not merely the call of animals and machines she so enjoyed. Above the groaning on of an existence she'd left behind came the sweeter songs of clattering chairs and moving bodies, talk and laughter. The music of company. Those had become the former Widow Cash's life now, and her one true purpose.

She heard George call out, "Mama, would you like some help?" and Dorothea smiled, George using that word when he had her by nearly a dozen years.

"You rest easy, George Grimm. Almost ready now."

Her eyes opened. Dorothea bent to pick the roast from the oven and placed it on a silver tray that she hefted with both hands, pausing only to wrinkle her nose at another window and the distant backup siren of a truck that came half a breath later. A chuckle too high and bright for her former self to have ever uttered trailed her to the dining room.

Tommy had already unsheathed the spoon from the

napkin Juliet placed at the side of his plate. His little legs swung free from the edge of his chair. He smiled through his freckles and tilted the bill of his cap high. George tossed his cigarette through the open window and grunted his body into a sitting position at the far end of the table. He ran a hand over the white scruff of beard around his mouth, eyeing the noon dinner. Laura Beth had taken her place as well and smiled (*As best she can*, Dorothea thought, *poor dear*) at Juliet, who poured glasses of iced tea at each plate. Dorothea took in their praise with all humility and returned to the kitchen for the rest of the food and let the others place it on the table where it would be best used—the greens beside Juliet, who never seemed to get enough of them, the corn pudding near Laura Beth. Tommy's heaping bowl of mashed potatoes came last. He accepted it with a watery smile and a kiss to Dorothea's cheek. She sat at the head of the table and gazed upon them all.

"Where's Junior?"

Tommy plunged the spoon into his bowl. "He ain't here yet, Mama."

"He's *not* here," George corrected. "Proper English, Tommy."

Tommy rolled his eyes.

"Mind your teacher," Dorothea said. "And take off your hat at the table. Have you seen Junior this morning, Laura Beth?"

The pretty girl adjusted the sunglasses over her face. "Not yet, Mama."

"Well, I'm sure he'll be along." She sighed. It was a happy sigh, one that felt good coming out. "No sense waiting. Are we ready?"

They were, all but George, who merely grunted his assent. Dorothea raised her eyebrows and forced a "Yes'm" from his mouth. How many dinners had she shared with that old codger? Cooking for him and granting an ear to his sadness, helping him through, and yet Dorothea *still* had to cajole George into showing respect for something greater than himself. In the moments she hated him, Dorothea tried to remember you could only truly hate someone you loved. And she did love him, though not enough to keep from wishing George one of his coughing fits as a reminder to be thankful.

She reached into the apron tied over her dress and drew out a plain white envelope. Tommy's mouth widened to a grin. Dorothea turned the envelope over and ran her thumbs over the smooth front, caressing this moment. With a single fingernail, she pried up the flap. The sheet inside lay folded into thirds. Dorothea's eyes wandered over the dozen or so words. She tried not to judge and searched for what to say.

"'My dear children,'" she began. "'Grace and peace to you all. My blessings to you this Turn.'" She looked up. "'Take care of each other today as you always do. Mind the balance. Keep your eyes upon Me, the Lord your God.'"

From up the street came an engine sound. Not Junior's truck. Not part of the symphony. Tommy turned in his chair.

"'Thank Me for the food you will eat and the company you will share.'"

The engine cut off. Now Juliet turned as well. Footsteps on the porch. Not one person. Two.

"'Love Me as you love one another.'"

The front door opened to the sound of Junior's voice, calling soft and pleading, "Come on now, it's okay," as though coaxing a puppy. He stepped into the room grinning, yelling, "Surprise—hey, everybody, surprise," and then pulled the other man in beside him.

George slumped in his chair. By instinct, he reached into his shirt pocket for a cigarette. Juliet's eyes blinked. Tommy

38

dropped his spoon. The room fell quiet but for the sound of Bobby Barnes clearing his throat.

Dorothea felt her fingers close around the letter in her hand. A blasphemy, she knew, though one not so egregious as what her eyes beheld.

"Junior Hewitt, have you lost your mind?" she screamed. "How dare you bring an outsider into this house? You forget everything I taught you?"

"No, Mama," Junior said. He dipped his head the way George should have for the reading of the Word. Bobby did the same, removing his greasy cap from his greasy head. "I ain't forgot, hand to God. I had to bring Bobby. Had to."

"And why?"

Junior's face lost its grin. "'Cause I caught'm," he said. "I went fishin' for fish and caught Bobby instead. He's one of us now."

-7-

Bobby didn't know what to do and so fiddled with his hat, watching Junior's head bend low. He swallowed. Thirsty, though not for the pitcher of iced tea sweating on the table. He'd found too much to take in and consider: Why Junior had brought him here and why these others had gathered in this house. How it was that a man like Junior Hewitt would cower and grovel at the feet of a frail woman such as the Widow Cash. And *He's one of us now*. What did that mean? And why was everybody staring like they were all at the zoo and he'd been stuck on the wrong side of the bars?

Dorothea's hands went to her chest, crinkling a piece of paper in her hand. "What?"

"I found him," Junior said. He smiled. Bobby guessed, as Dorothea had not shouted that question, it was okay for Junior to grin once more. "Inside Andy's where he always is. Come in to pay for his gas and I knew something was off, Bobby never says what he did. Asked Andy if stuff'd been going on because funny stuff been going on." He elbowed Bobby in the side like that was funny, nearly doubling him over. "I was scared," Junior said. "Know you won't believe that, but I was. Bobby tole me he knew what was gonna happen before it did. And it's *true*. Bobby said I was goin' *fishin'*, and how's he know that? So I brung him here."

Bobby glanced at the others, all of whom sat so shocked and confused they looked more like statues than people. George Grimm, his old science teacher, lit a smoke and drew deep.

"That true, Bobby?" Dorothea whispered. "I've gotten no word of newcomers."

He took a step forward and squeezed his cap. In the corner of the window, past where there sat the woman preacher Bobby had seen earlier, two heads bobbed in the bushes: Matthew's first, then Mark's.

"Miz Cash, I'm sorry to intrude on your . . . assembly . . . like this. I can assure you it was not my intent. I got some mixed up this morning is all, which happens to me from time to time. As I'm sure you know. Junior said we had to come to you about it. I couldn't well disagree, dangling in the air as I was."

Junior beamed.

The woman—that preacher—said, "Mama, maybe we should invite him to sit?"

Dorothea's face suggested no such desire. She looked different from when Bobby had seen her last, though still as skinny and with the same black dye in her hair. He tried to smile but only swallowed again.

"Is it true what Junior said, Bobby? Did you know he would go fishing today?"

"Well, he did have a can of night crawlers in his hand, ma'am. Anyone could've supposed his aim."

Junior said, "Naw," and elbowed Bobby again. "He knew a lot more'n he's lettin' on. Don't you be shy, Bobby."

Dorothea looked at George and said, "Why don't you fetch us another chair for our guest. I expect we all have much to discuss."

George stood up, smiling as he did, and disappeared into the kitchen with his cigarette. As he left, Bobby heard him call Dorothea the same name as the preacher had. *Mama.*

"You'll sit here," Dorothea said. She motioned to the spot next to hers on the left.

"Ma'am, I—"

"I know you have questions, Bobby, but we've found there's no better place to lay your worries than at a table full of good food and better friends."

Bobby wanted to say he had as many friends at that table as he had back in town. George returned with a plate and glass from the kitchen, along with a stool for which Dorothea apologized. He moved into the room, past where George had seated himself once more and past the preacher, who Bobby thought smelled better than any preacher should. Laura Beth looked on through her sunglasses. She offered a faint smile as Junior plunked down beside her.

Bobby gave a quick thumbs-up to the window and then flattened his hand, telling the twins to stay put. He sat between Dorothea's spot and a boy he recognized as Stacey Purcell's son, Tommy.

"Some tea?" Dorothea asked, though she'd already poured a glass and set it in front of him. "We were just sitting down to dinner. We always do, every day, and most times supper as well. Would you like some roast?"

"No, ma'am." He looked Tommy's way and was met with an expression of near adoration. "You'll pardon me, Widow Cash, I don't rightly know what's going on here."

Tommy chuckled. Junior, too. Despite their difference in size, they sounded the same.

Dorothea set her hands on the table. "Well now, I've found it best to ease people into that. Makes things go easier." She smiled. "Junior says you came into Andy's this morning knowing what would happen. Is that true? And before you answer, Bobby, know that truth and kindness are spoken at my table, nothing more."

Bobby took a sip of tea. "Yes'm, it's true."

"And how long has this been going on?"

"This morning, I reckon. Woke up just like always. I got Bea Campbell's car in the shop. I knew she'd call even before she did."

"You got a feeling," the woman preacher said. Bobby still couldn't remember her name. "Like a heaviness."

"How you know that?"

She smiled and took a bite of roast.

"I saw you earlier. I was going for gas at Timmy's and I went past the church and I knew you'd be out front. And you were."

The preacher nodded. "I was. Not always, though." She swallowed and looked past Tommy, meeting Bobby's eyes. "Funny how that happened."

"Then it was you, Laura Beth," Bobby said. He watched as George pulled a small notebook and pen from his shirt pocket. "I knew I'd see you coming down the walk, and there you come. I thought you'd be wearing a yellow dress. That's the only thing I got wrong. But I could *see* it. And then I almost—"

"Whistled," Laura Beth said. She hadn't touched her food, hadn't even picked up her fork. "But you didn't. That's why I stared at you. I kept waiting for you to do it, but you never did."

A cloud fell over Junior's face. "Why you calling to Laura Beth like that, Bobby?"

Dorothea said, "Now, Junior, I'm sure Bobby didn't mean anything by it."

"I didn't *do* it," Bobby said. "I didn't whistle." He had no idea why he felt compelled to stand in defense of himself to the likes of Junior, at least insofar as Laura Beth Gowdy was concerned. If anything, Bobby felt he owed Laura Beth the sorry. Or maybe he'd go down to the bank, say the same to Charlie. "I ain't never."

"You have," Laura Beth said. "More times than I can count, Bobby."

He looked at Dorothea. "I ain't never whistled, Widow Cash. I'll swear it."

"Maybe not this morning, Bobby. But in the others."

"But—"

She held up a hand. "In the other todays is what I mean. What if you've been going through this one day more times than any of us can know, and in all those times you've seen Laura Beth coming down that sidewalk and you've whistled at her, which is rude and demeaning, but I'll set that aside for now. But what if you have and you just don't remember it? What would you say?"

Bobby took another drink. He wished for something stronger. "I'd say you're crazy."

Junior rolled his eyes and made a *pssh* sound, like he knew a secret Bobby didn't. Bobby guessed the times Junior Hewitt actually knew something someone else didn't were so few and far between that they were deemed worthy of relishing, even if it meant leaving a bit of mashed potatoes hanging from the corner of his mouth.

"What Mama means," he said, "is you're dead." Junior spread his arms wide, touching a strand of Laura Beth's golden hair and nearly touching Dorothea's sleeve. "Welcome to heaven, Bobby."

## -8-

What Bobby wanted to do was laugh. It was the only way he could respond to what he'd just heard, and from such a man as Junior, whose sole knowledge of the world encompassed how to throw a baseball and catch a fish and where in the hollers and mountains could be found the choicest marijuana. And the way Junior appeared right then, arms stretched with that glob of mashed potatoes stuck to his mouth, that wide and maniacal grin, almost demanded the very snort Bobby felt compelled to give. But he didn't laugh, nor did the others. Dorothea took a sip of tea and dabbed her lips with an air of solemnity. It was as though the table had become a graveside.

"Bobby don't believe me," Junior said. His smile grew. "Ain't that right, Bobby?"

He could feel their stares, Dorothea's and the preacher's and Laura Beth's from behind those dark sunglasses, and Tommy's most of all.

"Well, Junior, seeing as how I'm sitting right here and

everybody's looking at me like I'm a bug in a jar, I'm gonna say I don't guess I'm much dead at all."

"Ha!" Junior's hands landed on the table, making the dishes and glasses rattle and Tommy laugh. "Knew it. That's what they always say."

Dorothea said, "That's enough, Junior." She reached for Bobby's hand. Her skin felt hard and stretched against the brittle bones beneath. "You'll have my apologies, Bobby. Junior's always wanted to give welcoming a try."

Junior bobbed his chin. Laura Beth reached over and dabbed his mouth. Of all the odd things Bobby had experienced that morning, somehow that seemed the strangest. He didn't even know Laura Beth and Junior were acquainted, much less well enough for her to go cleaning him.

"I think maybe I'm just gonna go."

There was honey in Dorothea's words, and a sharpness: "I'd ask you to stay, dear. At least until we have a talk."

George's cigarette had burned to near the filter. He coughed hard and deep, spilling ash onto his plate. Bobby glanced over his shoulder. Matthew and Mark were gone. A tiny hand gripped his elbow.

"You ain't gotta be scared, mister," the Purcell boy said. "You got us now."

And now Bobby did laugh, a short but harsh breath between his teeth, like he'd blown out a candle.

"Let's slow things down a bit," Dorothea said. "Okay, Bobby?"

He looked at her and nodded.

"Now, to your own words, you woke this morning same as always but with . . . *feelings*. Yes?"

"Yes."

"Can you tell me what you remember of last night?"

Bobby shook his head and said no. But in the brief space between, it seemed to him as if he *did* know, at least a little. Feelings rather than memories, pictures that came broken and blurred. A road and trees and the moon, a bit of song. He rubbed his chest.

"He ain't here yet," Tommy whispered. It sounded like awe. "Not all the way. Right, Mama?"

Dorothea rubbed the soft spot between her nose and upper lip. "So it seems."

"That's never happened," the preacher said.

Bobby shook his head. "What's—?"

"No, it hasn't," Dorothea said, "and here we are all forgetting our manners. I must apologize again. It's been a great while since we've had a new guest." She took Bobby's hand and spoke softly now. "I'll say it plain, Bobby. Plain is always best. Tonight your day will end. I don't know how or at what time, though I expect *you* know, or at least some part of you knows. And then you'll wake. But it won't be tomorrow you'll meet, it will be today. It will always be today. Now and forever."

"Because I'm dead." Not a question.

"Don't think of it as death. Think of it as a coming into life once more. One far more precious and beautiful than the one we've left behind."

"We."

"Me. Junior. Laura Beth. George. I believe you know us well enough, as we know you. George taught most of the town's young people his dark arts at some point. I'm sure you're no exception."

"Earth science, I believe," George said. He coughed again and pulled a handkerchief from his pocket. "That right, Bobby?"

"Yessir. Long time ago."

The old man smiled. "You've no idea."

"Though I suppose you've yet to make the acquaintance of our newest minister?" Dorothea asked.

The woman scooted her chair back and leaned behind Tommy. "Juliet Creech." She offered both her hand and a wide smile. Bobby took both and realized her touch was as lovely as the rest of her. Not as beautiful as Laura Beth, perhaps, but also more in a way he could not put to words.

"Pleasure's mine."

"Juliet pastored the Methodist church before she reached the Turn," Dorothea said. Then, more to Juliet than to him, "Bobby reached the point where he had no use for religion, much as our George. Beside you, Bobby, is our precious Tommy."

The boy thrust out his hand. Bobby shook it proper. "Tommy. Believe I know your mama. Stacey Purcell, right?"

Tommy's smile, constant since Bobby had stepped into the room, now vanished. His bright eyes leveled to the color of a spotted sky.

"Miss Dorothea's my mama."

Dorothea spoke up. "What Tommy means is he doesn't have a mother *here*. We're his family now, and the only one he needs. Isn't that right, Tommy?"

The boy's bright smile returned. "Yes'm."

"What do you mean 'here'?"

"Heaven," Junior tried again.

"But I ain't dead."

"You will be," Tommy said, "maybe even tonight! Then we can be friends." He tugged at Bobby's sleeve. "Will you be my friend?"

That was enough. For Bobby, that was about plenty. "Y'all quit messing with me."

Juliet's eyes were soft. Her face open as if to show that

neither lie nor malice could dwell there. "I'm so sorry, Bobby. There really isn't an easy way to tell you all of this."

"Lord knows we've tried," Dorothea said. "It wasn't easy for any of us, Bobby, and maybe that's the way it must be, passing between worlds."

"But I ain't *passed*."

"But you're passing," Laura Beth whispered. "Even now, you are. You just don't know it yet."

"I know what you feel, Bobby," Dorothea said. "I know your troubles. Those . . . *feelings*. Knowing what's to come before it does, and then having it come again and again. I was first here to this heaven. To our Turn. It was a slow waking and then it turned to madness. I was the only person in the world who knew what was happening. More people I told, the worse it became. I don't know how long passed. Years, maybe. Maybe longer. Then I found Junior, and in much the same state as I'd suffered at first."

"I was *crazy*," Junior said.

Bobby could only disagree with the verb tense.

"Mama saved me."

"Only because by then I knew enough to be of help. And having two of us certainly made Tommy's arrival better, just as the three of us helped Juliet, the four of us George, and the five of us Laura Beth. Just as the six of us will help you, Bobby. It's been so long since we've had someone new. George was beginning to think we were all there would be. Weren't you, George?"

"That's true, Bobby," he said. "I daresay we were all becoming a trifle lonely."

"Lonely? George, I seen you and your wife just the other day. You sure didn't look lonely."

George's face fell. "You saw my Anna?"

"Sure I did," Bobby said.

"And she was fine? How did she look?"

Bobby snorted. "What you mean how did she look? It was just the other day."

"To you," Dorothea said. "It was the other day to *you*, Bobby. But that day might well be a thousand years past for George. Anna isn't in the Turn."

George laid down his pen. He reached into his pocket with one hand and found another cigarette. With the other, he wiped a single tear.

# -9-

Dorothea left the preacher—*Juliet*, Bobby remembered—and Laura Beth to handle the rest of the meal, then asked Bobby if they could speak alone. She did not wait for his answer before rising to leave him in an awkward silence with the others. They stared with a kind of wonder, like they saw in Bobby not the man he was but the place from which he'd come, a land near enough to touch and smell and yet so far that it existed now only in their deepest memories.

She waited in the center hall on the other side of the kitchen, where a droning grandfather clock stood against a wide stair that led to the second floor. Two rooms sprawled to Bobby's right, one a formal living space and the other what Dorothea called the gathering room, where she guided him. Bobby had never been in that part of the house. So far as he had been led to believe, few had since Hubert Cash's wake some years back. Dorothea had looked sullen that day, frail and shriveling and unwilling to accept her husband's sudden absence.

Yet the person who showed him to a long leather sofa was no sickly widow, but a woman in full control. Bobby had seen her in the years following her husband's funeral, had noticed how Dorothea had taken to coloring her hair the dark black it had been in her youth and how she would only be seen in her finest dresses. Those things had done little to keep the Widow Cash from turning into a recluse. Had any in Mattingly paused in their doings that day to notice the yellow house at the end of the road filled with strangers seeking a good dinner, Bobby thought they never would have believed it.

"It'll be quiet here," Dorothea said, closing the door. "Just the two of us." She smiled and made her way to a small wooden cabinet in the corner of the room. The door made a soft *click* and swung wide to reveal a rack of bottles. Bobby's mouth watered. "I don't normally imbibe, especially this early. But I think this may be an exception. Bourbon fine with you?"

"Yes'm."

She brought a bottle and two glasses to the sofa and set them on the table, pouring Bobby's first and then her own. Bobby downed his in a single gulp. He had no qualms asking for another.

"What's happening to me, Dorothea?"

"What happens to us all, dear, sooner or later. Nothing but that. Most come when they've already made their crossing. All of them, actually. Junior snatched you in what I'd call midstream. One foot in one world, one in another. If he'd waited one more Turn, things would be a lot simpler." She took a sip. "This will all be as easy or as difficult as you make it, Bobby. You are passing. There is nothing to be done about it, and that's what you must know first. You will finish this day as you always have and wake to this day again, and you will enter into eternity."

Bobby shook his head. "Dorothea, this ain't how people die."

She raised her eyebrows. "You ever died before, Bobby Barnes? You expected pearly gates and streets of gold? Dark tunnel and a bright light? Tell me, did you expect to see heaven at all? And before you answer, remember I know you well."

Bobby could only drink. Dishes clinked on the other side of the house. Muted conversation, likely revolving around him. The room was comfortable but large. A desk that must have been Hubert's in the corner. An old typewriter sat on top alongside a telephone and stacks of papers. Framed pictures of Dorothea in her younger years on the mantel above the fireplace. The television sat beside two large windows facing the street. Outside, he could see Matthew and Mark peering in.

"You don't have to speak," she told him. "As I said, I know you well enough. There would be no heaven for you. Your soul would be snuffed like a candle, winked out, never to spark again. That's what you'd come to believe, even if deep down you feared a fate far worse. Hell's waiting on you. Believe I've heard you say that once or twice, though my memory of the former things is old and fading. But it's not to hell you've come. Instead, you've been given all this."

She waved her hands toward the walls and the windows.

"Not heaven, I suppose, but certainly the closest to it any of us deserve. I will not say I lived a holy life, Bobby. Far from it. I abandoned what faith I possessed after Hubert passed, just as you abandoned yours for your own reasons. As for the others . . . well, I won't have to say much. Junior was never a good man in the world. George placed what faith he had in his books. Laura Beth and Tommy were never brought up believing."

"What about Juliet?" Bobby asked. "Crying out loud, Dorothea, she's a preacher."

She raised her eyebrows. "You think preachers are so sure of what they proclaim behind a pulpit? Hardly. They are as doubting as any, and sometimes more. And yet we're here. No weeping and gnashing of teeth, no roasting over the devil's spit. It's grace, I suppose. A credit for lives that may not have ended well but that had, at least for a time, found good favor in the eyes of heaven."

"Heaven ain't Mattingly, Dorothea."

"Ours is," she said.

Dorothea refilled his glass. Matthew looked on, unseen by her, from the corner of the window.

"So you're saying, what?" Bobby asked. "You and me and all the rest in there, we died the same day? Seven people pass at the same time in a town this little? You tell me the odds of that."

"I'm afraid that's not how it works," she said. "I don't know how long I've been here, Bobby. As I said, it was ages before I found Junior. Ages more before Tommy. You ask me to explain it, all I can say is I can't. Logic and science, that's George's domain. Heaven's a matter of faith."

"Faith."

She moved from the sofa to the window just as Matthew's head ducked away. Her back to him, a slender figure in a navy dress and white apron. Bobby didn't know if she was broken or crazy.

"All those people out there, Bobby? Life will go on for them. They will pass through this day as they have all the days before. They will grow old in their hearts and minds and suffer as all the living do, trundle along as best they can toward whatever end awaits. But here is where our journey ends—our final stop, our eternity in a day. Part of the living, yet cut off from it as well. And that is our true and final gift, whether we deserve it or not."

"Gift?"

She reached for the remote and moved to the sofa once more, then turned on the news, flipping from one station to the next.

"I used to watch this. Even after I realized this was heaven, I never strayed far from this house. I did on my last day of living. Went to town on my very own for the first time since Hubie passed. Stepped out in the middle of an empty street and near got run over by a truck. Scared me half to death, Bobby, and that was the end of my travels. Even here, I don't go out. I watched the news instead at the beginning, watched it so many times that I memorized it all. We all do when we first come." She chuckled. "I remember after George had only been here a short while, he kept telling Tommy he needed schooling whether this was eternity or not. Tommy sat right where you are now and turned this TV on. *Jeopardy* was showing. Tommy ran through the whole show and never got a question wrong. Left poor George speechless and Junior rolling on the floor. That shut George up for a while, until he figured out Tommy had seen that show about a billion times. Watch this news this morning?"

"I did."

"War and death and sickness, children in grown bodies making messes of things. Horror, that's what it all is. The world is crumbling, but nobody cares to do anything about it. But look here."

Dorothea touched a button that made the screen go blank.

She tossed the remote across the room, where it landed upon the carpet with a soft *plunk*.

"That's our gift. The comfort of knowing we can finally turn our backs to the hard world. Our struggle is done, and what's out there doesn't matter anymore. War and government, want and pain, none of those things are ours. For them"—she waved somewhere beyond the windows again—"not for us. We've been saved from the furtherance of such things. No more surprises, no cares of how we will get by and what we shall do. This day will part with all the bluster and blow of a spring morning. Then it will come again, unchanged and unburdened. We call what happens the Turn. We live this day right along with everyone else, but when midnight comes we remain as they go on to face their unknown tomorrows. We remain where there are neither secrets nor dangers."

Bobby listened to this with a few small nods of his head. "All that sounds a mite fine, Dorothea. Nearly enough to make me wish it was so."

"I know you doubt. That's expected. Lord knows I did plenty of that for a long while. You're just not fully here yet. You have one more Turn yet to go, and it's not as bad as it may seem. I end my time brushing my hair. A silly thing, isn't it? But that's the last thing I did, so it will be the last thing I always do. Next, I'm dressed and in the upstairs hall with the bed already made. It goes more or less the same for the others. None of that's spoken much. It's a private thing, our Turns. But that is the only rule. We must end our every time in the same manner as we ended it the first, and we always begin the same. There are no exceptions. To try any other way is unwise."

"Unwise?"

"And impossible. Trust me when I say don't even bother.

Just go about your day as you see fit, Bobby. Do what seems best for you and end it as you are led. Let the Lord handle the rest."

"Lord?" Bobby asked. He chuckled and swirled his glass. It felt good, that tingling. "Well now, I ain't even thought of that. He around, Dorothea? I expect He would be, given as how I'm supposed to be sitting here in the beyond. Sure like to have a word. I got some things need explained."

Dorothea went rigid. She smoothed a wrinkle in her dress that Bobby couldn't see and set her glass on the table. When she spoke, it was with a tremble. "Right now, Bobby, the only thing that needs explaining is there will be no mocking the Lord in my home. I have to endure enough of that from George, and I won't abide another. The Lord is watching. Always watching. What answers you seek may be given in time or they may not, and that is not for you to decide. Dare I say such flippancy is what got you here in the first place. My advice would be to show a measure of gratitude that you haven't been damned with the rest of the drunks and molesters."

Bobby's glass stilled. He met Dorothea's eyes. She did not blink. Nor did he.

"I am no molester," he said. "Allie run off into the woods with Zach Barnett and they got themselves lost. I didn't have nothing to do with that, Dorothea, and you know it. They both said the same when they come back."

"Nonetheless, here we sit. What grace brought you here was certainly not my own, but it's grace I must accept. And I'm willing, Bobby. But you must do your part."

She reached into her apron pocket and pulled out a single sheet of paper, folded into thirds. She set it on the table by the bottle. Bobby couldn't make out the typed words on the page.

"Light cannot dwell with darkness, Bobby. I'm sure you at least remember that from your churching years. And we are still dark. Saved but sullied. God is in His heaven and we are in ours, and the two cannot mix. He made the Turn, but He cannot remain here." Dorothea reached out and touched the paper with all the care of a holy relic. "He sends me word every morning. I found one of these a very long time ago in my mailbox, soon after Junior arrived. Affirmations for the most part, praise and goodwill. He loves us, even you. After all our sinning and turning away, He loves us still enough to craft this place and not remain wholly apart from it."

"The Lord writes you a letter every morning." He had to bite his lip to keep from laughing. "That what you're trying to tell me? I'm in heaven, and God writes you letters?"

"As I said, the Lord is watching. This is only the heaven we've earned." She flexed her hands. "I died with this old arthritis. I was reborn with it. Poor Laura Beth in there came down with the pinkeye just before she passed. Now she views heaven through a pair of sunglasses. George still has a taste for his cigarettes. And given your level of inebriation when Junior brought you in and the bottle you've nearly drained, it seems to me you still crave your liquor. It's not perfect here, Bobby. It was never meant to be. But there is joy. More joy than you've ever known in your former life, and that's what you'll learn with us. Because we're together. You wonder why heaven is this day and not another, that's why. Junior has no work and no prospects. No friends. I suppose any old day would have suited him to die. You could say the same for me. But the rest?"

She held up one finger.

"Tommy's mother is gone, leaving him alone."

Another finger.

"George's Anna is visiting relations in Kentucky. She's returning home as we speak. Of course she won't arrive today and never will, at least as far as George is concerned. She didn't call before she left this morning, though I can promise George has tried to call her as many times as I can count. Those mountains, Bobby. No cell service. George, too, is alone today."

A third.

"As it's Saturday, Juliet has no responsibilities to her congregation, what little of one she had left."

And finally a fourth.

"As far as our sweet Laura Beth, her Charlie is away golfing with his drunkard friends and won't return until late tonight. We're alone, Bobby. Every single one of us. That's why the Lord chose this day. He knew an eternity in the Turn would be all the fairer with a family to share it with, and that's what we are. That's what we offer to you. We gather here in my home because no one wanted us out in the world. We let the great mass of people go on as they will, and we are unburdened. We have what they never can. We are free."

Dorothea hung that word in the air with a smile wider and deeper than Bobby believed her mouth could manage. Her anger over his mocking seemed forgotten. Or perhaps even forgiven, if such a thing could be offered him. And whether it was the bright autumn day or the liquor flowing through his veins or the sight of Matthew's and Mark's tiny heads lifting up from the bottom edge of the window, Bobby felt something in him give way. He let himself believe if only for a moment that perhaps he had indeed found heaven, that all his long years of striving and struggle had somehow come to an end. He felt Dorothea's hand upon him once more, heard the sounds of talk and laughter from deeper in the house. And the word Bobby then spoke sounded to him like a song when the note is struck just right and echoed, however briefly, in a place he believed long dead.

"Free."

# -10-

He didn't stay for a plate, saying there was too much for him to think over and he'd always done his best thinking alone. Dorothea knew that was a lie. Bobby Barnes hadn't conjured an organized thought in years; all he wanted was away. She rose to show him out, torn between the desire to have him gone and the desire to keep him there. Between wanting to keep the rest of the family safe and wanting to protect her heaven from a man she knew was more reckless even than Junior.

Bobby turned in the hall and looked at her, forcing Dorothea to smile once more. "I guess I should say my good-bye to the rest."

"I'm sure they'd like that. They're all fine people, Bobby. I don't want us to part with any unease. Maybe I could get you some coffee? Or a nice cup of hot tea? I grow the spearmint out back."

"I don't think so, Widow Cash. Thank you."

He didn't wait for her to lead the way. That only made Dorothea more anxious. Someone new, someone like him, leading her through her own home. She nearly offered once more when they reached the kitchen—*Wouldn't take but a minute to fix a plate, there's plenty*—but said nothing. Pride, of course, which Dorothea understood. She also knew that in the few feet between the gathering room and the kitchen, she had decided it best for Bobby to simply go. He was right, he needed to think. Dorothea needed to think, too.

What conversation the others had found around the table ended the moment Bobby walked in. There was no attempt to smooth the awkwardness; everyone knew Bobby had become the center of their talk, Bobby included.

He held his cap in his hand and said, "Guess I'll be going."

Tommy worked a frown. "You're leaving?"

"Yeah, well. Got stuff to do."

Junior snorted. "Ain't *nothin'* you got to do. Not no more. Mama tole you that?"

"Now that's okay, Junior," Dorothea said. She came forward and laid a hand to Bobby's back (if for no other reason than to show the others all was well) and felt the muscles between his shoulders clench. Dorothea told herself that had nothing to do with her and everything to do with what Bobby had become, though that gave her little comfort. She did not relish his falling under her care. Laura Beth was bad enough. "It's a lot for anybody to take in. I'm sure you can all remember that bit of dark before the light comes. Besides, we must all remember Bobby isn't fully among us yet. He can't remember the end of his Turn, isn't that right?"

"Yes'm," Bobby said.

But he did not look at her. He had the first time, but not now, and something in Dorothea wondered if Bobby was being entirely truthful when he claimed ignorance as to how this day ended for him. That worried her, though not as much as why he would lie about it.

"I expect tonight will be the end of it." She smiled at him and added, "As well as your beginning. Bobby simply has his doubts now, as we all did. I won't blame him for that."

"Certainly not," George said through the cloud of smoke around him. His grin faded only a little at Dorothea's stare.

"Nonetheless, all doubt will be gone next Turn, Bobby,

and you'll certainly be welcomed here. I'll be sure to leave a proper place for you at the table, right next to me. In the meantime, someone should go along with you."

Bobby said, "I'll be fine, Dorothea."

Here she refused to yield. "I'm afraid I must insist. Yours is a new circumstance, and I'll admit I don't quite know how to handle it."

"You mean God left that outta His letter?"

Silence from the table. Junior turned around and looked ready to rise.

Dorothea spoke slowly: "You are free, Bobby, just as I told you. But there are expectations here. Responsibilities. We all must do our part in tending to the blessing given us. There are things you must learn in order for us all to get along, and that is why you must have company this day. Junior?"

The man acted as though he hadn't heard. He was still turned in his seat, glaring. After a long pause, he said, "Don't guess I'll be the one, Mama. Me and Bobby had a little row down at the BP. Andy was calling to the sheriff. I expect Jake's looking for me. Can't go back for my truck. I was gonna get George to run me out to Boone's Pond so I can get my fishin' in. Don't really have a mind to spend the Turn in jail."

"Be glad to," George said. "I could take Bobby, too. If we should run across Jake, I'd simply explain it was all a misunderstanding."

"No," Dorothea said. "You go on with Junior, George."

Juliet's mouth opened to speak. Dorothea wasn't sure if letting the preacher babysit Bobby was any better than letting George, but Tommy beat her to it.

"Let me go, Mama," he said. "I'll show Mr. Barnes all he needs to know."

Laura Beth, silent until now, said, "I don't think Bobby is in much condition to drive, Tommy."

"I ain't drunk," Bobby slurred, "nor in need of fellowship."

Dorothea said, "You're wrong on both counts, but I'm sure you're better drunk behind the wheel than sober. You've certainly had more experience. Tommy will go with you, or I'll see to it you don't go anywhere. I'm sorry I have to say it plain, but not even heaven is without its dangers."

She supposed Bobby's desire to get away was stronger than his need to disagree.

"Fine," he said. "Come on, kid."

Tommy hopped up, shoving one last forkful of mashed potatoes into his mouth before grabbing his cap from the floor. He made a circle around the table and kissed everyone on the cheek, kissed even Junior, and saved Dorothea for last.

"You take care of him now," she said.

Tommy and Bobby answered, "I will."

"Nice to see you all," Bobby added. "And, Laura Beth, my apologies again for not whistling. Or whistling. Whatever the case may be."

Dorothea walked them to the door. "Don't you worry," she was saying. "Tommy will help you with the rest you need to know. You might see him as a boy, but he has the wisdom of far more years than I dare count. Just go about your business as you would. I'm sure there'll be no trouble. And when this morning rolls back, you come see us. I'll have a hot breakfast that'll warm your bones."

She opened the door. Bobby paused and said, "Dorothea, thank you for . . . this."

"It's what I do. And please call me Mama."

For all Bobby's bluster that he had to go think in private,

he didn't seem much in a hurry now. He toed the mark in the doorway between the wood of the foyer and the concrete of the porch as if his next step might send him off the edge of the world.

"I'm gonna die tonight?" he asked.

"Everybody out there's dying, Bobby. You're just going to finish. It'll be an easy thing. And when it's done, we'll be here to welcome you."

"Welcome me?"

"Why yes," she said. "We'll welcome you home."

Tommy took hold of Bobby's hand and pulled him on. Dorothea watched as the two of them made their way down the walk toward Bobby's truck, smiling as Tommy set to talking. She felt the boards beneath her feet give way and smelled Junior's cheap cologne.

"You believe that?" she asked. "Of all the people to wake up and be brought here, it has to be Bobby Barnes. I swear, Junior, sometimes the Lord is a mystery I tire of unraveling."

"What'd you tell him?"

"All he needs for now. We'll have to get with the others, though. Figure out how and when to say the rest. In the meantime, Tommy will do what's right. You keep that man away from Laura Beth, though."

"You don't want him knowing?"

She shook her head. "Something like that? No. Telling Bobby now will do nothing more than scare him off. It'll upset the balance."

"He'll be okay," Junior said. "Soon as he finds out he's got an eternal supply of drinkin' alcohol, Bobby'll be happy as a clam."

"I hope so," Dorothea said. She waved to Tommy as he climbed into the truck. Bobby had disappeared around the other side. She heard him talking, though to whom she had no idea.

She said it again: "I hope so."

# -11-

Bobby kept his voice low and soft and did his best to tell the boys Tommy could be a new friend. Neither Matthew nor Mark budged. They'd rather ride the three miles back to the shop in the bed than be squished in with a stranger. There had been enough of that already, having to come all the way from the BP with Junior. And so the boys left Dorothea's in the bed of Bobby's truck, their faces pressed against the back window, scowling at the boy occupying their seat. Bobby decided it was a good thing Tommy didn't see them.

Any worry of what he should say soon faded; the Purcell boy did enough talking for them both. Talking about Dorothea and Junior and Juliet, George and Laura Beth, how much fun they were all going to have now that nothing mattered any-more. All Bobby could do was drive. He watched the people he passed and wondered how many of them could see the strange boy in the passenger's seat—the kid riding with the pervert.

"You wanna sink down a ways?" he asked. "Don't think it's a good idea, people seeing you with me."

"Why?"

"Let's just say some might get the wrong idea."

"That don't matter none, Mr. Barnes," Tommy said. To prove it, he rolled down his window and began waving to those on the street, telling them good morning and hello and this was his new friend. Matthew and Mark went pale. Bobby tried snatching Tommy's arm, but the boy was too fast. It had become a game. Bobby thought that for Tommy, most things were. "See? Don't nobody care. Even if they do, they'll forget next time around."

"Next time around," Bobby said.

Tommy smiled. His freckles spread when he did that, almost such that they disappeared. Below his cap, red hair curled up like roses bending for the sun. "You'll see."

They made it back to the shop without incident, proving Tommy right. Nobody cared. Or at least nobody cared as far as Bobby Barnes went. He backed the Dodge into its spot and cut the engine. Matthew and Mark jumped from the bed and disappeared through the door leading into the waiting room. Neither turned to see if their daddy followed.

"Guess I got some making up in store this afternoon," he said.

Tommy cocked his head. "Making up about what?"

"Never mind. Well, Mr. Purcell, I thank you for escorting me safely to my abode. Now I'm gonna go inside and try to forget everything Dorothea put in my head. Guess you can see yourself home?"

"Mama won't let me. I gotta stay here and talk to you more."

"Stop calling that woman your mama."

"But she *is*. She's all our mama. Yours, too, Mr. Barnes."

"Your mama is Stacey Purcell. She works up at the factory and you two live in that little shack out on Gertie's Lane."

"She *ain't*," Tommy screamed. His eyes grew shiny. His jaw clenched. Then came a long and slow exhale, as though he was trying to push back a great pain. "I know what you're doing, Mr. Barnes. You're trying to get me away. They told me you'd do that."

"Who told you?"

"George and Laura Beth. Junior. Juliet didn't, but just because she don't know you and neither do I. But the rest of them. They said they known you in the old world."

Bobby took off his hat and rubbed his hair. Tommy did the same.

"So you gonna get in trouble if you don't come in awhile?"

"I don't get in trouble, only with George sometimes when I say I don't want to learn. I'm staying because I want to. I know you're scared even if you say you ain't, Mr. Barnes. I was scared half to death when I got here. But it's great now. It's the best thing ever."

"I ain't got no food."

"I ain't hungry."

"Ain't got no drink."

"Ain't thirsty."

Bobby sighed. "Fine then. But you mind what I say, and don't you step inside my shop. You'll like to hurt yourself."

Instructions given and accepted, Bobby got out. Tommy followed through the door and into the waiting room. The boy didn't pause to look around. Instead, he plopped into the recliner and smiled.

Bobby smirked. "Make yourself at home."

Tommy sat in the recliner and kicked the footrest up, sending one of the paperbacks across the floor. "I been here before. Wasn't this messy, though."

"You ain't never been here."

"Have so. This one time. Junior got a nail stuck in one of his tires. He come up here to get you to patch it. I come along."

Bobby searched his memory, which wasn't at all as clear and reliable as it once had been, but still could be counted upon for something as monumental as a customer. No recollection of Junior or Tommy occurred to him, much less the two of them together.

"It was a long time ago," Tommy said. "We weren't in the Turn long, so you were still mostly alive 'stead of sorta dead."

"You mean one of the todays?"

Tommy shrugged like that was as good a way of putting it as any other.

"You know how stupid that sounds," Bobby said. "Right?"

"Better not say that, Mr. Barnes. The Lord's watching."

Bobby snorted. He wanted to say something about that, something like what he'd said to Dorothea, but didn't when he saw how grave Tommy looked.

"Me and Junior had to ask Dorothea if we could come here to get the tire fixed. She said coming here wouldn't upset the balance. So we did. You was drunk like you are now. You let me sit here and watch cartoons, even though I already seen them all. Junior said I couldn't tell you that. Guess I can now."

The boy talked so much that Bobby had come to think he didn't really have to be present at all. He paused in the doorway, one foot in the waiting room with Tommy and the other in the shop with his boys.

"What's that mean? 'Upset the balance'?"

"That's one of the things I got to tell you about. God says even though this is heaven, you can't be goin' 'round doin' anything you want. Like get in trouble. Or do bad things. The balance keeps heaven strong."

"Balance between what?"

"Between us and the ones passing through to tomorrow."

"God says that, or Dorothea?"

Tommy's red hair bobbed. "Both. It's in the letters she gets. I seen some of them. Mama don't know. Sometimes

I look while she's makin' dinner. She thinks I'm doing the studyin' George gives me. You know he makes me learn, Mr. Bobby? I mean, it's *Saturday*. It's *always* Saturday. Ain't even no school day."

He held out his arms palms up, that universal childhood expression of *stupid adults*. Bobby knew that sign well. Matthew was doing much the same on the hood of Bea's car.

"Ain't for you to worry of learning anything here," Bobby said. "I ain't nothing to teach. You gotta stay to keep yourself outta trouble, I don't care. Sit there and watch the TV."

"But I already seen it."

"Seen what?"

"Everything."

Bobby pointed at the TV and didn't stop until Tommy sighed and pushed the button. He found a *Gunsmoke* rerun on one of the lower channels and began speaking lines of dialogue seconds before Marshal Dillon and Festus. Bobby watched, not knowing whether to laugh or run. The boy never missed a word.

"How you know all that?" Bobby asked.

Tommy rolled his eyes. "Told you, already *seen* it."

"Then see it again. I gotta tend to something."

Bobby left him there and walked into the shop. He felt Tommy stare and heard him talking, now mimicking not only Festus's lines but also the nasally way Festus talked. He got the sense the boy was possessed somehow, though who Tommy Purcell was and what had overtaken him Bobby could not know. It unnerved him in a way even Matthew's and Mark's stares could not. They sat motionless on the hood of Bea's car and tried not to look at him. Bobby held up his hands in surrender.

Matthew spoke first. He always did. "We decided we

ain't talkin' to you, Daddy. I'm just talkin' to you now so you can know."

"Guys, I'm sorry."

Mark crossed his arms and stared at a spot on the floor near Bobby's boots.

"I didn't mean for none of this to happen. Swear it. But after that mess with Junior, wasn't no way I'd let y'all in that house. I'm sorry you had to stand outside and worry, but I was fine. Everything's fine."

"*He's* here," Matthew said, pointing a thumb toward the waiting room. Tommy still stared, though he'd finished talking to the TV. "Ain't fine so long as *he's* here, Daddy. I ain't even supposed to be talkin' to you. Me and Mark pinkie sweared."

"Tommy's okay. He's nice. I let him stay because he's supposed to make sure we're okay, but sitting here arguing sure don't seem like we're okay now, does it? He can't leave, Matthew. He'll get in trouble. You wouldn't want him getting in trouble, would you?"

Mark said, "He ain't gonna get in trouble, Daddy." Still staring at the floor, arms still folded. "He *is* the trouble."

"What's that mean?" Bobby asked. He chuckled. "What? Y'all jealous?" He pointed toward the waiting room. "That's just some kid in there. You're my *boys*."

"Ain't been your boys all morning long," Matthew said.

Bobby looked over his shoulder. He lowered his voice, just in case Tommy could hear. "Well, that'll change right now. But I need to ask y'all something. Y'all remember what we did last night? Right before bed? It's important."

Matthew thought. "Went on a ride, I guess. We always go on a ride."

"But do you *remember*?"

"No, but we always do."

"Mark? You remember we took a ride last night?"

Mark chewed his bottom lip. "Why?"

"Because it's important."

"Why's it important?"

Bobby jerked his cap off and counted to ten. Counted to twenty. *Can't get mad. Can't yell. Not now, in front of the boys when they're already mad, and in front of the Purcell kid. Thirty. Can't tell the boys why. Why's too horrible and hurts too much, because unless a bunch of people in town who barely know each other decided to play a trick on your pa, we're dead, Mark. That's why. Dead or mostly dead, and from something that happened last night. And if it was a ride, Mark, that means it was something I did, and it don't mean I just killed myself, it means I killed you and your brother, too.*

"It just is, Mark. Do you remember what we did last night?"

"We went on a ride."

"You sure?"

"Yessir. You kept feeling funny and said you might get a lot'ry ticket at the store, and I told you to. I did, but you didn't listen. You never listen when I say it."

"What do you mean I never listen?"

He wouldn't answer.

Bobby bent down and put his hands on his son's shoulders. "Mark? Your daddy needs a little help right now, buddy, and you're just the man to give it. Please, son."

Mark looked up with two trembling lips. His brow had gone wet with fear, the part in his hair all but gone. A tear fell from his eye and raced down his left cheek.

"There's night on the other side, Daddy. And monsters. It's dark when it happens and we can't see and then the night gets nighter and we fall in. We fall in every time."

"When what happens, Mark?"

Another tear.

"When we die."

*　*　*

Bobby felt his shoulders curl forward. He bent his head from Mark's gaze, putting the bill of his cap between them. No counting now. He could pace off a thousand steps in his mind, there would still be a tremor to his next words.

"What you mean 'when we die'?"

Mark sniffed. "I don't know."

"You do. Tell me."

"I *can't*."

His hands shot out and grabbed hold of Mark's arms—Bobby's hands alone, not his mind and certainly not his heart, both of which had gone cold and numb at his son's words. It was as if those two hands had become possessed themselves, perhaps by the very thing that had overtaken Tommy. Bobby could do nothing as he felt his fingers sink into the soft skin, nothing as he pulled his son forward and pushed him away, rocking him for answers as he once had the Pepsi machine when it refused to yield a can. Mark crying harder now, begging his father to stop, it hurt. And now Matthew, flailing at Bobby's arms to turn his brother loose, weeping as Mark wept and as Bobby screamed all that Dorothea and Tommy and the rest had told him.

Bobby pulled Mark to himself a final time and held him there. He kneaded the back of the boy's neck with his fingers, using it as a kind of anchor to let Bobby know this was real, *they* were real, and whatever had happened to them had at least left them together. It had left them a family.

70

"I'm sorry," Bobby said. "Sorry. I didn't mean to hurt you, son."

He drew Matthew in as well, rocking them in his arms. Bobby turned and looked through the doorway. Tommy hadn't moved from his spot.

"I wanna go," Mark said. "I don't wanna be here no more."

"We ain't going nowhere. We're staying right here where it's safe."

He stared at Tommy, who had sunk into the recliner such that he looked stuck there. His breaths burst in and out against a trembling, pointed chin. Something had drained his confidence. The boys, Bobby thought. Or the arguing? Or was it that Bobby had somehow pieced together a little too much before it was time?

"Why don't y'all go play in the alley awhile? Won't nobody bother you out there. Just don't wander off. We stay here tonight, okay? Until this is all over. No ride."

Matthew looked at Tommy. "Tell him to leave, Daddy. Tell that boy he's gotta go away and not come back."

"Can't do that," Bobby said. "Not yet. Me and Mr. Purcell got to have us a little talk."

He hugged them both and turned. Tommy said nothing, only drew his legs tight against his chest.

# -12-

Tommy had never seen Mr. Barnes act like that. Granted, it hadn't been often he'd seen Mr. Barnes at all, even in the Turn, because Mr. Barnes hardly ever came out of his shop. The few times Tommy had (not just the time Junior blew out his tire but others, when Tommy took one of his walks or

Mama had an errand for him), he'd passed the shop and seen Mr. Barnes either sitting in his old chair reading or standing out front watching the world pass. Tommy had never stopped to speak. Not because it might upset the balance, but because he hadn't known what to say. How could he talk to someone who always looked so lonely and sad?

That's what had made him so excited when Junior brought Mr. Barnes to Mama's. Because Mr. Barnes didn't have to be lonely anymore and certainly not sad, not with such friends as he would have now and such a good family to love him. None of the others seemed to think that the case. Junior, maybe, though Tommy had gotten the notion that all Junior was really happy about was he'd have somebody to sin with now.

George had seemed okay with Mr. Barnes being there, but Tommy couldn't see what was going inside that old notebook. Mama asked him a lot to take a peek in there and see what all George wrote, but Tommy never could get a look. Laura Beth hadn't been too happy, though Laura Beth was hardly *ever* joyful. Juliet said to give Mr. Barnes a chance. She said there had to be a reason for all this to happen, which had made George laugh and Laura Beth get all teary eyed and Junior give Laura Beth a hug. And then, just before Mama brought Mr. Barnes back to the dining room, Juliet had said they all had to do their part to welcome him and get him settled.

Tommy knew all about that, which was why he volunteered to take Mr. Barnes home. Dying wasn't easy, and this wasn't the first time he'd helped people come into the Turn. But now he wished it would've been Junior who'd brought Mr. Barnes to the shop, or George or even Juliet, because Mr. Barnes was walking straight toward him and he was mad.

He made himself into a ball on the chair as Mr. Barnes came back in. "Everything okay out there?"

Mr. Barnes went around behind the counter and dug a beer from the refrigerator, then dug two more before shutting the door. Tommy got up from the chair to let him sit.

"We got to have us a talk, Tommy. No foolin' around."

He felt himself backing all the way to the door leading outside. All afternoon Tommy had the feeling Mr. Barnes wanted him gone. Now he thought Mr. Barnes would chase him down if he tried to leave.

"You answer me true now, boy." Bobby took a long swallow. "Anybody back at Dorothea's house tell you what the town says of me?"

"Nosir."

He belched. "Good, 'cause ain't none of it true. Sorry, I got no other chairs."

"That's okay." One step and a push against the door, he'd be gone. "You gonna try and hurt me, Mr. Barnes? 'Cause you better not. Lord's watchin'."

"So I hear. It's been brought to my attention maybe everything y'all said is right, though I still don't know how. People like tricking me. Lying to me. They prank call and write stuff on the shop sometimes when I'm sleeping. Kids mostly, teenagers, though the looks I get and the stuff gets said's from plenty of grown-ups, too."

"Anybody be mean to you today?"

"Just what Bea said when she called. And the sheriff, when I went to get my beer at Timmy's this morning. Jake's always had something against me, but I know the ghosts in his past."

Another swallow. Mr. Barnes crunched the empty and set it down beside the chair.

Tommy said, "Ain't nobody bothered you much today, means they won't ever again. You ain't gotta answer Bea's call no more, or go down to Timmy's neither. You got plenty beer in there to get you through the Turn."

"What about tomorrow?"

"Ain't no tomorrow. Tomorrow's today. All you drunk gets put back, just like the gas in your truck and whatever you eat and what clothes you change out of. You ain't even gotta go see Mr. Andy no more. It won't upset the balance. Mama says the Turn's a strong place."

Mr. Barnes reached for another beer. "The Turn. That what y'all call this?"

"Mostly we just call it heaven."

"'Cause we're all dead. You remember dying, Tommy? Come on over here outa that bright."

Tommy eased to a spot near the chair.

"Them feelings I got this morning," Mr. Barnes said. "I ain't felt them no more."

"That's because you're almost all the way here. You felt it 'cause you been doing the same stuff over and over again, but I don't know how long. Like answering your phone and getting your beer and your gas and seeing Laura Beth. Don't you whistle at her no more, Mr. Barnes."

"Why not?"

Tommy thought about that. He decided he'd better not say much else. "Just don't. You ain't felt the heaviness because all the other stuff you done was new. You ain't ever been to Mama's house before today or talked to me, so you ain't gonna get the feelin' you had. I don't ever get it no more. You got somewhere else to go today? I can go with you."

He crunched another can. "Nope. Stay here most days unless responsibility takes me elsewhere. Seldom does."

"Where's your house?"

"You're standing in it."

Tommy looked around. "You ain't got no home?"

"Home ain't nothing but four walls and a roof. Got a cot in back and a couple boxes clothes, some food squirreled away. Refrigerator and a TV. Phone. Bathroom, same as everybody else. Might not be as fancy as Dorothea's got, but then, I ain't a fancy man." He picked up another can. "Used to have a house out by the west bridge. Got tore up in the twister 'long with the shop and everything else. Insurance gave me money enough to rebuild both, so I did. But as you can see, business ain't exactly booming. Sold the house and moved in here, live off the money I made."

"So what do you do all day?"

"Read my books. Watch a little TV. Piddle on whatever car comes in, which ain't often but at least keeps my head above water." He lifted his can and grinned. "Keep myself—"

He stopped there and lowered his drink. Tommy saw Mr. Barnes's face turn white and his lips shudder, like a cold had passed through him. He looked at the phone.

Tommy whispered, "Somebody getting ready to call on you, Mr. Barnes?"

The phone rang. Mr. Barnes flinched.

"You gonna get that? I don't mind."

Another ring.

"No," Mr. Barnes said.

"You sure? Might be a customer to your shop."

"Carla," he said. "That's Carla callin' me."

"Who's that? You ain't gotta answer. It won't upset the balance. You ain't ever gotta answer it again if you don't want, because you already know what she says. You know, Mr. Barnes. All you gotta do is think about it."

"I can't—"

"Just think. That's all you gotta do."

The phone kept on. Mr. Barnes shut his eyes and bent his head like he was praying to the Lord who watched. His lips started moving. Tommy could hear the whispers:

"*Hello Bobby* Carla what do you want *Just to say hello* You don't ever say hello *You know what today is* I don't care *Yes you do* No I don't does Richie care *It wasn't Richie's fault* Well then it's yours *It could have been yours you do that all the time* Why do you think I do that I ain't got nothing no more *That's your fault this was never the way it should have been* Good-bye."

The ringing stopped. Mr. Barnes's hands shook.

"What'd I just do?" he asked.

"You remembered."

"Can't nobody remember something ain't happened yet."

"Did happen, Mr. Barnes. Who's Carla?"

"None of your business." He got up and fetched more beer, rubbing his head like it hurt.

"You ain't gotta talk about it if you don't want. It don't matter."

"Does matter, just not to you." He sat back down and stared. Not at Tommy, but out the window. "She's my ex-wife. Carla."

"Carla don't love you no more?"

Mr. Barnes chuckled. "Man I got to be wasn't the man she married, and that's all I'm gonna say. You're too young to understand it."

"I ain't young, Mr.—"

"I know, I know. You been here forever and a day, wherever here is. Quit calling me Mr. Barnes."

Tommy grinned. "We're in heaven, Mr. Bobby."

"Looks the same old world to me," Mr. Bobby said, "and just as dim."

\* \* \*

Little passed between them the rest of that afternoon, and it didn't take Tommy long to understand why. Mr. Bobby wanted him gone again. Tommy tried to make himself useful, helping to move all those spilled books into a nice pile, offering to sweep the shop and, more than once, getting Mr. Bobby a beer from the fridge. Then for a while he just sat at his place on the floor and watched Mr. Bobby read. He told Tommy it was a story about a drunk man who got turned into a monster. Tommy wanted to say he needed no story to know such a thing could happen. Heaven was a fine place and full of wonders, but not so many that they crowded out the former things. His old mama could drink so much that she got to be a monster, too, and that was one memory that would never fade.

Mr. Bobby drank more beer that afternoon and evening than Tommy's former mama ever could. Turned to a monster, too, though a sad one instead of mean. Most times, what he did was walk around his shop. He'd polish tools and mop the floor and look at Bea Campbell's car, thinking, Tommy supposed, that looking was about like doing. The phone rang a few more times. Mr. Bobby said he had no feeling about any of them. Tommy thought that was Mama calling or Juliet, or maybe George saying they'd have to double up on schooling the next time through the Turn. Once Laura Beth walked by the shop. Tommy waved and gave the okay sign.

Then there were the times he was left all alone. Mr. Bobby would say he had to go check on his own and he'd walk out to the alley and shut the door behind him, and Tommy could hear talking going on. On a few of those walks, he'd tell Tommy to watch some more TV or maybe find himself something to read. Others, Mr. Bobby would just up and disappear. Tommy would walk up to the door but never go out, though he did try to hear because Mama would want that. She'd want to know all about Mr. Bobby come next Turn. Tommy never did hear much of what was said, hushed speech about not worrying about things.

Supper that night consisted of a pack of crackers and beef jerky. They ate near the old radio in the shop that blared music Tommy had never heard before. Mr. Bobby said that was all the food he had, Tommy could go if he wanted. That was the first time Tommy almost did. He kept thinking about everybody sitting to supper at Mama's house, talking and laughing over fried chicken or baked spaghetti or a big pot of potato soup, and Tommy would have his mashed potatoes because that's all he ever wanted and mashed potatoes were what Mama called her *specially*. That would taste a whole lot better than crackers and dried meat. But he didn't budge. The food might have been awful, but not the company. The two of them talked long into the evening. Not just Tommy. Mr. Bobby, too. Once Mr. Bobby even laughed.

Tommy told what he could of the Turn, Mama's job keeping the balance and Junior's job helping her. How Junior and Laura Beth loved each other (which Tommy begged would go no further than the two of them and which Mr. Bobby could not seem to believe), and how George kept secrets and Juliet sometimes fought with Mama. Tommy even spoke of the Lord, how powerful He was and sometimes how frightening. The sad monster that Mr. Bobby had become began to slumber, leaving only the sad man Tommy had come to believe was his truest self. And as the hours ticked on and the beer in the refrigerator dwindled, Tommy's thoughts began to drift to this, the end of the best Turn in a long while.

"I'll be goin' soon, Mr. Bobby. Few hours. My Turn ends at eleven."

They were sitting on the hood of Mrs. Campbell's car, listening to something called Quiet Riot on the radio.

"What's that mean?"

"That's when everything ends and starts again for me. At eleven. Mama's 'bout ready to end hers, too." He checked the clock on the wall. "That's at nine. Laura Beth's already ended hers. Junior'll watch the ball game until just after that. Juliet's got awhile longer, least that's what she says. George says his Turn goes all the way to midnight, but I don't believe him."

"So what's that mean?" Mr. Bobby asked. "You gotta be home before?"

"Should. Don't matter if I'm there or not, though, that's where I'll be. What you do 'round this time, Mr. Bobby? You go to bed?"

Mr. Bobby looked down.

"Drop the 'Mister,' kid. Yeah. I go to bed."

A lie. Tommy had seen enough of them to know, both in the Turn and not. Some of him felt angered at that, some felt hurt. Friends didn't lie to each other.

"Guess you can run on now," Bobby said. "I appreciate the company, Tommy. Ain't had that in a long while."

"I can stay. I can see."

"See what?"

"Your Turn. Or you see mine. It's always good to see it at least once. That way you won't get so scared next time."

A man came on the radio saying this was 99.7, the valley's classic rock station. Bobby didn't hear it. He was too busy staring off into space as if trying to remember something he'd forgotten. Then the song came on. Tommy had never heard it before, but he could tell it was way old. He could tell Bobby heard it, too, because his eyes flew open and he started backing away.

"You hear that?"

"Hear what?" Tommy asked. "You mean the song?"

"Bad moon. I remember."

"Is this your Turn? It's okay if it is. It's just scary once. I swear."

"Hey!" Bobby screamed toward the door to the alley. "Hey, y'all come—"

He stopped then, or at least his words did. Bobby turned as his body began to wink out. Tommy saw arms and legs and body, then the bit of the wall behind, then the body again.

"You don't stay here?" Tommy asked. "Where you go, Mr. Bobby?"

Bobby opened his mouth to speak (*Or is he screaming?* Tommy wondered) and then winked a final time. Winked all the way and gone. The radio people kept singing on about a bad moon a-rising and a book fell off the table beside the chair in the waiting room, and Tommy stood in the middle of the shop alone.

"Good-bye," he whispered. "I love you."

# -13-

The world falls away. Bobby can't hang on.

He reaches for the door of Bea's car and for Tommy and for anything to hold him there, but then what *there* exists inside the shop is no more. It fades instead, winks away, walls swirling and blurring as though everything moves faster than his eyes can see, and then comes the terror of knowing it isn't the world that has gone missing, it is Bobby himself. A cold like ice falls upon him. Heaviness. Wind buffets him as he tumbles, not down or up but *inside himself*: collapsing, all that Bobby was and is and shall be pressed to a single mote of dust, to something whose breadth and height measures all he has given the world and all that will remain behind of him, Bobby being not born but unborn, leaving him only to pour every regret and unspoken plea into a single word that falls from his mouth:

"It's."

A road and the trees and the light coming for him, time twisting every moment into this final moment, a long screech and Mark—Mark!—pinwheeling away, Mark's brown hair on end and his tiny hand waving good-bye and Matthew floating away and metal strikes metal, the sound of glass shattering where there is no glass and Bobby's chest crushing and his screams for a God not there.

And then blackness, a dark silence beyond all reckoning and the realization that he is gone, completely and forever lost, left to drift in the meaninglessness he has embraced and the unbelief to which he has offered his soul as a sacrifice, a waking sleep of neither dream nor rest, left to suffer an eternity with himself, the man he had not lost but become. Alone and not alone, because there are monsters here.

An echo sounds through the swirling night—"It's."

Faraway, another echo answers:

*There will be*

# -14-

*stars.*

He jerked as if torn from a nightmare, every sense alive, gasping as one pulled from drowning. The rat that had crawled near to Bobby's arm scurried with a shriek. Empty beer cans clattered farther into the alley, kicked away by his boots. And there—there were the stars, hung bright in a silent sky already lightening with morning. Dozens of them, hundreds, each a beacon leading him out of the darkness into which he'd plunged.

The pain in his chest was not enough to keep him on the wet ground. Bobby stood, finding his cap. He pushed hard on the wood door to the shop and ignored the deep and true sense that struck him, a rabbit running over his grave. Moving as fast as he could on two shaky legs, aided by the single yellow bulb buzzing over the workbench, dodging the service pit and brushing the pegboard wall before entering the waiting room. Then came the horrible thought as he reached behind the counter: the bottle would not be there. He'd drunk it all the previous day, downed every drop.

And yet Bobby's fingers closed around smooth glass as though the bottle had never been touched. He raised it against the drawn blinds, watched the amber liquid inside curl and crash before settling to a mark midway on the label. He did not pause to consider how such a thing was possible and unscrewed the top. The bourbon seared his throat, gagging him. Bobby shut his eyes and willed it down. He paused only to breathe and then drank more, stopping only when he believed he would vomit and thus ruin everything.

"Hey," he yelled. *"Hey."*

Only silence.

The room lay undisturbed. Beside the recliner rested the table, upright and in place, an ordered pile of books stacked beside. Bobby wobbled there as the liquor took hold. He had not stacked those books beside the chair. Tommy had helped push them all against the window the day before. He felt between the seat and armrest. The Tom Franklin he'd been reading (and had moved, Bobby possessed a clear memory of that) lay wedged inside.

He turned to the counter as a timer he had not set on the coffee maker clicked on. Panic built but did not bubble over, for the simple reason that Bobby wanted one more and supremely important verification. He walked around the counter again and, giving the coffee maker a wide berth, pulled on the refrigerator handle. Inside, he found a miracle. Bobby counted them to make sure, touching each and saying the number aloud. By the time he finished, the room had filled with his laughter.

Twenty-two beers. Twenty-two beers that took up most of the three narrow shelves, saving room for only a quart of spoiled milk.

He drank two in quick succession and waited to make sure they would stay down. Then Bobby took the nearly empty bottle of bourbon to the bathroom and studied the mirror. Everything of him was there, arms and eyes and face. The only addition was the bruise on Bobby's cheek. He pressed a finger there and felt the throb.

His head began to swim. His arms felt heavy. He didn't go to the toilet and didn't wash his face, didn't brush his teeth for fear of even the slightest chance it would hitch him to the reality of things. What Bobby did was turn and open the door. He stepped out into the shop with what he could only call hope and let his eyes wander. The back door and the wall next to it, hidden by a pile of tires. The workbench and the floor jacks and the service pit. Bea's car. And just as Bobby's mind bent with such fear and worry that he had even begun a notion of prayer, there by the first bay door stood his children.

"Boys?"

A lump welled in his throat. He wiped at his tears, making sure.

"Boys, that y'all?"

They sprinted to him in step, little legs pumping all the way to where Bobby stood, and he smiled under the belief that Matthew and Mark were racing not each other, but away from the very fear that had gripped his own self. He fell to his knees as they fell into his arms. Bobby held them tight and kissed their heads.

"Thought I lost y'all," he said. "Last night, after all that. But we're here. We're okay."

Matthew began to cry. Whispers came through the hollow place between his chin and Bobby's chest like moaning. Bobby squeezed him more.

"It was dark, Daddy. I couldn't see and I couldn't say anything."

"I know. It's okay now."

"Where were we?"

"The mountain," Mark whimpered. The words came clear, even as Bobby heard the pain beneath. "We were on the mountain. I remember it now. There's a car and we hit it. We always hit it. We went on a ride after all."

"The mountain," Bobby said. "That's it. That's where we were." Smiling or trying to smile. That was what Matthew had meant. The mountain and not the deep and lonely after, that dark place between worlds where monsters dwelled. "Come on, let's get y'all sitting down."

He carried them to the recliner and set them there, wiping their eyes with his hand. Morning broke full and bright. Mark slipped his hand into his brother's as Bobby fumbled with the remote to find a distraction. Not that there were many options on Sunday morning, unless the boys had a mind for news roundtables or infomercials or preachers lying about the beauty beneath all the ugliness. He settled on the news first. A leggy blonde smiled from behind a glass desk as she recapped the morning: an outbreak of some disease and more mistrust of the government, a dead woman near Stanley. The Series and murdered schoolkids and a man holding a sign, screaming for war.

Mark turned to him. "Daddy, we saw this yesterday. This is yesterday."

Bobby kept his eyes to the little TV. He told them of the bottle under the counter and the beer in the fridge and how things had been cleaned up from the night before. Not like it had all been put back, more like it had been reset.

The phone rang. Outside, a boy in long pants and a Red Sox cap walked past the shop with his mother. Neither stopped to peer inside. *Because I didn't fall*, Bobby thought. *The phone didn't scare me, so I didn't fall.*

Matthew said, "You better tell Miz Campbell you ain't done a thing yet to her car, Daddy."

"That Bea calling again?" Mark asked. He rolled his eyes like a proper adult.

"No," Bobby said. "Not again. Not exactly. I think it's the first time for Bea, just not for us."

A worried look crept over Matthew's face. "I don't even know what that means."

"Means they were right. Miss Dorothea and all them others. Tommy."

Mark said, "We need to go there, Daddy. They can help us."

Bobby got up to fetch another beer from the fridge. "Don't need nobody, boy. Never have." He popped the tab and took a swallow, smiling as he did. All the beer in the world lay right on those shelves. Whatever he drank that day would be there again the next. He had food enough in the back and his boys in front of him. Shoot, if all this was true, they'd never have to step foot outside again. "Nosir, we're just gonna sit tight and relax."

-15-

The Turn had never dictated that Dorothea take her morning tea on the back porch overlooking her expansive yard; she did so by her own choice. The neighborhood (if four houses spread over twenty acres of trees and open space on the back side of town could be called such) lay quiet in the early day. Sunlight reached well enough over the mountains to warm the spot where she sat, tapping the edge of her cup with a fingernail. October had always been Dorothea's favorite days. Let others favor the sweet winds of spring or the Christmas cheer; they could have them. But give Dorothea Cash those middle days of autumn, their clear mornings and crisp nights.

These had been Hubert's favorite days, too. He and Dorothea had chosen the fourth of October to wed, this after he'd returned from fighting the red menace in Vietnam. Sixty-eight, that had been. He'd gone to work selling insurance and the two of them built what life they could, one with plenty in the way of comfort but lacking in the way of children. Neither ever bothered to discover where the blame lay, whether Dorothea had been cursed with a barren womb or Hubie (as he had been known to all) had been born into the world with faulty equipment. The two of them had simply accepted their fate as the Lord's will and kept company together for the next forty-one years, and then the aneurysm claimed him in an instant.

He had been a good man. Better, Dorothea thought, than she'd deserved. Hubert had devoted his life to providing, and now that provision would stretch on through eternity. Wasn't a run-down camper like Junior's for her to spend heaven in, or a little cottage like Juliet's or a shack like poor Tommy's. Dorothea had instead a grand home fit for filling, something she had little chance of accomplishing in the old world. The loneliness and grief with which she'd met her end had been turned to company and joy on the other side. Dorothea missed him with every breath. And often as she sipped and stared at grass so green it shone like emeralds and maples and oaks and willows in their finest fall colors, Dorothea wondered about Hubert's heaven—the real one rather than the pale imitation she had been given. She wondered if her husband was at peace and if he missed her, but never once did Dorothea wish to trade her heaven for his. The Turn held her purpose. That's what she told the others, even if deep down the better truth sounded too selfish to utter: better to rule over a flawed world than be ruled in a perfect one.

Her mind drifted to the Turn's newest resident and what Bobby Barnes's arrival meant. No word had come from Tommy. Dorothea had called the shop several times after he and Bobby had left the Turn before, though all her calls went unanswered. Laura Beth, who had objected to Tommy's going on the grounds that Bobby was a known pervert (but had not objected to the point she volunteered to go instead), finally went to check. She'd returned soon with news that Tommy was fine. That was the last any of them heard.

Dorothea shuddered, even with the warm sun and the cup of hot tea in her hands. Supper the last Turn had been a strange affair. Chicken and dumplings and cornbread had always been a family favorite, but not even that had been enough to fill the void of Tommy's absence. The meal had been picked through with little conversation; all had left early. Dorothea well imagined Junior and Laura Beth and Juliet—even George, and maybe George especially—going out of their way to pass the shop on their way home. To check. To make sure.

She would have her answers soon. They would all be up by now, Junior buying his bait at Andy's and Laura Beth on her way to the grocery, Juliet leaving the church to go home and change. George would be doing his best to remember (*and good luck with that*, Dorothea thought through a grin) and, this Turn, to make his foolish drive over the mountains. And Tommy. Tommy should be here just about now, and hopefully carrying with him all Dorothea would need. The two of them would have a little talk and then she would feel better.

The front door opened and shut. Dorothea grinned as Tommy's voice called, "Mama?"

"Out here."

She rose and opened the screen door. Tommy bounded out, followed closely by Juliet.

"Met Tommy on the way," the preacher said. "Thought we'd walk together."

Dorothea fetched Juliet a coffee and Tommy a glass of chocolate milk, all she could offer until Laura Beth arrived with food. They sat around the patio table and succumbed to business. Dorothea took the lead.

"Well, Tommy, tell us what you know. Was there trouble?"

Tommy wiped the brown mustache from his lips and set the glass down. "No'm. It was fine. Mr. Bobby's really nice. We listened to the radio."

"Where did you go?"

"Just to the shop. Mr. Bobby hardly ever goes nowhere else. Some people called, but not many. Did you call, Mama?"

"I did, checking in. Juliet as well. What else?"

"Nothin'," Tommy said. "He just read all day. Mr. Bobby likes that stuff. Somebody named Carla called—"

"Carla?" Dorothea asked.

"She's the woman Mr. Bobby used to be married to, but she don't love him no more."

Juliet asked, "What did they talk about?"

"He didn't answer. He already knew what they'd say."

Dorothea leaned in close. "He knew? Did Bobby say so?"

"I *heard* he knew. He said it all under his breath, and I heard it but I didn't know what any of it meant. I said he don't have to talk to her no more if he don't want to—it won't upset the balance. That's right, ain't it, Mama?"

"Very likely," Dorothea said, though she wasn't sure. Time wouldn't tell, but the Turn would.

"What about after?" Juliet asked. "Did you see Bobby's Turn?"

Tommy fell quiet. He reached for his glass and took a long drink, then set the glass down and stared at it.

"Tommy?" Dorothea asked.

"That's how Mr. Bobby does it. He drinks his beer like I drink my milk. He drinks it even more than my old mama did. I think that's how he died. He must've drank and drank and drank and then when he wanted to drink more, the Lord must've said that's all you get, mister."

"Did you see? Was it after your Turn, or before?"

"Before." He wouldn't look at them. Tommy sometimes did that with Juliet, but never with Dorothea. She knew why when he said, "Mr. Bobby winked."

"He did what?" Juliet asked.

"He winked. This song come on the radio. Mr. Bobby knew what it was. I think he *remembered*. And then he winked away."

Dorothea leaned in again. "You mean he disappeared?"

"I looked everywhere, Mama. Out in the alley and in the waitin' room, back where Mr. Bobby said he sleeps. Even the bathroom after I knocked three times first like you taught me. But he weren't there. Had to be close, though, 'cause I still seen his truck out where he parked. What's that mean?"

Dorothea didn't know, but that didn't mean she could give no answer. She was the prophet, the one given the ear of the Lord. And there sat Juliet, staring with that self-righteous look of pity on her face.

"People like Bobby and your old mama," she began, "they're different from us. When they get in their cups, they . . ."

"Get to be monsters?" he asked.

Dorothea nodded. "A fine way of putting it. Hard to say where he wanders off, but you'll take comfort in knowing he's back where he's supposed to be now."

"I hope so. I don't think he even took his friends with him."

The two women exchanged a brief look of panic.

"Friends?" Dorothea asked.

"Yeah. Mr. Bobby was hollering fierce for them before he winked away. Telling them to come here. But I don't know if they did because I couldn't see'm. I never could, even though Mr. Bobby was talking to them 'bout the whole day."

"Bobby was talking to people who weren't there?" Juliet asked.

"Yes'm."

Dorothea drained the last of her tea much as Tommy had his milk. The cup rattled against the saucer as she set them down. "Tommy, be a lamb and fetch me another cup?" She waited until he left and whispered, "Dear Lord in heaven."

"What is it, Dorothea?" Juliet asked.

She did not bother to correct what Juliet had called her. *Mama* Dorothea was and *Mama* she would always be, to everyone inside the Turn. She had grown tired of repeating such to Juliet Creech. But this time Dorothea let the slight pass. She had other worries.

"Long before you were called to Mattingly," she said, "Bobby was married. Carla Jenkins, she was. They had twin sons, Matthew and Mark. You would think those names would not be of the biblical sort given the sourness of Bobby's view of the Lord, but Bobby was much different those dim years ago. Then something happened. He fell away is best I can put it. Fell away and fell into a bottle. Lost Carla. Lost the boys. Carla married a man who turned out to be much like Bobby. He was in prison when I came to the Turn. But I suppose Bobby's come to lose more than just his family in the time since. He's lost himself, too. I knew the man had problems. Whole town knew. But going mad?" She shook her head. "That man is far too wounded. He won't come here. Not willingly. Bobby Barnes has shut the world out, and that means this world, too."

"Should we go see him?"

"We?" Dorothea grinned inside. *That's what you'd love, wouldn't you, dear? Take a crack at Bobby first and poison his mind. All sweetlike and innocent, the way you just happened to come across Tommy on his way here.*

"I could take George."

"George is leaving for the day. And even if he wasn't, I'll have no one visiting Bobby. Not yet. Give him time, he'll come around. If not, I may coax him. A man such as him hasn't had a good meal in a long while. He mustn't be forced, Juliet. It'll only make what comes after harder for him to know."

"And we'll tell him everything?"

"We'll tell him the truth."

Juliet looked at her. "Whose truth would that be, Mama?"

"Mine, dear." Dorothea patted her apron pocket, making the envelope inside crinkle. "The only truth that matters."

# -16-

They left as the clock tower struck two, after the dishes were done and Junior and Laura Beth had gone upstairs and Mama had settled for a nap. Heaven or not, Juliet thought, the old woman still tired after a long morning's toil. Talking Tommy into sneaking away wasn't difficult. The trick was convincing him of the lie they would have to tell if Mama found out.

Neither of them minded walking the three miles to town. Juliet thought of how she never would have done such a thing in her old life. There (or was it *then?* She'd lived long in the Turn but had yet to decide if where she'd been taken from was best described as a place or a time), Juliet would have hopped in her Volvo even to fetch the mail at the end of her lane. She never checked that box now. It was always the same collection of bills she no longer had to pay and junk mail she would've thrown out anyway. Unlike Dorothea, she never had to concern herself with whatever missives the Lord might send via heavenly express. Juliet smirked. She always did when pondering such a thing.

"Ain't right to lie, Juliet," Tommy told her. "Mama says the Lord's watching and He'll know, and then He'll tell her and *she'll* know."

"Mama won't know so long as we're careful. The Lord knows how to keep a secret."

She held Tommy's hand as they strolled, watching a groundhog munch clover and a mockingbird chase off a crow, their shoes crunching gravel at the road's shoulder. Tommy spoke of the few cars that passed, where those people were going and how one thing someone did would ripple out and touch others. It was always a wonder to Juliet how much of the Turn the boy noticed. Dorothea had taught Tommy much.

They stopped at the bridge so Tommy could spit into the river. Talk was pleasant and focused upon the man he called Mr. Bobby. That Tommy had become so taken by the Turn's newest member and in such a short time struck Juliet as odd. Tommy had never acted that way when she arrived, nor George or Laura Beth, choosing instead a hesitant indifference until he'd decided they meant no harm. Juliet smiled as he reached for her hand again, his tiny fingers slick with sweat, pondering the long process of winning his trust. If she could gain that from Tommy, Juliet felt certain she could do the same with Bobby. It would take time. She smirked again, thinking time was all they had.

They reached downtown and the weathered sign out front of the shop. A huge red truck sat parked in the corner. Bits of weeds and grass pushed up from cracks in the lot's concrete. The blinds had been drawn tight, the bay doors closed.

"Doesn't look like he's here."

"He is," Tommy told her. "Always looks this way."

He kept his grip on Juliet's hand and pulled her across the street, dodging the midafternoon traffic. Past the big truck and across the lot, to the door leading into what Juliet guessed was the waiting area.

"Shouldn't we—"

*Knock* was how she'd meant to finish, but Tommy didn't

give her the time. He pushed on the door and walked in, dragging her behind.

What struck Juliet first was the smell, sweat and stink and alcohol that made her want to brush her teeth. The room was tiny, dark with the drawn shades. Somewhere close, a radio blared. Her eyes adjusted to empty beer cans scattered along a floor of fading green carpet and a worn recliner in the middle of the room. And on that recliner Bobby, an open book in his hands and one leg hung over an armrest, naked but for a soiled pair of briefs and a look of shock.

Juliet spoke the first words that came to mind: "Oh my sweet Lord in heaven."

Tommy shouted, "Hey, Mr. Bobby!"

For what seemed an eternity itself, Bobby sat motionless. Then he jumped up and, holding the book below his waist, filled the air with curses and screams as he ran behind the recliner.

"What the world y'all doin' here?" he asked.

Tommy said, "Come to call on you. You okay? I missed you."

"No, I am not okay. Y'all can't just come up in here. This ain't no barn, it's my *home*."

"Door's unlocked," Tommy offered. "You miss me, Mr. Bobby?"

Bobby didn't say, though every indication told Juliet no.

"I'm sorry," she said. Her eyes went shut. The hand that still held Tommy's was across her face, making the boy look as though he had an answer to a question. "Tommy said you lived here. I should have called. Or we. Oh my sweet Lord. We'll leave."

"We ain't leavin'," Tommy said. "You don't want us to go, do you, Mr. Bobby? We just come."

"Just . . . ," Bobby stammered. *Drunk*, Juliet thought. Angered and embarrassed. "Y'all just stand there. Turn around so's I can get some clothes on. Go on, Tommy, turn around."

Tommy huffed. Juliet took her hand away from her face and turned the boy's shoulder, pointing them both toward the door. She heard Bobby stumble, then cuss, then stumble again in another room.

"Was he dressed all last evening?" she whispered.

"Yes'm."

She heard Bobby coming back into the room and him saying okay, they could turn around. Juliet did so first, taking her time, and found Bobby tucking a T-shirt into an old pair of jeans. He'd draped a work shirt over his bony shoulders; it hung from him unbuttoned.

"What y'all doin' here?" he asked again.

"Comin' to call," Tommy answered.

Juliet turned him around. "We just wanted to stop by and make sure you were okay," she said. "Dorothea didn't think you'd take up her offer for company. Tommy told us how last night . . . went. With your Turn?"

"He did?" Bobby stared at the boy. "That what last night was all about, then? Come up here and get ol' Bobby drunk, listen to what he says so you can be a little spy for everybody else?"

Tommy's lips puckered. Juliet put an arm around the boy's shoulders.

"It's not that way," she said, and with a harshness she regretted. "That's not how we are, Bobby."

"Where'd you go off to, Mr. Bobby?" Tommy asked. "You winked out, and I couldn't find you no place. Truck was here, though."

"My truck was here?" Bobby asked.

"Yeah. Where'd you go?"

"I don't know. It was dark."

He kept behind the chair as though it was a shield. Juliet felt less like a stranger than an intruder.

"Tommy," she said, "do you think you could give Bobby and me a little time to talk?"

He didn't seem to want to but agreed anyway. Bobby sent him into the shop with orders not to mess anything up. Though to Bea Campbell's car, he said, Tommy could do as he wished.

Juliet watched him bound off and said, "He's a good boy. Our boy. We all look after Tommy. He's had a hard life."

"It's a hard world. What brings you here . . . ?"

"Juliet. I'm sorry we didn't have the chance to speak more the last Turn. I know it was a lot to take in."

Bobby grinned. "You could say so. Have a seat, if you like. I'd offer you something, but I'm afraid all I got's beer and some sour milk. Pepsi machine's been empty for years."

"Beer's fine."

She took the recliner as Bobby's grin fell into a laugh. "Well all right then."

He went behind the counter. Juliet looked out into the shop and spotted Tommy behind the wheel of a little car against the wall. She couldn't hear much over the din of the radio and so only watched as he mouthed noises, pretending to drive. A can appeared in front of her eyes. She popped the tab.

Bobby said, "Woman havin' a beer this early don't sound like a preacher to me."

"Guess that's because I don't know what sort of preacher I am."

Bobby paused in the doorway, nodding toward Tommy.

"Figured y'all'd get him to tell everything he seen. Tommy run his mouth on anything else?"

He looked at her with eyes Juliet took to have once been a deep blue. But something had died there, inside him. She remembered the boys. Bobby's twins, Matthew and Mark.

"No." A lie, but an allowable one. Besides, Juliet had gotten the sense that Bobby wasn't being entirely truthful himself. "Except that you like to read." She pointed to the stack of books beside her. "You have interesting tastes, Bobby."

"Gotta have something to pass the time. Looks like I got plenty of that now." He grinned again, spreading the spider lines across his cheeks the way Tommy could spread his freckles. "You a reader?"

"Am," she said. "Always have been. Growing up, books were my best friends. Met some good ones and some great ones. Know the difference between a good book and a great one?"

"What's that?"

"Good books tell us how we're all different. Great ones tell us how we're all the same."

"Huh," he said. "Guess I never thought about that. Mostly because I don't agree with the sentiment. Might even have to get me a library card now, though. Always got my books 'round the corner at the used bookshop. Dorothea tell me right, Preacher? Is this heaven?"

She had to be careful here, say the right thing. Bobby was of the Turn now, but he was not of the family, not yet, and Juliet couldn't know where his allegiance would lie.

"Right now, Bobby, it's more important what you think."

He drank. "Never thought I'd see it, to be honest. Heaven. But I woke up this morning with half a bottle of bourbon and a fridge full of beer, and it looks like I ain't never gotta do nothin' I don't want from now on. Sounds like heaven to me."

Juliet grinned, nodded. She didn't have a lot of time. Mama would wake soon, and the longer Tommy lingered, the more likely he would let slip where they'd been. Tommy knew to keep a secret, but Dorothea had her ways. The Lord always watched.

"It's more than that," Juliet said. "Whatever you come to think of the Turn, it's a mirror most of all."

"Got one a them in the bathroom. It don't get me free beer."

"Nothing's free, Bobby. Not even here."

"What you telling me, Preacher Juliet? And you take that beer just to get on my good side? You ain't tipped it once."

Juliet raised the can to her lips and swallowed. "I'm telling you that this is all new right now, and as long as a thing is new, it's wonderful. But it won't be new long. You're going to crave company more than you crave this." She held up the can. "That's why Dorothea would like you to start visiting. So we can help. I can help. Doesn't have to be every day, but we're all here together, Bobby."

He shook his head. "Got all I need. Don't need nothing else. I appreciate you coming by."

That was all he said and all Juliet needed to hear. She called for Tommy and said it was time to go. He went along with some hesitation. Before leaving, he wrapped his arms around Bobby's waist and, when Bobby wouldn't bend down, kissed the flat of his stomach. In all the ages that followed and in both the darkness and the light of what was to come, Juliet would look back and consider that the moment everything began to change. That tiny kiss did more than all her words could.

She opened the door and felt the sunlight on her arm, then turned a final time.

"I want you to know I'll be here for you, Bobby. Whenever you're ready. We all have regrets here, and they're all laid bare with no consequence. That's what family does. They love regardless. No matter what you did or who you were, you have the chance to do different. Be different. It's the only way to keep on. You don't have to be alone anymore."

"Appreciate it," he said again.

Juliet smiled and turned away. The door opened wide on the same dull world. As it closed, she heard Bobby call out.

Saying, "Y'all can stop hiding, they're gone now."

# -17-

Only one member of Dorothea's family visited in the Turns after. That's how Bobby and the boys had come to measure their time in heaven. "Days" or "weeks" implied the passage of time, and time passed not at all.

Then came the morning Bobby heard the door to the waiting room swing open. He and the boys were in the shop, Bobby with the mop and Matthew and Mark arm wrestling on the workbench, faces straining as their feet threatened to topple from the wooden stools they stood upon. When they heard the voice call out, Matthew flinched just long enough for Mark to pin his hand. Matthew cried his protest and leveled a charge of cheating that both boys forgot about when George walked inside.

"There you are," the old man said. "I was beginning to think you were closed to business, Bobby, even though your truck's out there."

Bobby laid his mop into the bucket beside him. "Told Juliet and Tommy I don't need no company, George. I'll tell you the same and ask you pass it along to the woman who sent you."

"Can't do that today. And Dorothea didn't send me. I'm here on business."

"And what business would that be?"

"I need an oil change."

Bobby looked over his shoulder to the boys. Matthew stood questioning. Mark's face broke into a grin Bobby didn't like at all.

"Been a long while since I had your truck in here, George."

He shrugged his shoulders. "You're a drunk."

"So why you here now?"

"Oh, I don't know. Your place is closest, and my window of time is short."

Matthew said, "He's a mean man, Daddy."

Bobby picked up the mop again and wrung it, then made two swipes across the floor by his feet. "Seems to me time's all we got. Also seems I take the old oil out that Toyota of yours and put fresh in, it'll be back to old once the clock tower strikes a tomorrow that won't never come." He stilled the mop and looked up. "Unless I'm mistaken."

"True enough. But I could use that new oil this Turn. Might give the truck a little extra oomph going over the mountain. I'm leaving for the day."

Bobby stopped mopping. "You mean you can leave?"

George began with a chuckle and ended with a cough. "Of course I can. World's still as wide as it ever was, Bobby. Junior drives down to Lake Moomaw to fish, though I suppose he's the only one other than me. Dorothea hasn't been away from her house since I arrived here. Told me once she went out and almost got run down. Tommy has no need to travel beyond Mattingly, nor I suppose does Laura Beth.

Juliet walks everywhere. Says it keeps her feeling good. She suggested I try, but my old lungs won't let me."

"So where you going?"

"Kentucky."

Bobby cocked his head. "You looking for your wife? Dorothea said something to me that first time I was over to her house. Said Anna's visiting kin."

"Was." He coughed hard into his fist. "She's somewhere between there and here. West Virginia, I expect." His face went drawn as he whispered again, "I've tried calling her more often than you can know. Cell service. We have telescopes that can peer into the farthest reaches of the universe, Bobby, but try to talk to someone in those mountains, all you get is static."

"So you, what? Go looking for her?"

"What else is there for me to do? Oh, I have the others. Juliet and Laura Beth and Tommy and Junior. Even Dorothea. Pardon me." He smiled. "*Mama*. They all keep me well in their own ways, but so long as I'm here and Anna is not, a part of me will always wander. So, interested in making a little money?"

"Money don't matter. Just like your oil, it'll be gone in a few hours."

Behind him, Mark said, "Don't be so mean, Daddy."

"True enough," George said. "You're learning, Bobby. That's a good thing. I always considered you a bright boy, though your grades never reflected it."

"As I recall, you gave me a D-minus."

"And well deserved," George said. "But nonetheless. Suppose I'll be going, then, and leave you to your work. I've searched many a road, but there are many yet and many more times to pass upon them. She asked me to go, you know.

Anna. I didn't. Never did agree much with her family." He paused, then added, "Though I would gladly spend eternity with them so long as I could have her in the bargain."

He turned away. Bobby looked over his shoulder again to the boys and then back. He set the mop back in the bucket.

"Go ahead and pull in," he said. "Right over the pit there. Just need to get me another couple cans from the fridge first."

George smiled. "I would appreciate that, Bobby."

Bobby raised the door and guided George's little truck inside. He grabbed the tools he would need and stepped down into the pit. It had always been Matthew's favorite place—"my fort," he called it—and yet this was the first time it would be used for actual work. George stood at the edge as Bobby worked, removing the oil pan and changing the filter. He asked if Bobby minded that he smoked and Bobby said no, mostly because of the beer he'd brought down into the pit with him. They spoke generally and in short sentences, Bobby wondering how to steer their conversation to the deeper things that plagued him and knowing that George wondered the same.

"How long you been here?" he finally asked. "With Dorothea and the rest."

"I've lost track of the days. That'll happen, no matter how hard you try. Long, best I can say it. A very long while."

He could see nothing of George but his shoes. Bobby stared at them and pretended to work. "You remember dying?"

A long pause. "No. Do you?"

The mountain and the road, John Fogerty singing of the bad moon, headlights and the dark filled with monsters. Was that dying, or was that something other?

"No," Bobby said. Then, testing, "Dorothea says this is heaven, though. We must've died."

"Tell me, Bobby. That day Junior brought you to Dorothea's. What'd you do before?"

"I don't know. Nothing, I guess. Bea Campbell always calls me. That's her car over there I'm supposed to work on, but I'm waiting to pry a little more money out of her for the labor it'll take. Went to Timmy's and then Andy's. That's where I saw Junior. The rest?" He shrugged even if George couldn't see. Aboveground, he could hear the sound of pages turning. "Why?"

"Making sure," George said. "I wrote down much of that already from what you and the others said that first day."

"Why you do that?"

"Oh, don't worry. I do that for everyone. Just to keep track. To . . ." He didn't finish. "Of course, everything I write down gets erased with each Turn, so I have to write it all down again. It's my way of figuring things, old habits and whatnot."

"You mean your science stuff," Bobby said. "Don't think Dorothea takes too kindly to that."

"Dorothea's afraid."

Bobby laid down his wrench. "Afraid of what?"

He coughed again, hard and wet. "I like to keep my mind sharp. Writing all this down helps. Turn's been kind to me that way. You may not know this, Bobby, but my retirement from teaching wasn't wholly voluntary. They made me leave. Budget cuts is what they said, and they simply had no use for someone who had devoted so many years to teaching. It destroyed me. Left me, I don't know . . . aimless, I suppose. I only found my purpose when I arrived here."

Bobby listened, turning those words over in his mind. He realized George hadn't answered his question.

"So this is what I do now," George said. "Study. Gets me

out of the house most days, which is a blessing considering the racket that goes on. I wouldn't say faith has ever been my strong suit, but I have enough to blame the Lord for mocking me."

"What you mean?"

"It's nothing. A small aggravation, though one that ends up driving me from the house early in the day for some peace and quiet. Even if it's to Dorothea's. You know the river goes right by our house. That little outcropping of rocks there?"

Bobby nodded and remembered George couldn't see him. "Sure."

"There's a cat there every morning. Out in the middle of the river, out on those rocks. Cold and wet and bothered to no end. Makes so much noise it drives me crazy. Even with the windows down."

"Cat drives you out your house?"

"Ridiculous, isn't it?"

"Little bit."

George shrugged. "You're not the one getting a hole bored into your head by an animal's screeching every morning."

"You ever think about going out there, getting it off the rocks?"

"You want me to crawl this old body out in the middle of freezing river water to fetch a cat? No thank you. Just turn out like this oil change and the money I'll pay you."

Bobby couldn't disagree with that. George could take that cat away all he wanted, it'd still be back come sunrise.

"Sure would be nice to see you at Dorothea's," George said. "We'd all love to have you, Bobby. Tommy's taken quite a shine to you."

"Don't know why that'd be. Been on my own a long time, George. On my own's how I like it."

George snuffed his cigarette on the bottom of his boot and placed the butt in the palm of his hand with the others. He tried saying something and was stopped by another cough, this one so hard that he winced and doubled over. Bobby stood watching as cigarettes and ash tumbled to the already-mopped floor. George reached into a pocket for his handkerchief. When it came away from his mouth, the white cloth was stained with blood.

"Pardon me," he said when he found his breath again. He dabbed his lips.

Bobby looked up through the narrow crack between George's tires and the pit. "You all right?"

George waved him off. "Dorothea would call it the sins of my past, though as I said, I never put much faith in faith. The doctors found the cancer a few months before"—he waved into the air—"all this. Maybe I did die and simply have no memory of it. Regardless, at least I can smoke now without it killing me."

He smiled. Bobby could see the blood on the old man's teeth. He thought of his own drinking and Laura Beth's pinkeye, thought of Dorothea's arthritis.

"How much do I owe you?"

"No charge," Bobby said. "You go find your wife."

"Believe that's just what I'll do. Much appreciated."

George moved to the truck. He eased inside and rolled down the window before backing out. "Think about my offer. No family's perfect, but then, we can't choose them, can we? No one should spend eternity alone."

"Why is it I get the feeling spending all day at Dorothea's won't exactly promise a good time? Only been there once, but it was enough to get the sense not all y'all get along sometimes."

"There may be a difference of opinion on a few things here and there, but it's still company. You think this is heaven, it can turn to hell with loneliness."

"Well, I'm not," Bobby said. "Alone, I mean." He grinned. "After all, Lord's watching, right?"

George looked at him hard. He put the truck into reverse and started to back away. "Never seen the Lord here, Bobby. But you can bet Someone's watching, oh yes. And that Someone sees all."

# -18-

He stayed away as long as he could and very nearly proved Juliet wrong about craving what he had never craved before: Company. Family. The boys provided all of that he'd ever needed. Bobby had been alone long before that final ride to the mountains. He had been dead long before his death.

The Turn that George arrived was the last he had seen of them. Not even Tommy visited, leaving Bobby to suppose Dorothea had convinced them all to let him be. Bobby and the boys agreed no longer to avoid the ride at night. He didn't know which of Dorothea's words to believe and which to cast aside, but the part about ending each day in the same fashion proved nothing but fact. Mark said if they had to be on that curve, it was better and braver to go willingly. Matthew wasn't so agreeable but said facing it together was better than facing it apart.

And so from that Turn on they took their usual route once the sun died and the town fell to sleep, winding that big truck through the hills to Route 237. Matthew would punch up the volume on the radio as John Fogerty began to sing. He still liked that song, even if he knew what that song wrought.

Those rides were often quiet. Sometimes Bobby would try to choose otherwise on the mountain. He would turn right onto Route 237 rather than left, aiming for Camden way. He tried slowing down and speeding up to avoid the brake lights they always came upon in the distance. None of it worked. Going right would only take them left, as though the curve hung free of time and place and moved instead, following Bobby everywhere. Speeding up or slowing down proved impossible. Once the wheels were firmly set upon that stretch of road, it was as if the truck drove itself. Bobby could pump the brake and push the gas, pull the wheel with all his might, but he could never alter their path. A path, he came to believe, that had been set in place long before the night of his death. What choices Bobby had been free to make in his old life ended there. The three of them would hold hands as the truck entered the high point in the curve, and Bobby would break the silence long enough to tell Matthew and Mark to hang on as best they could. Don't be afraid, he would tell them, I'll see you right soon. Then would come the headlights and the screams, those flailing limbs and the bottomless dark. Then would come the stars.

He needed no company. He had his boys and his beer and the half bottle of bourbon. Eternity promised Bobby more than he'd ever expected.

And yet as the Turns went on, Bobby found the blinds were kept wide to the street and the sign on the door always read Open. What time not spent drinking and playing with Matthew and Mark found Bobby looking out windows or pacing the lot, watching for those who never came to check on him. Only Bea and Carla called. Sometimes Mark would tell Bobby to answer, if only to have someone else to talk to. Matthew always provided reason enough to ignore those rings. Their arguments were many. Bobby began taking the phone off the hook when he stumbled in from the alley. It seemed easier that way.

Mark said there was no reason for hurt and anger. The rest were only abiding by Bobby's wish to be left alone. Bobby paid him no mind. His heart began to close under the weight of the same TV shows and the same radio songs, nothing ever changing. All the world seemed relics of things rotted and spoiled. *Time* became a word forgotten. Bobby tried keeping track of the Turns by scoring a mark on the alley door with a knife, yet each time he woke again, he found that door untouched.

The shop became less a home than a cell as his eternity wore on, forcing him out in ever-widening circles. Sometimes in the truck, sometimes on foot, but always with the twins and always to sneak a look at Dorothea's home. He would take stock of Junior's truck and George's Toyota, catalog glimpses of Laura Beth and Juliet and Tommy in the backyard. Always at a distance, never too close, kept away by what Bobby could call the fear of finding peace and losing it once more and what he came to call pride. Bobby Barnes needed no one, and yet he did.

But then came Tommy. Dear Tommy, whom even after that long time of quiet Bobby hoped would call upon the shop again. It was an early afternoon, that time in the Turn when Bobby's drinking slowed and the boys slumbered. He was under the hood of Bea's car when he heard the knock at the waiting room door. Bobby stepped out and saw the back of Tommy's Braves cap and a shock of red hair before both were lost in the sidewalk crowd. He found at his feet salvation in the form of a covered basket containing Dorothea's fried chicken, slaw, and biscuits, along with a used milk jug full of her sweet tea. A note in Tommy's boyish hand folded inside, saying the Lord had sent a letter to Mama asking that she invite him to the house again. The Lord was watching, and the Lord was worried. Bobby ate and drank that night as though Tommy had delivered the flesh and the blood.

\* \* \*

He waited until the morning of the next Turn. Matthew and Mark watched in pensive silence as Bobby combed his beard and hair before donning a fresh pair of jeans and an unused work shirt. He said they could come along and they did. It took nearly an hour of driving past Dorothea's street before Bobby finally turned in, then another twenty minutes along the curb well away from the house before he finally got out. Laughter drew him, the low hum of table talk through the open window. Even from that distance, it reminded him of song.

The boys trailed behind and refused to go in. Bobby knocked at the door alone. He shifted the basket and the clean dishes inside from one hand to the other. Tugged at his collar. Debated the merits of leaving. He hoped Dorothea would answer or Tommy, anyone but Junior. Juliet came to the door smiling. Bobby paused before stepping inside, biting back tears.

It was to his mind the finest meal in any world and any eternity, though it had little to do with the food. Mama's family welcomed Bobby as the prodigal he was, showering him with kindness and attention, sharing his joy. None asked where he had been and why he had taken so long in coming. Those things mattered none. He spent all that afternoon and evening with Tommy at one side and Juliet at the other, laughing at Junior's jokes and George's attempts at them, watching Dorothea smile. Even Laura Beth once moved a manicured finger behind her sunglasses to wipe her eye.

From then on, Bobby was no longer alone. He visited the yellow house as often as the rest, speaking long to Dorothea of the former things. George began to look upon him as another student, which pleased Tommy to no end. While the boy continued to while away eternity mired in history and math and science, Bobby's curriculum became centered upon chess. A ridiculous game, he thought, filled with too many rules that put too much strain on his thinking, but one George felt necessary.

Laura Beth would often sit with Bobby in the early afternoons under the careful watch of Dorothea and Junior. The two of them would look back upon the old world and their youth, those years they spent together in school. Bobby, still being new to heaven, had to do much of the remembering.

He played tag and football and hotbox with Tommy and Junior, which more often than not left the others in hysterics.

Sometimes he listened in secret as George and Juliet and Dorothea argued about the higher things that Bobby did not understand. Families often fight, Dorothea reminded him. They fight because they love.

Junior took him fishing. Rankin's Creek and even Lake Moomaw, where Matthew caught his first fish. Mark applauded. Bobby could not. He didn't want to risk Junior seeing and so opened another beer to keep his boys close. Junior kept talking about the time he struck out Chipper Jones on three pitches. Bobby kept drinking.

But it was those moments with Juliet that Bobby secretly came to cherish most. Her kindness charmed him, her warm eyes and quick smile, how she never called him a drunk or a pervert but treated him instead as an equal. Of them all, she was the one Bobby had come to nearly trust. Nearly. Matthew warned Bobby that none of his new family were what they appeared. Mark never went that far, though he often said something along those lines—they all held secrets: Junior and Laura Beth and George and Tommy. Juliet. Dorothea especially. They knew things Bobby didn't, and they were all vying to be the first to tell those hidden things when the time came.

Turns began with a feeling akin to expectation, that long and eternal day promising a full belly and a deep rest. Whiling away the hours puttering around town with Junior or playing ball with Tommy or stealing away for a picnic with Juliet.

Turns ending with the boys high above town on Route 237, enduring what must be done the same as Bobby had endured one of Doc March's injections as a boy—grit your teeth and suck it up, it'll feel better after. He asked Juliet if he could start calling her near the end of their night. Her yes came with only a flicker of *Why?* in her eyes. Bobby would put her voice on speaker so the boys could hear. They spoke of things now and things gone and things that now would never be, and Bobby would always say his good-bye just before the curve. Though the words never passed through Juliet's lips, Bobby understood she had come to love him. And though he believed he would have loved her back at one time, Bobby would take the curve and see those headlights and know this last act of his old life could never be forgiven. Dorothea and the rest may have had their secrets. That was fine. Bobby had a secret of his own, one that damned him.

Yet eternity soon softened the hard edges around him, taking away rather than adding to the thick walls Bobby had built around himself. The world grew larger and brighter. Tommy went from calling him Mr. Barnes to Mr. Bobby to Bobby and finally, one day, to Daddy. Meant as a joke, Bobby thought, though he suspected one Tommy had not intended. He never asked Tommy not to call him that again. Matthew hated them both for it.

He drank more and then less and then more again, always arriving early at Mama's. Before dinner, Dorothea would gather everyone and read what the Lord had left in her mailbox. Bobby would watch more than listen. He would see the way George sneered at those words and how Juliet seemed to study them with her mind, how Junior and Tommy would smile and Laura Beth would listen stone-faced. He would see how the sunlight played through the page and lit the typed words, then glance over his shoulder to where Hubie's old typewriter sat on the desk. He saw this new world as neither new nor a world at all. Tiny things such as the fading paint on the walls of his shop and the cracks in the foundation of Dorothea's house, things that could be repaired but never fixed. How Juliet fretted over the flowers in front of her church, which were pretty enough on the outside but brittle, given to some sort of disease. *Rotted*, Mark said on one of their rides. *Not just Juliet's flowers, but everything. That's everything, Daddy—pretty on the outside but brittle underneath. Can't you see it? Can't you feel it?*

Yes. Bobby could. He saw it in the stars that greeted him and felt it in the blackness that claimed him. Dorothea had been right. This was heaven, but a soured one. And then it became not even that.

A mirror was what Juliet had once called the Turn, and such was what Bobby's world soon became. What was once large and bright began to shrink and fade in a whisper barely noticed. Those moments of happiness and belonging still came, and yet what always followed were moments when the Turn only seemed to magnify the life Bobby thought he'd left behind. In such times the emptiness of his old life followed like a shadow, and not even Juliet could lift his spirits. The early call from Bea. The late call from Carla. Sheriff Barnett, warning he would someday have to peel what was left of Bobby off the road. Tommy was right in saying Bobby could keep away from those things without upsetting Dorothea's precious balance. Yet Tommy was also still a boy, too inno-cent to know that Bobby could never truly remove himself from Bea's accusations or Carla's regrets or Jake's insight. These things stalked him whether he picked up the phone or not, drove to Timmy's or stayed far away.

It was a truth Bobby could not help but come to believe: he could run forever, but never from what lay inside himself.

# Part II

# Hell

## -1-

Stars.

He woke cursing in his mind what had once been a source of comfort. For longer than Bobby could imagine, that early sky had been a counterbalance to the darkness on the mountain. He tasted something like death at the end of his Turn, quick and violent. Now there seemed death, too, at the beginning, one so slow it made him question his own eyes.

*Those eyes lie,* Mama would say. *They fool you into seeing too much.*

But seeing too much had not become Bobby's problem. It was seeing too little.

The stars were gone.

Not all and certainly not many, but some. Vanished. Winked out, the same as he had that first night with Tommy.

He tried to remember if the empty spaces above the pharmacy and the hardware store had always been such. Bobby told himself yes, of course yes, where could stars go? He imagined asking George that in the middle of their next chess match, just as George was about to make a crucial move— *Say, George old bean, where do stars go when you can't see them anymore? And exactly how can they go in a world where nothing is supposed to ever change?*

Two tiny paws touched the hem of his jeans, two more, all four crawling up his right leg and across his wrist, down his left arm. He waited until all but one paw had stepped off.

"Mornin', Mr. Jangles."

The rat turned its head at the sound, seeing Bobby for the first time even if Bobby had seen it . . . how many? He'd lost count. Enough times to give a rat a name. Bobby sat up and reached for his cap as Mr. Jangles raced for the trash bags against the opposite wall. He pushed through the wood door and walked to the front for his coffee, then to wash up. The blinds on the waiting room windows were left alone. Bobby wouldn't be in the shop long enough that Turn to bother.

He stopped midway to the bathroom, stunned at that word.

*Shop.*

Those four walls had never been that, not since he'd sold the house. That half acre in the heart of Mattingly's pitiful excuse for a downtown had been *home. Home* to him and to the boys, even if also a place near dead but for the memories it trapped. Did that mean home now lay at the yellow house across town, just as Mama had wished so long ago? Bobby stood there, listening to the empty shop. He wanted to answer yes to that question but found he couldn't and wondered what had come to lie in his heart.

The phone rang (Bea, right on the dot) as he studied the bruise on his cheek. There, too, something was different.

They had all at some point asked where and how he'd gotten that mark. Tommy had been first, of course, followed by the rest. Bobby's story was he'd been drunk and run into one of the shop's beams the day before he died. It seemed a plausible scenario. Much like Laura Beth's pinkeye and Dorothea's arthritis and George's cough, that bruise had followed Bobby into the afterlife. No one noticed it had gotten larger since he'd first come to the Turn. More mottled looking. Not by much, but enough for it to be the first thing Bobby settled on in the mirror. He thought maybe Juliet had noticed it as well. She'd certainly gotten close enough.

He leaned in close to the glass as the phone fell quiet. No sense fretting over his face now. Dorothea had called an early dinner the Turn before, and Bobby had agreed to help Junior with Tommy. More schooling, though a much more entertaining education than George could provide—baseball. It was the only real contribution Junior could make in the boy's life, seeing as how Dorothea forbade him from teaching Tommy how to smoke what she called "the weed."

With no sugar and only soured milk, Bobby drank his coffee black. He nursed the first cup as he walked back to the waiting room, finished it in silence. Not even his books could occupy him. His thoughts remained on the mountain road from which he'd returned and would return to again, the curve and the headlights and all that followed.

His end had become no less a change than the winking stars and the growing bruise. But it was not the horror of that place of monsters between eternities that made Bobby stand in the middle of the waiting room as the sun woke the town. It was that he no longer felt horror at all. Death—if that was in fact what he brushed against at the end of each Turn—had lost its sting. And what of all the horror he had once felt *before* that black? The helpless sense as he rounded the curve to find nowhere to go and the hopelessness of watching his sons wave good-bye, the scrape of metal upon metal like a million fingers upon a million chalkboards? Those, too, had been lessened, made bearable by the sheer repetitiveness of it all. Bobby and the boys now approached their ride at night with equanimity at best and fools' hearts at worst, laughing as they took the curve or making plans for the next Turn or saying good-bye to Juliet over the phone. Caterwauling along with the radio of rivers overflowing and a voice of rage and ruin.

Yet the end never came soon and never would. No hurricanes a-blowing. No rivers overflowing. But what of the rage and ruin?

It was then he realized those last moments of his old life had become a small thing, nothing more than a chore to be checked off, a mere trivial hour tucked inside an endless stream of others. He had long considered his ability to fashion a sense of normalcy in the midst of any hell; such was how he had finished his days, alone with the boys. And yet he considered for the first time that the ability might be less a mark of his good character than evidence of his wretchedness.

He dumped what was left of his coffee. For a small window of the very time George said no longer existed, Bobby thought of leaving. He could be at Dorothea's early, help her get things ready. The boys would never know the difference, couldn't come until bidden. He reached beneath the counter for the bottle, half full as always, and set it on the counter.

Tommy would often ask if he felt guilty, getting drunk all the time. He'd tell Bobby his old mama had done that and now she wasn't in their heaven and maybe she was in hell. Bobby knew the others felt the same. He saw the way they watched him, Dorothea especially, and how they whispered when they thought he wasn't looking. Mama to Junior and Laura Beth, Juliet to George, Tommy listening to them all. His family, they said. His friends. And yet would friends coddle in mystery while setting him aside? They had welcomed Bobby into their lives and Dorothea had opened her home to him, but was that all family meant? He didn't know, had gone too long with neither. What Bobby did settle on was that even after all that time, he still felt a stranger to them. Like a stray dog allowed to rest and eat but never fully trusted. He knew they kept secrets, even Juliet, all of which Bobby excused because he had kept a few of his own. Not simply what happened each night on the mountain. As misunderstood as that would be by Juliet or Dorothea or Tommy, it would pale against the other, worse skeleton he hid: Bobby felt no guilt in partaking of the devil's wine. The shame came in leaving it alone.

He unscrewed the top and took three large swallows. Quicker, he had found, was better. The beer came next. Though in times and lives past it would have taken much more to get Bobby drunk, three swallows and a single can had become enough. He sat in the recliner and waited as the alcohol rushed through him, muscles warming and relaxing, the world slowing down. It was not long before the alley door opened and closed. The sounds of running feet echoed from the walls, laughter that had come to bring Bobby as much sadness as joy. The Turn was a mirror.

Mark bounded in first, Matthew close behind. The sight was not unlike the stars or the growing bruise on Bobby's face—Mark at the forefront, not only in deed but in word as well. They leaped together onto Bobby's lap and covered him in kisses he could not feel.

"Where we goin', Daddy?" Mark asked.

"Miss Dorothea's got a little gathering. Figured we'd head over there."

"Why we always gotta go over there?" Matthew asked. "I don't like it over there, Daddy. It's creepy."

"It's company," Bobby said. "And I don't mind seeing Juliet and Tommy. Maybe I'll whip old George today, become a grandmaster. What y'all think of that?"

"You ain't gonna beat'm," Mark said. "You play wrong, Daddy. Could we stay here? Please? We can play hide-and-seek and sing to the radio and you could read out your books." His face had gone long, and there was a weight to his eyes. "Like we used to."

"Maybe tomorrow. Day's too bright to spend shut up in here. I need to get away awhile. Do some thinking. Maybe Mama's is the best place."

"She ain't your mama," Matthew said. "The Widow Cash ain't what she seems."

"I'd ask the origin of such a sour view of humanity, son, but I know that answer. Something buggin' me is all. Sometimes if you do something to get your mind off what it is, you get your answer."

"Maybe you're just askin' the wrong question," Mark said.

Bobby grinned. "Thanks there, Riddler. I'll keep what you and the Penguin have to say in mind."

"Don't you laugh, Daddy," Mark said. "You always go to Miss Dorothea's. You act like they're your friends but they ain't, and they act like you're their friend but *you* ain't. And we tell you, Daddy. Me and Matthew. We say things you need to listen to but you never do, because you're always listenin' to Miss Dorothea or Juliet. Well, you need to listen to *us* and not make fun, because there's bad things in heaven."

Bobby's smile disappeared. "What's that mean?"

"It means there's secret things. There's monsters." His tiny voice cracked before adding, "Even here."

Bobby held them close, trying to feel their arms and heads.

"Y'all seen me through some hard times, you know that? Times I thought wasn't nothing I could do no more. But we got through, huh? Three of us. And we'll get through this, whatever it is. You got my promise. Okay?"

The boys nodded, though without conviction. Matthew's bottom lip puffed over his top. Mark looked at the floor. It was good enough, Bobby thought. Good enough for now.

He got them up and brushed his teeth to get the smell of bourbon and beer off. The boys waited in the truck, somber and still. Bobby took another can before he left, thinking of what Mark said. Then he grabbed a dozen more. That should do if he spread them out enough. Thirteen should keep the boys with him, right where they needed to be.

## -2-

"Bad move."

Bobby glanced up to see George shake his head like an old wrinkled dog just out of the water.

"What?"

"Bad move," George said again, clearing the board of Bobby's remaining knight. "You have to *consider*, Bobby. I might've just now taken your knight, but in truth you lost it three moves ago. This is no game for an apathetic mind. You have to plan. The little mistakes you make early are dearly paid for in the end."

Bobby sighed. He muttered under his breath, "Mark says I never play right."

"What's that?"

"Nothing."

"Then quit your blathering. Mind the center of the board. Control the center, you control the game."

They sat at a small table beneath a towering willow not twenty feet from the back porch. The Turn had colored the leaves a pale yellow that felt somewhere between life and death. Juliet and Laura Beth constituted their audience. Junior and Tommy played catch nearby. Dorothea sat alone on the porch, enjoying her tea and the day's letter. Bobby looked her way. Dorothea did her best to smile, though her grin faded into a troubled look. The letter maybe. Then Bobby thought no—Mama was troubled over him.

"Careful, Bobby," Laura Beth said. "I smell a trap."

He opened his mouth to say something (though what, exactly, Bobby didn't know), then realized she was speaking of George. Sunlight glinted off her sunglasses. Laura Beth produced a tissue and eased it behind the black lens covering her left eye. She balled up the tissue to hide the gunk. In matters of chess, Laura Beth had become Bobby's biggest champion, more so even than Juliet.

"George always got something up his sleeve," he said.

The old man raised his eyebrows and smiled. Beneath the table, Juliet's hand touched Bobby's thigh. She squeezed as her lips grew to a grin.

"Everything okay with you, Bobby?" George asked.

"Till I sat down here with you, yes." He studied the board.

"Plan. The beginning seals the end."

"Always been more a checkers guy, George. This stuff don't make no sense to me."

"Checkers." George tugged at his beard and gave the same look as he did when Dorothea read her letters. "A child's game."

"Tell that to Junior. He gets me to play every day."

"As I said." George cast a look into the yard where Junior and Tommy played, then reached across the table and patted Laura Beth's hand. "No offense, dear. I know where your affections lie."

Laura Beth watched her man. Even with all the time Bobby spent in their company, he still could not understand her fixation upon Junior Hewitt. Someone as beautiful as that, latching on to such a man. He had once suggested to Juliet it was loneliness. Juliet had only shaken her head and said it was more than that. She'd refused to say more.

Dorothea called, "How goes the game, Bobby?"

"Same as always," Junior yelled. "Bobby gettin' beat. I can see it from here, Mama, just as I hear his whinin'."

Bobby moved a pawn that George gobbled with a sigh. Juliet squeezed his leg again. Not an admonishment, a concern. They had all picked up on his silence that morning. Even Junior had offered what compassion he could, chuckling as he asked Bobby who he'd killed. It was all Bobby could do not to leave.

"Sure you're okay?" George asked. "You keep this up, you'll be in the kitchen helping Dorothea make dinner."

They all chuckled, drawing Dorothea's gaze from the letter in her hand. Bobby had no desire to help with dinner. That's how Doro—*Mama*—tended to family troubles, and troubles weren't rare. Bobby had spent enough time in the Turn to know there may not be seasons in heaven, but they lived on in the heart. Joy and despair ebbed and flowed if nothing else did, driven less by the steadfastness of the place in which they'd been marooned than by the weaknesses of those marooned there. Bobby had witnessed times when Juliet fell into a quiet even he could not penetrate. Whole seasons of Turns when George mourned his separation from Anna. Laura Beth would sometimes isolate herself from all but Junior, and Junior would sometimes leave for days without notice, only to return with little explanation. In their quiet moments together, Juliet said that Junior was running from something he'd glimpsed in the mirror. To her, all in the Turn were running from something.

He kept his eyes on the board and asked, "What y'all doing tonight?"

"I don't know," Juliet said. "Supper, I guess."

"I don't mean supper. I mean . . . after."

"You mean when our Turn's over?" George asked.

Laura Beth straightened in her chair. It was plain to Bobby this wasn't a subject she wanted to discuss.

Juliet's hold on his leg tightened. "You want to talk about your Turn, Bobby?"

"No," he said. "No," again, making that point. "Just, you know. We don't ever say anything about it."

"I guess none of us ever saw the need," George told him. He looked toward the porch. The old man had never been given to nervousness, yet Bobby thought he looked plenty nervous then. "I read. Nothing else. Not always the same book, of course; I at least have that freedom. But that's the last thing I do, then I'm awake again."

"Staring out my window," Juliet said. "That's how I end."

Laura Beth whispered, "I'm with Charlie," and Bobby felt Juliet's hand disappear.

"And you, Bobby?" she asked.

"It's not . . ." He shook his head. "That's not what I mean. When you wake up, are the stars out?"

They all shook their heads. George said, "I think only Junior's up that early. Maybe Tommy."

"True enough," Junior said. He tossed the ball to Tommy. Bobby hadn't thought the big man could hear.

"Why?" George asked.

Bobby lowered his voice. "Something's wrong with the stars."

For a stretch of time enough to make Bobby uncomfortable, George only stared at him. Then he leaned forward and shot a look toward the porch once more. "What's wrong with the stars, Bobby?"

Junior said, "Need a catcher here."

"I'll do it," Bobby said. He set a finger atop his king (a shaky one, he needed a drink and his boys) and toppled it.

"Bobby?" Juliet asked.

He pushed his chair back and rose. Dorothea watched while George reached for his little notebook. Junior moved the garbage can lid that he and Tommy used for home plate, positioning it down closer to the house. Tommy held a bat nearly as long as he was tall. Bobby grabbed a glove and squatted into his stance.

"Gonna put one out there today?"

Tommy grinned. "Gonna put'm *all* out there."

"Gimme a batter," Junior yelled.

He stood in an awkward stance that turned into a fluid motion as he lobbed the ball. Tommy swung, grunting as he did, and bounced the ball past Junior's left. Laura Beth clapped. The next one went near all the way to the maple at the edge of the backyard. The one after that, even farther. Tommy beamed. Everyone clapped. Junior curled his brow.

"I tell y'all 'bout that time I struck out Chipper Jones?" Junior yelled.

Everyone answered yes (all but Tommy), though Junior seemed not to hear.

"Back in '91. South Atlantic League? He was for the Macon Braves, me hurlin' for the Gastonia Rangers."

He wound and tossed again. Harder, making Tommy miss and Bobby's hand sting. Dorothea cheered anyway.

"Scrawny little thing," Junior said. To him, everyone looked scrawny. "Come up to the plate actin' all cocky-like, well, I showed him. Three pitches all it took. I can show you. Let me throw one in there, Bobby. Hard, like ol' Chipper got. Boy might be a Hall-a-Famer, but he never seen gas like that before or since. Lemme throw one in there, Bobby."

Bobby said, "Don't think so, Junior."

"Come on now." The voice low but somehow whiny at the same time. "Can't let that little runt have all the cheers today. Just one. Step on in, Tommy."

Tommy wasn't sure. "You ain't gonna wheel it, are you?"

"Nah," Junior said. "Come on. Scared?"

"I ain't scared."

Tommy looked back at Bobby, who shrugged and said, "Go on, I guess. But don't plant your feet."

Bobby crouched down as Tommy stepped back in. Junior took his stance, leaning forward with the ball hidden behind his right leg. He looked to where Laura Beth sat.

"You watch this, sweet knees."

His glower was enough to sink Bobby's heart. Junior wound slow, kicking his leg high, and Bobby knew what was about to happen even if he had no idea why. He barely had time enough to tell Tommy to get away before the ball shot from Junior's hand like a rocket. Bobby saw nothing but heard an angry hiss like hot steel plunged into cold water. The blur was on him before he could react, cutting left to right as it glanced off the tip of his glove, caroming away as Junior's deep grunt finally reached him, the grunt arriving *after* the pitch, and Bobby had no time to ponder how fast that meant the throw had traveled because the ball then cracked against Dorothea's home and shattered the siding like a cannonball. Juliet's mouth hung free of her face. Laura Beth whooped as George rose to inspect the damage.

Mama leaned forward in her chair. The calm demeanor she had kept all morning was gone, leaving behind a hard woman's rage.

"Junior Hewitt, what you thinking you can do something like that to my *house*?"

"Don't you worry none, Mama," Junior said. Bobby felt him walking forward, caught his shadow closing in on his own. "Hole'll be gone next Turn." He gripped Bobby's elbow, helping him toward the house. His smile was all teeth, his voice low and stupid. "Sorry 'bout that, Bobby. Accident. That can happen, 'specially when you go start talkin' what you shouldn't. Don't you worry none about no stars, and don't you go stickin' your nose into everybody else's Turn. You unnerstand? Lord's watchin'. So am I. I'm the one you gotta be scared of."

-3-

Dorothea willed him to stay, just as Bobby knew she would. Asked him to come into the house in that singsong voice of hers while George and the rest gaped at the hole Junior had made. Tommy didn't look to know whether to be angry or amazed and so showed some of both, but Bobby only wanted to leave. Not just because of what Junior had said (which hadn't made Bobby angry or amazed but mostly scared), but because Matthew had been right. He should've stayed at the shop.

What he said was he didn't feel well. Nothing of importance, a headache and a stomach that wasn't sitting right. He couldn't stay. Because of the head and the stomach, he'd told Dorothea, though the truth was that Bobby had to leave because he couldn't be around *them*. Not Junior with his threats or George with his notebook or Dorothea with her stares, not even Tommy and Juliet. Could not bear to sit with a smile he had to hammer and shape into existence as Dorothea gathered them all to listen as she read the Lord's letter. Could not bear to stand in Dorothea's kitchen and listen to her go on about putting aside whatever preyed upon his heart to ponder instead the safe home he enjoyed.

And so it was back to the shop he fled, those four empty walls that had become no more a home to him than the yellow house. Bobby drank long that afternoon and tried to forget. When Matthew and Mark appeared to crown him with kisses and sweet words, he drank still. He drank and told them what he believed of heaven, things he could tell no one else, and that secrets could kill a man as sure as any beer.

* * *

Dinner was the beef jerky and crackers the Turn always restocked, with a side order of blaring radio. Matthew took his hand at air guitar, Mark a set of drums he fashioned from some old buckets. Bobby took lead singer, bellowing songs he had heard over and over before. They were in the middle of "Paradise City" when Bobby spotted Juliet standing in the doorway between the shop and the waiting room. Her hands were clasped at the flat of her stomach. She grinned, not so wide as to seem presumptuous. Bobby reached for the knob and turned down the radio.

"I knocked this time," she said. "Promise. Mind a visitor?"

Matthew walked forward, putting himself between them. "Tell her to go away, Daddy."

"No," Mark said. Sometimes Bobby wondered if his oldest by thirty seconds had grown even more smitten of the town preacher than he had. "It's okay, Daddy."

"Don't mind it," Bobby told her. "Just blowing off some steam. Need a bass player, if you're interested."

"Don't think I am. Glad to see you're feeling better."

"Want a drink?"

She stepped inside and waved him off. "Mama fed us so good I don't think I can swallow another thing." Matthew held out his arms, palms up, demanding she halt. Juliet strolled through him. "I've never been in here. Isn't that weird? All this time? Waiting room is as far as I've gotten."

"Guess it ain't. Weird, I mean. I ain't ever been to your house."

"That's not for want of asking on my part."

She smiled. Bobby studied his shoes. He was never sure what existed between them, but it was something and it frightened him. He had lost everything the last time he fell in love. Mark had told him once that love was the only thing he could risk again. He'd said the heart could bear what the soul could not, and that had made Bobby wonder how a boy could know such things.

"Not sure what to make of this." She pointed to the sticker on the front of the toolbox. "'Mary should have aborted Jesus'?"

"Been there a long time. Don't even see it no more." The way Juliet looked at him brought a shame. "Ain't like I can't peel it off. Just be back next Turn."

Matthew looked ready to explode, for what good it would do.

"There's much you don't know of me, Juliet, and much I'm ashamed to speak."

He expected anything but her chuckle. "You'd have a horned head and a spiked tail if all I've heard was true, Bobby Barnes."

He looked at Mark, who only shrugged.

"Heard from who?"

"Dorothea and the rest. All but Tommy. He wanted to come along. Begged me. I had to tell him I wanted some time alone, in case you wanted to talk. He's quite taken with you. You've been good for him."

Bobby wouldn't say it, not in front of the boys, but his thoughts were clear enough—*Tommy's been good for me, too.*

"What'd they tell you about me?"

"Not much more than I knew the first time I saw you," she said. "Nothing I haven't put out of my mind. Dorothea said you were a good man until you went away, though she didn't mention where you went or when or what happened. George said you're divorced. Junior called you a drunk. The man stays high as a kite, but that's Junior, stating the obvious while displaying his own hypocrisy. Laura Beth called you a molester."

"I ain't—"

She held up a hand. "They don't speak of you in such terms now. They love you. Truly."

"Guess our first meeting wasn't my finest. I didn't know what was going on when Junior brought me in there."

"Oh, that wasn't our first meeting." Juliet studied the toolbox, the floor, Bea's car. "I saw you once before. When Allie and Zach were lost. I was in the square one night after the search, trying to be the preacher I knew I wasn't. Trying to be strong, even if I didn't believe myself strong anymore.

Somebody said something had happened down here. Sheriff Barnett and everybody else went running. I did, too. Found you lyin' on the sidewalk in a bed of glass from your window, just after Hank Granderson found his Allie's scarf in your truck."

He repeated the same line he had for so long: "I didn't do nothing to them kids."

"I know."

Bobby shoved his hands into his pockets. Matthew glared at Juliet. Mark smiled.

"I brought a stuffed bear," he said low. "When it was all done and she was laid up in the hospital, I bought Allie a stuffed bear. Never told anyone. Guess I thought maybe that would square me or something. I was drunk when I dropped it off."

She leaned against Bea's car. Bobby studied the bare legs sprouting from under her skirt.

"I knew you were drunk as soon as Junior brought you in the house. And I can never be one to chastise anyone for what faith they have or don't. As for the rest . . ." Juliet shrugged as though the rest didn't matter. "I don't think anyone ever thought you that sort of man. Sometimes a thing gets whispered so much it takes on a life of its own. After a while, it grows to a monster no one can slay for good. Whatever you were doesn't matter, Bobby. That person's died. You don't have to be him anymore."

Matthew muttered, "She's lyin', Daddy. You think you can trust her, but you can't. Can't none of'm. They ain't no different than anybody else, and this ain't no better place than the one we left."

Juliet took his hand. Her fingers were soft and warm and made Bobby wonder whether the rest of her felt the same.

131

"What's wrong?" she asked. "And don't say you're sick. George only noticed today, but I've seen it for a while. Something's hurting you, Bobby. Is it me?"

He shook his head and smiled, wanting to change the subject, even if he knew this was the only one he could ever tell and the one person he almost trusted. Also the one person he could not bear to disappoint. "Nothing I can't handle."

"Doesn't look to me like you're handling it."

"You need to tell her, Daddy," Mark said. "Miss Juliet's supposed to know."

Bobby said "No" too harsh, making both Mark and Juliet flinch. She let go of his hand and looked to where his eyes had gone.

"Bobby?"

"You need to go," he said.

"I'm not going anywhere until you tell me what's wrong."

"You wouldn't understand."

"I would."

She stepped closer, reaching again for his hand, yet Bobby pulled away.

"Some things follow us from one place to the next, Juliet. Sometimes even another world ain't far enough away."

"What's followed you?"

"Don't say nothin', Daddy," Matthew said.

"Bobby? What's followed you here?" Another step, backing Bobby against the little car. And then Juliet uttered the eight words that sent him reeling. "Is it the things you think you see?"

"What?"

She kept her voice even and low, that soothing tone that Bobby had come to hear as a salve for his hurt. "Tommy told us about them. Me and Dorothea. That first night he was here with you, he said you were talking to things that weren't real."

"We're real!" Matthew screamed. He bolted from his place beside Mark and leaped, through Juliet again and out the other side, landing in a pile on the concrete. He rolled, yelling, "You tell her we're real, Daddy. Tell her we're *true*."

Mark inched his way to Bobby's side, wanting to be held. Juliet backed away as she watched Bobby open his arms.

"That what you're doing?" he asked. Fire lit his belly. Matthew lying on the floor and cradling a knee that had already begun to bruise, Mark shaking in Bobby's arms, pale-white and scared. Because of her. "You spying on me, Juliet? You and Dorothea? That why you come?"

"No." Her smile had vanished. "Bobby, that's not what I—"

"She send you here to tell me the Lord's watching? Say I should come on back and be a good boy?"

"What? *No.*"

"You think you know me, Juliet Creech?" He laughed. "You think I can *change*? I can't. I'm who I always was and who I'll always be, and that's what I get to see every *day*. You come up in here acting all holy, telling me things you don't know nothing about."

"I just want to help."

*"Well I don't need your help!"*

Juliet's lips trembled. Bobby held his ground. She took an awkward step away as though fighting for balance and said, "I'll leave you to your beer and your ghosts, then."

She turned, staggering toward the waiting room. Bobby felt Mark go limp in his arms. Matthew cursed Juliet's going, screaming that he never wanted to see her again, that he was *real*. And even in the midst of all that screaming and holding, even in Bobby's drunkenness, he understood he would lose

133

Juliet if she walked out that door. What they had, that great mystery, would fade. They would sit at Dorothea's and talk and laugh and eat, but they would never be the same. Bobby doubted his heaven and his place in it and what counted as his new life, but he did not doubt that. It was the only reason he could think of that made him tell her the truth.

"I kill somebody in my Turn."

*   *   *

Juliet stopped but did not face him.

"At the end," Bobby said. "Every time. You call and talk to me on the phone because I asked you to. Because I needed someone to help me through. Because every time I hang up it's because I'm about to kill him, and I couldn't bear it no more."

Now she turned. "Who?"

Matthew tried, "No, Daddy."

"I don't know who." His voice cracked. Bobby felt Mark squeeze his tiny arms around his waist. "I don't mean to. Not now, not then. I'm up in the mountains because I always go up there every night, me and"—*the boys*, he nearly said—"and it always helps me set aside my burdens. You don't know what it was like for me, Juliet. That time Hank tossed me through the window wasn't the start of it and nowhere near the end. You imagine what it's like, being the man everybody hates?"

Tears now, and it didn't matter how tight Mark held him or if Juliet saw because Bobby could hold his despair no longer. "Ain't nobody supposed to be up *on* that road, Juliet. I try to get out of the way but I never can and I kill him. Every night, and now he's gone and I'm here and I don't know where *here* is, and in between." Bobby dropped his voice, afraid to speak it. "There's a darkness. There's night between the worlds, Juliet. That's where I go. It's my judgment and my fate and now it's longer. Every Turn, that dark grows and it's gonna swallow me someday and I don't know what to do."

He knew she couldn't help. The shock had gotten to her. Juliet stood no more than ten feet away, and yet she may as well have been back in the old world for the distance between them. Her posture had gone rigid. Her fingers touched two parted lips. "Bobby . . ." was all she could manage.

"Don't hate me," he begged. "Please, Juliet?" He left Mark and closed the gap between them, searching for some way to lessen the horror in her eyes. "I've tried so many times to stop it, but I can't. I can't. I'm always there and I can't get out of the way and I don't—"

And then she took him. Bobby felt Juliet's arms at his back and smelled the perfume she wore, let his hands find the soft cotton of her shirt. He sank into her embrace as one would a baptism. Yet these were sins Bobby knew water could not wash away, and the blood that covered him spoke to his own damnation.

"This can't be heaven," he muttered.

Juliet tensed in his arms. "What?"

"This can't be heaven. I don't know what this place is, but it ain't that. Heaven wouldn't feel this bad."

She released him but kept her hands on his elbows. Bobby saw hurt in her eyes and he saw hope, and he supposed the two of those together made something like love.

He said, "Don't you tell Dorothea. I already said too much. Junior heard me asking y'all about your Turns. That's why he threw that ball like he did. He made it a warning."

That looked to worry her. Bobby thought he saw a flicker

of something out of the corner of his eye. Matthew saw it, too, and took a few steps toward the waiting room.

"Daddy, I think somebody's—"

"We've all been waiting," Juliet said. "Me and George. Dorothea."

"Waiting for what?"

Mark stepped closer to his brother. Their eyes locked onto the recliner and the soiled carpet.

"For you to say what you thought. What you believe this place is or isn't. We didn't know how to do it any other way. None of us were counting on you showing up. Or anybody. It's been so long, Bobby."

"Juliet, I don't understand."

"Dorothea said none of us could tell you until she got a letter saying it was time. She doesn't like us spending so much time together. She's told me, 'The Lord's watching, Juliet.' If that doesn't sound like a warning, I don't know what is."

"George told me it ain't God that's watching."

"It isn't. That's one thing he and I agree on. But it's something, Bobby. Something powerful. After that, I was afraid to say anything. But now . . . after what you just told me . . . she's going to find out, Bobby. Mama'll know I told you. But I have to—"

A voice screamed *"No!"* from the waiting room. Bobby and Juliet flinched. The boys ran for the alley door.

Tommy stepped from behind the near wall of the waiting room into the shop. His face had gone white, his eyes as wide as saucers.

"You can't tell him!" he screamed. "You can't!"

She put a hand to Bobby's chest and eased him back. Bobby understood it as an act of protection, though he couldn't understand from what.

"What are you doing here, Tommy?" she asked. "I said I needed to talk to Bobby alone."

"Because of this?" he asked. "You can't tell him, Juliet. You *can't*. You gotta do what Mama says because Mama knows."

"It has to be from us, Tommy. Not from her."

"What has to be from you?" Bobby asked. "Would somebody please tell me what I'm supposed to know?"

She turned to him and paused as if considering her words. Tommy began to speak. Juliet beat him to it.

"About Laura Beth."

## -4-

It felt strange, being alone.

He waited on a cracked and rotting bench in the shadow of the wide pine that had given the quiet avenue its name. Evening had turned to night in the last hour, streetlights ticking on one by one. The few vehicles that passed pulled into paved drives set in front of trimmed and painted homes. On the other side of the fenced and manicured lawn behind him, a dog sniffed but did not see.

Juliet had said the bench on Evergreen Avenue would be the best place to wait. There were things like pockets in the Turn, places people either drove or walked by but never really saw, and those made good hiding spots. *People don't see everything, Bobby. When I got here, I realized just how much of the world I'd never seen at all.* That had led Bobby to ponder a question for which he had no answer—if a place remained open and yet unseen, did it exist? He'd have to ask George that one.

His gaze kept to the fancy Tudor three doors down on the

opposite side of the street. A single lamp burned from the post at the Gowdys' drive. The house stood dark.

*Stay there and don't move. We'll do what we can. And for heaven's sake, don't let Junior see you if this all goes wrong.*

She had said more, most of which Bobby forgot once Tommy started screaming again. Yelling *No* to Bobby and *No* to Juliet, *No* to everything. Bobby had half a mind to follow the twins out to the alley. At least it would have been quiet out there.

Headlights down the street. He leaned back and peered through the branches.

Everyone in town knew Charlie Gowdy's yellow Corvette. It rumbled past in a blur and braked suddenly, nearly locking the tires before it swerved into the drive. The top was down in spite of the cool air. To make room for the golf clubs, Bobby thought, which looked to have cost Charlie as much as Bobby had paid for his truck. He watched as Charlie stumbled getting out of the car, lurching and grabbing hold of the lamppost, then knew the other reason. Charlie needed the air because he was drunk.

Sandy hair, thinner and grayer than it had been in high school, spilled down over his eyes. An empty bottle fell from inside the car and rolled down the driveway and into the middle of the street. Charlie righted himself as best he could and aimed for the house. He left the Corvette's door open, the top down (*Guess you'll pitch a fit when you wake up in your tomorrow and find it's rained*, Bobby thought) and the golf clubs in the seat. There came a muffled *thump* as he bumped into the front door, forgetting to open it. He tried twice to get the key into the lock and then disappeared inside.

Was this why Juliet had asked him to wait? To show him that Laura Beth's husband was a no-'count? If that was the case, Bobby had no need to spend half his evening sitting in the dark. Everyone in town knew Charlie Gowdy was a fool—everyone but Laura Beth, leastways—and what money he'd managed to collect over the years could be accounted to his sly bank dealings with the sort of folk even Mattingly's criminal element wanted no part of.

He eyed the bottle Charlie had left in the road. Juliet had said no beer and Bobby had grudgingly agreed, but then Juliet wasn't there and Bobby was thirsty. Could be a swallow left in that bottle. An import no doubt, nothing like the cheap stuff Bobby got from Timmy's. Charlie Gowdy always had the best in life. The thought occurred to Bobby that maybe it was common knowledge inside the family that Charlie would come home drunk, and that's why Juliet had wanted him there. So Bobby could see in someone else the way he himself acted so much of the time, and so he could stop wondering why it was that the people in town had always shunned him with upturned noses and eyes that looked anyplace but where he stood.

So he would stop talking to things that weren't there.

If that was the case, he might as well get up and leave. Because Juliet didn't understand. None of them did.

*  *  *

Still he waited, watching the house and thinking about how alone he felt. No beer meant no boys. He kicked a rock near his boot, making the dog in the yard behind him growl. Bobby decided maybe he shouldn't do that again. Lord might be watching.

He snorted a laugh that died in his throat when he heard shoes coming down his side of the walk. He felt panic grip him, thinking it could be Junior or Charlie, even Dorothea, thinking that all the promising Juliet had made Tommy give her about keeping quiet hadn't been enough. Bobby slid off the back of the bench and huddled between it and the tree limbs, listening to the footsteps that approached.

The figure stopped at the tree's edge. A soft voice called, "Bobby?"

"Laura Beth?" He raised his head. "Girl, you near scared me to death."

She moved beneath the tree and sat on the bench, back straight and legs angled beneath her dress. *Just like they taught you at cotillion.*

Her face went toward the house and her hand to her sunglasses. "I don't have a whole lot of time. My Turn's almost up."

He lifted himself over the bench and took a deep breath before speaking, wanting to keep his voice from catching. "You heading home? I seen Charlie come in. Hope that man swings a seven iron better'n he can hold his liquor, Laura Beth. That's what y'all trying to show me, forget it. I don't act like that, and I ain't giving up my drink."

"You keep quiet about Charlie," she said. "Let me do the talking here. Bad enough this was sprung on me the way it was."

"What's that mean?"

"Means if anybody should've been clued in on what was going to happen tonight, it should've been me. Guess I shoulda known, though. After what you asked earlier about our Turns." She sniffed. "I know you don't care much for me, Bobby."

"That ain't true."

"Shut up. I don't have time for you to be sitting here filling the air with words you don't mean. You don't like me. You never have, not even when we were in school. So just hush now."

Laura Beth dabbed her eye with a tissue. Bobby could almost smell the stink from under her glasses.

He said, "You know, back when I was a kid, I'd give about anything for a good case of pinkeye. Gets you outta school but you don't feel sick. Ain't got no fever or sore throat, get to play all you want. Shoot, pinkeye's about the best break a kid can get." He shut up. "Guess something like that wears when you get to have it forever, though." And when she said nothing, "Bet it's awful, having to keep quiet to your husband on being dead and all."

Bobby did not speak of the other thing Laura Beth had to keep silent of as well. Didn't seem right, seeing her spend all day with Junior and now seeing her about to go back to her own house. Not that Bobby thought he was in a position to judge. At least Laura Beth wasn't going to kill anybody in a couple hours.

"I never knew you, really," he said. "Before, I mean. Not like I do now. Guess you're right, I didn't much like you. You always had people falling all over you and just about had everything. All I ever had's nothing." He shook his head. "Jealousy's a hard thing. But I like you now, Laura Beth. Truly."

Laura Beth wouldn't look at him. "I don't know what all you said to Juliet. Whatever it was, you put a fear in her. Tommy, too, but he did his part." She let out a chuckle that was more worry than mirth. "Shoulda seen us all tonight, trying to be sly. Mama's worried you didn't come to supper. Juliet was near convinced she knew something was up. Mama has that way, you know. Don't nothing get past her knowing. It worries me, what might come after this. Juliet and George kept her occupied as best they could. Tommy was trying to get Junior to watch the ball game. That's when I snuck away.

141

Junior always drives me home. Drops me there at the end of the street so Charlie won't see."

She looked toward the house.

"You can't tell Dorothea, Bobby. You hear me? Don't tell Mama you know or there'll be trouble. You can be mad or stay away if you want, but I wish you'd come back. We all do. This is a hard place, but harder on your own."

"I'm used to having things hard on my own."

"Not like this. Mama was the one wanted to tell you when it came time, but George and Juliet said that couldn't be. I had one person telling me one thing and another person telling me another, and none of them ever asked what I wanted." She shook her head but kept her face away. "You think I got everything. Maybe in my old life I did, but not here. Here I get pulled every which way. Got Mama and Junior on one side and Juliet and George on the other, me and poor Tommy stuck in the middle. Makes me feel like, I don't know."

"Like a pawn?" Bobby asked.

She nodded. "Like that. Oh, they left it all up to me. Juliet and George. Like I had a choice. But they're right. Mama'd twist it all around, give it a name it ain't supposed to have. Call it the Lord's will and try to convince you to come over to her side of things. That's what all this is about in the end, Bobby. Everything comes down to what you believe this place is and where you'll stand, with Mama and Junior or Juliet and George. There's balance to the Turn, but there's balance to the family, too. That got upset the minute Junior brought you into that dining room. Because you'll slide one way or the other, and the other side's going to be outnumbered." Now she did smile. "Kind of funny, ain't it? You had to die to finally be popular."

"Laura Beth, I really don't under—"

"Charlie rapes me," she said, still looking away. "Every night. I can't stop it. I've hid and blocked the bedroom door. Don't matter. Whatever I do, it only makes what happens worse. He still gets that door open. It's my fault. I deserve it. Charlie comes home mad because of something I didn't do. Something stupid and petty." She pointed to the window at the corner of the second floor. "He busts in that room right up there. And turns on the light. And then my husband rapes me."

The clock tower began to toll. Laura Beth bowed her head as though praying. Bobby watched as she bit down hard on her lip.

"Time's up," she said.

She laid one hand to his leg. The other went to her face. Laura Beth eased her sunglasses away, letting Bobby see the black bruise that covered the entirety of her left eye. Her lid was so swollen that only a narrow slit showed. Blood pooled where there should be white, surrounded by a fogged green iris. More blood caked around the gash beneath her brow. The glow of the streetlamp made the wound almost shimmer. She winced as Bobby drew back. Five chimes from the clock, six. Laura Beth's body began to wink. The sunglasses fell from her hands.

"He rapes me every night and beats me every morning. That's what Mama doesn't want you to know. It's a lie, Bobby. All of it, everything she told you. This ain't heaven. It's hell, and it's forever."

The final chime sounded over town. Somewhere a dog barked. Bobby stared at the sunglasses at his feet, trying to find thoughts and words that had gone hidden inside him. He reached out and grabbed only empty night. Laura Beth had winked away.

In the big Tudor home just down the street, the bedroom light upstairs turned on.

## -5-

Junior was last to leave. He'd remained behind to help Dorothea clean the dishes and set the house right, mumbling he'd never understand why she bothered with what the Turn would put back on its own. Dorothea tried again to explain such things were done out of thanksgiving. Truly the Lord heard the words of men, but the toil of the hands made a sweeter supplication than the pattering of the lips. An act so small as wiping the dining room table could become a meditation if done in the proper mind. When she received no response, Dorothea let the lesson be. Junior had been cursed with a mind that could never truly understand such depth. Besides, it was not gathering the trash and sweeping the foyer that he railed against. It was that Laura Beth had snuck off for home without him.

He'd left the ball game on in the gathering room and stood rapt at all of that scratching of groins and spitting of tobacco, as though seeing it for the first time. Dorothea wondered if in some way that was indeed the case. Junior was a sweet boy, much like Tommy, but with an innocence masked by a brutish strength he'd never fully controlled. One look at the back wall of the house would confirm such. She'd been angry with him over that until Junior had taken her aside to explain himself. Bobby had been seeking answers to things he had no right to question. Dorothea didn't enjoy pondering where that might lead.

She took the broom from his hand and said, "I'll get the rest, dear. Why don't you go on home and finish the game?"

"Thought maybe to drive by Laura Beth's. She's still got some time."

"You know that's not best. Laura Beth's fine, and I'm sure she didn't mean nothing by leaving on her own."

"Tommy wanted to watch the game with me to learn things. Fastball in fastball in slider away, that's good pitching. Told him that. Got to keep them batters off balance. Laura Beth didn't even wait. She never told me was time to go. Didn't even tell me bye, Mama."

That did seem strange upon reflection. Dorothea couldn't remember the last time Junior hadn't escorted Laura Beth home. Poor girl said having him there until the very last gave her a measure of strength she wouldn't otherwise possess. Dorothea didn't doubt that. Laura Beth's end was always a hard thing. Her beginning came none easier. The Lord watched, but He seldom acted.

"I'm sure she said good-bye. You and Tommy were probably so into that ball game of yours that you just didn't hear."

Junior stood gaping. Dorothea could almost hear the gears churning in his brain. "You didn't hear neither."

"No. I was in the kitchen making coffee. George and Juliet wanted to talk of the letters."

"George an' Juliet ain't never care about your letters. Tommy says they don't even think they're real."

Dorothea cocked her head. Of course they didn't. They never had. George's lack of faith was something Dorothea had long given up bothering over, though Juliet's was something else entirely. The woman had once been a *preacher*. She should know better than to succumb to heresy. Why neither of them could accept their blessings and be happy had always been beyond Dorothea, which was why she'd been so willing to sit and witness to them that night. Junior stared at the television, mumbling again. Not about Laura Beth, but about why the batter had just doubled to left center. Fastball out fastball out fastball out, double. Didn't keep him off balance, he said. Gotta do that.

"Off balance," she said.

"Huh?" A bubble of spit formed at the corner of his mouth.

"They never ask about my letters, and Tommy never asks about that ball game. Maybe that's what they were all doing, Junior. Pitching well."

He thought that over. "You think this got something to do with Bobby, Mama?"

"They don't yet trust him enough to go spilling secrets. We got as much claim to Bobby as they do. We have Tommy. Bobby Barnes was always a no-account, but he enjoyed being a father. Juliet might have pretty legs and a healthy chest, but lust can't hold a candle to love. Bobby loves that boy, and that boy loves us."

"Bobby weren't here tonight. Tommy was."

"Bobby's in a season, nothing more. He'll pout and wallow and then he'll come back. They all do. Even you, Junior. We've time yet. Tommy is what bothers me. If George and Juliet are hatching something—and I wouldn't put it past them, never have—Tommy should have let me know. That boy's always been on our side."

"Maybe he didn't know. Maybe George just put it in his head that he needed to watch the game."

Maybe. But Dorothea didn't think so.

"Well, it's no matter. I'll go to the Lord. He'll know what's been done and what needs done about it. We're in His hands. So don't you worry none about Tommy and the rest, because I'm not. And don't you fret Laura Beth. She knows where her heart lies. Go on. I'll see you in a bit, and things will be brighter. You have a mind, though, swing by George's place. Let me know if you see his light on."

"Yes'm."

The crowd roared. Junior cut his eyes to the television and watched in silence as a lanky pitcher walked off the mound, head down and fist pumping. Dorothea watched him swallow. In that moment, the man in front of her looked a boy.

"That coulda been me," he said.

"I know. Lord had other plans for you, Junior. Better plans."

He bent low at the waist and moved his melon head close, letting Dorothea peck his brow.

"Love you, Mama."

"Love you right back and more."

He grinned and ambled for the door, boards creaking beneath his weight. Junior could go on and on about the Turn taking care of the dishes and dirt, but he still made sure to lock the door each night upon his leaving. He waved a last time and disappeared off the porch, down the sidewalk to where his truck sat, and Dorothea thought yes, she did love him. She loved all the children heaven had given her, the ones there and the ones yet to come. Some, like Junior and Tommy, were easy for her to fawn over. Others, like George and Juliet, could try Dorothea's patience, but never her devotion. Earth had taught her the heart was to be guarded lest it break, but heaven had taught her love. It had taught her that love was the only power that grew stronger the more it was given away.

\* \* \*

She watched the dark blur of Junior's truck race by and allowed herself a flicker of pride. There were times when Dorothea's heart felt full to bursting, when she wanted nothing more than to bang upon every door in Mattingly and share the good news that their jobs and lives and dreams counted for nothing in the face of eternity. Eternity was what they were made for, that and naught else. Yet Dorothea knew that folly. People were ignorant of what they could not see and cast aside what they could not understand. The most precious of wisdoms were those gained not by seeing and hearing but by living and dying. A good mother knew such things.

She did not feel full to bursting now. Dorothea could not give Junior evidence of the panic that had built at the thought of George and Juliet's trickery. There was only one reason they would want to sneak Laura Beth out of the house. To meet someone. And there was only one someone for her to meet. Bobby.

The grandfather clock tolled nine. Forty-seven minutes until her Turn ended.

She shut her eyes and listened. Some nights Dorothea could still hear an echo of the talk and laughter that had filled her house. George's bantering and Juliet's soothing tone. Tommy's high laugh and Junior's booming cackle. Laura Beth's quiet singing of "Peace Like a River" and "Softly and Tenderly." Even Bobby's slow drawl seemed heard now. They were here, Mama's family, even when they were not.

The game droned on in the gathering room as Dorothea sat at Hubert's desk. An announcer called out a score that never changed. She thought of Junior and the lasting wish he had to discover who won. A press of a button brought the typewriter to life, filling the room with a low electric hum and the faint smell of something burning. From the side drawer, she pulled a single sheet of paper and a plain envelope.

Dorothea rolled the page in and tabbed five spaces. Her fingers ached as she typed. She worried none of spelling or coherent thoughts, focusing instead on tapping the keys. For the next half hour, she poured forth every fear and worry and strain. She asked for help in dealing with whatever evil intent George and Juliet possessed and confessed her weakness of fear. She begged for wisdom and strength to keep her family together. When Dorothea finished, she sealed the page in the envelope and made the long trip to the mailbox.

Aside from cooking the meals and straightening the mess her family left in the evening, the walk from the porch to the mailbox constituted the only exercise Dorothea allowed herself. It certainly had come to mark the farthest reaches of her travel. She had never ventured far from the yellow house even when Hubert had been alive. Such a place as Mattingly held its share of dark and danger, Happy Hollow and Boone's Pond and the patch of woods on the Daniel farm where the rebels fought their endless war. Now it was the Turn itself that kept her close to the comfortable walls and quiet back-yard. Junior and George had come to the conclusion that heaven was impregnable. Juliet, Dorothea believed, had not yet become so convinced. Only Dorothea knew the truth. The Turn was a fragile thing in its own right, so much like the world she'd left. As strong as a spider's web once it caught you, but just as apt to be pulled apart by any strong breeze. It had happened to Hubert, who'd gotten up one morning to shave and shower and then sat down at his desk, dead from an aneurysm. Heaven needed protecting, just as they all did. She placed the letter in the center, faceup, and raised the flag.

The walk inside was always hardest, made so by the slight incline of the driveway and the sense of weariness that always gripped her near the end of her Turn. Inside the yellow house and up the stairs, wincing at the throb in her hands and knees. At the second-floor landing, Dorothea turned left into the bedroom and clicked on the lamp beside the vanity that had been Hubert's wedding gift. There she sat until thirteen minutes and twenty-six seconds before the town clock struck ten, looking upon a face that would have been altogether unknown to the woman she'd been in life. Dorothea's last lonely years in the world had been spent mourning a reflection that seemed to fade with each passing day. The gray, brittle hair. That deep-lined face. The sagging eyes desperate to close and never open again, if only to have an end to things. What more could an old and lonely woman have to look forward to than death?

But no more. What small time Dorothea's family spent away from the yellow house was known to her only in pieces, but she knew most of her children thought their Turns hollow. George and Juliet certainly, with their constant longing for elsewhere and their refusal to accept what they had not earned. And of course Junior, who never did make it to the end of his baseball game. Tommy and Laura Beth had their problems, of course. Bobby still had not offered enough of his Turn for Dorothea to form an opinion of its blessedness, yet she felt his view of things would be no different. Only her end held meaning, only her beginning. Two moments that served as bookends of what she had become responsible for and what was expected of her.

Juliet had once said she believed the Turn a mirror. If so, what Dorothea saw was a woman reborn from the ashes of a failed life. She saw smooth skin and hair the color of a raven's wing, eyes as piercing as a sage's. She saw strength that refused to wilt against what mischief her children could concoct and the lies they could tell. She saw in that glass the face of someone powerful and mighty. She saw a woman loved by a God who would not fail her.

That above all was what allowed Dorothea to breathe deep and grin. She glanced at the clock. Thirty seconds. Enough time for her to walk to the window and cradle herself against the cold, look down into the road at the mailbox.

God would know what to do.

He always had.

# -6-

One blink, that was all.

There were times when Dorothea believed even that too long a phrase to describe the distance that lay between her Turns. It was as if both end and beginning formed halves of a single beat of her heart—one beholding the reflection of the woman she had become, night pressing in and a chill foretelling a winter that would never be seeping through the gaps in the windowpane; the next, out on the landing once more with one foot stretched out to take the stairs down and a dawn like spring beginning to unfold outside. And in the small blink of time between those two, what? Dorothea had long pondered just that, yet she understood it would remain a mystery. Perhaps the nothingness she'd so feared in her old life. Perhaps the hell she'd feared even more.

She had no time to go back to the bedroom and change out of the plain clothes she always woke wearing. This Turn, Dorothea had more pressing matters. Downstairs the house smelled of mildew and desertion. She left the windows closed and the kettle cold on the stove and opened the door, cursing her fear and her doubt, asking a forgiveness she knew had been given as soon as her eyes met the lowered flag on the mailbox.

She went back inside long enough to reach for the sweater she must have draped over the kitchen chair on her last day of living. As Dorothea shrugged it over her bony shoulders, she wondered not for the first time if she had somehow known on that long-ago day, had a thought or a feeling the way an old cat does just before it roams off to die alone, that she would need that sweater on all the mornings of the life after.

Flowers caught in a purgatory between bloom and wilt lined the walk. Dorothea stepped off the porch and into the shadow of the maple she and Hubert had planted when they'd first moved in. Its leaves shone an almost electric orange against the morning's rays. She allowed herself to slow now, knowing the Lord had answered and that His guidance waited. The faint hint of smoke from a nearby chimney caught her nose, mixing with the clean and crisp air. Robins and sparrows sang from the trees and bushes that ringed the house. The mountains beyond lay clear, the sun close and warming. Dorothea often thought this was the very sort of day she would have wanted frozen in place in her former life—a prayer she'd never asked, yet had been answered nonetheless.

She made it to the driveway and down, keeping her feet light over the cracks and chips in the pavement, minding both the mailbox and that queer sense of dread bubbling once more inside her. A pull on the lid. The envelope lay faceup in the center, Dorothea's name typed and centered in capital letters.

Dorothea felt her heart swell at the sight of her own name writ large. She swallowed her tears with a deep breath that came out a huff against the still morning and plucked the letter out without the usual care. Ripping the envelope open to free the page inside. No one watched, she knew. Her family would not arrive for hours and her neighbors were either asleep or unconcerned. She could let herself go brittle here at the edge of her drive. Dorothea could let go of the happy and wise person she showed the others and suffer no consequence of the frightened woman she had been all along. There were no mirrors at the mailbox, no reflection to convict her.

She read the Lord's message, moving her lips over the words. Reading even the white spaces between them for some secret message. None was there. There had come no answers in the night. Nothing of what Juliet or George had done (if they had in fact done anything; Dorothea still left room for the possibility that whether the three of them disagreed with one another or not, neither Juliet nor George would ever go against their mama) or what Dorothea was to do now. No plan, no unfolding wisdom.

Do not be mad. Love.

Only that. Nothing more.

The page shook in Dorothea's hand. Heat bloomed on her cheeks and the back of her neck. Her head began to throb. All that she'd written the Turn before, every worry and fear and concern poured from her heart, poured from her own sore and swollen fingers, and this was His answer?

Do not be mad?

Love?

"Curse Your infernal obtuseness," she muttered. "Do You not see what is happening? Can You not understand my hold on these people remains tenuous? I need comfort. I need hope."

Tears again, no deep breath and no huff.

*Help me*, she thought. "Help me," she whispered. And then Dorothea shouted those two words in a rage to the wide sky above her, silencing the birds. Her fist struck the side of the mailbox, cutting her hand. She remembered Abram, that good man of Israel, and all the words the Lord had given him with neither rhyme nor reason. Pick up your things and leave your city, but I'm not telling you where to travel. I'll make your descendants as sand on the beach, but only after you're dead. They will have a land, but the only land you will ever own will be where you are buried. I'll give you a son, but I'll wait until you're an old man and then I'll command that you kill him. Yet Abram had prevailed. Abram had shown faith.

Dorothea wiped her eyes and cringed at the blood on her hand. The cut was deep, a chunk of skin hanging from one knuckle. She folded the letter back into the envelope and smoothed it against her breasts, closing her eyes as an apology rather than speaking the words.

-7-

He drank and told the twins of Laura Beth, how she'd looked beneath those sunglasses and what Charlie did to her every morning and night. Bobby felt no guilt. Pain was something better borne when shared, and his boys were old enough to know the truth of the words. He emptied can after can from the refrigerator and the entire half bottle under the counter, telling them. And when the boys looked to cry, Bobby understood that he must look the same. The Turn was a mirror, after all.

Matthew said to stay. He would rather they carry on

together, on their own. Bobby sympathized but knew things could never be as they were. A thousand souls lay in Mattingly, but only six mattered. Dorothea and her little family were the only people in the Turn that Bobby considered free. The other 994 were little more than stage props acting according to scripts long ago written. The family wouldn't let him be, Juliet and Tommy especially. Besides, Bobby didn't think he could ever get the image of Laura Beth's broken and bruised face out of his memory until he'd said his piece.

He was so drunk by the time they left that the truck drove with a mind of its own. Bobby joked along the way the miracle wasn't they'd all ended up in some sort of hell, but that he hadn't killed anybody else yet that Turn. Mark told him to park a ways down from Dorothea's house. He warned Bobby of what Laura Beth had said Dorothea would do if she found out. Bobby didn't care.

Maybe once. Not now.

* * *

The three of them kept to the side of the yellow house, not wanting anyone to see them through the windows. Matthew said he smelled chicken. The clock tower tolled noon.

Bobby snuck around to the porch and up the steps, knowing which boards creaked and which would hide his movements, keeping his shadow away from the windows. He wanted to go straight inside, get this over with. Mark put a finger to his mouth and motioned Bobby closer to the window. Dorothea's voice was the only sound inside, the bright and cheery tone she used whenever she read her letters, the voice of a Sunday school teacher reading a lesson to her class of toddlers.

"'Do not strive against one another,'" she was saying, "'but accept each other in love. Be one, as I am one, for I am the Lord your God, and I love you all greatly. I have brought you to this good place so that you may find rest, not restlessness, and so that you may be filled with joy rather than anger. So then, put aside all of your selfish ambitions and vain questions. Cling to Me, for with Me is truth and love everlasting.'"

Matthew shoved a finger down his throat and mouthed a gag. Mark was quicker to the point—"She's lyin', Daddy. That ain't what that letter says."

Bobby moved away from the window and opened the door, shutting it hard behind him. Dorothea's voice went quiet as he strode into the dining room. They were all seated in their accustomed places, Dorothea the head and George the tail, Juliet and Tommy to Bobby's left, Junior and Laura Beth on the right. Bobby's own place had been set beside Dorothea's, silverware gleaming against a white cloth napkin, both plate and glass empty. Juliet's smile faded only a little when Bobby did not return one of his own. He took a step into the room and stumbled, excusing himself with a curse and watching Laura Beth grow pale. She lowered her head (*Don't bother praying, Lord ain't gonna answer you, girl*) as George reached for a cigarette instead of his notebook.

Tommy leaped from his spot between Juliet and Dorothea with such force that he toppled the chair. He put his arms around Bobby in a hug Bobby could feel, nearly knocking them both off balance. Bobby patted the boy on the head and eased him away.

"Bobby," Dorothea said. "How nice of you to join us. Juliet and George weren't sure if you'd have the mind, though I've no idea why they would think such a thing." She cut her eyes to Juliet, who balled and then smoothed out her napkin, balled it again. George stared through a cloud of smoke. "But I had a feeling you'd come. I only hoped you'd arrive in better control of your faculties."

"What's that mean?"

"Means you're drunk," Junior said. He'd been sitting quiet, brow creased and mouth open, trying to understand what was happening. Bobby supposed the drunk part, at least, had been clear. "That right, Mama?"

"Drunk?" Bobby asked. "Oh, no, ma'am. Passed drunk an hour ago."

He reached for the top of George's chair, missed, reached again. Matthew and Mark flanked him on either side, giving Bobby strength enough to keep going.

"Why don't you come sit before you topple over?" Dorothea said. "I'll brew some coffee, get you straightened out. I was just reading the Lord's words. Serve you well if you gave them heed."

Tommy moved back to the table, picking up his chair and pulling Bobby's out. Bobby held his place. He couldn't look at the boy, couldn't bear that smile.

"Don't think I will," he said. "Just come to say my words, then I'll be on my way. Heard enough of what you got on that paper before I came in. Soured me for any food you might provide."

Junior's eyes went from soft to hard. "Don't like the sound of what you're sayin', Bobby. I done warned you watch your mouth."

"Might not like the sound of my words, Junior Hewitt, but they tasted fine coming out."

George said, "Maybe you should just go on back to the shop, Bobby. Come back when you feel better."

"Oh, I'm fine, George. Right as the mail." That made Bobby

laugh and, he realized, more than a little mad. He pointed at the paper in Dorothea's hand. "You'd know all about that, wouldn't you, Dorothea? Mail. How long you been getting those things?"

Dorothea's fingers curled around the page, making a crinkling sound. Her cheeks had gone as red as the bloodstain on one of her knuckles. Bobby wondered where she'd gotten that.

"Long," she said. "When it was just me and Junior and heaven was perhaps not so crowded. And I'll expect you to address me proper, Bobby Barnes. I believe I've earned that right for the meals I've cooked and the ears I've lent."

From the corner of Bobby's eye, Juliet shook her head slowly.

"Just wondering is all, Mama. Always thought it funny how you get them things. 'Member I told you that when Junior first brung me here? Still think it. I think it's awful funny the Lord speaks in such a way. Been a long while since I rested my bones in a church pew—and, Juliet, you can maybe help me if I'm remembering wrong—but I don't recall the Almighty typing up the Ten Commandments before handing them off to Moses. That sound right to you . . . Mama? Figured His own hand'd be good enough. Or a quill. Lord always seemed a quill sort to me. Little pot of ink on His desk, like them old monks used to use. You reckon the Lord's got such poor penmanship He's gotta break out the old Selectric to get His point acrost? *Mama?*"

Laura Beth uttered a weak, "Please, Bobby." Head down and lips trembling. Maybe she was crying, Bobby couldn't tell with those sunglasses hiding her face. Junior rose from the table, rage growing at the places where confusion had been. Something as hard as a pebble lodged in Bobby's throat.

Dorothea's eyes felt like nails, her voice the hammer. "Drunk or not, I will not have you blaspheming the Lord."

"Sorry," Bobby said, as much to Junior as to her. He tilted his head to the peeled ceiling and toward the kitchen, over his shoulder into the foyer. "Sorry," he called louder. "Forgot You's watching."

Junior crept closer, nearly past Laura Beth. George tried to stand. Bobby pressed down on the man's shoulders, keeping him there.

Tommy's elation had gone to something between the fear Bobby saw in Juliet's eyes and the fury in Junior's. "Why you bein' so mean, Daddy?" he asked.

"Ain't mean, s—" He cleared his throat. *Did I almost call him son? Did I?* "Tommy. I'm talking about love here. That's what's in your letter, right, Dorothea? How we're all supposed to love each other?"

Dorothea stood motionless.

"That the word the Lord give you?"

"It is," she said.

"Do you love, Dorothea?"

"I am *Mama*," she yelled. "And I love each of my children."

Bobby looked at Junior, freezing him in place. "How 'bout you, Junior? You love?"

Tommy said, "I love you, Daddy."

Bobby only nodded at that. "I don't know what love is. Used to think I did, but that's all gone now. Got took. Now I think maybe I never knew it at all." He felt Matthew's hand at his back, could swear he felt it. "Love's a thing I guess you can't never lose once it takes hold of you. But I did. Lost it. So maybe that means I never had it in the first place."

Dorothea moved to where Tommy stood, where Bobby's place at the table sat. "Come sit," she said.

"No, ma'am, I won't. I know what lives in this house. Snakes. Spent most of my years trying to bear up under the lies this town said about me. I come here, you the one told me this was heaven. Said I was free. All y'all told me. Well, it ain't heaven, and I ain't free. That's what I found. More lies. Found out *all* y'all been lying to me. This ain't no heaven."

"It *is*!" Tommy screamed. "It's heaven, it's my heaven."

"Ain't nobody's heaven," Bobby said.

"You'll leave," Dorothea said. "I won't stand here and be a party to your own ignorance, Bobby. We've come to love you dearly, but—"

"Don't speak to me of love." Pointing at her, unmoved against her ire. "Was it by love you told Laura Beth to wear them sunglasses? And was that love your own, or was it the Lord's?"

Laura Beth began to sob.

"You get that in some letter you stuck in the mailbox and pulled right out?" Bobby asked. "What was it, Dorothea? You couldn't bear to look upon her ruined face because you knew deep down that heaven could never hold such a thing? Or will you tell me this is all the heaven Laura Beth deserves? Y'all should've *helped* her. You should've *done* something."

Junior bolted. Laura Beth lashed out a hand and caught his sleeve. Screaming for him to stop, leave Bobby alone. "You'll strike the only man who's stood for me?" she asked.

Quiet fell over the room. Bobby felt his chest thrumming and that pebble growing larger in his throat. He would have to leave soon, before his boldness failed.

"This what last night was about, then?" Dorothea asked. "So you could see Laura Beth's Turn?" She looked at them all. Bobby watched Juliet bow her head and George stare at a spot out the window. Tommy reached for his mama's hand. Dorothea took it with reluctance.

Junior glared at Laura Beth, who shrank to a timid child in front of them all. Then he stared at Tommy with what Bobby could only describe as a look of hurt. "You didn't really want to watch the game with me?"

"I did," Tommy said. "They made me lie. Juliet and George." He gripped Dorothea's hand with both of his. Bobby saw her wince. At the betrayal, perhaps, certainly at the pain in her fingers. "I told Juliet not to, Mama. I swear. I said you had to be the one to tell Bobby about Laura Beth, just like we agreed."

Bobby shook his head and offered a chuckle. "Like you agreed. She's a *person*. Laura Beth's sitting right *here*. Y'all talking about her like she ain't even real."

Juliet looked as though she wanted to speak, but no words came from her mouth.

"You know not what you speak," Dorothea said.

"I know heaven might not be such a bad thing if not for all the folk in it. I'm done with the lot of you. I don't care who says this is paradise and who says it's hell, who's spying on who and who's making plans in this poor excuse for a *family*. I'm gonna go back to my shop, and I don't wanna see any a you again."

"You can't do that," Tommy said. "You got to stay here."

"Can and will."

Tommy's eyes went glassy, two sparkling blue holes, the same as Bobby could see on Matthew's face and Mark's. "You let me come see you?"

"Don't think that's best," Bobby said.

Tommy's sobs only made Dorothea angrier. Junior, too, though Bobby suspected not to the extent it would have if

Tommy hadn't tricked him. George snuffed his cigarette on the mouth of his spoon and stared at the ashes.

"Bobby," Juliet said.

He cut her off. "Don't want to hear you, neither. Anybody should've helped Laura Beth, it's a preacher."

With that, he turned back to the foyer. Dorothea called his name. Bobby stopped but wouldn't look at her.

"You do anything to help Laura Beth, Bobby? When her Turn came, did you follow her into the house? Confront Charlie? Try to stop the evilness he does? Because we have. We've tried. Did you?"

Mark took Bobby's hand and whispered, "We need to go now, Daddy."

Bobby walked for the door. He opened it and said, "Laura Beth, my shop is always open should you need refuge."

She did not answer. Bobby thought that best.

-8-

George thought it was bad enough the idiot had showed up drunk at Dorothea's, worse that Bobby had in a matter of fifteen minutes done more to anger her than he himself had ever managed. But none of that compared to the other damage Bobby had caused—he had split the family and then run off, leaving George to gather the pieces.

He could endure Tommy's crying and Junior's ultimatums, threats to him and Juliet for lying and Tommy for sneaking, and the ones Junior made to Laura Beth, yelling that Charlie Gowdy would be the least of her worries if she ever went behind his back again. George understood that was simply Junior showing his rotten core—all bluster and no bite. Threats were all that man-child could offer, words raised enough to make them wince but nothing more. All things considered, George knew Junior was just as afraid as they all were.

It was Dorothea's reaction after Bobby left that troubled him. Her silent refusal to look at anyone, as though the very sight of them sickened her. No one moved from the table. The chicken grew cold, the gravy lumpy, and the cornbread— always George's favorite—hardened into rocks the size of his hand. He smoked, filling the room in a cloud. Juliet offered no explanation as to why she'd decided the time had come for Bobby to know of Laura Beth. She offered no apology. George believed neither would have been accepted.

Laura Beth excused herself first, leaving Junior in mid-rant. She went upstairs to one of the spare bedrooms and shut the door. In the silence that followed, George heard the lock click. That wouldn't offer a large measure of safety—if Junior could throw a baseball through Dorothea's house, he could surely bust through a flimsy wooden door.

"George," Dorothea said, making him blink. "Take that cigarette outside. I've endured enough filth this morning."

He looked at Juliet, who nodded and made something of a grin. George rose without a word and went for the foyer. His last sight upon stepping onto the porch was Tommy sobbing on Dorothea's lap. Junior held a fork tight in his hand, tines pointed to the ceiling. Glaring at Juliet, who had gone back to balling up and unfolding her napkin.

The cigarette had only been half smoked before the coughing began, loud and deep and bloody. George crushed the butt under his shoe. He turned for the door and realized he had no good reason to go back inside. Laura Beth would remain upstairs. No harm would come to Juliet so long as Tommy stayed close. More yelling, more empty threats, all of which George believed Juliet more than capable of handling. She'd endured plenty since arriving in the Turn. They both had.

He stepped off the porch instead, walking to his truck as though going for the morning paper. The only hurry came when the engine fired. George threw the gear into reverse and watched the door as he backed out. When he reached the end of the street and pointed the truck toward town, he let himself breathe once more.

\* \* \*

The door to the shop was locked, but Bobby's Dodge was out front and George could hear the music inside. Banging on the glass only made that music louder. He tried the small windows on the bay doors but could see little through the grime and so walked to the end of the block and around, finding the alley. The wood door there swung free. George grinned and stepped inside. Bobby had never been one of his brighter students.

He was sitting on the hood of a ruined little car. A can of beer rested on one knee. George made his way over and turned off the radio. Bobby spun his head.

"Closed, George, case you didn't get the hint."

"You have to come with me, Bobby. Right now."

"Don't wanna see you no more." He flashed a drunken simper. "Guess that means you'll have to teach Junior chess. Or Juliet. Bet she'd be good, what with her conniving mind."

"You're done, fine. They're not. Dorothea and Junior. You're an idiot for the way you acted this morning."

"Told the truth was all," Bobby said. "You call me an idiot for that, reckon this place even more screwed up than I thought. Now get on. I got a lot needs doing today." He tilted his head to the right and left of where he sat, nodding at the chipped paint on the hood. "And I got all the company I need."

"You'll have more soon. Dorothea's sending Junior here."

George didn't know from where that lie had come, but it served its purpose when he saw Bobby's eyes cut. And who knew, maybe Junior really had left the house. The way Dorothea had been acting, George wouldn't put it past her ordering Junior to give Bobby another lesson in the art of being a family.

"What's Junior coming here for?" Bobby asked.

"Not to listen to your music and drink your beer."

Bobby bent his head to the left as though listening. For the sound of Junior's truck, George guessed.

"Where we goin'?"

"Someplace else. Come on. I'll drive. Even let you drink on the way."

\* \* \*

Bobby locked the door to the alley and the one to the waiting room on their way out. George said nothing of those precautions being pointless. Even if Junior did visit, whatever damage he might do would be erased by the next Turn. Unless it was the beer Bobby meant to protect. George thought about the pack of cigarettes in his shirt pocket and the two others in his truck—all he'd need for one day. But if they would somehow come up missing? If he'd have to go even a few hours without the sweet sound of his lighter clicking and the feel of that flame, the sheer pleasure of inhaling deep? Maybe then the Turn would truly be hell.

Out of the lot, left on Main. Past the sheriff's office and

the council building and the square, over the bridge toward Stanley.

"Thought I taught you better," George said. "What have I always told you about chess, Bobby?" He answered when Bobby didn't: "Have a plan. You have a plan when you climbed up on Dorothea's porch this morning? Or were you too stupid drunk? Laura Beth tell you not to let Mama know you found out?"

Bobby's head lay against the glass. He said, "Ain't Laura Beth's fault. I was mad. Y'all lied to me."

"Everybody lies. You think here'd be any different? What you did was selfish, pure and simple."

"Selfish?"

George looked at him. "Were you so mad because we lied, or was it seeing what Laura Beth has to go through?" He waved Bobby off. "All you thought of was the only thing you've ever thought of: you. You said your piece and took off, leaving the rest of us to take the brunt of Dorothea's rage. And it was rage, Bobby. Laura Beth had to hide upstairs, for crying out loud. Junior started screaming. Juliet looked like her whole world was coming apart. And Tommy. Standing there bawling, not able to understand. That boy loves you, Bobby. So let's dispense with all the righteous indignation."

Bobby took a drink. "Dorothea told me this was heaven."

"It's no more heaven than it is hell."

"What's that mean?"

George fished a smoke from his pocket and punched in the truck's lighter. The road widened from two lanes to four as neighborhoods yielded to fields of dying corn flanked by solitary farmhouses and clumps of cattle lazing under the sun. Mountains rose up in the distance, swaddled by the first wisps of the front that would bring rain sometime in the night.

"It's a heaven to Dorothea," George said. "This place, it has everything that woman always wanted but never had. Hell to Laura Beth. Juliet puts her own spin on what this place is and why we're in it, as a preacher is wont. But the Turn isn't any of those things."

"Then what is it?"

A car flew past, teenagers on their way to a Saturday in the city. They blew the horn.

"I thought it was a loop in the beginning. A loop in time. Don't ask how such a thing is possible outside of some cheesy science fiction movie, because I don't know. But here we are. There's been work, Bobby, theories put forth. I've read what I could. Online, the library, that sort of thing. Some of those times when I say I'm going after Anna, I go up here to Stanley instead. Stop by the bookstore and get what I need, memorize what I can. Books are gone the next Turn when that infernal beast starts caterwauling in the river, of course, so I have to go back and buy them again."

Bobby rested the can on his leg. "You really don't go after Anna?"

"On occasion. It's the only thing that eases my despair." He coughed and flicked the cigarette through the window, lit another. "I'll never find her, Bobby. Took me a long while to accept that, but I have. Anna's lost to me until I find a way back."

"Find a way?"

"Back," he said again. "*Home*, Bobby. I won't allow myself to believe this is the end, and for this simple reason: I don't remember dying. Do you? Dorothea and Junior are adamant that not only is this our final destination, but to consider otherwise is to invite ruin. Those two could come face-to-face with the truth, they'd still turn from it and wave the banner of faith. But I believe if we can *get* here, then we can get *away.*"

"How?"

"I don't know. Can't leave this place until we know what this place is. That's what I've set myself to answer." He pointed out Bobby's window, where a ribbon of water twisted beyond a field. "Think of that river as time, Bobby, and us floating on its surface. But the current isn't uniform. The river isn't the same depth in every place, nor as wide or narrow. There are places where the water flows fast, where the depth is shallow. But there are also deep places where the water doesn't seem to flow at all. The Turn, Bobby, is one of those places."

"Then how can it be only us that's in that slow place, George? You ever thought of that? Everybody else keeps right on going."

"Do they?" He took his eyes off the road. "Is that what they do, Bobby? Because I don't know. I said we're at a slow place in the river. I didn't say we were all in the *same* river. We may have somehow slipped into another river entirely, for all I know. Maybe we've drifted into another channel somehow, some backwater. You know there are pockets in the Turn. Maybe there are pockets in time as well, an eddy in the current that keeps swirling back on itself. I think that's what happened to us. The other people here, they're just . . . passing through. They were themselves on this day, that first time through. But all the times after? I don't know. Maybe it's them, maybe it's images of themselves as they lived this day. Regardless, they've spun out of the eddy and moved on down the current. They kept living their lives as they were intended. We haven't. Not yet."

"What's that mean, then?" Bobby asked. "You trying to say if this ain't heaven and it ain't hell, then we're . . ."

He stopped.

George looked away from the road and grinned. "We are still in time's river, or at least a branch of it. In a deep part, where the water is nearly stagnant. But that water still *moves*. It circles, but the current still pushes it forward. Even in an eddy. That bruise on your face, it's getting larger. Juliet said something to me about it once."

"The stars," Bobby said.

"What?"

"I tried telling you last Turn before the thing with Junior and the baseball. I wake up looking at the sky. First time, there were stars everywhere. Now there ain't. There's . . . patches. The stars are leaving, George. I swear it."

George slowed and flipped on the turn signal. The truck left the main road onto one of hard-packed dirt, where the trees were so close they scraped the sides of the windows. Limbs and leaves brushed against his arm. "Juliet told me some of your Turn," he said. "Not all of it. Enough for me to understand it's something on par with Laura Beth's."

"Juliet likes to run her mouth. I trusted her."

"You still can."

"Give me one reason."

George smirked. "I'll give the only one that matters—she loves you. She had to tell me, Bobby."

"Why?"

"Because after Laura Beth, she knew it wouldn't be long until I brought you here."

Ahead the road sloped to a small hill. George moved the truck nearer the shoulder and slowed, stopping when they reached the top. Near a clump of trees below were the remains of all the mornings before and ones yet to be. Strips of yellow tape tied to the trunks. Deep tire marks in the mud.

"What's this?" Bobby asked.

"The other half of everything I've told you. You remember last Turn? Sitting on that bench with Laura Beth?"

"Don't think I can forget it."

"Well, you're supposed to. If this was a loop in time, everything would reset. Not just my smokes and your beer and where everybody goes or what they do. *Everything.* Even our memories. But our memories follow us. We remember, Bobby. The seven of us, and we're the only ones. Caught in a tiny eddy of time in that big river, turning in a circle. Someone like Dorothea? Junior? They don't feel time passing at all. But you have your bruise and I have this infernal cough, one that I confess is becoming worse and much more bloody. We know, Bobby. Time's still moving, and that means that time will eventually run out."

He pointed to the yellow tape below. "And then there's that. Long before you and Laura Beth arrived, Dorothea received one of her letters saying she and Junior needed to come here. I was at Dorothea's when they left, there when they returned. Even now, after this morning, I've never seen her so upset. She and Junior left again early the next Turn. She wasn't even there when I arrived seeking out breakfast. Cat hollered something awful that morning; I had to get out of there. They got back around dinnertime. Juliet and Tommy were at the house by then. That's when I found out. Dorothea told Juliet and me while Junior was out in the yard with Tommy."

"Told you what?"

George lit a cigarette and inhaled deep, forcing down the cough.

"Dorothea and I have our differences, Bobby. We argue and fight and at times curse the other's very existence. But that was when I learned Dorothea was right about one thing: here in the Turn, we only have each other. I'll never forget her sitting Tommy down in the gathering room with all of us around him, saying what she did. I don't believe any of us had ever been close back in the old world. Familiar, yes. Civil. Even friendly. But that day bound us to one another. It made us a family. We are a family, Bobby. That's what you need to understand."

"Dorothea writes those letters," Bobby said.

George shook his head. "You know she burns them? I've seen her. Burns those letters to ash with a match and a little bowl. I've never been able to figure why. One Turn, I managed to pick up a scrap before Dorothea threw it out. Wasn't even a whole word, just the letter *E*. But it was enough. I checked Hubie's old typewriter. The *E* on his made a different mark on the paper. Juliet and I have gone over every inch of that house. That's the only typewriter Dorothea has. Whoever's writing those letters, it isn't her."

"Then who is it?"

"I don't know. Can't be Junior, he can barely talk, much less write. And it was just the two of them here when the letters first started coming. Someone else is watching, Bobby. Someone who knew how important this spot of woods would be to us. Dorothea truly believes it's God. And given the knowledge whoever it is has of the Turn . . ." He shrugged. "That's what scares me. There's little difference between gods and monsters. You still watch the news?"

"Used to."

"You remember seeing something about a woman found dead on an old service road between Mattingly and Stanley?"

Bobby nodded slowly.

"We were fighting then. Dorothea and I mostly, though

Juliet was a part of it, too. The whole heaven thing, you know. Then that letter came. Dorothea and Junior were too late that first time, but like I said, they left early the next. Got here before the police left, said maybe they knew who the woman was. The police let Dorothea look. Afterward, all our quarreling went away for a long while. Until Laura Beth. And you."

Bobby's voice dropped low. He fumbled for a beer but didn't open it. "Who'd they find down there, George?"

George drew on his cigarette. He blew out a long stream of smoke that hit the windshield, then curled out of the truck and into the sky.

"Tommy's mother."

# -9-

Morning came with soft light on warm blankets, one arm under the pillow and the other dangling over the bed. The smell of coffee from downstairs. Quiet. Safe. The sort of morning one would pray for if one ever prayed. Then the voice, two words made into a single that carried up the stairs and through the half-open door, shattering the peace:

"Laur-Beth."

She balled up in reflex, the hand that had dangled over the bed now cold against the warmth of her shoulder. Charlie's heavy steps ascended the stairs. She hid beneath the covers. That wouldn't work. It had never worked, just as locking the door had never worked, or trying to climb out the window or shutting herself in the bathroom or the closet, just as apologizing had never worked. Charlie's shadow, a wisp of gray shadow. Her name again, no less loud than the first

time even if the distance between them had grown shorter—
"Laur-Beth." The fingers of his hand curling around the door,
pushing it wide.

Laura Beth gripped the edge of the comforter. Charlie
yanked it from her fingers, making it billow off the foot of
the bed to the edge of the fireplace. She imagined that cover
a sail caught in the wind, tied to a boat that would take her
far away.

"Where's my shirt?" Charlie asked. Charlie always asked.
"My golf one. The polo? It isn't downstairs."

She shut her eyes and remained in a ball, protecting her
stomach and chest and face, those parts of her that would
soon be bloodied and bruised.

"Hey." He slapped the side of her leg. "You awake? I said
where's my *shirt.*"

Her eyes opened. Charlie loomed over her, all hundred
and sixty pounds of him, blond-going-to-gray hair spilling
over hollowed eyes, his bare stomach paunchy despite the
skinniness of the rest of him, the stink of his breath and body.
This was the real Charlie Gowdy. Not the dapper man in the
three-piece and the yellow Corvette, sitting behind his big
desk smiling, telling the bank customers to have a blessed
day. Laura Beth's leg tingled but did not hurt. That smack
had been nothing, a skim of his fingers. She curled her body
tighter, not wanting him to see her nakedness.

"Hey," again, louder and with a harder smack, not to the
leg but to the left cheek of her rump. "Get out of the bed,
Laura Beth, and get me my *shirt.*" His eyes narrowed behind
the wisps of hair. "My *clean* shirt."

She sat up. In the great trial and error that had become
Laura Beth's hell, she'd learned sitting up was best. It never
changed things but at least made them quicker. She showed

him her body, watched his eyes widen enough to flash the searing green irises she had fallen for so long ago. Like emeralds, she'd once thought.

"I forgot," she said. "I'm sorry, Charlie. I forgot to wash it."

Just as quick as those emeralds had appeared, Charlie's eyes collapsed back into the black slits Laura Beth had come to know so well. "You forgot?" His voice came as one of mock surprise. "That was the only thing I asked you to do yesterday, Laura Beth."

"I know."

"Do you? So you remember now but you didn't before?" Charlie curled the forefinger of his right hand into his thumb and reached out, flicking her between the eyes. "I need that shirt today. It's my lucky. Shirt."

"I can wash it now."

*"You can't wash it now."* The words boomed, silencing the birds. "I have to *go* now. My tee time is nine, Laura Beth, and I still have to drive to Stanley. You think I can be late? Do you have any idea who I have to spend my day with? The sort of men I have to smoke stinking cigars with and drink fancy beer with and laugh at stupid jokes with? The kind of men I have to make sure I *lose* to?"

She did. Bad men. Men from Richmond who bought and sold people like Charlie like chattel, who dealt in drugs and guns and whores and would sooner put a bullet in you than call you by name. Charlie's men. Charlie's good guys.

Laura Beth didn't answer. She'd learned that, too. Mama had told her never to resist, to do like the Bible said a wife should do. Submit. *It'll make things easier for you, dear.*

"Do you have any idea what I have to do?" he said. "The things they *make* me do? Just so you can have this house? So you can saunter down Main Street in your pretty clothes and

I can sneak us some money in my safe? What I have to turn a blind eye to and what I have to put up with? Do you know what would happen if anybody found *out*, and here you can't even remember to wash my *shirt*?"

(*It's coming. It's coming and then it'll be over and then he'll leave. He'll leave and I'll be—*)

She felt his hand closing in her hair and her head tilting back and yelped at the pain, saw Charlie's fist and the glimmer of the gold band on his finger, the 24-carat one he'd bought for them both because *My baby deserves the best*, he'd said, and then Laura Beth felt her face explode. She heard the hard thump of his knuckles boring into her cheek and saw the stars (*stars Bobby said the stars are missing but they're not they're all here ha-ha*) and felt blood pouring from her brow. She fell backward onto the mattress. Meeting it felt like being thrown onto bricks.

"One thing," he shouted. "I ask you one thing, Laura Beth. I have to do a million things to keep us going, keep us *safe*, and you can't do the one thing I ask you to do? What am I supposed to do now?"

The world began to tunnel.

Charlie climbed atop her as he had done so many times before, not in love but hate. Laura Beth didn't flinch when he hit her again. In the stomach and between her breasts, once more in the eye. *A shirt, it's just a stupid shirt*, she thought, and then she thought no, it had never been about the shirt.

He climbed off and stumbled toward the closet, knocking over the poker and the brush next to the fireplace, throwing clothes onto the floor. Charlie chose a blue polo instead of the dirty white one and disappeared into the bathroom, walked back out and tossed a towel onto the bed. When he left, it was without a word. In the time before Mama and Junior and

Juliet, when it was Laura Beth alone, she had believed that towel the apology Charlie was too proud to give and the love he was too sorry to admit.

\* \* \*

She stared at the ceiling, numb as life drained from her. Birdsong echoed far. Charlie slammed the front door. When her strength gathered again, Laura Beth cleaned herself in the bathroom and winced as she put on as much makeup as she could bear. Junior never liked seeing her bloodied, and he would see her that day. He would want them to be alone and they would have to talk—punishment for what she'd let Bobby see. She stumbled downstairs and found her purse and the money and sunglasses inside, then began the long walk downtown. Mama hadn't said what food she wanted that Turn. Laura Beth had stayed away from her and Junior both after Bobby had left. She'd gone upstairs and locked herself in the bedroom and hadn't even opened the bedroom door to Juliet.

Her legs hurt and her stomach ached from where Charlie had beaten her, making the walk difficult. Laura Beth wasn't yet to the end of her block when she saw Junior's truck turn onto the street. She stopped, the pain fading. Fear took hold. Not just fear of Junior, but of the others with him. Tommy in front, Juliet and George in the cramped row of seats behind. And in the passenger seat, eyes already bearing down, sat Mama. Mama, who in all the time Laura Beth had been in her hell had never once stepped beyond the yellow house.

Junior stopped on the curb. Tommy's hand rose, waving. Dorothea only said, "Climb in, child."

George opened the door and got out, helping her. He did not smile. Juliet stared at the long line of expensive houses beyond her window. She laid a hand to the spot Charlie had smacked on Laura Beth's leg and squeezed soft.

They drove to Bobby's shop. Juliet wanted to get out, but Mama said, "Don't you dare," and sent Junior instead. He banged on the door and hollered. Mama told him to try the back. People passed on the walk, some holding bags and others on their phones, faces down into flashing screens. Few looked their way. Laura Beth heard two quick booms from behind the shop.

George whispered, "Guess Bobby locked the door this time."

Tommy turned his head. Dorothea laid a hand to the boy's neck, patting him there. The front door of the shop opened. Junior came through first, Bobby after, straining against the two big hands that gripped his shoulders.

"You'll ride in back, Bobby," Dorothea said. "If you'll not have our company in my home, you'll not have it here."

He grimaced as Junior gripped him harder. Laura Beth saw the look on Juliet's face, a stare of sadness and want that she knew well.

"Go on," Junior said, shoving him. "Won't take long and you won't suffer."

Bobby climbed in back. He sat at the end, as far away from the others as he could manage. Junior got back in the truck and drove one block down and parked on the left side of the street. Ahead lay the town square. The council building and sheriff's office stood to the right.

"Here good?" Junior asked.

Dorothea reached into her pocket and bent her head. Laura Beth could hear the crinkling page. "Pull around. It'll make it easier to leave."

Junior did as Mama asked. Dorothea looked at the thin

watch on her wrist. She said go and Junior went. He got out and checked the traffic on both sides, crowded on that Saturday morning, then walked across the street. Looked back and grinned.

Dorothea opened her door but didn't move. "George," she said, "if you would be so kind."

George opened his door and helped her out. Tommy followed with a grin on his face that Laura Beth likened to someone expecting a surprise. Juliet got out on the opposite side. Laura Beth followed.

Dorothea said, "Bobby, you come on and stand with us. Won't take long, then you can go back to where we found you."

Bobby didn't budge. "What are you doing, Dorothea?"

"It's Mama," she said. "And I'm doing nothing. I'm only the vessel here."

Bobby stood but didn't leave his spot. People passed, men tipping their hats and women and children saying hello. Junior stood by crates of apples and peaches in front of the grocery across the street. He kept his hands to his back as though standing at attention. His gaze wavered from Dorothea only to look at Laura Beth.

Dorothea unfolded the letter once more and motioned for Junior to take one step left. She checked her watch again, lofting a single finger. Laura Beth watched Dorothea's lips move, counting. The finger lowered. Junior took one step into the middle of the sidewalk. He dug into his pocket and flashed a penny to the others, then stooped and placed it on the pavement. Mama gave a nod. Junior smiled and took two steps back, where he disappeared into the shadow of the awning over the storefront.

"What's happening here, Mama?" Juliet asked.

"What must, child."

Laura Beth stared across the street. She saw Jake Barnett come out of the sheriff's office with his wife, Kate, and their boy, Zach, who had come out of the woods not two years before after being lost for days. The whole town had aided in that search. Charlie had helped organize things, had even pledged the bank's help in any way possible. Those had been horrible times, and better.

Jake paused on the sidewalk to speak to Mayor Wallis. Down from the grocery came a mother and her two children, a boy and girl no older than Tommy. They'd reached the front of the grocery when the boy spotted the penny. He stopped quick and bent as an older woman Laura Beth did not know exited the store, arms full of paper bags. The woman didn't see the boy and clipped his knee with her foot. Groceries sprawled, toilet paper and canned vegetables in every direction. A cry of hurt and surprise, drawing those near to help.

One of the spilled peaches broke free and rolled into the middle of the street. The girl, Laura Beth swore she knew her name but couldn't remember, ran to retrieve it. She never looked. No one saw her, not her brother sitting on the walk and rubbing his leg, not the mother saying it would be okay or the others trying to help the old woman to her feet. Only Laura Beth saw, and her family, Junior in the shadows with his hands at his back. The driver of the car was looking at the commotion on the side of the street rather than the road. Laura Beth wanted to scream, cry out, but it was too late. The girl bent to pick up the peach, looking first to her mother and then to the road. She screamed.

The three of them ran—Laura Beth and George and Juliet. Tommy stood transfixed. Bobby, numb. Dorothea screamed for them to keep still.

The car swerved at the last moment. Laura Beth stood

in shock as the little girl's hair swirled in the breeze made by the front bumper rushing past her. Those on the sidewalk scattered as the car jumped the curb. Zach Barnett stood frozen as the car barreled toward him. Laura Beth heard Kate scream for Zach. Jake pushed his boy out of the way. She saw the look of horror on the sheriff's face as his mouth formed a *no* that would never be, and then the car slammed into him. The force threw Jake backward into the wall of the sheriff's office. The sound of his head meeting the brick doubled Laura Beth over.

Dorothea whispered, "Dear Lord in heaven," as townspeople converged on the scene. Kate screamed again, for Jake and God and someone to help. Zach Barnett stood alone and still and shattered of mind.

Bobby's hands went to the top of the old cap he wore. Someone hollered for an ambulance.

"What did you do?" he asked. "God Almighty, Dorothea, what did you *do?*"

"God Almighty." Dorothea held up the letter. "Not me."

The whole of downtown converged on that corner of the square, people running and shoving and crying. Juliet began to sob. Tommy's eyes went wide with glee, having his surprise.

Junior sauntered through the crowd as the distant siren of an ambulance rose, hands shoved into his front pockets. His grin made Laura Beth fear him as she never had, more than she feared even Charlie. He reached the sidewalk and touched the tip of her chin.

"That was something, huh?"

"Is he dead?" George asked.

Junior snorted. "You see that? That's about as dead as a man can get."

"He's dead," Dorothea said. Her voice sounded frail and

tired. "For this Turn, at least, our sheriff is no more. His wife and child will mourn him as will we all, and next Turn Jake will be back, coming out of his office this time as he always has, living his day as he has all the times before and to come. But in the old world . . ." She waved a shaking hand at the mass of people. "Where they reside still, I cannot say. Jake may now be away from there, gone to his heaven."

Laura Beth could take no more. She wheeled, seething, and said, "You didn't have to *allow* that, Mama."

"But I did, child. The Lord instructed it. I took no pleasure, but His ways are hard. Balance, Laura Beth. The Lord speaks of balance and so do I, and now you all see the reason. A single penny, that's all it took. One coin laid to the ground becomes the death of a good man, because that coin never should have been there." She turned to Bobby now. "And now you see, Bobby Barnes. You see why we can offer Laura Beth only comfort in her trials and nothing more. You cannot know how many times we've stopped Charlie from his evil acts, and yet Laura Beth only suffered more the next. Because the balance was upset, and it must correct. That's what I've learned, and I will not upset it more. I am the keeper of heaven, son. That is a responsibility I hold dear. Do you understand?"

Bobby looked as though he would faint. All that spirit Laura Beth had seen in him, all that anger over how she had been treated and would be treated again, lay as broken and dead as Jake's body.

"You are cast out from us," Dorothea said. "You will spend your eternity alone in your hovel of a shop, and you will mind my balance. I forbid any of my family to seek you out, nor will you seek them. If they see you, they will turn away. Now leave my sight and let me mourn."

He left without so much as a good-bye, neither looking

back at Tommy or Juliet, nor again offering refuge to Laura Beth should she need it, looking instead across the street.

* * *

Dorothea told Junior to take them home. The ride was a quiet one, interrupted only when Tommy asked Mama why Bobby had to go. Junior dropped the rest at Dorothea's house and told Laura Beth to stay behind. They were going somewhere alone, he said. To talk.

His camper sat on four deflated tires propped level by a stack of cinder blocks in a ruined patch of woods outside town. Junior said nothing as he parked. He got out and left Laura Beth to do the same. The narrow door was unlocked. No one had the nerve to steal from him, and Junior had nothing worth stealing.

Laura Beth stepped inside. Unwashed plates of moldy food were piled in the sink. The toilet in the bathroom had clogged long ago, leaving Junior to do his business outside. She sat on the mattress in back, the only place she could. Junior took a beer from a cooler by the door.

"What'd you want to talk about?" she asked.

Junior emptied half the bottle and belched, jiggling the roll of pale fat that poked out from the sides of his Bib-Alls.

"What you think?"

"I didn't do anything."

"You showed him your face."

She said nothing.

"You showed him your face," Junior said again.

"They wanted me to. George and Juliet."

Junior tilted the bottle again. "Got Mama riled."

"Got Jake killed."

"Jake ain't killed. Jake ain't even Jake."

He set the beer on the counter and stared at her. "Don't like you alone with Bobby. He's got Juliet if he wants her, but he wants you. Whole town wants you, Laura Beth."

"Bobby don't want me. Maybe before. Not now."

"Take them glasses off."

She did. Slow, wincing at the light coming through the windows. Only one eye worked. The other wouldn't but for those few minutes in the next Turn.

"I love you," Junior said.

"I know."

"You love me?"

She nodded.

"I'd like to hear it."

"I love you."

"Show me, then."

He unsnapped his overalls to reveal the mass of flab and hair on his chest. Laura Beth lay back on the mattress and inhaled the stench of sweat and a thousand showerless nights. She heard his approach and felt her legs sink as he met her. He was a kind lover; Junior never harmed her. Laura Beth let him take her and let him say his words, how he loved her and would never let her go. She stared at the ceiling, numb as the life drained from her.

They spent the rest of that afternoon and evening together. Sometimes talking and sometimes in silence, the little radio on the counter their only distraction. Junior called themselves gods and people like Jake playthings. He had weed. He never told her where he'd gotten it all and she never asked. They smoked as much as they could until it was time to take her home, and Junior took her hand as they rode. He kissed her soft at the end of Evergreen Street and said he would see her soon. Things would be fine now, just the way they used to be.

Laura Beth got out and took the sidewalk, feeling the cool air against her skin. Under the streetlights and through the shadows, past the bench where Bobby had waited. Charlie wasn't home yet. She went upstairs to the bedroom and waited by the window, her head light from the drugs. That was good. That helped. Likely, she wouldn't feel a thing.

Charlie came home as drunk as she was high. He said he was sorry for the morning and touched the side of her face, making her grimace. He wanted to. She said she was tired and he said he wanted to. He struck her again and shoved her against the dresser, pushing her head down onto the hard and polished wood. Tearing at her clothes. Ripping her from the inside out.

She did not scream and did not know if she had on her last night of living. There was only the dresser shaking beneath her and the sound of Charlie's drunken grunts and the silent plea echoing from Laura Beth's hollowed heart. Shouting, *Help. Please, someone help.*

# -10-

It seemed a pattern Bobby hoped wouldn't be repeated much longer, rising to count the missing stars and then examine the bruise on his face, ignore the ringing phone and get drunk. The Turn before had been the worst one yet. Seeing Jake die the way he had, all because of a *penny*. Hearing Kate scream like a madwoman. The blank, shocked look on Zach's face. Bobby had gotten drunk again when he got back to the shop, had locked the waiting room door and moved the Pepsi machine in front of it and rolled the big toolbox in front of the broken door to the alley. He had gotten so drunk that he'd vomited and passed out before he could even tell the twins what had happened.

He drank upon waking that next Turn as well, though only enough to steel himself against what might be found at the house across town. Matthew and Mark went along. Mark suggested they wait and go to Timmy's instead. Better that than going out to the Barnett house and risk Kate (or worse, Zach) answering the door, crying and sullen and numb, still mourning the violent passing of her husband and his daddy. Bobby agreed with much of that, but he couldn't wait. He had to know now.

The town was only then beginning to wake, the streets all but bare, and what Bobby felt was a taste of the loneliness that would now likely shadow him forever. He saw no more of the family after Jake's death. Junior had not come to break into the shop and drag Bobby out. George had not arrived with his notebook or his chessboard. Tommy had not come to talk. Not even Laura Beth had visited, wanting a place to hide for the day. But what had struck Bobby hardest was that he and the boys had to take the mountain alone at the end of the last Turn. Juliet had not called. The darkness between the worlds had been blacker and deeper than ever, and Juliet had not called.

"You think he'll be there?" Mark asked.

"I don't know. Dorothea said he would be. Said he'd be *here*. I don't know if that means Jake's still alive where we came from."

"So he'd be here maybe," Matthew said, "but just a shadow. Like a memory."

"That's what we need to see."

The road was wet and puddled from the night, the fields and woods quiet. Bobby took the two hills just down from the Barnett home with the right side tires off the shoulder, partly because of the beer and partly to avoid any oncoming traffic. He turned left off the road a few miles on up the Barnetts' lane to the small farmhouse on the knoll. Kate's truck had been parked near the side door. Jake's was beside hers.

"Was his truck in town before?" Mark asked. "Yesterday, when he died?"

Bobby shook his head. "I don't remember."

He cut the engine and sat there, knowing he had to get out but afraid of what he'd find. No one inside bothered to look out; not a single curtain fluttered. The three of them got out and climbed the porch steps together. Bobby took a deep breath and rapped on the door.

For a long while no one answered. Matthew said maybe they were all out back and then Bobby heard the hardwood floor inside creak. The door opened to Kate. Her expression was one more of confusion than sadness.

"Bobby?"

He took off his cap. "Morning, Kate. Didn't wake you, I hope."

"No. No, we've been up awhile."

"We?"

"Me and Zach."

Bobby lowered his eyes.

"And Jake, of course. He sleeps better than he used to, but still not enough."

"Jake?" he asked. "He inside?"

"Sure."

He smiled. It felt wide and stupid and good.

"You don't mind, Kate, could you get him for me? I sure would like a word."

"You want to come in?"

"No. Thank you. Won't be long."

She nodded, concerned, and left the door open to the screen. Bobby looked down at the boys, both of whom smiled as wide and stupid as he.

The boards creaked again. Bobby looked in, waving. Jake opened the screen door as alive as ever. He carried a cup of coffee in one hand.

"Bobby?" he asked. "What you doing up this way? Everything all right?"

Bobby chuckled, couldn't help himself. "It is. Didn't mean to intrude, Jake. I's just piddling around, thought I might stop by and say hello."

"Don't recall you ever stopping by before." He took a sip.

"No, reckon not. Guess I've more often tried to steer away from you than seek you out. Today's just a little different."

"How much you had to drink this morning, Bobby?"

Bobby stared at him, not knowing what to say.

"Know we had our problems, Jake. In the past. But that don't mean I don't view you as a friend, because I do. 'Member you caught me out in Hollis Devereaux's woods, buying that shine? You let me go."

Jake looked down into his cup and nodded. Bobby knew that was a memory the sheriff would rather set aside.

"And that whole mess when Zach and Allie come up missing. I didn't have nothing to do with that, Jake."

"I know, Bobby. Kate does, too. We do what we can to make sure you're left in peace. There's no ill will here."

"And I appreciate it." Bobby grinned. Happy, just happy. "Well, I'll be getting along, then."

"Everything okay, Bobby?"

"Nothing I can't handle. I expect things'll be quiet now." He stepped off the porch, bringing the twins along. "Jake? It's okay that you take your Blazer to Camden for them new brakes. I unnerstand. You won't 'member none a this when the Turn's done, but I'll say you can bring your truck or Kate's to me anytime. Work I do'll be top of the line. You got my word."

Jake had raised his cup halfway to his mouth before holding it there. "What's a Turn, Bobby? And how'd you know I'm taking the Blazer to Camden this morning?"

"Don't matter. I'll leave you to it."

"Bobby?"

He turned around.

"You lay off that drinking. Okay? Don't wanna have to peel you up off the road one day."

"I'll do that, Jake."

Bobby got back in the truck and pulled away. Jake took another sip of his coffee and waved when Bobby reached the road.

"He's alive," Matthew said. "That's good."

"It is, even if all I could see while he was talking was his head exploding on that wall. But he's still here."

"What about there?" Mark asked. "Back in the world?"

"I don't know. Guess it don't matter."

Mark shook his head. He rubbed his mouth like he was worried. "'Member what you told us George said? About there bein' a way home?"

"That ain't home," Bobby said. "Neither's this."

"Back, then. A way back. If Jake gets killed here, he still comes back. Because the Turn repeats itself each time. But if he gets killed here, he might die *there*, too. In the old world.

It works different there, Daddy. Nothing happens over again. He's just . . . gone."

Bobby looked away from the road, to him.

"Do you see?" Mark asked. "There could be a way back, Daddy. But if you die here, might be it won't matter. You'll be dead for real."

# -11-

Tommy woke to the moon high in the early clouds outside his window. The bedside clock glowed 4:37. He reached for the memory of how many Turns had passed since the letter had killed Sheriff Barnett and Mama had driven Bobby away. Not even Tommy could reckon how long ago that had been, how many times since day had repeated day. Like a chain, he thought. Like a long and brittle chain.

He counted to seven and heard the slam from the other side of the wall, the sound that marked both the end and beginning of his Turn. The front door closing each night as his old mama came home from work, hands full of the day's mail, voice sobbing. Tommy would have to go to sleep in the midst of that quiet wailing. He no longer loved her, not after what she'd done on that old road halfway to Stanley. (*Ate a gun*, Junior had told him the day Mama and the rest sat him on the sofa. *Ate the whole damned barrel, boy.*) Yet he mourned her. Tommy often wondered if that meant he loved his old mama still. He didn't think so. Mama—Dorothea, Tommy's real mama—said love meant less about saying and more about doing. If that was true, then Tommy didn't think he loved his old mama at all anymore. It was like an echo, hearing her tears. And while he had once held the pillow tight over his ears or hummed a song to drown their sound, now Tommy would most times lie still and listen to every sniff and warble. Those cries had become a reminder of all he had gained and all from which he had been saved.

Now that door shutting again, his old mama not coming home but going away forever. He remained in his bed, a broken one with the slats missing from part of the bottom, leaving Tommy to sleep at an angle, head higher than his legs. The Turn never allowed him to leave his room at night. He'd tried when he first came to heaven, so hard and often that his memory still bore the scars. The door was always stuck shut and the walls would somehow grow thicker on his side, letting Tommy hear his mama cry but leaving her deaf to his screams and pounding on the door. Yet here in the Turn's early day, the knob would swing free. Tommy could call in little more than a whisper, his mama would hear. He could run after her even if he never had. Too afraid at first. Too unconcerned now.

The car door shut. Tommy rubbed sleep from his eyes and rolled from the bed, moving the bent slats on the blinds in time to watch her pull away. It was better she was gone, fine that living with him had left her so hungry that she'd eaten a gun. Heaven wouldn't be heaven otherwise.

He changed into his clothes and turned the light on in the hall, walked through the kitchen past the stack of mail on the table. Tommy still didn't know what those letters meant. He could read the words fine (though he'd never thank George) but could understand none. Once he'd taken the whole pile to Mama, wanting to know what could be so bad. She'd gone through them while they sat on the back porch, drinking tea and chocolate milk. All Dorothea had said was Tommy had been blessed to come to heaven when he did. She'd said the

Lord had rescued them all from a mean old world and set them down in a fairer one.

Those letters meant little after that—echoes, nothing more. Tommy ignored them and reached for the stool next to the sink, then went to the small closet off the living room and reached to the high shelf. He carried what he needed to the kitchen table and swept away the piles of old clothes and his old mama's full ashtray and the empty bottles of beer. His only chore in the Turn never took long. Cheese and milk from the mostly empty refrigerator came next, along with a knife from the drawer. Tommy shoved them all into the knapsack he'd once used for school.

He donned his Braves cap and headed out for the long walk into the night. Following, perhaps, the very streets his old mama had just traveled and would travel again. George had once confessed that was surely the case, there being only one way from Mattingly to Stanley. Gravel crunched beneath his tennis shoes as Tommy shut his eyes and tried to recall her face. He no longer could. Those Turns when he rose as soon as the front door shut, Tommy could only see the back of his old mama's red hair and how she slouched in either drunkenness or despair. When she turned to climb into the car, she did so in darkness.

It didn't matter now. Tommy had traded his old family for a new one, a family bigger and better and filled with people who loved him. He had Dorothea for a mama and Juliet and Laura Beth for sisters and Junior for a brother, George for the crazy uncle nobody as much loved as endured. And Tommy finally had in Bobby the father he had never known. It hadn't been right, Mama sending him away. She said maybe Bobby would come back one day. Tommy hoped he would. Maybe if Mama didn't start missing Bobby or Bobby didn't

start missing everyone else, the Lord would send another letter. One *telling* Mama to make peace. Wasn't right, splitting
everyone up. When Juliet first came to the Turn, she asked
Mama once where the streets of gold were, and the holy city,
and the light of God to replace the sun. Tommy didn't need
any of that. Heaven wasn't beautiful, heaven was family.

He took the short way there but the long way back, winding his way along empty streets. In those small hours it was
easy for Tommy to think all of it had been made for him
alone, every tree and star and puff of breeze, a whole world to
play both in and with. He leaned his head back and breathed
the cool air, ran a finger through the rainwater that had
beaded along the top of a newspaper box on Main. A right
at the blinker, then a left into the alley. Hands in his pockets
and his hat tilted back, humming a song he didn't know as
the knapsack kept rhythm with his steps. He fell quiet as he
spotted the shape on the ground ahead.

It had taken Tommy longer than he could reckon to find
the place where his daddy's Turn began. Even then, it had
been on accident. He went to his knees on the wet gravel and
slipped out of the knapsack, wondering where Bobby went and
who he killed. It had taken Tommy only a few years' worth of
Turns to discover everything about the town, but there were
still things he didn't know about his family. In many ways, he
understood they were all as separate and closed off from each
other in heaven as they had been in the world. There were
still secrets. That troubled him. But maybe secrets helped
make a family, too, right along with love.

Bobby never talked as he lay there. Tommy had tried
waking him before, shook Bobby's shoulders and poked him
in the side and screamed in Bobby's face, but the Turn kept
him asleep. Most times now, Tommy would just talk and

hope his daddy could somehow hear. He'd say whatever was going on with the others and how Laura Beth was fine and that Juliet missed him because she was in love, Tommy knew that, he'd heard Juliet tell Mama. But that was the sort of love a wife had for a husband, and that love was a lot less than the kind a child had for his father. He brushed Bobby's cheek with his hand, then twisted the Braves cap to the side to kiss his daddy's forehead.

Home now until the day broke and it was time to go back to Mama's. He took the bridge, pausing to spit over the side, and made for the long field beside the railroad tracks that would lead him to the house. At the edge of the field stood an abandoned barn that had somehow survived the tornado years before. Tommy hopped the old cattle gate along the road and approached the barn slowly. He knelt in the grass and whistled once, then used his coaxing voice to call out.

"Percy. PercyPercyPercy."

From the barn came a familiar mew. The filthy tom poked its head out between the slats, one dark shadow set against a myriad of ones lighter. Tommy kissed the air. The cat didn't move. He opened the knapsack and set down the milk and cheese, then used the knife to cut the empty beer can he knew would be near his feet. Percy squeezed through and out, his fear deep but his hunger deeper, casting its one remaining eye toward a boy it had never seen. He began to eat as Tommy reached to stroke the matted fur and the stump of a chewed-off ear. Finding Bobby in the alley had been a matter of chance. Finding Percy had not. There wasn't a stretch of ground in all of Mattingly that Tommy had not covered in his time inside the Turn, not a truth he did not know. Only the mysteries troubled him. Just the secrets.

The dark sky began to wane over the mountains. Tommy

waited until the cat had finished and stood for home. He walked off, telling Percy good-bye, then stopped when his eyes wandered through the crack in the barn door.

Something was in there.

Air caught in Tommy's throat. He forgot how to breathe and took a step back, wanting to look away and yet afraid to do so. Percy nuzzled against his leg, making Tommy jump. He bent his head to see past the shadows inside.

There it was again.

Not moving.

*Glowing.*

He stepped closer. Waited, stepped again.

"What's in there, Percy?"

The cat looked at him as if to say, *You're the one so smart.*

The handle on the door had long ago rusted and hung by a single screw. Tommy reached out and pulled slow to the right, sliding the door only wide enough to see inside. Cobwebs hung from the posts and stalls. The musty smell of dust and dirt and mold nearly overpowered him. He walked farther in, nearing the back wall, then stopped when his eyes settled on what stood in the corner. Tommy's legs turned to jelly. He turned to run and tripped, landing on the hard earth with a sound part scream and part cry that chased Percy away. And in the deep silence of the Turn's early morn, no one heard.

## -12-

It had taken Dorothea longer than she'd anticipated to return her family to a semblance of what it had once been. Much prayer and much toil and not a few lies, though for the good of all and thus sinless to her mind. It was no sin, she reckoned, to smile as one weeps inside or keep one's voice light when it would rather rage. *I must be strong now, more than ever,* is what she told herself at each Turn's start, one foot ready to take the stairs down. *I must show them this is best.* "Them" being all the family aside from Junior, who had been fine with Bobby's going. "Them" being God as well. The Lord had not been pleased that she had sent Bobby away. The letters in the Turns after had come with angry words full of condemnation, and Dorothea's letters back had been full of her tears.

Time could not wholly erase Bobby from their minds, but time would help and time was all they had. Junior made sure Bobby remained close to his shop and everyone else remained far from Bobby. He had spied no one there, not even Juliet. Dorothea was certain the preacher would be first to test the rules—still a young girl, barely out of her twenties. Junior had already been spoken for, and George was too old and mournful over his own wife. Bobby, drunk and dim as he was, remained the only viable option for a woman not yet above longing for a man's touch. But there had been no sign of that, nor of George or Tommy finding their way downtown. Not that Dorothea could ensure the others were always watched. There were gaps, of course, long hours when one or any of them could sneak to Bobby's or Bobby could sneak to them. Dorothea didn't think that had happened. She would know.

Then came the Turn well beyond Dorothea's counting, when the threat of losing both God and family became too great a burden for her to bear. She cried out long to the Lord that night, using most of the ink in Hubie's typewriter to confess sins both now and past. Begging for things to be made right and swearing she would never go against the Lord again. As a testament to both her seriousness and devotion, she had cut the tip of her thumb with a kitchen knife and left a smeared print at the bottom of that letter, sealing that promise with her own blood.

The words from the Lord became less threatening afterward: kinder, if not wholly forgiving, much like the rest of the family. Juliet and George ended their constant whispering. Even Laura Beth returned to some sense of the woman she'd been, though the marijuana Junior gave her to smoke played a hand. Poor girl had come to reek of it now. Juliet had come to Dorothea about it. Dorothea promised she would have words with Junior and Laura Beth both, though she never did. The weed had been Dorothea's idea. Just for a bit and only enough to put Laura Beth at ease. It had worked well enough. Calming Laura Beth had in turn calmed the rest, leaving Junior to speculate that if pot would've been around in Bible times, the Israelites would've ceased their desert grumblings and reached the promised land a mite sooner.

But not all had fared so well. The person everyone considered the family's heart remained sullen and distant. Dorothea had once believed the Turns would tend to that as well, and in fact there had been an abundance of dinners and suppers when much more laughter than silence filled the yellow house. But as she sat on the back porch beneath the midmorning sun and watched the others play and visit, she could avoid the obvious no longer.

Something was wrong with Tommy.

She called him away from his ball practice, saving them all from another rendition of how Junior had once struck out someone named Chip Jones. Tommy came willingly enough. George and Juliet watched from their place beneath the willow. Dorothea supposed Laura Beth watched them as well, though she couldn't be certain. There had been a long string of Turns after Jake died and Bobby had been cast out that

Laura Beth went about the house naked in the face, as though she'd meant to remind everyone what Charlie did to her and what Bobby had found so offensive. Junior's doing, perhaps. Or maybe it had been the slow realization that some things simply must be.

Dorothea had asked Tommy to help with dinner enough in the past for him to understand that brewing the tea and mixing the biscuits were simply busywork to gloss over the real reason he was there. She would not patronize the boy and pretend otherwise. He sat in one of the hard chairs by the kitchen table where Dorothea had sat alone all those years after Hubert died. She gave him a bowl of potatoes to peel and started in with how pretty the day was and how the birds sounded like angels, then how well heaven treated them and what the Lord had saved them from, Tommy especially.

"Can you imagine?" she asked. "Having to face what the days beyond this would have promised, dear? Knowing what lies in wait? And you would be all alone."

Tommy kept peeling. All he said was if he had to peel the potatoes every Turn, he'd like them nowhere near as much. Sunlight streamed through the windows and mixed with steam from the pots, creating a bright and moving fog. Dorothea tasted the filling for her apple pie. She brought a knife from the counter and sat across from Tommy, picked a potato from the bowl. The work made her wince.

"Your fingers hurtin', Mama?"

"Only some. Hurt the day I passed, so I suppose it's my cross to bear. I'd count that another blessing in your favor, Tommy. You passed young. You'll never have to suffer the pains and humiliations of the old, like my rusting fingers. You'll never have to see the ones you love most go away."

"Bobby went away."

Dorothea glanced up. Tommy concentrated on the potato in his hand.

"You miss him."

"I love him. He's my daddy."

"The Lord is your daddy, son."

Tommy didn't appear satisfied at that prospect. "You miss him, Mama?"

"I miss the man Bobby showed us he could be. I thought Bobby could be important to us, me and you and Junior. The Lord thinks George and Juliet sometimes have too much say over this family, especially with Laura Beth. You saw how that all went. Poor Jake got killed, then Bobby had to go away. Because of them. There are times when I feel it's only me and Junior keeping things together. I know you love George in spite of the schooling he makes you do, and I'll not fault Juliet for her kind words and sweet disposition. But they peddle lies, Tommy. You must understand that. I'd hoped we could sway Bobby to the same belief, but that didn't happen. He showed us the man that hides in his past, a selfish man with no concern for anyone but himself. For that, it's best he's gone."

"The Lord didn't tell you to make him go," Tommy said.

"The Lord trusts me to do what's right."

She got up to stir the green beans and check the roast. Junior came inside for a glass of tea and asked if he could take Laura Beth a nip of Hubert's whiskey. Dorothea said fine. She waited until Junior left before continuing.

"I'd hear your thoughts, Tommy. Bobby makes you sad and I'd say he makes us all sad, but you're not acting sad today." She kept her eyes to the stove. Not looking might make Tommy more inclined to state the truth. "You ask me, you look scared."

He said nothing at first, though Dorothea didn't hear him peeling.

"You ever wonder, Mama?"

"I know what I need to and don't have to guess on the rest."

"Sometimes I wonder," he said.

"Of what?"

"Heaven. Like if something bad will happen and heaven will go away."

"Whatever gave you that idea?"

"Nothing."

"Tommy?" She looked at him now. His eyes had gone wet and glassy.

"This really heaven, Mama?"

Dorothea went to him, wincing as her knees popped and cracked as she bent, letting Tommy see her face.

"Of course it is," she said. "Don't you ever doubt that, Tommy. Don't you ever even think about it."

The words struggled off his lips, brought forth only by the weight of the sobs behind them, spit and snot and tears that stained his freckles. "Tell me it is, Mama. Make me believe."

She pulled him to her chest and let him cry. Behind her, the door opened. It closed with a whisper. She didn't know who that had been.

"Has George been talking to you?" she asked. "Or Juliet?"

"No."

"Tommy?"

"No," he cried again. "I just had a nightmare. After I woke up, I mean. I mean my old mama woke me up and then I went back to sleep, and then I dreamed bad."

"A nightmare about what?"

"About heaven ending. About the world coming apart."

Dorothea rocked him, feeling Tommy sink into her. She

took his fear and pain and returned safety and love. She shut her eyes, thanking the Lord for making her a mother.

"A dream isn't real," she said. "Just the mind playing tricks, Tommy. Nothing more."

"Swear it."

"I swear."

She would have remained there forever if Tommy had asked, no matter the hurt in her knees or the boiling pots, no matter who walked inside. Dorothea felt Tommy pull away. She broke the embrace, wanting to see his smile. Only worry streaked his face.

"Can I be excused?" he asked.

"If you like. And if you're better."

He answered yes to the first and remained silent to the second.

"Go tell the others dinner's almost ready."

"Can you save my plate?" he asked.

"Why? Where are you going?"

"Just on a walk. I don't want none of them seeing me cry. Juliet'll wonder what's wrong, and everybody's happy now."

She thought about that. "Be back for supper."

"I will."

Tommy reached for his cap beside the bowl of potatoes.

"Tommy? I love you."

"Love you, too, Mama."

Dorothea watched him go. The way he walked, down the middle of the street with his head down and shoulders slumped, troubled her. She didn't like mistrusting the boy. George yes, even Juliet, but never Tommy. And yet Dorothea found herself in the backyard not long after, pulling Junior aside. Telling him to find Tommy and follow him, because that boy was going for no walk.

# -13-

It wasn't hard to lose Junior. The man was too big and stupid to go unnoticed.

Tommy reached the bridge when he first spotted him, easing up behind in that big truck of his. Trying to sneak. Tommy shoved his hands in his pockets and made like the thing he was supposed to be—just a kid out for a walk. He stopped in the middle of the bridge and spit off the side, counted to five as the stream from his mouth wadded to a ball and plopped into the current below. Then he walked on easylike, ambling really, planning to stay as far from things as he could.

At Juliet's church, he left the sidewalk and plodded up the parking lot to around back. Junior's truck rumbled at a distance. Right after the Methodist church had been rebuilt, the congregation had taken up a special offering to build a prayer garden behind the church in memory of the old pastor who'd been killed in the tornado. Tommy's mama—the old one, he reminded himself, Stacey—had even given a dollar to the cause. *God don't care about people like us*, he remembered her saying, *but maybe He'll leave us alone if we're good*. He guessed what the church had come up with was once pretty enough. All that sat behind Juliet's church now was an overgrown patch of yard with more weeds than flowers, a few rotting benches, two groundhog holes, and a wood cross in sore need of staining. At the opposite end of the garden stood a patch of trees. Tommy went there, cocking his head for the sound of Junior's truck.

Inside the trees lay a path Juliet had once shown him that snaked all the way to the Dumpster behind the grocery. Tommy ducked there as Junior rounded the building. He heard a sharp curse and squatted down, not wanting to rustle the fallen leaves. Junior walked the whole way around the church and back again. He hitched his thumbs into the front pockets of those stupid Bib-Alls he always wore, studying the ground for prints. He wouldn't find any. Tommy had known just where to step. Junior called out Tommy's name once, and that nearly brought a giggle so loud it would've ended things right there. When no answer came, Junior turned back for his truck, head low, like he was already pondering what Mama would do.

Tommy followed the path to the Dumpster. He came out at the spot between the grocery and the sheriff's office where Jake had died all those Turns before and kept a wary eye out for Junior. Just as it had been at the church, Tommy knew where to move and when. He drifted among the hidden places where people never looked. Pockets, George called them. Tommy liked that word.

He couldn't risk going the front way and so crossed the street, skirting the blinker light. Once, Tommy swore he heard the sound of Junior's truck. He ran faster, dodging men and women who cared to see him in heaven as little as they'd cared in life, then nearly leaped into the alley as if that narrow stretch had become the only safe place and the only part of the world not in danger. He looked over his shoulder and saw no one, then looked ahead and stopped.

Bobby sat atop an overturned bucket just outside the propped-open back door of his shop. His hands were on his spread knees, with the remnants of what Tommy thought may have been a smile on his face. He wore the same dirty ball cap and work shirt as the last time Tommy had seen him, though his jeans looked newer and maybe even clean. The bruise on his face was bigger. His eyes looked more hollow and tired. Tommy saw a pyramid of beer cans stacked against the wall.

Neither of them spoke. Bobby didn't run inside or tell Tommy to get away. Tommy tried thinking of something to say, how much he'd missed Bobby or how many times he'd sat and watched Juliet cry, how Laura Beth and George would sometimes still speak of him and even Dorothea, when it was her and Tommy alone. Those words failed him. There was just him staring at Bobby and Bobby staring back, and what Tommy spoke was what he supposed any boy in need would say to his daddy.

"You gotta help me. I'm in trouble."

Bobby licked his lips and drew the bottom one in, chewing on it.

"Please, Daddy? He can't find me."

"Who?"

"Junior."

"What's Junior want with you?"

"You won't find out if you don't let me in. You said you'd give Laura Beth aid. You love her more'n me?"

Bobby's eyes narrowed. He stood and kicked the bucket inside, gathering up his cans. "Come on. Here's safe as any."

Tommy ran after him and inside the shop. Bobby shut the door and moved him aside, rolling the big toolbox across the entrance. He locked all four wheels and pushed. The box didn't budge.

"Ain't nobody gonna back-door me no more," he said.

He'd pulled his truck into the first bay, over the service pit beside Mrs. Campbell's car. Tape covered the windows on both bay doors. Tommy could barely see.

"Stay along the wall," Bobby said. "Waiting room's at the end. Got the blinds shut, but there's light enough. Junior can stop but he won't see anything. And since I got the truck in here now, he'll think I'm gone and you never come this way." He stopped. "You didn't tell him you were coming here, did you?"

"No," Tommy said. His voice echoed in all that quiet. "Promise. All I told Mama's I was going for a walk."

Bobby told him to sit in the recliner and left again, returning with the beer and the bucket he'd been sitting on outside. He turned the bucket over and sat in front of the chair, putting them at eye level, and took a long drink.

"What happened?"

"Mama made me go in and cut the potatoes because she knew something was wrong, but when I tried tellin' her, she got mad and told me not to think about it."

"Think about what?"

Bobby's breath stunk like beer, like Tommy's old mama's breath used to stink. Tommy smelled the sourness and wrinkled his nose. Dorothea had once said his old mama went away because she must not have loved him anymore. Bobby had gone away, too.

"It's a secret."

"Must be a bad one," Bobby said, "send you runnin' here."

"It is."

"How bad?"

"Real bad."

Bobby grinned. It looked an ugly thing, rarely practiced, yet it eased Tommy's fear.

"I've missed you, Tommy."

"Missed you, too."

"How is everybody?"

"Fine."

"Juliet?"

"She misses you," Tommy said. He added, "Not more'n me. Do you miss us?"

"Some of you all the time. All of you sometimes." He looked around at all that dark. "I thought it would be easy, going back to the way things used to be. It ain't. Some days not even the . . ."

"What?"

"Nothing," Bobby said. "It's a secret."

"How bad?"

"Really."

"Well," Tommy said, "I'll tell you my secret if you tell me yours."

Bobby looked to think that over. "You first."

"Nuh-uh. You."

Bobby dipped his head, and when he looked up, a tear ran through the center of the bruise on his face, and the smile he gave looked even more horrible than the one he'd given before.

"You first," Tommy said again.

"'Kay." Bobby cleared his throat. "Used to have two boys that reminded me lot of you. 'Specially one. Mark. Sometimes talking to him is like messing with a Rubik's Cube, but he always told me straight. That kid's like my conscience, you know? Much as I strayed, Mark would always try to lead me back to the straight and narrow. Not like Matthew. He was my other boy. All Matthew wants is to have a good time. Kinda like me, the way I was. They had their hair parted to the side instead of leaving it shaggy like you do, and theirs was brown instead of red. But I look at you, I see them."

Tommy wiggled in his seat. The air inside the shop had been cold when he'd first come in. Now he felt hot and didn't know why. "Where they at?"

Bobby took another swallow. "What if I told you they're sitting right beside me?" He looked down to his right, "Mark." To his left, "Matthew. Y'all say hi to Tommy."

Tommy heard not a thing. "Ain't nobody there, Daddy."

"They don't like you calling me that. Not a lot they can do about it but tell me to make you stop. But I won't."

"Stop foolin' me."

"Ain't foolin'. You can't see'm. I can't either, 'less I'm drunk. I'm drunk, they show up. They talk to me and we make jokes and watch TV and listen to the radio, all the things we used to do. They tell me stuff and I tell them stuff back. Stuff I don't tell no one." Another tear, a quick one that raced from Bobby's eye to his chin and then off before Tommy could blink. "You want to see them, guess you'd have to walk over to Oak Lawn. Both them are buried up there side by side. Carla, you know Carla, that woman I was married to, she left me and took the kids because I got forsaken. Married some guy in Stanley who turned out to be just as big a drunk as me, and that would be what I'd call justice if things hadn't turned out as they did. They were all at some kind of office dinner a few years back, got in a wreck coming home. He was fine, not a scratch on him. Carla got hurt bad. The boys . . ." He shrugged, struggling for the words before deciding he'd said enough. "They were eight when they died. Carla calls me. Calls me in heaven. That phone'll ring in an hour and thirty-four minutes, and I never answer because I know what she's gonna say—'Our boys died seven years ago today, Bobby. Do you know that? Do you ever think about them?'" He took another drink and wiped his cheek. "Almost poetic, ain't it?"

Tommy felt about to cry, too. "Why you telling me this?"

Bobby shrugged. "Heard about your mom right before Dorothea and the Lord kicked me away. Thought about it a lot. I promised myself the next time I saw you, I'd tell you. That's the first thing I thought when you came bounding down the alley. Figured I'd let you know you ain't alone in the things you might feel, all that anger and hurt."

"Lord didn't have a say in you leaving. Just Mama. We're supposed to be a family. All of us. That's what the Lord wants."

"Be that as it may," Bobby said, "I gotta live in fear and darkness now, waiting for something awful to happen like it did to Jake. Except maybe this time, it'll be real. There's my secret, Tommy Purcell. Now give me yours."

"I can't."

Bobby snorted. "What you mean you can't? Deal's a deal."

"I mean I can't tell you," he said. "I have to show you. And you gotta bring your phone."

# -14-

Bobby didn't want to take the truck and risk Junior seeing them, but Tommy promised his secret was close enough to reach on foot. The boys refused to come along. Neither was speaking at the moment, not to Bobby and not to each other. Shocked to silence, Bobby thought. Or angry. There would be a lot of making up that night, but telling Tommy had felt the right thing. Bobby didn't know when he'd last spoken to someone of flesh and blood. The day with Jake, he supposed. Things had gotten to the point that he'd even considered picking up the phone when Bea called. Or worse, Carla.

Tommy led him back through the shop and helped move the toolbox. He said they'd have to be careful, not only of Junior, but of everyone else, too, because Junior might go asking if anyone had seen them together. That might upset

---

the balance, Tommy said, though he wasn't sure. He seemed more sure Junior would risk upsetting the balance before upsetting Mama.

They went left, through the alley and to the corner. Tommy counted to ten and took Bobby's hand as they crossed to the next block. Down that street and then left again, skirting the flower stand and ducking into a sliver of shade outside the used-book shop—a pocket, Tommy said, and even though the area was open and they were both plain to spot, those who passed did not so much as look their way. Tommy counted to fifteen and took Bobby's hand again. Across the street, past the post office, then across the street again. Weaving their way back to the bridge and making a cautious walk across, then cutting a hard right along a tottering fence that surrounded the field between the railroad tracks and the river. Old Man Moser's field, which had long survived Old Man Moser. All told, Bobby guessed their circular route had made a mile through town in the middle of a Saturday afternoon, and not a person had spotted them.

"How you know to do that? Sneak around such?"

Tommy shrugged and lifted his cap, letting the sun strike his pale skin. "Gotta stay to the pockets is all."

"You mean like the bench on Evergreen?"

"Yeah. That where you sat that night with Laura Beth?"

"Juliet told me to wait there."

"That's a good spot," Tommy said. "There's plenty others. Like outside the bookshop? George says he taught me where they're all at, but I showed'm more than he showed me. There's whole parts of town people pass right by but never see. I don't think Junior knows about the pockets. I ain't never told him, and George never would. Mama probably knows. Mama knows everything. But I still use them sometimes, when I want to hide. Like Juliet wanted you to hide from Junior that night when you seen Laura Beth's real face. We're almost there."

"Where?"

Tommy pointed in the distance, to the barn leaning by the tracks. "There."

"What you doing at the Moser barn?"

"You'll see. You bring your phone, Daddy?"

Bobby felt his pocket. "Yeah. Why I need my phone?"

Tommy kept walking. Bobby slowed but followed. He asked, "Juliet still the same?"

"Told you she was. We all are. Everybody's sad when you left, but I was saddest. They were sad about Jake, too." He turned around and put a hand over the bill of his cap, blocking the shine. "What'd you think of Jake dyin', Daddy?"

"Think it's about the worst thing I ever seen. You okay with it?"

"Sure," Tommy said. "I didn't mind. Sheriff Barnett's got ghosts in his past. And he wasn't kind to you. I think that's why the Lord made him die that day. You took it like it was bad, but the Lord was trying to show He loves you."

"Lord's got a funny way."

They swung around to the front, giving the barn a wide berth. The field shaped a square of no more than five acres. A few trees and bushes struggled in the rocky soil, hamburger wrappers and empty bottles and plastic bags rolling like tumbleweed in the breeze. Bobby figured the Lord could've at least taken out the trash in the next world. He heard the cars passing and the clock tower droning, but they were as alone here as any two people could be.

Something moved inside the barn. Bobby reached for Tommy and took a step back.

Tommy shook him away. "That's just Percy."

"Who's Percy?"

Tommy made a kissing sound and bent at his waist, putting his hands on his knees. Bobby heard the mew. A cat's head eased out between a gap in the boards near the door. A filthy thing, ugly and deformed and half starved.

"I feed him," Tommy said. "Give him milk, too, every morning after my Turn starts. He's my pet. I love him." He kissed the air again and whispered, "C'mere," in a sweet asking voice. The cat ducked its head inside, ignoring him. Bobby guessed Tommy could come here every day, it'd always be the first time with Percy. An animal like that was more wild than tame.

"Why you come all the way out here every morning?"

"I don't know. My old mama wakes me up when she leaves. Guess I don't want to stay around there, knowing what she's gone off to do. I followed her once after she left. Couldn't ever catch her. Like George can never find Miss Anna. But I liked coming into town before everybody woke up, so I forgot about my old mama and just did that. Juliet says walking brings you closer to the Lord. She walks everywhere. I ain't ever seen her drive a car, but Junior says she's got a Volvo. They good, Daddy?"

"I don't work on foreign. This what you brought me down here for, Tommy? Show me a mangy old cat? 'Cause this here ain't no secret worth keeping. Worst thing Dorothea'll do is tell you watch out for the rabies. Ain't like she'll banish you to the nether regions like she did me."

"It ain't Percy, it's what I found." Tommy pointed at the barn. "In there. I was here this Turn before it got light, feeding Percy like I always do. Saw it when I was leaving. You got your phone, Daddy?"

"Told you I did, but I don't know who you expect me to call."

"Don't want you to call nobody."

Tommy walked to the front of the barn and took hold of the handle on the door. "You coming?"

"Not until you tell me what's in there."

"I can't. I don't know what it is, I just know it ain't supposed to be."

He slid the door open, letting in the light. Bobby stepped forward and felt a darkness he could not know, an undefined something that grew a lump in his throat and set his knees to shake, made the stab in his chest that came every night from the steering wheel and every time he grew afraid. He wished the boys were there.

"It's in here," Tommy said. "You gotta be careful, Daddy. Bunch of old wood and nails on the floor."

He disappeared inside. Bobby followed, not out of good sense, but from the desire to make sure Tommy didn't get himself hurt. Bars of sunlight fell through the rafters and gaps in the sides, making the dust shine like pixies in flight. Percy hissed and darted from his hiding spot and through the door, wanting nothing to do with them or whatever lay in wait. Bobby kept his eyes to the floor, watching for nails. He looked up when Tommy said, "There."

What lay in the back corner of that barn struck Bobby with a terror he had never known, one more visceral than watching Jake Barnett die and deeper than even that fresh day when Carla had called in tears, saying their sons had died. Tommy didn't speak, didn't move. Bobby felt the boy's fingers reaching for his own. He took them and squeezed hard.

"What is this, Tommy?"

"I don't know. It ain't supposed to be here because it never was before."

"You gotta tell Mama about this." Bobby needed a drink,

needed his boys, needed away. He stared at the edges, knowing what it was. What it meant.

"Mama won't listen."

"George, then. George'll know what to do."

"George would tell Mama, and Mama won't believe anything he says. It's gotta be you, Daddy."

Bobby wanted to look away but couldn't.

"You have to come with me," Tommy said. "We have to show them. If you go, they'll all listen. They got to, Daddy. Lord's told Mama you can come back. She has to take you. You need to be with us again, Daddy. Because it's bad. This is bad, ain't it?"

Bobby stared. Those edges.

"Bad," he said.

# -15-

Junior's truck sat in the driveway behind George's, and Tommy said Junior would be mad. He'd let Tommy get the better of him way back when Bobby had found out about Laura Beth, now again that morning. The kid was smart, smart like Mark. But Tommy's brains could not stand against Junior's brawn, and Bobby guessed that was what scared them both so bad now.

Bobby walked in uninvited. Tommy lingered, following but trying to appear like he wasn't. Bobby understood and tried not to think about what Dorothea would say when she discovered where Tommy had gone. He tried not to think of Jake Barnett. If this all went south, if he couldn't convince Dorothea something in the Turn had gone terribly wrong, he might have to get Tommy out of there. The house smelled of roast and potatoes and baked fruit—apple pie, Juliet's favorite. Of all that had gone through his mind on the ride over, everything he had to say, the words to give Juliet remained the most vague.

"Guess they're all out back," Tommy said. "Mama's gonna be mad when she sees I brung you."

"You let me take care of that."

Bobby hoped that sounded stronger in his voice than it had in his mind. He wanted Tommy out the back door first, especially when he spotted Dorothea at her little table on the back porch, but Tommy had left his courage back at the barn. Bobby went ahead through the kitchen, past the dirty pots and plates soaking in the sink. Trying to make enough noise so Dorothea would turn and see him coming, yet keeping his steps slow and soft so she wouldn't. He could see no one else in the yard. Dorothea's back was to him, head down. In prayer, Bobby thought, until he saw the breeze flutter the page in her hand. For the first time, Bobby hoped that paper had indeed come from the Lord, and that the Lord had sense enough to warn His prophet who would be stopping by that afternoon.

The door squeaked open. Dorothea folded the page before Bobby could study the words. She turned as he stepped out and saw Tommy at his elbow and then stood, raising her hand. Junior called out from across the yard. He came running with a bat in one hand and a ball in the other, reminding Bobby of a little boy longing for playmates. Over by the willow, George stood and Laura Beth, still in her sunglasses. Then Juliet. The sight of her was enough to chase Bobby's fear and every bit of doubt. Her eyes caught the light as her lips parted to a hesitant smile, as if wanting to believe the answer to a prayer long asked. Bobby no longer smelled the remnants of dinner, no longer heard Junior running for the porch with his bat and ball or felt Tommy tugging at his arm. There was only Juliet. She brushed away the black curls that had swept over her forehead. He would not believe he loved her, and yet love seemed to Bobby the only answer as to why someone he had known for what he still judged a short while could shine over such a wide space of his heart.

"You ain't supposed to be here," Junior yelled. He stopped at the three wooden steps that led from the yard to the porch. The bat hung high in his left hand.

Dorothea stopped him from getting closer. She used no words, only the hand she'd raised to Bobby. It shot out with a single finger pointed at Junior, holding him where he stood. She looked at Bobby first, then Tommy.

"Knew that's where you'd run." She huffed a laugh that sounded like sandpaper over wood. "You've never been a good liar, Tommy. I'll count that among your many virtues. But unless Bobby has come to apologize for what he's done and renounce his sin of doubt, I've no choice but bid him go."

The others, George and Laura Beth and Juliet, made their way closer to the porch. The women stared at Bobby. George, at Junior. Bobby believed the old man would do his best to keep Junior away should he must, even if it came to George lying unconscious in the middle of all that green grass with a baseball sticking out of his head.

"I'm sorry, Mama," Tommy muttered.

Bobby took the boy by the shoulder and moved him aside. Close to the door, in case they both needed to run. "Tommy's got nothing to say sorry for, Dorothea. I made him bring me. Just this once." He looked at Junior, holding his gaze for as long as he could. "Hear me? Tommy got nothing to do with this, so you leave him alone."

Junior showed his teeth. "Bobby, you threatenin' me?"

"Guess I am."

"That's enough," Dorothea said. "You say your piece, Bobby, then move on. It's taken more Turns than I care to count for this family to get where we were. I'll not have you ruin it as before."

"I found something," Bobby said. "Out near the railroad tracks." Tommy started to speak. Bobby stilled him with a finger not unlike the one Dorothea had used to still Junior. "Something that shouldn't be here. You need to see it . . . Mama."

"You want me to go traipsing off to town, Bobby, I'll say I won't. Last time I did that, a good man died."

"Jake ain't *dead*," Junior said. He rolled his eyes. "Keep tellin' y'all. Them people don't ever *die*."

Dorothea pointed her finger again. "Junior, you'll shush. Bobby wouldn't even be gracing my house if you'd had brains enough to match wits with a ten-year-old boy."

"I ain't no boy," Tommy said.

Bobby had reached his limit. "Doesn't matter if Junior could have followed Tommy or not, I'd still be here. And you don't have to go anywhere to see it, Dorothea. I can show you here."

He pulled the cell phone from his back pocket, holding it out. Bobby wouldn't look at the picture himself, couldn't bear it. He didn't want to ever step foot inside that barn again. Dorothea took the phone. She held it close and put her right hand over it to shield the screen from the sun. Fear streaked across her face, then was gone. Junior came up the steps. The others followed.

George went to Dorothea's side. He bent his head and reached for the phone. Dorothea surrendered it without a word.

"Where did you find this?" he asked.

"The old Moser barn. There's a cat lives in there. I've taken to feeding him." Bobby glanced at Tommy, who bent his head. "Name's Percy."

Juliet brushed her hair behind one ear so she could see. She looked away from Bobby only long enough to look at the phone. The others joined her. Even Tommy, telling them it was true. It was real. Dorothea backed away as if removing herself from the temptation of some sin. Bobby couldn't blame her.

The fear on Juliet's face mirrored Bobby's own. "What is this, Bobby?"

"That ain't nothin'," Junior said. "What'd you do, make that up on some computer thinkin' it'd scare us?"

"Didn't make it up. Tommy saw it with his own eyes. I found it this morning, ran back to town. Then I stumbled on him. Tommy tried going the other way, but I wouldn't let him. I made him come and look himself, then I made him bring me here. Something's wrong with the Turn, Dorothea. Something's happening."

Her black hair—*black from a bottle*, Mark would say— sparkled in the sun. She kept her jaw set and her back straight, but there was no denying the worry in her eyes, plain to everyone.

"What would you have us do, Bobby? If such a thing is even real. Junior's right. This could all be some ruse to get you back in our good graces."

"Ain't no ruse," Bobby said. "Go on down there, look for yourself."

"I will do no such thing, nor will anyone else. Who's to say what it is or how long it's been there? Besides, you're *drunk*. You're always *drunk*. The heavens could fall, you wouldn't know a difference. You mean to tell me that just now showed up? You mean to state you've been in that barn every Turn since your first to feed some mongrel cat—"

"Percy," Tommy said.

"—and been in that very spot every time? You mean to convince me you've been in heaven as long as me and know what belongs where?"

"It wasn't there," Tommy said. "It wasn't, Mama."

"So Bobby says. A man known in the old world to lie as quick as he'd open his mouth. Who sees and speaks to dreams conjured in his mind."

Bobby cleared his throat. "Whatever I may do to lessen my burdens, Dorothea, I'm telling you the truth. Something's wrong. I think the Turn is failing."

"The Turn is *not failing!*" she screamed. "It is and was and always shall be, Bobby Barnes."

Laura Beth took the phone from George. Bobby wasn't sure how much of the picture she could see through her glasses. However much she could, it was enough to make her smile.

"I'm going," George said. "I have to see for myself."

"You won't," Dorothea announced.

Juliet stepped forward. "I'm going, too." Laura Beth said the same. Then Tommy, who said he could show them all. Only Junior remained in place.

Dorothea stepped forward, pleading, "Listen to me, all of you. Please, George. Don't go. Juliet, Laura Beth, stay with me. Stay here. I don't know what's in that barn. Maybe it's not a thing, a trick of light or Bobby's imagination or a million other things. But whatever it is, it's the Lord's. We don't need to go looking for trouble. Tommy? Stay here with your mama. You, too, Bobby. Stay and we can talk. We cannot tempt destruction."

But only Junior remained. One by one they left, Bobby first and the others close behind. Tommy alone looked back, telling Dorothea he was sorry and they would only be gone a little while. He blew his mama a kiss she did not catch, then asked her to please make extra mashed potatoes for supper.

# -16-

George's little Toyota truck barely held two and would never hold four, so Tommy and Laura Beth climbed in back. Juliet took the passenger seat. Bobby had already pulled away, leaving for the shop. He'd told George and Juliet he'd done all that could be asked, then said he understood why they had to go down to the field but they shouldn't get too close and should never go there again. George took turns throwing the gear into first and reverse, trying to maneuver around Junior's truck. He backed out of the drive and spotted Junior watching from the dining room window. A look of hate had fallen over the big man, rage and anger mixing into one long glower.

"Look at him," he said.

Juliet did. She lifted her hand slow and waved. Wanting to show, George supposed, that no hard feelings were had. Junior lifted a hand of his own, fingers closed into the shape of a gun. His cheeks bulged and then his lips mouthed a *POW*.

"Don't just sit here," Juliet said. "*Move*, George."

He did. Not so fast as to knock either Laura Beth or Tommy from the back of the truck, but enough to make the back tires bark. He turned left at the end of the street and checked the mirror. Junior's truck remained in Dorothea's drive. Tommy looked just as afraid as he had on the back porch. Laura Beth grinned from beneath her sunglasses.

*Grinned.*

"I'm sorry," Juliet said. "I didn't mean to yell."

"It's fine."

"He was gone for so long," Juliet said. "Bobby could have reached out to me. He could have called."

"You could have called."

She chewed her lip and said, "It's complicated."

He looked at Laura Beth in the rearview. "People always are."

"That's not what I mean. He could have called. But he didn't, and instead he just shows up with . . . that. What was that, George?"

"I don't know, but we're about to find out. Barn's just up here." He reached over, patted her hand. Smiled. "Don't worry, Juliet. It'll be fine."

Juliet said, "You're a horrible liar."

At the field's edge, George flipped on the signal and waited for the oncoming traffic to pass before pulling parallel to the rusted cattle gate guarding the entrance. Laura Beth was out before he could unbuckle. When she raised herself over the gate, her dress hitched up to reveal a blackened thigh. Tommy remained back, waiting for George and Juliet. Cars and trucks slowed but never stopped, their drivers no doubt confused as to why such a group as they would be gathered in such a place. George waved. It was a sight that never failed to amuse him, people gawking while he stood in the company of those no one had ever known him to associate with but who in the Turn had become closer to him than any family aside from his Anna.

Laura Beth had made it halfway to the barn by the time the others stepped into the field. Tommy called for her to wait. She did, hands on her hips, telling them to move faster.

"You got to be careful," Tommy said. "When you get in there. There's stuff like nails and wood all over. And don't get too close. Bobby almost did. I thought he was gonna fall *in*."

George stopped, leaving Juliet and Tommy to drift ahead and Laura Beth to throw up her hands. "Why would Bobby do that?"

Tommy turned. "Do what?"

"Touch it. Why would he try to do that with you this morning? Why not the first time he'd found it?"

Juliet shielded her eyes from the sun. "What do you mean, George?"

"Why would Bobby even be out here anyway? Rummaging through some old forgotten barn just to feed a cat? That doesn't sound to me like something he would do. Bobby's never been the sort to have time for people, much less stray animals. I'd call it a wonder he even bothered finding you, Tommy. But he *brought* you here? And then he cares so much that he makes you come with him to Dorothea's?"

"You calling me a liar?" Tommy asked.

"That depends. Did Bobby bring you here, Tommy? Or was it you who brought him?"

Juliet took her hand away and looked at the boy.

"It don't make a difference," Tommy said. "All that matters is you see."

He turned away before George could ask his next question and ran for Laura Beth, pulling on her arm to make her wait.

"Tommy," Juliet said. "Tommy found it."

"My guess. Come on."

He led her to the others and then all of them to the barn. They'd almost reached the door when Percy crawled through a gap in the boards. Hissing first, then easing close enough to rub against Tommy's leg.

"Never took you for a cat person," George said. "Know where there's another one that could use some tending to. Some shutting up. If you're interested."

"Where?" Tommy asked.

"My place. You should come by."

Laura Beth said, "I don't care about a cat, I care about what's inside." She pulled on the handle. The door slid open in a series of squeaks and sighs. "Y'all can stand out here long as you want. I'm gonna see this."

George stepped in first, followed by Laura Beth and Juliet. Tommy remained with Percy away from the barn's shadow, saying he didn't want to go inside. Sunlight floated through the boards and played with George's eyes, casting shadows that seemed to move. He felt Juliet's hand at his elbow and inched forward over the dirt floor toward the back, where Bobby said the thing appeared. Laura Beth's breathing came quick and short, reminding George of building excitement. That breathing stopped when the three of them came upon it.

A crack. That's what Bobby had said. A crack in the Turn. But what George saw was more than that.

It looked as though the air itself had been flayed open. Like some great hand had picked at the thin scab over the world to reveal the meat underneath. Hanging there, suspended in the air, a long and jagged line that began at what George judged a meter from the barn's floor and stretched almost to the rafters. Thirty feet at least, and as wide as him and Juliet together.

A *wound*.

That was the phrase his mind settled upon. A wound in

the Turn. Light poured from the center, so white it looked a pale blue and so shining that only Laura Beth could look at it. The light gathered in each lens of her sunglasses, making her eyes look like a cat's. George looked back, squinting. At the edges, strips of black darker than night ran in lines marking the light's reach. Angling up, out, down, in, and in directions George believed impossible, ways that could be described in no words of any language. He felt his very mind twist under the strain of that sight: something neither wholly evil nor wholly good, but alive, and of no world he knew.

"I have to go," Juliet said. "I can't . . ."

She ran before George could speak, stumbling over the hidden things strewn over the floor as she ran and tried not to run. George looked back at the glowing mass, wincing. He knew he should circle it, get a better view. Reach for his pen and notebook. But it—that wound, that *tear*—was too horrible to study and too overwhelming to consider. His head began to swim. His hands tingled. George realized he had forgotten to breathe.

"It's different."

He turned. Tommy had crept inside and taken a spot just inside the door. The light cast a beam that encircled him.

"What's different?" George asked.

"That thing. It's bigger. Bigger than before."

"You're sure?"

Tommy said yes. George backed off, awe giving way to fear. He took Laura Beth by the arm to lead her away. She wouldn't move. Her glasses kept the glow of that light and the darkness surrounding it. George believed it a terrible sight, though it didn't chill him nearly as much as the smile on her face.

"Isn't it beautiful?" she whispered. "I hope it kills us all."

Bobby told the boys what he could and why he had left them behind, but forgiveness would be a long time coming. For the first time, they felt like strangers. Worse, he knew they'd come to feel the same way about him.

The twins could do much in the world they had left that first night on the mountain. They could comfort Bobby and guide him and give him some faint reminder of the family that had once been his, could protect him from the madness of being alone. Yet the three of them had come to understand separately that in the Turn, their protection meant less. It had been slower for Matthew than for Mark, who had always been sharper of mind and more aware. Bobby had discovered it last. The comfort his sons provided here never reached the level of Juliet's or Tommy's. They were the ones who brought Bobby joy and purpose now, the ones to whom he'd turned. And though he had never meant for that to happen, Bobby knew it could be no other way. There was no going back to the way things had been. He had tried after Dorothea's banishment, had *wanted* it, but in the end Bobby had discovered that flesh was sometimes more valued than spirit, and that the real was more precious than the imagined.

He drank, both out of fear and to keep the boys close, even if Matthew would only look at his cartoons and Mark would only stare out the window. Neither had spoken since he'd returned. He couldn't bear to look upon the crack in the world again. Tommy could show them. He had been the one who found it.

"You lied," Mark said. He wouldn't turn from the window. "You said you took Tommy there, when it was the other way 'round. Why'd you do that, Daddy?"

"How you know I lied about that?"

"Just 'cause you can't see us don't mean we can't see you. We still know."

Bobby took a drink. "Didn't want to get him in trouble. Tommy was scared enough as it was."

"You never cared about that before, people getting in trouble. Or even people. Take care of you first, that's what you taught us."

Bobby said, "Guess I did say that, once ago."

"You love him?"

"Maybe so."

"You love Juliet?"

A pause. "Yes."

"Do you love us?" Matthew asked. He didn't look at Bobby, only the TV.

"I do. More than anything."

"I think you're lyin'," Matthew said. "You don't love us no more."

Mark turned from the window. "Come on, let's go out back and play." He pulled Matthew up from the floor and looked at Bobby. "It's okay, Daddy. You got to be brave now."

Bobby watched them leave through the shop. Matthew hung his head. Mark's hand went around Matthew's shoulders. It was not the first time Bobby considered what they were, conjurings of his mind. But it was the first time that he understood that he had used his sons in the same way he had used everyone in his life, and had hurt them just as bad.

He turned at the knock on the door. Juliet stood outside in the sun, peering in. Her mouth curled downward in a look of pain balanced by her warm eyes. Bobby kicked the footrest down and went to the door, opening it. Juliet didn't step inside.

"Sorry," she said. "I didn't mean to come here. Just kind of . . . did."

"Come on." Bobby held the door wider. He thought of Mark standing by the window, how he'd said to be brave. "I won't mind the company."

He stepped aside. The way Juliet walked in, slow and awkward, made Bobby wonder if she wanted to be there at all. She didn't sit when offered and wouldn't accept a beer. She stood near the wall by the telephone with her arms tight at her sides, as if afraid to touch anything.

"Did you see it?" he asked.

"Yes. What of it I could bear. I've never seen George so taken aback. Tommy didn't even want to go in. I've never been in that barn and I don't think I've ever really paid attention to it before today, but you're right. It isn't supposed to be here. That crack. What's it mean?"

"I don't know."

"It scared you," she said.

"Didn't it you?"

Juliet lowered her eyes. "I've always believed we had time, Bobby. All the time we needed. But seeing that made me realize maybe we don't. Maybe time's running out."

"I don't know if it's running out, but I know it's changing. George says there's a river the universe is on, and we're all stuck in a slow place. Or something."

"George does say that." She smiled.

Bobby moved toward her in a graceless dance of steps and pauses. Wanting to be near her. Needing it. "You think that's right?"

"I should go. They're probably waiting."

"I missed you. More than I knew." He wanted to reach for her, brush her arm and caress her face, yet he wouldn't. Not until he told her everything about the barn, and not until he knew that touching her was what she wanted. "Miss me?"

"We all do. Even Dorothea, though she's too proud to admit it."

"I didn't ask about Dorothea."

Juliet's hands moved from her sides. Not to him, but across her chest—an X made of flesh and bone, warning him to come no farther.

"Things are different now," she said. "I need time, Bobby."

"You just said time might be running out. Is it because I've been gone? I couldn't try and talk to you, Juliet. Not after what happened to Jake. I couldn't let that be you. Lord or no, somebody sees what happens here."

He waited for her answer. Juliet only stared at him. Bobby saw want in her eyes and something he couldn't comprehend.

"I should go," she said again, though she didn't move. "I'm sorry about Laura Beth. It wasn't that any of us were keeping that from you. It all just got so *big*. We thought we could wait until things were right. But something like that, there's never a right moment. When you told me what happens to you each night, I couldn't handle it. But I had to put it aside because you were hurting and I hurt for you. That was the first time your walls came down, Bobby. You let me in. I wanted to give you hope, and I thought letting you know about Laura Beth would help. It would show you that you're not the only one who hurts here. That's why George showed you where Tommy's mom dies. All of us, Bobby. We all hurt. Maybe not like Laura Beth, because that's different and worse and—" Her voice broke. "I don't know."

She kept her arms where they were and Bobby where he stood.

"What about you?" he asked. "How do you hurt?"

Juliet shook her head. She moved away from the wall and away from him, toward the door.

"Stay with me," he said. "Please?" He went not for her but for the handle on the door, pulling it closed as hard as he could. Frantic, wanting her to understand. "I need help."

"I can't."

"The thing in the barn. I wasn't lying when I said I don't know what it means. I don't know about that light, but I know about the black. The black around it, leaking through. I see that black every night, Juliet. That's the black I see after the crash. That's the black between the worlds, where the monsters are. And now it's here, too. It's here for us."

# -18-

She woke with her head down and Bobby's words echoing in her ears, his voice charged with exultation, saying again over the sound of truck and wind that he was sorry and would see her early the next Turn. Before she could say no, her eyes had shut and opened again.

The room was quiet, warmed by the morning sun through the window. Juliet lifted her head from the piles of paper on her desk—overdue bills and a tally of worshippers and tithes from a long-forgotten Sunday, an anonymous note decrying the sorry state of the flower beds out front. And her notes, three pages of handwritten scrawl, long paragraphs and underlined phrases, lying next to her Bible, opened to the book of James, chapter 3, verse 1. It would have been a fine sermon, maybe her best. Certainly her last.

She leaned back in the chair and rubbed her head to get the sound of Bobby away, looked around at the bare office.

The desk, two chairs, a bookcase filled with tomes of college texts and commentaries that had gone utterly unread until recently, pictures of college friends who had drifted away where those of family were meant to go. If that tiny space behind the sanctuary contained an abundance of anything, it was dust. Juliet never spent much time here while alive, and certainly not in her death. This was only where she woke, where she could look upon the meager bounty of her old life. The church was her tomb. Not where Juliet had died, but surely where she had rotted.

Down the street, the clock tower tolled eight. She always left at those bells, home to change and freshen before heading to Dorothea's. Anywhere but downtown. Yet that was the direction Bobby wanted her to go that morning. A surprise, he'd told her on the phone at the end of the last Turn just before he murdered. Juliet was done with surprises, but Bobby brushed those words off because he couldn't understand. She'd told him George would need to talk about the barn. Bobby said as important as that was, it could wait a few hours. And when Juliet had said Mama would wonder where she was and could even send Junior looking for her, Bobby answered that didn't matter because he'd have her back by dinner. His answers were arrows he pulled and loosed, shooting down Juliet's every objection. Then he'd told her again of the black leaking from the center of that wound in the world, and how he'd seen that black before and would again. He needed to talk, he said. He needed help. And though Juliet loved him and hated him and wanted Bobby away, she had said yes because that was her duty.

The verse stared up at her. She'd highlighted those words in some long-past time, a yellow that ghosted through to the next page. And just as Juliet had done ever since God—the real God—had revealed her purpose, she balled her notes and tossed them into the plastic trash can in the corner.

\* \* \*

Those she greeted on the sidewalk were polite but aloof. There were no more courteous people than those of the South, many of whom lived by rain and sun and plow and whose possessions were few but cherished. Life here was hard. She'd been warned of that—the people were proud and their lives hard, and they would show kindness but never acceptance. Juliet Creech was a woman preacher and she was from Away.

That had been the beginning. The Turn had been the end.

Her pace was slower than usual, feet already hurting. She never should have gone back to the shop. Juliet knew that now as much as she had then. She should have stayed at the barn with Tommy and George and Laura Beth. But that . . . thing, that *tear*, had repulsed her. It had been too horrible to look at and too beautiful to draw her eyes away, and what Juliet had seen was their end.

Bobby waited at his truck, dressed in a clean pair of jeans and a denim shirt tucked in at the waist. His beard had been trimmed and his hat was gone, showing hair wet and freshly combed. He saw her and waved, making more than a few people nearby turn their heads in question. Dorothea called Bobby a selfish man and said those he had been drawn to in life had suffered for it. Some people were poison, a rock upon which others broke. Juliet had once thought that wrong. Now she knew Bobby had already hurt her and would no doubt hurt her again.

"Mornin'," he called.

Juliet crossed the street. She couldn't help but grin as she pointed to his clothes. "What's this?" she asked. "You taking me to church?"

"Might. Least the only one I know."

There was only a faint smell of beer. His hands shook as he took them out of his pockets and took Juliet's elbow, showed her to his truck.

"Thought I'd take you on a picnic," he said. "Got one stop first."

"Where?"

"Diner. Can't picnic without food. Crackers and jerky don't qualify."

"The diner?" She stopped and pulled her arm away. "No, let's not go there, Bobby."

"Don't worry about Junior or anyone seeing. I expect after yesterday, Dorothea's got more to worry about than us spending time together."

"It's not that. I just . . ." *What am I doing?* "I go there. Or I did. Like you going to Timmy's and seeing Jake, I go to the diner. I haven't been in a long time, and that's how I'd like to keep it."

"Fine. But I'm hungry and I know you are, too, so you can sit in the truck. Should be okay, right?"

She shook her head, wanting to say more. Bobby cut her off. He scratched his hairy chin with another shaking finger and spoke in a voice far from the exalted one of the last Turn, just before he met the black again. "Trying not to drink this morning, Juliet. Okay? I gotta eat something. I eat, my mouth'll be too full to want to drink. I want this to be a good thing. I want to talk to you and be with you with my whole self."

"I can't go in."

Bobby's cheeks dimpled. "Well all right then." He slapped the hood of the truck. "You just stay right in here."

He opened her door like a proper gentleman, then climbed into the driver's seat. The diner stood only a couple blocks down, facing the square. Bobby parked out front and said he'd be right back. Juliet leaned forward to look through the diner's long window, spying the old woman with the curly white hair who had just gotten up from her table. *She's going to see. I don't know how but she will. She'll see me and she'll say the words and I'll say no but I'll do it anyway, and I won't have a choice in what happens.*

The air inside the truck smelled like Bobby's shop and like Bobby, like the stale and bitter dregs at the bottom of a beer can. Juliet saw the woman paying. Bobby stood behind her, tapping his leg. Juliet pulled on the handle and eased out, deciding to hide in the square until Bobby returned.

She hadn't taken two steps into the street when she heard, "Pastor, oh, Pastor."

She shut her eyes. "Hello, Marjorie. Good to see you this morning."

The woman—Marjorie Duncan, eighty-five years old, near deaf and blind and infirm to the point where even Doc March marveled at her continued existence, stepped forward. Her white hair puffed in the breeze like a fallen cloud.

"Did I see you getting out of Bobby Barnes's truck? Lord, tell me that ain't so."

"No, ma'am," Juliet said.

"That man is a craven, Pastor. Had to stand in front of him in the diner just now. Near took my breath away. You can *feel* the devil in'm."

"I'm afraid I'm not that well acquainted."

"A molester's what he is," Marjorie stated. Her jaw was set, eyes narrowed. "A fiddler of children and a selfish man.

Do not cast your pearls before such swine, Pastor. There's no redeeming him."

"I won't."

The old woman brightened, satisfied. Or perhaps over-joyed at the bit of gossip Juliet knew she'd just stumbled upon—their preacher cavorting with a devil-worshipping sex criminal.

"You've heard Nolan has taken ill?"

Juliet took a deep breath. "I have."

"He's near to the Lord. I hear it's a matter of days now. A shame, the way he left the church. Took all those people with him."

"It was."

(*You should go see him, dear. A good preacher mends fences . . .*)

"You should go see him, dear. A good preacher mends fences. There's no saving Nolan for this world. But if you settle with him and admit to change, he may spend his last breaths giving you his forgiveness and swelling your pews again. That church has been my home . . .

(*since I was knee-high to a*)

". . . grasshopper, and I tire of sitting there mostly all alone every Sunday. Got tore up in the tornado and we rebuilt it with our own sweat and tears. I'd never abide by seeing you . . .

(*fail*)

". . . so you go to him. Tell him you'll be better and you're sorry. He lives in Camden. Do you know where that is?"

Juliet looked up to see Bobby standing at the curb. He held a paper bag in one hand and had a funny look on his face.

"I know where it is," she said.

"Marbury Street. The big house. You go," Marjorie said. "Go tonight. Promise?"

"I will."

Marjorie nodded and turned—two separate actions, the dexterity required to do them both together had long passed—and eased on down the sidewalk. Juliet looked up at Bobby.

"You ready?" he asked.

"More than you know."

＊ ＊ ＊

"You know they say this place is haunted?"

Juliet watched Bobby bite down on the egg sandwich he'd brought from the diner. Her own lay untouched, still in the wrapper. A crumb had lodged in the part of his beard just below the bruise. It made him somehow more handsome.

"Whole place is," he continued. "But the water mostly."

Boone's Pond looked to Juliet more like a small lake. She'd always hated the water, couldn't swim. Sank like a rock. But she'd said nothing when Bobby led her to the end of the rotting pier that jutted a third of the way into water that wasn't the brown she'd suspected, but a deep and terrible blue.

"They say pond's got no bottom and there's things down there. Ghosts of those the water's swallowed." He took another bite and chewed. "Been plenty of those. Ain't you hungry?"

"Not really," she said. "Guess I had my appetite ruined back at the diner. Should save room for dinner. Dorothea'll get suspicious if she doesn't see me eating."

"What was that about, anyway? Marjorie Duncan." He shook his head. "Seem to recall she was always pretty high up in your church."

She looked out over the water. "Junior likes to come here."

"Not anymore. Told me once he gave it up because the fish here taste spoiled. Said it's from the ghosts."

"You believe that?"

"Fish? No. Ghosts?" Bobby shrugged and took another bite. "Never seen any myself, but I know people who have. Whole town's supposed to be haunted. There's a place up the mountain, Crow Holler? They say the devil's come there. Say the people's trying to beat him back, but it ain't easy. Not even Jake'll go. People up there tell us to keep out, and we do."

"I haven't heard that."

"Don't know why."

"Why'd you bring me up here, Bobby?"

"Wanted to spend time with you. Talk."

"About what?"

"Leaving. George thinks there's a way out of here. Told me so right before Jake died."

"George is wrong," she said.

"How you know that?"

Juliet opened the wrapper and picked at the sandwich. She tossed a bit into the water, where it floated until it was gobbled. By fish or ghost, she didn't know. "He's told me the same. Time's a river and we're in a slow part. I remember taking a physics class in college. All of it went completely over my head. But I remember a few lectures the professor did about quantum theory and all that. About time. I loved it. Didn't understand it, but I loved it." She smiled. "Sort of like how I am with God, I guess. Anyway, that river analogy George uses is about thirty years old. Lot's changed since then. Science always does. Guess that's what drew me to being a preacher. God doesn't change, you deepen."

"Ain't got much use for religion." Bobby balled up his

wrapper and shoved it into the bag. He looked out to the far shore where the trees rose in a long line toward the mountains. "Guess Dorothea and the rest told you that when I first come here."

She curled her legs in and wrapped her arms around her knees. "Can I tell you something?"

"Sure."

"I hate this place. I'm not talking about the Turn. I hate that, too, but it's not what I mean. I mean Mattingly. The mountains. Life in the sticks. Lot of churches, the preachers start there young and full of life and keep going until they're dead. They help raise up families and generations. Churches like mine, the higher-ups like to move preachers around. That's what happened to me. Right out of seminary. I thought I could do good work here. But I came, and I hated it."

"Why?"

"Nobody wants a woman preacher. Marjorie was talking about Nolan Reynolds. You know him?"

Bobby nodded.

"Head of the deacons. An elder. Or at least he was. We never got along. He ended up saying I should step down and I told him no, it was my flock and I wasn't going to abandon it. Well, he was the one who ended up stepping down. Left altogether and took most of the congregation with him. The Sunday before I came here, you know what the attendance was? Twelve. Twelve people in that big old church. Wasn't even enough to take up two pews. And the thing is, I can't blame him. Nolan. Wasn't right for him to ask me to step down because I don't have the right plumbing, but it was right for other reasons. I've never lost my faith, Bobby, but I was close then. The harder I tried to make things work, the less the Lord did to help me."

"I can sympathize," Bobby said.

"So I finally decided I was done. I sat down this Saturday morning, that first one, I guess, and started writing out my sermon for my twelve faithful followers of the Lord. Even had a verse: 'Let not many of you become teachers, my brethren, knowing that as such we will incur a stricter judgment.' Book of James, if you don't know. Because I was quitting. I was going to stand right there and quit in front of everyone, and then I was going to leave. Run away somewhere. And I guess that's what happened, because I came here to the Turn. That's why I didn't want to go to the diner. I knew Marjorie would be there, and I knew she would ask me to go see Nolan. That was all part of my first Turn, way back whenever."

"Nolan lives in Camden," Bobby said.

"He does."

"You ever go see him?"

"No. Tried, but I never knew the way and always got lost. It doesn't matter. My congregation might be smaller now, six now instead of twelve. You and Dorothea and Junior, George and Laura Beth and Tommy. But for the first time in my life, I feel like a pastor."

"Took you dyin' for God to give you what you never had."

She smiled. "Dorothea says this is heaven. George says it's some backwater in time's river. It's not either. It's more."

Bobby plunged his hand into the water and drew it up slowly, watching it spill through his fingers. "Now, Juliet, I brought you out here to have some alone time, and here I get a sales pitch."

"I offer nothing of the kind."

"Good, because it won't work. You say you almost lost your faith. I did lose mine, and I had more than a piece of paper from some fancy college. I had experience. Used to go

on mission trips. Dorothea tell you that? Used to go everywhere, take Carla with me. Good soldiers going off in service
of the risen Savior. Used to go wherever something bad happened, you know? Went down to Louisiana after Katrina hit.
Carla, she didn't go then 'cause we had the boys and they were
only little, too little for any of that. I seen a lot of bad in my life,
Juliet, but I ain't never seen nothing like that. All them dead
people, starving people, their whole world washed away. Seen
little kids all bloated up and stiff, seen gators and snakes eating
bodies like they was snacking on bait. It was too much . . ."

He trailed off, watching the water. "Changed me, Juliet.
Something like that would change anybody. I left a soldier in
the army of the Lord, but I came back someone who didn't
want a thing to do with a God who'd allow something like
that. Ended up costing me everything. Carla left me. We had
two boys, twins. That hurt the most, them leaving. Then
they both died. That day in the shop, right before I told you
what I do every night up on the mountain? You asked if what
was wrong had something to do with the things I see. They're
the things I see, Juliet. My dead boys. See them when I drink.
I only had a little bit this morning when I was getting ready,
just enough to let me tell them where I was going and who
I was going with. They're both waiting back at the shop, or
somewhere in my head."

She turned away and rubbed a cheek, not wanting him
to see. "Bobby Barnes, that's just about the saddest thing I've
ever heard."

"Ain't sad. It's interest on a payment I made every day
since. Wouldn't have lost my boys if I'd've been there, if Carla
had still been with me. I really did think this was heaven for
a while, Juliet. But it ain't. It's a punishment for my sins. And
that's why I got to leave, because I paid for them all already."

"This place isn't punishment," she said. "It's a chance."

He snorted, she knew he would. But he said nothing and only looked at her, watching for what she would say.

"Dorothea calls this heaven, Laura Beth a hell. George thinks it's something out of his science books. We all try to make what's happened fit our view of life."

"What about you?"

"I'm a preacher. Never thought I was, but I am. You remember the story of Jonah. God tells Jonah go to Nineveh, Jonah says no. Runs off and gets on a ship bound for the end of the world. Then a storm comes, and Jonah gets swallowed by a whale. That's us. You. Me. The rest of the family. You call that a punishment. I guess Jonah thought so, too. But it wasn't. Jonah changed in the belly of that whale. His whole life stopped for three days, and that gave him time to figure out who he was. God was saving him, Bobby. God snatched him before the storm could take his life. I think that's what He's done with us. I think He knew a storm was coming, and He wanted to give us a chance to survive it."

She waited for him to say something. Make a joke. Toss her off the pier. But Bobby didn't. He didn't even move.

"How were we before we all got here, Bobby? George had been forced to retire. Dorothea's husband was gone. Junior took up with drugs. Tommy's mom killed herself. I'd lost my way and most of my faith. You'd lost almost everything. And I don't even want to talk about Laura Beth. We'd all reached the end. None of us were dead, but we might as well have been. What sort of future awaits people like that? What troubles and sorrows? We're here to fix that. To . . . I don't know . . . change. George can find all the ways he wants to get us out of here, but the only way we will is if we learn that. The Turn is a mirror, Bobby. It strips away everything but who we are deep down, and it leaves us naked and makes us look upon ourselves. That's the only way we can change."

Bobby smirked. "Guess I'm stuck, then. I gotta listen to my heart, and my heart says only thing worth believing in's me."

Now Juliet snorted. She rocked on her backside and flitted a hand out, striking him on the arm. "Listen to your heart?" she said, mocking him. "I've learned a lot living the same day over and over. I know what works and what doesn't, all my truths and lies. I never figured out how to live until I died, Bobby, and the one thing I know is never *listen* to your heart. *Talk* to it."

He went quiet. "I heard what Marjorie said about me."

"I know it's not true."

"Part of it is. I'm a drunk and I'm selfish, but there's reasons for both. Spent so long looking after myself, I don't know no other way. That why you turned away from me, Juliet?"

"I never turned away from you. I guess after you told me what happens to you, what you're going to do tonight, I just needed some time."

"And now?"

She shrugged. It was a sad slump of her shoulders, the kind Juliet knew meant she didn't know at all. "I know you're not selfish. You told Dorothea you found what's in the barn. You didn't. Tommy did. You didn't go to him, Bobby. He came to you. And the only reason you said otherwise was to protect him."

"Don't tell Dorothea."

"I have to." She smiled. "Dorothea and me being so close and all."

He snorted and slapped her arm. She slapped him back. He took her arms and she wriggled free, laughing and trying to push him away, and even as her mind screamed, Juliet let herself go. Their kiss was long and soft and everything she had once hoped it would be. Her heart sang. Juliet only listened and never talked.

\* \* \*

He would have stayed that whole Turn if Juliet would have allowed it, but there was only so much she could endure. Everything was too perfect. They were on a sliver of warped boards in the middle of water that might or might not be both bottomless and haunted and it was too perfect. The sun hot on their shoulders and the breeze smelling of wet leaves and pine, the birds calling and the sound of ripples striking the wood. Bobby kissing her, touching her. He was sorry, he said again. Juliet didn't know if that apology was meant for touching her or for what he was about to do on the mountain in only a few hours more, for when he'd shown up at Mama's drunk to confront her about Laura Beth or the things that happened in between. Maybe his apology was meant for all of those things. Juliet knew those words began in Bobby's own heart, just as she knew him a broken man trying to heal. And she would help him, but not there.

They left midafternoon, long after dinner. Mama would be worried and so would Tommy, but there could be no fixing that. Juliet had spent the first part of that Turn exactly where she was supposed to be, and that was enough to endure whatever feelings she battled now and whatever battle might wait with Mama later on. Bobby drove in silence. His body shook from the beer he had not drunk, but his expression looked serene, pondering. Once he reached his hand onto the seat between them, fingers creeping in slow inches. By the time they'd reached Mattingly, his hand held hers.

The tiny house served as the church parsonage and was tucked inside a group of aging trees at the end of a long lane just outside town. Bobby didn't invite himself inside; Juliet didn't ask. It would only make things harder later on. He blushed and said he'd never kissed a preacher before, then waved as he pulled away.

The truck hadn't even made it to the road when Juliet turned her phone back on. There were three messages, all from Dorothea. Juliet sat in a rocker on her narrow porch and dialed the number. The line didn't even ring once.

"Juliet? You worried me something awful."

"I'm sorry, Mama. Just needed a little time to myself. I should've called."

"Everybody's been asking about you."

"Tell them I'm fine," she said. "Though don't expect me for supper."

The line went quiet. "What's troubling you, dear?"

"Nothing. Bobby. Everyone and everything. What I saw yesterday in the barn. I suppose George has done his best to talk to you about it."

"And I've done my best to ignore him," Dorothea said. "I couldn't stop you from going down there, Juliet. Now you see why that was my aim. It's none of our concern what's down there, and now it's gotten into your heart. Just as Bobby has. You been alone all this Turn?"

"I have."

"You wouldn't lie to me, Juliet."

"The Lord's watching," she said, barely able to speak the words. "I saw Marjorie today."

Another silence. "I'm sorry, dear. I know that pains. You go on and keep yourself there. But you'll come by next Turn?"

"I will. Thank you, Mama."

"And, Juliet?"

"Yes?"

"Bring Bobby."

The line cut off before Juliet could answer. Juliet tossed the phone onto the small table next to the chair and looked out down the lane, a strip of dirt and rock between her yard and a fenced pasture of sheep. The sun had begun its slow arc downward. Shadows of the trees reached the tips of her shoes. She waited there until darkness took hold, rocking as she prayed and pondered and simply sat as the world fell asleep. Then she went inside long enough to find her keys and began the drive to Camden.

She wondered if anything Bobby had said that day had been a lie, bold or small. So much had passed between them, things Juliet had told no one before and hadn't planned to tell him. The gravel road yielded to pavement and town and then openness beyond. Camden lay fifteen miles on. Juliet had been in Mattingly only a few years before the Turn found her. She had visited parishioners in the hills and in Mattingly and even Stanley, but never Camden. Marjorie would have been glad to offer her directions, but Juliet had always thought the GPS on her phone would serve better than a route scrawled in an old hand upon a napkin from the diner. Of course, GPS only worked where a satellite could reach. Juliet would have known that if she weren't from Away, would've realized all that made this backwater hole was trees upon trees and narrow roads that climbed and dipped but never lay straight. She had made this drive every night since and gotten lost each time. Never finding Nolan Reynolds had been the end of her Turn.

She didn't want to call. Juliet knew she had promised, but a promise in the bright of day with Bobby smiling at her was easy to make but harder to keep now, when everything lay dark and lonely. She waited until the last moment before picking up the phone (*Searching for satellite,* the screen said) and dialing Bobby's number, more out of duty than want. He picked up in the middle of a laugh.

"I was just staring at my phone," he said. "Thought you wouldn't call."

"You could've called me."

"No. Don't want to bother."

"It's not a bother, Bobby."

"Maybe. I know things between us aren't quite what they used to be yet. Better in some ways, but not all the way. I've been thinking about what you told me today. About seeing myself. Changing. I have a lot to change, Juliet."

"We all do."

"Not like me. The changing I'd have to make, it's something won't get done on my own."

She gripped the wheel. Lost again. Lost forever. Juliet slowed to the road's shoulder and turned the car around. Giving up. Going back home. Was this the way it would always be? "You won't have to do it alone."

"Good. Juliet?"

*He's going to say he loves me now. He's going to say it, and I'll die inside.*

"Yes?"

Bobby cleared his throat. "I guess I should go. Will I see you the next Turn?"

"Mama called after you dropped me off. She wants you to come by. I think she's ready to have you back, Bobby. With everything that's going on, you should at least try."

"I will. Good-bye."

"Good-bye, Bobby."

Juliet shut her eyes and set the phone down, moving the

gearshift from reverse to drive and letting out on the clutch. *He didn't say he loved me.* That was both better and worse. *He didn't, but I would have. God help me, I would have.* Her car moved toward the other lane and lurched. Flooded. She pushed the clutch in and started the engine, easing the car toward the opposite lane just as the headlights appeared around the curve. Big truck, moving fast. Juliet shut her eyes. Unlike the man who killed her every night, that would be the only dark she saw.

## -19-

The yard rested quiet that early Turn, the chairs beneath the willow unoccupied and the wide swath of grass empty. It wouldn't be that way long. They'd all arrive soon. Tommy and the rest and even Bobby, if Juliet could convince him, and Dorothea knew she would. She had seen the looks between them, the sort she and Hubie once exchanged.

On the table beside her cup of tea sat the day's letter, short and to the point. The Lord did love His brevity. But those few words had been enough to frighten Dorothea of the coming battle she wasn't sure if she was strong enough to fight:

Everyone is scared. You must be brave. I will be with you.

She didn't have to be told everyone was afraid. Dorothea was not the idiot God sometimes took her to be. She had seen the worry on her family's faces, felt her own horror. That thing in Moser's barn. It was something beyond all thinking and faith. Something Other.

And the Lord hadn't told her. If the wound (the word

George had used and the word Dorothea had thought of when she'd seen that picture) had been there all this while, the Lord would have told her.

The front door opened and shut. She heard Tommy's footsteps and folded the letter, tucking it inside the envelope. Tommy came out carrying a bag of cat food and half a gallon of milk and set them on the table.

"That for George's?"

He bobbed his head. "George wanted me to come straight-away 'cause he starts his Turn early just like me, but I waited. I wanted to come here first. Tell you I'm sorry."

"For what?"

"For everything, I guess."

She slid her cup over and let him take a sip.

"Things don't feel right, Mama. You need to go down to the barn and see."

"I won't. I know what's there."

"Really?" He set the cup down. "What is it? George thinks the Turn's sick."

"Not the Turn that's sick, Tommy. Us." She tapped a finger on the envelope. "Know what the Lord told me today? Said I have to be brave. I have to be brave, because everybody's scared. Are you scared?"

"No," he said. "Not so long's I got you and everybody else."

"Amen. The Lord has told me often heaven was made for us to enjoy together. To be as one. A family. And we were just that for a long while, weren't we? When it was just you and me and Junior and even after, when Juliet and George arrived. Then Laura Beth came and all that horror with her. In some ways, finding Laura Beth was even harder than finding out about your old mama. Because it meant the older things hadn't been left behind. They can follow us."

245

"Like your fingers," he said.

She smiled. "Yes. Like my fingers. Our family became less when that woman arrived. I don't blame Laura Beth for that. She can't help what happens to her and can't do a thing about it. But she cracked the bonds between us, Tommy. Got some of us doubting. I wanted Bobby to be the one to bring us all back together. I thought the Lord had a plan. Now Bobby's ended up being the one to tear us apart. First he passed judgment on us, and now he's brought news of our great test."

"Bobby didn't mean nothing bad. He just wanted to show you what he found."

"And it was the Lord's will that he did. That wound, what's in that old barn, it's not the Turn failing. Heaven can't be *sick*, Tommy. That's only George's lack of belief talking, and that's what we can't have, especially now. The Lord is testing our faith. Warning us."

"About what?"

"About falling away. The old world was once a heaven. One day it will be a heaven again. But Adam and Eve spoiled heaven through their own selfish desires. They were cast out. I believe the Lord is saying the same could happen to us if we're not careful. I won't allow that. We have to be strong, and we have to be *together*." She sipped. "I spoke with Juliet last Turn with the hopes that Bobby will come back to us."

Tommy's eyes lit. "Really?"

"It's time we put our quarreling aside. Families can disagree, doesn't mean they have to be apart. But now I want you to be honest with me. Can you do that?"

"Yes'm."

"I need to know his secrets. Bobby loves you. When people love each other, they say things they wouldn't to anybody else. I'd never tell, Tommy. I just need to know so that I understand him. Hearing a man's secrets is the best way."

Tommy looked down at the food and milk in front of him. Dorothea realized she hadn't asked from where all that had come, whether he'd found money enough in all that squalor he'd once lived in or if he'd stolen it from the grocery. That didn't concern her now. She needed other truths.

"Tommy? You know I love you. I would never do anything to betray a trust."

"He kills somebody."

She leaned forward, thinking she'd misheard. "He what?"

"Bobby takes a drive on the mountain and he kills somebody. I heard him tell Juliet. And those people he talks to that I can't see, it's his boys. They're dead. He talks to his dead boys and kills somebody on the mountain, and he starts his Turn in the alley out back of his shop. That's all I know, Mama. Promise. Can I please go?"

Dorothea nodded, not able to speak. Tommy grabbed his groceries and left without even kissing her cheek. Too ashamed, she suspected. He had always been a good boy when it came to reporting the goings-on of the others. It had been different with Bobby, who had somehow become a father in Tommy's eyes.

"I forgive you, Tommy," she called, though the front door shut before Tommy could hear it.

So that was it then, Bobby's secret. Dorothea had suspected it was his boys that Bobby's mind had gone twisted enough to see. Matthew and Mark. She remembered them. Sweet and innocent. But Bobby killing someone? That came as a surprise, though not wholly. Everybody in Mattingly held an opinion of when and where Bobby Barnes would run someone off the road and into a grave. Dorothea could use such information.

Oh, yes, she could use it well.

She finished the last of her cup and rose to go inside and wait for Laura Beth to bring the makings for dinner. Perhaps things weren't so lost after all. She could make Bobby see. Make him understand.

Her hand was on the knob of the back door when the sound came. Low and soft and from somewhere distant. Dorothea spun around, listening. Not a truck sound, not Junior or Bobby or George. Not machinery or the clock tower in town. Thunder. *Thunder.*

She peered up to the cloudless sky and the sun hovering over the east. The sound came again, a slow rumbling that ended as soon as it had begun. Dorothea dropped her teacup and saucer. They shattered into a hundred tiny pieces as she stumbled to the edge of the porch. Looking up and over and out, craning her neck. Hollering for Tommy and for anyone, screaming, begging the Lord's forgiveness.

# -20-

It was the first time Bobby woke without casting his eyes to a draining night sky. He kept them closed instead as Mr. Jangles crept up and over without regard for the man he used as a mat and with no concern that in a life marked by hard days, this would surely be that man's hardest.

A notion occurred to him inside the blackness of his own eyelids: he could pray. No one would know. Not Juliet, not Dorothea (whom Bobby thought would be exceedingly glad that he had found the fault in his former ways and turned to the One who had saved them all). But of course Bobby would know and so would the Lord, and it was the Lord who had

sent him to this terrible place and arranged things such that
Bobby had been forced to do the one thing he did best other
than crawl under the hood of a car—hurt those who loved
him most.

He stood, knocking beer cans farther into the alley, and
reached for his cap before pushing on the wood door. He took
the phone off the hook and turned off his cell, not wanting
the distraction. Nor did Bobby visit the bathroom. He had
done enough gazing into the mirror the Turn before, both
with Juliet at the pond and then on the ride to the mountains
that night. He needed no polished glass to know his ugliness.

The bottle went first and then six of the beers, which
curdled his stomach and brought an ache to his head that
matched the one in his chest. He dreaded the sound of the
alley door opening, the quick steps of tiny, racing feet. The
laughter. Yet when the boys came, it was in just that way, and
though Bobby mourned it, he found himself happy to hear it
one last time.

Mark bounded in first, Matthew at his heels. Both smiled
as they held out their arms to their father's embrace. Bobby
remained at his spot behind the counter. Mark's grin faded
only a bit. When it returned, Bobby suspected it was more
for Matthew's benefit than Mark's own.

Matthew stopped midway between the door and the counter, still with his arms out. He eased them down. "Something
wrong, Daddy?"

"I guess some."

Mark remained by the door. He blinked, flashing those
blue eyes. His face carried a knowing that was part sadness
and part relief—the look of one who had always dreamed of
an end to his long journey and, now that it had been found,
wished to keep journeying awhile longer.

"Y'all come on over here," Bobby said. "Let's sit down a minute."

He went to the recliner and kicked up the footrest as they settled in, nuzzling the hollows where his shoulders and chest met.

"Love you, boys," he said. "Y'all know that? Love you more than the world."

Matthew: "Love you, too, Daddy."

"You two saved my life when you showed up to me. Don't think I ever told y'all that." He squeezed them both and felt nothing but his own bony ribs. "I was so happy, never thought to question how or why. Asking things like that, guess I was afraid it'd be enough to send you back away. So I just accepted it. On faith, you know? About the only faith I had left."

"You needed us," Mark said.

"Did. Would've done something horrible any other way. Drunk myself to death. Pulled my old truck in the shop maybe, stuck a hose from the pipe through the window. Gone to sleep. Sometimes I think that would've been best, me dyin'."

Matthew shook his head. "You'da gone to the bad place. Where the monsters are. You'd never see us again."

"But I'd never come here. That's one thing. Wouldn't have come to heaven and found it hell. Yet here I am and here y'all are and there's no getting around it. There's somebody here says they're God. Maybe that's so. I think whoever it is made that crack out in Moser's barn, and I think he'll do a whole lot worse than that before it's done. So I got to figure a way out of this, boys. I got to do all I can to get away from here before it's too late."

Mark asked, "What you gonna do, Daddy?"

"George says Turn's a slow place in a river we can't see. I

think he might be right. Juliet told me only way we crawl out and get going again's take a hard look and see the bad we done is because of the bad we are. I think she might be right, too."

"You'da never met that preacher if you never came here," Matthew said. "Ain't that right, Daddy?"

"Likely not. But I'd say she's my one bright spot, her and Tommy."

"Because you love'm."

"Yes," Bobby said. "Because I do."

"You love us."

"Yes. But now I think I got to love you from afar, Matthew. Mark. I seen myself with Juliet yesterday and on our ride. That's the best I can say it. I seen myself whole, not just in pieces. I gotta get away from here, kids. I stick around, I'll end up like Jake. Dorothea's God'll come get me, I know He will, and I won't even know it until it happens. Till it's too late. Don't know how it'll be if that happens, whether I'll just start out all over again here or if I'll be dead for real, and I can't take that chance. You try to keep to a slow spot in a river, sooner or later you'll tire and drown. Y'all don't want me to drown, do you?"

"Nosir," they said.

"Man's drowning slow, he'll do all he can to get out. Even if what he does is something that hurts. Something he don't want to do at all."

"What's that mean?" Matthew asked.

Bobby swallowed hard. "Y'all ain't real."

"You made us real," Mark said. "'Cause you needed us."

"I know. But now I gotta go, and so do y'all. Y'all know I took my first drink down in New Orleans? Never had a drink in my life before then. But it was a hard day and I seen too much bad, and so I took a drink. Fella I was with said it'd calm me. Said if I had enough, I wouldn't have my nightmares no more. And I didn't. Ain't a prayer in the world that chased them away, neither. And you know what I thought? I thought God sent me drink. So I drank more the day after and more the day after that, and then I started drinking all the time. Everything I lost in my life, I lost in a bottle. Your momma, y'all, my honor in town. Traded it all for a drink so I wouldn't have to hurt no more. That's what the mirror showed me last night. Turn's a mirror. Juliet told me that. So if I'm gonna get out of here the way Juliet says, I gotta put down the bottle. I can't drink no more."

Matthew's face went dark. "But then you won't see us."

"I know, son. But it's what I got to do."

Matthew raised his head, shaking it at his brother. "You can't, Daddy. Mark, tell him he can't. Tell'm it's selfish. You're *selfish*, Daddy. You're hateful and selfish, just like they all say." Matthew's eyes clouded with tears. "You can't kill me again after I already died. I like it here."

"I don't," Bobby said. "I don't like it here. Took me dying to want to live. That's why I got to do this."

Matthew struggled from the chair—*"I hate you"*—and stomped toward the shop. Mark went after him. He paused at the door and looked back.

"It's okay, Daddy," he said. "Matthew don't understand because he's the part of you that never will. But I do. I'm the part of you still livin'."

Bobby looked at him, eyes welling.

"Love you, Daddy. Be brave now. There's this world and the other, and others still."

He could hear Matthew's sobs from over near Bea's car, but Bobby didn't move. He couldn't go to them and say it would be all right, couldn't apologize like all the times before.

Because things wouldn't be all right now, not for them, and all the sorries in the world wouldn't change it. He felt thirsty and reached for the can on the little table by the chair, just as Bobby had done far more times than he'd been in heaven. The can reached his lips before he set it down again. He swallowed, throat dry, and stared at his boys. Bobby watched them for an hour before they began to fade. An hour more, they were gone. Mark held his brother as they both disappeared. He cast a final look into the waiting room and smiled just before winking out, and that was when the thunder rolled.

## -21-

The cough woke George every Turn at 5:53 a.m. The cat began its horrid speech eight minutes later.

He rose from bed and shut a bedroom window he always found open and proceeded to do the same with the others in the kitchen and the living room, then made his coffee. The television drowned out the birds, but never the cat. Even when George could no longer hear it, the cat kept on.

What he'd once kept for an office wasn't an office at all, but more a maze of papers and books in a corner of the living room that over the years had spread outward like a creeping fungus. Aside from his bed, that was the only part of the house still in use. The miscellany of a teacher's life lay piled atop a scratched oak desk in the corner at each Turn's start: old textbooks, binders stuffed with notes and lesson plans, yellowing papers from past students who had never bothered to collect them—reminders of what he once had been and what he was no more. It was a ritual of sorts to remove those stacks each Turn, the closest George had ever allowed himself to a religious act. In their place went his notebook and a picture of Anna, smiling toward the camera from a far-back time when the world had been ordered and sane and good.

He sat and leafed through pages that had been filled and erased and filled again with a pen that never ran out of ink, muting the television to the screech from the other side of the yard. Most Turns would yield him half a notebook of theories and suggestions, notes from books and Internet searches, memories, observations. Yet George found his pen quiet that morning, his mind cluttered. All he produced was a rendering of a shining wound growing bigger. He would find no answer for what had appeared in the barn, no explanation. And it was not merely its presence—that such a thing could be. It was also the feelings that looking upon it had birthed inside him: that sense of deepness. Of *transcendence*.

The word made him uncomfortable. He found he had written it and crossed it out once. Again. Then George emptied half of the ink left in the pen to ensure each letter and stroke had been covered. Still, the notion remained. He had long prided himself on being a logical man. If what he knew lay in the Moser barn not a mile down the road could be nothing found in nature, then logic dictated its origin must be beyond nature.

He tossed the pen down in disgust and walked to the door, flinging it open and stepping onto the porch. The acre-and-a-half front yard sloped downward in an easy grade where it fell away to the riverbank, giving the illusion the house had been built atop a cliff. The morning brought a mist that floated above the water's surface, what all in Mattingly called the ghost river. Far to the right, the river bent and continued on toward town. Below and out of sight, George could hear the churn of the water against the rocks and the cat calling out.

*"Shut up!"* he screamed. *"Shut up shut—"*

The rumble silenced him. George spun so hard that the heel of his bare foot sank in the wet grass, nearly costing him his balance. He winced as his knee buckled, bringing him to the ground. It was his heart that kept him there, hammering so hard and fast that he believed standing would risk a heart attack. One cough flew from his mouth. Others followed, deeper, making him belch blood into the green grass. The cat wailed more. George had never felt so alone.

After, he would tell Dorothea and Bobby that he likely would have lain there until his Turn's end had it not been for Tommy. The boy came running with a sack in one arm and what looked like a carton in the other, glancing over his shoulder every few strides. George could not yell and so lifted his arm, waving him over. He managed to stand as Tommy came up the gravel drive. Tommy dropped the food and milk both and crashed into him with such force that George nearly fell again.

The boy's face had flushed so red that his freckles were almost nonexistent. When he spoke, his words came fast and jumbled with fear. All George could make out was, "You hear that?"

"It's okay." Rubbing the top of Tommy's cap, trying to quiet him. "It's okay. We're okay."

"That was thunder. George, it's *never* thundered."

"It's okay," he said again, all he could. Because whatever he and Tommy had heard wasn't thunder, at least no thunder George knew existed. *But we're well beyond that now, aren't we?* he thought. *Oh, yes, down the rabbit hole.* "We should get to Mama's. Assuming the rest of us heard the same thing, that's where everyone will gather."

Tommy wouldn't let go. George ended up escorting him

inside the house in a clumsy version of a three-legged race to get his keys. They left the food and milk lying in the grass. Tommy sat as close to George as he could, the gearshift between his legs. As they pulled away, the cat called.

## -22-

Only one of the headlights on Junior's truck functioned in working order, leaving half of the road dark and the other in a dim sort of haze, but that had always been enough and maybe even too much. Once, sometime between Tommy's arrival and Juliet's, he'd even tried to make the long shot of pavement past Boone's Pond to Hersey's trailer with his eyes shut. Wasn't much risk when Junior hit that straightaway. Morning was only a thought on this side of the mountains, no one out but him, and he could lose nothing that the Turn wouldn't put back.

So he'd done it, driven that stretch on feeling alone. Junior didn't look until he'd heard the thump and felt the right side of the truck shimmy over something. Turned out to be Ben Hickam, the little runt who delivered papers out that way every morning. The kid wasn't much older than Tommy, always wore glasses and khaki pants rolled up so they wouldn't get caught in his bike chain. When Junior pulled over to take a look, those glasses were broken down the middle and the pants were stained with excrement. That was sorry work, having to haul a busted bike and a boy who'd messed himself in his dying far enough into the woods that no one would find him. It had been the last time Junior tried driving without looking. When he'd passed Ben the next Turn, he made sure to wave. It had been a dangerous thing, running over that boy. Something like that could upset the balance. Mama never knew, but the Lord watched. From then on, he'd waited until well past sunrise to go to Hersey's, avoiding the dark and Ben both.

Hersey Childress's place stood high on a hill well off from the road and was reachable only by a wood-and-rope bridge strung across the river. The little shack had been gifted down from one generation to the next, along with what most considered the primest pot-growing land in the county. Junior parked past the lane just inside the trees and took what he needed from the glove box, then aimed for the swing bridge in the distance. Thinking about what all had happened those past Turns, Bobby coming back and that picture and the strange way Laura Beth acted. She'd come back from the Moser barn all worked up, laughing and being silly. Junior hadn't even had to give her any weed and still didn't know what to think of that. Laura Beth told him there really had been something in that barn. She'd called it a sign from the Lord. Junior didn't know one way or the other and didn't really care so long as she was happy. That Turn had come out to be the best in the many they'd spent together.

He took the bridge in baby steps with his hands gripping either side, trying not to wobble even though he always did. Junior never had liked heights. Often he would think it was well he never had made it out of A-ball. Playing in the majors meant flying all about the country, miles and miles in the air. Would've turned him crazy, he thought. Better to be here in Mattingly, where he could feel the earth beneath his boots and where he'd found heaven and Laura Beth. Those were two things far better than standing on a mound in the show, listening to all those screaming fans. That's what Junior told himself as he walked that bridge, what he whispered every night in front of his little television as he watched the Series from atop the soiled mattress where he and Laura Beth made love. He had heaven and he had her and he had all he ever needed. A part of him almost believed it.

Hersey wasn't on the porch. Junior didn't have to look to know that. He'd come at other times in the Turn, eight o'clock or seven thirty or six fifteen, Hersey was always around. But he was always somewhere inside at 8:37, in the bathroom maybe or breaking his fast. Counting his money. Junior crossed the bridge and climbed the stone steps up to the shack's front door, knocked twice. Counted to fifteen. The door cracked to Hersey's skinny face.

"Say there, Hersey."

"Junior? What you doing out here this early?"

"Don't know." He shrugged. "Woke with a hankerin'."

"How much you need?"

"Couple ounces."

The door opened wider, though not all the way. Hersey wore a faded pair of jeans and what Junior called a wifebeater. He stunk like the Hickam kid did after Junior had hit him with the truck. "Anybody follow you?"

"No."

"Need cash, Junior. No more credit. You never pay."

"I got it." He patted the back pocket of his Bib-Alls.

"Lemme see."

The door swung open. Junior reached into his back pocket and drew the pistol. Three rounds sank into Hersey's chest, knocking the skinny man backward into the living room. Junior stepped inside over the body and went into the kitchen, picking up four of the dozen or so plastic baggies that covered the table. He'd learned there was no sense in being greedy.

"Don't need so much as usual," he said. "Laura Beth's okay now."

A stack of cash lay beside the coffee maker. Junior took that, too, enough for his bait at Andy's. By the time he finished, Hersey's blood had oozed over most of the John Deere mat in front of the door. Junior stepped back over it, tipping an imaginary cap.

"See you tomorrow, Hersey."

He tucked the drugs and the money inside the big front pouch of his coveralls and the gun in his back pocket. The return walk across the river came easier. Junior reached the end and stepped onto the bank, humming one of Mama's hymns about being there when the roll was called up yonder. He'd made it near all the way back to his truck when the sky rent itself in a single roar. Air moved in a wave outward, striking Junior's back and throwing him forward into the mud. Junior reached behind for the pistol and rolled, waving it across the river, thinking Hersey hadn't been dead this time and had gone for the sniper rifle he'd brought back from the war.

The pistol fell from Junior's hand when he saw it. He pushed himself back from the river's edge, sliding on his backside farther up the bank and into the trees. Wanting to look away and finding that impossible. The horror of it, the beauty. His chest hurt, his head and his eyes. It was the thought of Laura Beth that finally made him stand and run. He had to get to Laura Beth, get to Mama's. He cast a final look over his shoulder as he flung open the truck's door. The crack was still there. Hanging in the air just above the middle of the river and reaching high above the trees, a light so pure that Junior mourned himself and black edges so dark they reminded him of death itself.

# -23-

They came after the Lord had called forth from His heaven in those morning hours. They came to Dorothea. Laura Beth first, bags of groceries quivering in her arms and a look of hell fixed across what part of her face the sunglasses did not hide, crying, *Did you hear that, Mama?* and *That noise?* Juliet, fresh from waking at the church, arrived in much the same fashion and with much the same words, saying she had tried to call Bobby but there had been no answer. George and Tommy next (Tommy running straight to his mama's arms). Bobby soon after, this time knocking at the door as a proper gentleman should, stepping inside only with Dorothea's permission. He looked agitated, as if he'd gone a day and night without a meal. Sweat gathered at his brow. When he walked, it was as though he'd forgotten how. He sat at the table and asked Dorothea ("Mama," the word came) for a cup of coffee and drank it with a twitching hand, wanting to know what that noise had been.

Junior arrived last but not long after. He stumbled into the dining room stricken with fear and said nothing of Bobby's presence, only hugged Laura Beth and his mama and then sat with his head in his hands. No one had a mind to eat. Dorothea prepared more coffee and some tea. For a long while they sat in a silence broken only by Tommy's occasional sniffle, the others too afraid to talk about what they had heard from the sky, Dorothea too overcome by what had happened since. She had never known any who did not bend toward the familiar in the face of tragedy. In spite of what all had been said of hell or deep places in time's river, they had each come to the yellow house in their hour of need.

They had all run home.

George first broached the subject. Mama allowed it. Tommy and Bobby agreed it sounded like thunder, though they didn't know how that could be, given the closeness of the noise and the clear sky over their heads. Juliet said it had sounded like a crash. Laura Beth, still weeping, declared it had reminded her of Charlie's slaps. George put forth the sound had not come to him as thunder at all, but more a tray of ice larger than he could comprehend cracked by hands even larger. Junior sat quiet the whole time. He gripped Laura Beth's hand and cast his eyes to Dorothea, pleading. She met his look and nodded—*Later.* She would not have him talk and thus destroy the fragile bonds beginning to strengthen them all, nor would Dorothea allow herself to interject. The letter crinkled in the pocket of her apron (I love you, it had said, nothing more and nothing more needed). She did not offer to read it aloud. When Bobby spoke and said time still moved forward in the Turn, he'd seen it himself and offered his bruised face as evidence, Dorothea did not admonish his lack of faith. People like Bobby Barnes possessed no faith to lack. Such things had mattered to Dorothea once, but no more. The Lord could abide disbelief but never a family divided and cut off from one another.

Dorothea did then what she should have done from the beginning—offer her home as a place of comfort and safety to all who called upon it. Dinner that day was a feast they all took part in cooking. Junior huddled with Laura Beth as Juliet kept a little too close to Bobby to remain proper. Tommy peeled his potatoes, leaving George and Dorothea together at the stove. George stirred the pot slowly, murmuring to himself.

"Something's happening, Mama," he said. "That sound shouldn't be."

"It's the Lord's doing, dear," she answered. "There lie all the answers you've sought. You think you're so smart, but you're not. All this while, you've been looking in the wrong place."

For the first time in memory, George did not respond to that mention of faith. There came no derision, no mockery. Only silence as he stirred.

Patience. That was what Dorothea decided would be needed here. Patience for her family to see that all would be well and would stay that way so long as they remained together. Some of that was proven over dinner. Tommy offered the prayer. He made a small mention of "And, God, please don't let the sky fall again" that made Dorothea smile but nothing more. The rest had been given over to how thankful he felt that they could all gather at the table again and for the mound of mashed potatoes on his plate. Dorothea offered to shut the windows. Her family asked she keep them open. Every sound from outside, large or small, was met with turning heads and forks hitting plates. But there was no thunder that noon nor in the hours after, and the afternoon showed itself no different from all the ones before. Juliet laughed at something Bobby said as the plates were passed. She covered her mouth with her hand as if sorry and then took it away, laughing again. That tiny note became the keystone pulled from a dam of pent feelings. The room bloomed with the chuckles and high-pitched speech of togetherness, and these things filled Mama more and better than any food.

\* \* \*

They spread out over the backyard after the dishes were done. Dorothea took her accustomed place on the back porch. The thought that perhaps the crack in the Moser barn had not been a test at all struck her with a suddenness that sent a shiver across her shoulders. As she looked out across the lawn, it indeed appeared the case. Junior tossed the ball to Tommy in a high and easy arc. George and Juliet huddled beneath the willow. Laura Beth sunned herself in a spot between the two groups, alone but (it appeared) content. And huddled over the small chessboard in front of George sat Bobby, the prodigal son returned. The sky above them had been colored a peaceful blue that was empty of even a wisp of cloud, and Dorothea thought no, all that had happened in the past Turns hadn't been a test of faith at all. It had instead been the Lord's way of succeeding where she herself had failed.

She heard Juliet call, "Ooh!" and saw her bend to kiss Bobby's cheek. He grinned out of yellow teeth and lifted his filthy ball cap. "Everybody come here."

Laura Beth tilted her face away from the sun. She rose from her chair and moved toward the others with a grace that almost stole Dorothea's breath, bare feet in the grass, walking as if according to some unheard music as the wind played with her blond strands and her red dress billowed and bent in the breeze. That woman could have been something, Dorothea thought. In another world and another time, Laura Beth could have done great things. Tommy tossed the ball back to Junior and ran to the willow as well, asking Juliet what was happening. Dorothea didn't hear the response but gauged the reaction. It seemed as though that Turn had yielded two miracles. Not only a splitting sky and a family reunited, but Bobby winning a chess match.

Junior kept his spot in the yard, tossing the ball into his glove. Dorothea looked out that way and waited for him to see her. When he did, she nodded him over. He grunted into a chair too narrow for his wide body and wiped the sweat from his brow.

"You've been awful quiet, Junior. Everything okay with you?"

"No, ma'am, it ain't," he said.

"Was it earlier? You hear the thunder?"

He shut his eyes as though wanting to crush the memory away. "Yes'm, I heard it. Seen it."

"Seen it?" She looked down into the yard. Everyone huddled around George and Bobby.

"Seen it," Junior said again. "I was up to Hersey's. That's where I get my weed. Come back acrost his rope bridge and heard it. Thunder. I said I gotta get out of here and so I did, but then I turned around to look because I thought it was Hersey trying to get me with that long rifle he's got. Hersey's real good with that gun, Mama. But it weren't Hersey. It was what was on top the river."

"On top of the river?"

"Yes'm. A hole. Like the one they say's in the Moser barn."

Dorothea's hand went to her mouth. She gasped just when Juliet screeched, making the sound unheard even by Junior. "You mean to tell me you were way out past Boone's Pond to Hersey's place, and that thunder we heard was—"

"World crackin'," Junior said. "Yes'm."

"Have you told anyone of this? Laura Beth?"

Junior shook his melon head. "Thought about it. Laura Beth sure did like knowin' that first crack was there. She didn't need no weed to make her happy after, and when we got back to my camper, she was lovin'. Extra lovin'. Figured maybe if one crack'd do that, two'd do double."

"Now listen here to me, Junior." Dorothea took his hand,

as heavy as an anvil and twice as hard. "Don't you say a word now. You hear me? Not even to her."

"Sure would like more a that extra lovin'. It was fine."

"You might want it, but that isn't what you need. Look out over there, Junior. Go on."

He did, just as the call went up that Bobby had captured George's queen.

"You see that out there, son? That's joy. That's happiness. That's those people being right where they're supposed to. You tell any of them what you saw, all that'll go away. George will be back to his funny ideas and drag Juliet off with him, and where Juliet goes is where Bobby follows and Tommy's right behind. Do you love me, Junior?"

"Yes'm. Love Laura Beth, too."

"Then do as I ask. For the both of us."

Junior thought about that as much as Junior could, then gave a soft nod. "Bobby says time's movin' on. Things is changin'. Said the stars are winkin' out one at a time."

"Nothing is changing. Just the Lord bringing us together. Lord would tell me if things were otherwise. You know that. Time doesn't pass here, else by now we'd both be so old we'd be nothing more than shriveled-up bones. Do you feel older, Junior? Even by a day?"

"No, ma'am," he said. "Feel as strong as I did the day I musta died."

Tommy yelled from under the tree, "Mama, Junior, come watch this. Bobby's winning."

Dorothea smiled and waved. "Come on," she said. "Let's do our best to keep up appearances. It isn't my job to love these people, Junior. My love is reserved for you and Tommy alone. It's my job to save them."

Junior helped her down the stairs. By the time they reached the willow, the noise from the others sounded not unlike the rancor of the baseball game that would show that evening. Bobby grinned like a fool through the sweat dripping from his face. His arms twitched. Dorothea thought not for the first time that day that something was wrong with him. Juliet hung on him like some love-starved schoolgirl, Tommy like a proud son. And for a moment, Dorothea truly did believe Laura Beth would succumb to some whorish cheerleader dance. Only George looked perplexed. His shoulders had gone slumped as he stroked his white beard. At his feet lay a pile of spent cigarettes. A bloody handkerchief poked out from the front pocket of his gray pants. Dorothea watched as everyone fell silent. George fingered a piece that looked like a horse's head, let go of it, touched another. Bobby's grin widened and then burst as George touched a tall piece topped with a cross and tipped it over.

"He won," Tommy yelled. "Daddy won, Mama."

More cheers. Even Dorothea smiled, though not so much for Bobby's victory as for George's defeat. It was a fine thing, seeing someone so sure of his own ways finally brought low.

George looked up from the board. "How did you do that?"

Bobby shrugged. *No*, Dorothea thought. *Not a shrug. A spasm.* It occurred to her that she hadn't seen Bobby take a drink all day. Had brought none with him, hadn't asked to dip into Hubie's cabinet.

"I don't know," he said. "Guess I had time on my hands while I was gone. Got on the computer some." He winced. "Studied up a little. Figured out my opening was wrong. Like you said, George, the beginning makes the end."

\* \* \*

Everyone stayed. Dorothea couldn't remember how long it had been since that had happened. Before Bobby found out about Laura Beth, maybe longer. They all remained close to the yellow house instead, as if the world outside had suddenly grown too big and wide for them to travel safely. They talked and played (though not chess; George had fallen into melancholy and said his chess days may be over) and loved one another. Even Junior and Bobby got along. Even Dorothea and Juliet.

Yet it was not long after supper when the slow realization came that they could remain there no longer. That Turn was drawing to an end, and with it would go what Dorothea believed was the most frightening and pleasurable twenty-four hours any of them could recall. Tommy and George left first, George saying they could try feeding the cat next Turn and telling Tommy to be there early, seven at the latest. Junior took Laura Beth back to the house on Evergreen Avenue. Laura Beth looked so at peace that she didn't even mind what awaited her there. Juliet and Bobby went together with the promise that they would speak to one another soon. On the way out, Dorothea asked Bobby if he felt well. He replied no, then said he had never felt so fine.

The letter she wrote that night proved the shortest she had ever typed. Long had Dorothea cursed in her mind the seeming unwillingness of the Lord to write back anything more than a few phrases, thinking Him detached at best and uncaring at worst. Now she understood. It took not many strokes of the keys to impart what she most felt, but only a few. *I love you* worked just fine.

She placed the letter in the box and lifted the flag, then made the long walk back up the driveway to the door. The stars were out, all of them, the sky quiet. She thought not of the crack in the Moser barn or the one Junior had found along the river. Such things didn't matter, and Dorothea had the only things that did. She took the steps upstairs and sat at her vanity, waiting for her Turn to end as she listened to the silence of the house and the hum of memories beneath it. She picked up the pearl-handled comb beside the mirror and began brushing her hair. One hundred strokes, as she had done every night since a child. The vanity light captured each freckle and inconsistency of Dorothea's face, every minute flaw. She did not mind. She was a strong woman. She was loved. Her smile gathered at the corners of her drawn mouth and spread, showing her teeth. Such a pretty smile. Not a come-hither one like Laura Beth's or a beautiful one such as Juliet's, but a smile born of . . .

The brush stilled in her hand. Dorothea's eyes narrowed to a spot along her hairline where the smoothness of her scalp met the wrinkles of her forehead. Staring as she felt her heart against her ribs and the very blood coursing through her body. A trick of light, no more. She set the comb down and felt the silence of the house, four walls drawing a breath. Light. The sorry light, the one Dorothea had griped to Hubie for years should be brighter and clearer or else she would never get her makeup right. She saw her hand moving in the glass, pulling her hair back away from her face. Felt her back creak and moan as she bent closer to the mirror. Remembering, *Fix that light, Hubie, I'll look ugly* and *No, you won't, my dear, not ever,* remembering the day she'd sat in that pale light to fix her face for Hubert's funeral and the day not long after, hands stained with black coloring as she looked upon her new self. Her fingers working now, separating the strands, thinking back to how she'd smiled for the first time since his death when she had found her hair the color of her youth, those better days never to be had again.

She looked deep into the mirror and thought of Junior, what he'd told her.

*Bobby says time's movin' on. Things is changin'.*

The Lord would tell her if that was so. Surely He would.

Silence around her, the world going to sleep. And within minutes of her Turn, all Dorothea heard were her own whimpers, and all she saw was the faint line of gray reaching up from her scalp.

# -24-

Bobby said good-bye and then he said, "I love you." He thought he heard Juliet answer before the line went dead, a single word he couldn't understand over the rumbling tires. The truck's front wheels banked hard to the right—not trying to avoid the car hidden around the turn, more Bobby's arms failing him. His head ached and his muscles felt afire. A puddle of vomit sloshed on the floorboard, the stench making him more nauseous. Sixteen hours had passed since his last drink. He missed his boys.

Metal against metal, the steering wheel shattering Bobby's chest. He thrust out a hand to stop Matthew but Matthew wasn't there, turned to the empty window where Mark should have tumbled out. When the black took him, it was almost a relief.

There would be stars, yet when Bobby woke in the alley, he did not look. His headache not only remained but had intensified, along with the sweats and a rage that threatened release. The salty taste of his purge coated his tongue. Bobby rolled over, chasing Mr. Jangles away. George said memories were kept in that deep part of the river. Bobby had hoped his withdrawals would be something other. Repeated, perhaps, but only as a singular thing rather than one compounded. He had not begun to shake until he'd arrived at Dorothea's the Turn before, hadn't felt sick until after dinner and hadn't wanted to kill himself until halfway up the mountain. The one small hope Bobby carried into the world between the worlds was he would wake and the cycle would repeat instead of build. He should have realized the Lord of the Turn wouldn't be so merciful.

He stumbled into the shop and the waiting room, counted to a hundred before the coffee maker dinged. The first cup went down in a series of gulps that burned his mouth and tongue. Bobby imagined the half-empty bottle beneath the counter or a can from the fridge. He fumbled for his cell phone and dialed Juliet's number. The call went to voicemail. Bobby asked her to call as soon as she could. His hands shook. His teeth hurt. He needed help.

The refrigerator hummed. Bobby clenched his jaw as he looked that way, thinking, *One beer wouldn't make the boys come, but it would let me function.* He opened the door. The light clicked on, revealing tiny aluminum soldiers lined in perfect formation that clanked when he slammed the door shut.

He couldn't stay. Not with the alcohol there. Nor could Bobby trust himself to take the beer and bourbon and pour it down the sink. He would carry it all into the shop and lock the bathroom door behind him, pour one can and maybe two down the drain before spilling some of it and then what would he do, clean it, clean it because Bobby had always kept a clean shop, and then it would get on his hands and his fingers and it wouldn't be long before the boys knocked at the door wanting in, wanting to give their daddy a hug. The longer Bobby remained inside the shop, the more the beer called like a siren song, leading him ever closer to the rocks and shoals of his former life. He tried Juliet again, cursing that he'd never asked what time her Turn began or where. The message he left contained only four words—"I'm coming to you." By then, he felt his throat closing.

The air outside was crisp and clean and chased the fog from his eyes. Morning had broken over Mattingly. Bobby heard the phone ring—Bea—as the waiting room door shut behind him. The road was all but bare. Bobby pulled off the road at every approaching vehicle, not only braking, but adding the emergency brake as well, no longer trusting his judgment. He took the middle of the bridge so he would not drive off either side, keeping the yellow line in the middle of the hood. Thinking of how the boys used to help him drive when he'd had more than needed, wondering where they had gone.

A stab of pain flared behind his right eye. He winced, trying to rub it away. The right-side tires drifted into the gravel along the shoulder, and only that allowed Bobby to see the figure ahead at the side of the road. Not walking, standing there, eyes turned toward the long field that ran parallel to the railroad tracks. Bobby mashed on the brake, shooting a cloud of gravel skyward.

It was terror that loosed Bobby's rage and drove him from the truck. He left the door open and nearly stepped out in front of a passing car, horn blaring in a fading echo.

"Dorothea?"

The figure didn't move.

"Mama? You got to get away before you get killed."

Bobby looked behind to make sure no other traffic

approached, then went back to the truck long enough to flip on his hazards. Dorothea still did not move. She stared across the field, eyes unblinking as the breeze made tiny circles in her hair. Bobby may have been sick to the point of death in that moment, and yet enough of his reasoning remained to understand the last time he had seen Dorothea so old and broken, she was burying her husband.

"Mama?" Softer now, no longer in a rage but still very much afraid. "What you doing all the way out here?"

She turned slowly and blinked as if surprised to see anyone there. "Bobby?" she asked, taking his hand and winding her gnarled fingers about his, squeezing as much as he believed she could. Her eyes were wet. "I had to see. I had to see it for myself."

"See what?"

"The Lord called me here last Turn." Her voice cracked. "He sent me a sign to come see for myself. I thought it was a test of faith, a test of family, and now I just don't know."

"Come—"

She released his hand and pointed across the field. Bobby followed her finger, unsure what she wanted him to see, until he realized there wasn't anything to see at all.

The Moser barn was gone.

# -25-

George came alive as first light crept over the ridge. Beyond the open bedroom window called the soft churn of the river and the rustle of dying leaves, a crow cawing in the distance. And the cat. Already, the cat. He rose but did not shut the window, too concerned with his pressing bladder and the other business at hand. He went to the bookcase beside the TV and took down the folding chess set he and Anna had once, then placed the pieces in the position of the last few moves of his game with Bobby.

A teacher's proudest moment should come when his student rises above, becoming a teacher to the teacher. George had never known such a moment. He had taught both the gifted and the cursed in his years, Mattingly's cream and its dregs, and in all that time had never been humbled in word or deed. His pride had not allowed it.

The memory was still fresh: Bobby sitting stunned and happy, that stupid smile spread over his face, hand trembling as he'd doffed that filthy cap of his; Juliet kissing him hard on the cheek; Laura Beth clapping as she jumped up and down, her sunglasses lifting up each time she landed to show a bit of the ruin beneath; Tommy's face, a beam that said, *You just got beat by a stupid man you ain't so smart at all*; and Junior's look of either disinterest or contempt, *What's winning some stupid game next to striking out Chipper Jones back in '91?* And Mama, silent with her hands on her nonexistent hips, smirking.

*You think you have this all figured out. But do you, George? Do you really?*

His hand paused in the air, hovering over the bishop Bobby had used to pin George's last rook. Those words hadn't come from Dorothea. He leaned back in the desk chair and rubbed his beard. No, Dorothea hadn't said that at all. That had been his own mind, questioning.

*You think you're so smart, but you're not. All this while, you've been looking in the wrong place.*

Those had been Mama's words. At any other time, George understood he would have batted that nonsense away with some stroke of flowery phrase, half sugar and half salt, reminding Dorothea that she may choose to live in the shadow of superstition, but he would rather bask in reason's open sun. A part of him had always loathed her insistence upon following some unproven faith, for failing to *question*, and yet George now found the sharp intellect with which he'd always viewed others turned upon himself. Had he kept the very open mind he demanded others embrace? Had he ever paused in his life inside the Turn to consider another viewpoint rather than twist and bend circumstance to his own? Once he had thought no, before he stepped into the Moser barn and found something reason could not explain. Standing there by Dorothea's stove, stirring a pot of corn into a tight eddy that wound back upon itself time and time again as she spoke of greater things George knew not, he believed for a moment maybe yes.

Anna smiled from the picture in front of him. George had tried calling her in this part of the Turn, had tried earlier and later. He could take his cell phone from his pocket and dial her number; there would be no ring, only a recording of Anna's smooth and honeyed voice, begging forgiveness for missing the call but promising to call back soon. The cat wailed in the river, and George knew the reason he could not bear that sound was that sound was him, his own heart breaking and his own cry for help. He closed his eyes and coughed, felt the blood at his lips and his own hands beginning to fold and his head bow. There was no question in his mind of what he was about to do, no reasoning for or against it. He tried remembering the words he'd been taught as a child, *Our Father who art in heaven* . . . something of trespasses and kingdoms coming, words that felt wooden and hollow on his tongue.

"Please," he said, "I don't—"

The knock at the door stole his next words. Tommy curled a hand around the side of his forehead and leaned into the screen. In the other hand, a grocery bag rattled.

"George? You here?"

He coughed and nodded, though he didn't think Tommy could see, then stood from the desk in the corner. "Morning, Tommy."

"It ain't too early for me to be here, is it? Your cat's callin' something fierce, George. Heard'm all the way down the road."

"Not my cat, not anybody's cat as far as I can tell, but yes. Does make a racket." He went to the door and opened it, letting Tommy inside. "Guess you can see why I spend so little time here during the day."

"What you doing?" Tommy moved to the desk. "You playin' your chess alone, George?"

"No, replaying. My game with Bobby."

"Daddy beat you good." Beaming as he said it, the proud son.

"I taught him well."

"You busy? I can go down to the river myself."

"No," he said. "I wasn't doing anything."

\* \* \*

They walked across the lawn to where it sloped hard to the riverbank, guided by the noise of the cat. Tommy carried what he'd brought from home. Cheese and milk, he said, Percy had always come to those. At the slope they stopped and looked down into the river, which flowed wide and fast over the smattering of rocks that had been deposited in an age when the land there lay wild and untouched. The center rock stood at an angle in the water with a top nearly flat some two feet from the current. That was where the cat lay, curled and shaking. Fur clung to its body, soaked through to reveal a line of narrowed ribs. It saw George and mewed loud and long.

"Think somebody tossed it in upriver?" Tommy asked.

"Likely. A stray someone wanted rid of. Would've drowned if those rocks hadn't been there."

"You ever try to feed him?"

"Once. Some lunch meat Anna left me in the refrigerator. I couldn't toss it out that far."

Tommy put his hands on his knees and bent forward. "Looks wild. You ever try throwing a rope on him or going in?"

"I'm a science teacher, Tommy, not a cowboy. And that water's too cold and I'm too old to be going in after him. Current would sweep you all the way to Stanley."

He led Tommy down where the angle wasn't so steep. The bank was wide enough for them both but little more. Tommy opened his bag as the cat watched and mewed. He said he guessed the milk would do no good unless the cat came to shore, but he broke off enough of the cheese to try making the rock. The first two throws went short, plopping into the water and floating away. The third hit the rock, making the cat flinch and hiss.

"This isn't working," George said. He grabbed some of the cheese and tossed it. The cat called out in a high sound that came over the water like a scream, whiskers shaking. "Take it!" he screamed. "Take the stupid food and shut up."

Tommy said, "Don't yell at him, George. He's just a cat."

"He's making me crazy is what he is."

George plunged his hand into the bag so hard that it almost slipped from Tommy's grasp and threw more, watching it hit the water like yellow rain. The cat raised up and arched its back, *Get away* and *Help me* at the same time.

George felt his foot go wet and cold and then the other and then his knees, heard Tommy screaming, *What are you doing?* and *You can't go out there!* and *Come back!* It was too late. George felt the river pushing against him, wanting to drag him under. He kept moving and dug his boots into the muddy bottom, cursing the cat's stupidity, wailing at it. The cat curled into a ball again as George made it to the river's center. He put one hand on the rock to pull himself the last few feet and reached, meaning to grab the cat by the scruff. A paw shot out, and in the midst of all that cold came a flash of heat along his arm. He screamed more in anger than pain and reached again, harder this time, sinking his fingers into the cat's back as the cat cried out, one claw slashing and then another, raking George's arms and making him let go.

"You're hurting him, George, *don't hurt him.*"

The cat backed away to the edge of the rock. George tried pulling himself closer and slipped on the bottom, nearly sinking under. Frigid water flowed into his mouth and throat, choking him into a cough. His head began to lighten. Tommy shouted again, a commanding voice demanding he stop hurting his new pet. George's hand reached for the cat again

(*I'm trying to save you can't you see I'm saving you*)

as needlelike white teeth sank into his skin. The sound he released echoed across the water, an arching wail that George felt in his very bones, and in that wail he knew the cat was him and he the cat, they were the *same* and he couldn't let go and wouldn't, no matter the pain. Teeth bit and claws tore as he lifted the cat from the rock, a handful of screaming muscle and terror, trying to make the shore as quick as he could as his boots sought purchase along the slick and rocky bottom. Tommy's face had gone as red as his hair, the tendons taut in his neck. He screamed words George could not hear as the cat struggled and howled, threatening to tear free of his weakening grasp and fall into the current. George reached shallow water where the current moved slower and reached only his knees. With what strength remained he threw the cat toward the bank, away from Tommy. The cat landed paws first in the mud and bounded up the slope toward the house, where it disappeared.

\* \* \*

"You almost *killed him*."

George tried taking a step and found the task impossible. His waterlogged boots felt like cinder blocks on his feet. Water flowed over them in tiny whorls that threatened to pull him back into the current. He wanted to ask Tommy to stop yelling and start helping but only spoke a cough. Blood dripped down his chin (*You almost killed my cat I hate you I'm not helpin' you no more*) and from the scratches and bites on his arms. A great ringing sounded in his ears. He made it to the bank only because that promised a shorter walk to the house than from elsewhere downstream. His breaths came in deep, rattling heaves.

"Inside. Tommy, help me."

Tommy did, though at first George believed the boy wouldn't. There wasn't much helping he could do being so outweighed and so did little more than offer a shoulder for George's hand to rest upon and a few halfhearted words of encouragement as they climbed the slope again. He saw the blood on George's arms and asked if it hurt, said he could hurt George if he wanted to and maybe he should. Maybe would.

"I was trying to save it," George told him through the wheezes. "I was trying to save that cat but the cat couldn't see."

He had to shower first, clean the wounds and bites. Even if the cat had been riddled with disease, George believed there was no need to worry of infection. The wounds would be gone next Turn. He stopped just inside the door, knees weak and eyes wet from pain and exhaustion, thinking of the bruise on Bobby's face and the hidden horrors under Laura Beth's glasses. If time indeed still crept forward, then maybe the cuts to George's body would remain. Maybe it would be years before even the scabs formed and years still until those scabs fell off.

"Stay here, Tommy? Don't leave me just yet."

Anger flooded the boy's face. George understood. From Tommy's small perspective, he supposed it did look as though he had been trying to harm the cat. "We'll be late for Mama's. You're always on the way there by now, George. She'll be worried if you don't go."

"We'll explain. It'll be fine. I just . . . I don't want to be alone right now, Tommy. Be a good boy and stay."

Tommy's cheeks flared again. He stared at his shoes, muddy and wet from the riverbank. "I ain't no boy."

George left him in the living room with a stack of *National Geographics* from the shelf and the television remote. He limped into the bedroom, leaving a trail of sopping clothes, then turned the shower on as hot as it would go. The water made him spit more blood. George watched it gather and twirl down the drain. Tommy knocked at some point, asking if he was okay. He said he was and Tommy answered it had been twenty minutes, they were now not late but truly late, and besides he couldn't find the cat anywhere. The phone rang as Tommy ranted. George turned his head beneath the spray from the shower, trying to drown the sound. He asked Tommy to answer and tell Mama they were fine and would be there soon. Tommy sighed (George could hear that sigh all the way through the door and past the water, and how it sounded like the sigh of someone tired and much older) and said fine. He knocked again a few seconds later. His voice was lower now and without indignation, almost frightened.

"It's for you."

"I'm in the shower."

"That's what I said. She said she'd wait."

George turned the water off and eased out, wrapping himself in a towel from the rack. His arms hurt and his legs, though not in the same way—more tired than wounded. Tommy stood outside the door with the phone in his hand. He gave it to George and walked to the bed and sat, staring at him.

"Yes," he said into the phone. "I'm sorry, we were trying to help the cat and—"

"George?"

George's knees buckled. He gripped the edge of the dresser beside the bathroom door to keep himself upright, knowing otherwise would mean a fall from which he might not be able to rise. The static on the line made the voice sound faint, almost as if the call had come from

(*another world*)

somewhere far. Tommy got up and helped him to the bed. George sat as bathwater fell from his elbows and feet, puddling on the floor.

"George?" the voice asked again.

He cleared his throat of phlegm and said, "Anna?"

"George, who was that boy answering the phone?"

"Tommy," he said. "Tommy Purcell. He was helping me with something."

"Stacey Purcell's boy?"

"Anna, where are you?" He felt his eyes tighten and burn and wiped his nose. Tommy stared at him, shocked and pitiful but still angry, still wanting his cat back. "I've called, Anna. So many times. Gone looking. I've never been able to find you."

"Find me?" She laughed, long and loud and with a sweetness so pure it sounded like life unspoiled. "Told you I was coming back today. You missed me so bad, you should've come along. I'm just about to leave, dear. I'll call you when—"

His voice broke. "You won't get here, Anna. Something's going to happen."

"Oh please, George, I am a grown woman and more than capable—"

"No, you don't understand—"

"—of caring for myself." The line broke again. ". . . home soon."

"What?" He stuck a finger in his free ear. "Anna, I can't hear you."

"I said I'll be home soon. No worry now. You just have the house nice when I get back. Can imagine what you've done to the place, playing the bachelor. I love you, George."

Tears tumbled from his eyes.

Tommy sank farther back on the bed.

"I love you, Anna. I love you so much. And I miss you."

She got *miss* and part of the *you* out. The line scrambled and buzzed. Anna was gone.

## -26-

Bobby hadn't answered when Juliet called from church. The message she'd found on her phone upon waking sounded frantic, the words of a man not only in trouble but in anguish as well—*I'm coming to you.*

She left the church in a fast walk toward the shop and found Bobby's truck gone. Her stride turned to a near run by the time she met the bridge, then it warped into a stumble at what she saw in Moser's field.

No—what she didn't see.

She shuddered to a stop at the bridge's midpoint and forced her feet forward in heavy, loping steps that made her toes catch the rocks along the shoulder. Beyond where the barbed-wire fence began, she stopped and tried to catch her breath. Only a few Turns had passed since George had brought them there, her and Tommy and Laura Beth, to gaze upon the crack Tommy had found in the barn. Mama had willed them all away from the field since. Juliet hadn't visited, nor to her knowledge had anyone else, and that had turned out to be a wise decision because now the barn was gone. Not removed—she shielded her eyes from the sun and saw green grass where the barn had stood—but . . . erased. As though the old Moser barn had never existed.

Juliet's hands folded, the tips of her fingers touching her bottom lip. She closed her eyes and opened them again to that same nothing. Her periphery caught an oncoming truck slowing and crossing the lane, coming to a stop by the cattle gate. She turned her head, keeping her body to the field, and watched Sheriff Barnett ease out.

"Pastor," he called, "what you doing out so early in the a.m.?"

Emotion flooded her, sadness and grief and confusion and fear most of all, fear of what had happened not only at the barn but up on the mountain road, what had happened to her and to Bobby and now what would happen to them all

because something was indeed wrong with the Turn, something horrible, and the only way Juliet could respond was to
hug herself.

"Juliet?" Jake's smile was like the barn, there and then
erased. He walked to her and held out a hand he didn't seem
to know what to do with that landed on her arm. His touch
was strong and real and everything she needed. "What's
happened?"

"I don't know." Shaking her head, tears ready to spill. Cars
and trucks eased past, country folk gawking in that way they
do, judging, shaking their heads at the crazy preacher woman
from Away. "I was at church working on the sermon and I had
to go see Bobby—"

"Bobby Barnes?"

"—but he wasn't there and—yes, Bobby Barnes—so I
came here and then I . . . Jake, there used to be a barn in that
field."

Jake lifted his hat and turned his head to where the railroad tracks made a straight line that faded in the distance.
"Used to be the old Moser barn out there. Tornado took
it years ago. You weren't even here yet. One of your flock
tell you?"

"It didn't get taken. Jake, that barn was *there*—" She
stopped, unsure of what word to use. Yesterday? Before? Last
Turn? "Lately. I could swear it."

Jake raised his eyebrows and rubbed his jaw. Trying,
Juliet guessed, to find a way to not call her crazy. "No. Been
gone since that day. Anything I can do for you, Juliet? You
don't look well."

"No," she said. Then, "Yes. Could you give me a ride? I
need to get somewhere faster than my legs can carry me."

"Need me to take you home?"

"No, I need you to take me to Dorothea Cash's house."
"Widow Cash?" That look again. "You got business there?"
"I do."

She let him guide her by the elbow, still thankful for his touch and thankful, too, that the road had emptied. Jake shut her door and went around the other side. He cast a long look toward the field before turning the truck around.

"Just out on my morning run," he said. "Glad I saw you."

"You're just coming back from Timmy's?" She watched for his reaction, wanting to gauge if anything else had changed besides the barn. "You have Kate's truck because yours is getting brakes."

He looked at her. "How'd you know that?"

"I don't think you'd believe me."

"Been sheriff here a long time, Preacher. Raised in this town, and here I'll die. You might be surprised what I'd believe."

Juliet might have told Jake everything had the drive to Dorothea's been a few miles longer. In the end, it was the notion of balance that kept her conversation general. Dorothea had long spoke of heaven's delicate equilibrium. Juliet had always believed that to be Dorothea's fear alone, her way of keeping things just so. She'd since changed her mind. Jake turned into the neighborhood, past homes that had been put back together in the time since the tornado had taken both them and Moser's barn (*At least here*, she thought, *wherever here is*). He guided the truck to the curb in front of the yellow house. Too many vehicles had parked in Dorothea's drive.

"Widow Cash throwing a breakfast party?" he asked.

"Something like that."

Jake looked at the assortment—three trucks, Junior's and Bobby's and George's, along with Laura Beth's car. "Bobby in there?"

"Yes. You haven't seen him this morning, have you? At Timmy's?"

He shook his head. "Widow Cash decides to serve some Bloody Marys, you make sure he don't fill up and take off to town behind the wheel."

"Bobby's not drinking anymore."

"Since when?"

Juliet didn't know. "Awhile."

She got out, thanking him for the ride and promising again that she felt much better, she must've just been mistaken in seeing that run-down barn. Jake didn't look convinced.

"Anything you need to be telling me, Juliet?"

"No. Nothing that can't wait." She shut the door and said through the open window, "Thanks for the ride, Jake."

"Anytime." He nodded toward the yellow house. "Quite the motley crew you're having breakfast with."

"They are," she said. "But I love them like family."

* * *

Dorothea sat at the head of the dining room table, drying her eyes with a cloth napkin. She refused the cup of tea Bobby tried to offer. Oddly enough, Juliet found them the only people near one another. The others had drifted to opposite sides of the room, Junior alone at the far end of the table and George near the kitchen, Tommy near the wall by the foyer. Laura Beth stood at the edge of the bay window, over Mama's shoulders. Her eyes held a faraway look, her mouth a wide grin. She turned with the others as Juliet walked into the room. Bobby smiled in a way that felt more genuine, more *good*, than Laura Beth's, yet his face troubled Juliet just the same.

Tommy spoke for them all: "The barn's gone, Juliet. The whole thing. Even Percy."

"I know," she said. "Just came from there."

Dorothea slid a hand to the chair beside her. "Come, Juliet. Family needs a preacher now. As you're the closest we have, you'll have to do."

Juliet sat. Dorothea patted her hand with fingers that had gone as cold as the tea in front of her. The day's letter lay unopened at the table's edge as though it had almost been discarded there, forgotten.

Bobby put his hands on Juliet's shoulders and said, "Things are happening." He went into detail of all that had been shared before her arrival, not only of him finding Dorothea at Moser's field, but also of her graying hair, Junior finding another crack, what had happened that morning with George and Tommy. This last shocked Juliet most of all. George remained at his spot by the kitchen. His body had gone bent at the waist; his every movement, no matter how small, punctuated with a wince. He had opted for long sleeves to cover the bandages on his arms. Anna. George had spoken with Anna. The thought seemed as impossible to Juliet as it must have seemed to them all.

He looked at Juliet through bloodshot eyes and said, "That cat always drove me away. Anna must've been calling at that time ever since I got here, I was never home to know it. I was never home, Juliet. But I saved it, me and Tommy. I changed something."

Laura Beth kept her gaze to the window. Juliet heard her whisper, "Things are happening."

"What do we do?" Tommy asked.

"I don't know, dear," Dorothea said. Juliet blinked at the words, the first time she'd heard them from Mama's mouth.

"I fear this is a test for us all." She looked down at the sealed letter in front of her. "For me most of all."

The room fell silent. It seemed as though even the birds outside had ceased their singing. The breeze, warm and nearly ever present in the Turn, now failed to reach through the screen. It was as if the whole of the Turn held its breath against the force of what blow it might meet next. Bobby laid a hand to Juliet's shoulder and squeezed. She laid a hand to his. Thinking about that great river. About time.

# Part III

# Stars

## -1-

Tommy didn't know if George would be up and didn't care either way; he wasn't going to George's for George. He'd waited longer than usual to start his Turn, keeping under the covers and peering into the dark as the blankets turned his hot breath back to him. It had felt safe but also suffocating. Tommy wondered if that was what heaven would come to be if everything kept cracking and going away.

Mama always said heaven had stood long and would stand longer still. She thought Tommy a boy, but he was old enough to know that what Mama Cash said and what she believed deep down were sometimes two different things, and that made her less a prophet and more like everyone else in his eyes. If Mama really thought heaven would last forever, she wouldn't have spent so much of the last Turn crying with Bobby and Juliet and even George, asking them what they should do. George, still rattled from finally getting to talk to his Anna, had suggested Dorothea reach out to the Lord. Even under the covers, Tommy still marveled at that memory: Mama sitting down to Hubert's old typewriter with the family gathered around, all of them peering over her shoulder and suggesting things to say and ask. That Turn, everyone believed in the Lord.

It was a sense of love rather than courage that finally got him out of bed. He dressed and found his hat and did half of his chore at the kitchen table, then took what food he could. The milk, Tommy let be. He lingered long enough for first light to stretch its long fingers across the valley before leaving and decided to try George first. All lay still along that stretch of road, Tommy listening to the gravel under his shoes and feeling the cool air on his face and the soft *thump* of the plastic bag against his knee. He heard no thunder. Far to his left he spotted the empty space between two long rows of trees where he knew the river lay. A faint mist had grown atop the water, casting the bottom half of the trees in fog. The ghost river, some would say. Tommy never feared that. In a way, he was a ghost, too. They all were.

A single lamp burned in George's living room window. The rest of the house lay dark and dead. Good. Tommy skirted the house and made for the bank, listening for a screech or a frightened mew. Everyone had been so caught up about the barn disappearing and what Sheriff Barnett had told Juliet about the barn that they'd never said a word about Percy. Worse, no one had taken a moment to tell Tommy how sorry they were for his loss. That had made him mad more than anything else, even madder than the way George had treated that poor cat in the river, because Percy had been *family*. Maybe not to Mama or Juliet or Junior, but to Tommy for sure.

Only the water called, fast and swirling over rocks hidden

by the bank. A lump sat at the edge of the yard. Tommy stopped, trying to remember if he'd seen that the Turn before, an old chair or a stump. Then the lump moved. Then the lump stood. The bag fell from his hand, bread and crackers spilling as the thing walked toward him from the fog, calling his name—George crying out between coughs.

"Come here, Tommy. Come see this."

George took him by the shoulders and pulled Tommy toward the slope that led to the river's edge. They crossed the spot where George had been sitting. His notebook and pen sat in the wet grass. George pointed far below and managed a single word:

"Look."

Tommy peered into the mist, swirling thick and thin in a current of its own. It parted long enough to reveal the empty rocks below.

"Where's my cat?"

"Gone." George smiled through bloodstained teeth. "*Gone.* I woke up and heard nothing but sweet silence."

A panicked thought rose up in Tommy, red and sharp. "Why's he gone? Is it 'cause you hurt him yesterday?"

"No." He shook his head. "Because I saved him. *We* saved him. Do you know what that means?"

Tommy didn't.

"It means I know what we have to do, Tommy. I know how to get us out of here."

"Ain't no leavin', George. This is heaven."

"It isn't. It's what I said. It's what Juliet said. And it's something . . ." He flung his arms up, joyous, George's hoarse laugh aimed at the wide sky. "Other. Go, Tommy. Find out where the others are and tell them to come here. I need some time to figure it all out, but I *know*."

Tommy didn't move. Couldn't, until George pushed him. "*Run*," he said. "Bring them all, soon as you can. We're going home, boy."

* * *

He did run, though not to Dorothea's or Bobby's or to the church, not to Junior's little camper or Laura Beth's big house. Tommy ran home.

The sun already shone above the Blue Ridge. If he didn't hurry, everything would be lost. He took what shortcuts he could, side streets littered with cans and bottles and backyards patrolled by barking dogs, patches of woods slick with dewed leaves and bare branches that poked and stabbed. By the time he reached the bowed front porch of his old mama's house, his lungs hurt worse than George's. Thankfully, Tommy had no need to haul the old typewriter back down from the high shelf in the closet. It sat waiting on the kitchen table, right where he'd left it.

He dug the letter to Dorothea from his back pocket and tossed it into a tray of half-smoked cigarettes, found another clean sheet of paper. Tommy had long run out of words the Lord would say. Countless minutes at his little kitchen table, recycling some form of *I love you* and *You are blessed* to keep them all happy, keep them together. But now words poured forth, the levers smacking hard onto the page:

STOP GEORGE. HURRY! HE WILL KILL YOU ALL.

He yanked the page free and fished the envelope from the ashtray, exchanging the letters. Then Tommy ran again. Out the door and up the street, racing the sun and the Turn and time itself, hoping Mama wasn't awake and George would be too preoccupied with thinking to remember he could go in the house and call everyone himself. His sprint became a tired lope by the time he reached Dorothea's street. He only allowed himself to rest when he spotted the mailbox flag still raised. Tommy studied the windows for movement inside, then sprinted the last few feet. He flipped down the lid and grabbed the letter Mama and the rest had left him, put the Lord's response inside, and pushed down the flag before running off again.

Sweat stained the front of his shirt. His legs cramped. Tommy heard the crinkle of the envelope in his pocket. He pulled it out and felt its smooth front, remembering how they'd all gathered as Mama had typed it, how they'd all been a family. He shuddered a deep breath as he balled the envelope in his hand and dropped it into the gutter.

## -2-

Could it be so simple as this? Untold months and years of searching, all George had read and studied, only to find the answer lay not in his books but on a tiny island of rocks not fifty yards from where he woke? An answer that had in fact *called* to him all this while with a shout he had been too stubborn to hear? And yet it felt true. All of it felt true.

He would pause in his writing and stare down the steep slope to the water, making certain the cat was no longer there. Each time the rocks were bare. George reached back into his memory (still sharp in spite of his age) to that first day in the deep part of time's river. He remembered the cat and leaving for town, finding Tommy—as if the boy was waiting for him, as if he'd *known*—and then Dorothea. But there had been something else, hadn't there? Something before? He sat, cross-legged as he'd sat as a boy, the wet grass soaking the seat of his pants. Yes. There had been the mayor. The cat had driven George from the house and he had met Mayor Wallis in town, and the mayor had asked George to consider taking a substitute teaching position at the high school. And George had said no, of course he'd said no, the school board pushing him out only to ask him back. But he should have said *yes*. He should have saved the cat and spoken to Anna and said yes to the mayor but he hadn't, and then George had been brought here. To the Turn. The only question now was why. Why for him, why for them all. Had Juliet been right in believing this place was some sort of temporal time-out? A place to question the whys of their own selves, to see that the tiny and insignificant choices they all made could turn to large and horrible things later on?

Could ripple. Could ripple in the river.

He turned to a fresh page in his notebook, thinking with his pen. Remember. They would all have to remember. Everything George could recall of the others who'd arrived after him and every snippet of conversation he'd had with those who'd arrived before went into his notebook in scribbles and phrases, arrows connecting them all—Juliet and Nolan Reynolds; Dorothea and her near accident; Bobby's talk with Bea Campbell and his ex-wife, his visit to Timmy's; Laura Beth and Charlie; Tommy and his mother. Only Junior's name stood alone. So far as George could reckon, what had brought that dim brute to the Turn remained a mystery. Junior had spoken of nothing in his former life except his ball-playing days. And beneath those George scrawled something else, underlining it, a quick remembrance of the reason Bobby had given for finally winning their chess match:

*The beginning makes the end.*

A rumbling sound stopped his pen. George flexed his neck toward the empty sky, thinking thunder and wounds in the world, the Turn rending itself. Then his gaze turned to the road and the sight of Junior's truck pulling into the drive. He waved. Junior climbed out and walked across the lawn. Pale fat jiggled where his Bib-Alls did not cover. A stupid grin spread under his cheeks.

"You're first," George said. "Others coming?"

Junior's pace stuttered. He answered, "Mama sent me."

"Did she tell you why?"

"Nope. Said it was important. My duty."

"Come on over here, Junior. Got something to show you." He closed the notebook and tucked it in his pocket. "Remember that cat, the one stuck in the river?"

"Tommy's?"

"Yes. Come here. You have to see this."

Junior followed. He said he'd never liked cats when he was alive and still didn't now that he was dead. George thought that a good enough opening.

"Do you remember being alive, Junior? What you did the first day you came to heaven?"

"Went fishin'. Went to Boone's Pond to fish because I didn't know the fish there were spoiled. Caught some and et it, but it weren't no good 'cause that pond's cursed. Went to get weed. Hersey said he needed cash but I didn't have none. Not for bait, neither. So I shot him and took his money."

George stopped. "You shot Hersey? Hersey Childress?"

Junior kept walking toward the slope. "Was gonna kill'm

the last day I was alive. Figured I'd do it first day I was dead. All the days after. Hersey charges too much for his weed."

George could only look at him.

"What?" Junior asked. "It's just Hersey."

"You ever wonder what happened after you did that? Hersey would've been found, Junior. Jake would've come after you. You'd spend the rest of your life in prison."

"Didn't," Junior said. "Come to heaven." They reached the lip of the yard. "Steep here, George."

"You don't have to go down. See those rocks there, in the middle of the water? That's where the cat was."

"Cat ain't there."

"Exactly. Tommy and I rescued it last Turn. Because we were *supposed* to. You see? The Turn keeps us here so we can right the wrongs we did. Not so much deeds, but decisions. *Choices*. Little things we might've done or answered or said the same way at any other time in our lives, but on this day, those choices somehow travel out and lead to something bad. Like you and Hers—"

Everything happened at once, the two of them looking down over the water and then Junior's hands at George's back, a push like being ejected, like a shot from a cannon, stealing George's breath and making his eyes bulge and his mouth open. George flying, the ground falling away in a spiral and the feeling of being turned upside down. The sound of water rushing not out but up, meeting him, bones crunching and the pain (*PAIN*) and the taste of blood and dirt in his mouth. Stars filled George's vision. He wanted to call for help but made only a gurgling sound at the water's edge.

Junior turned and disappeared. Ages passed. George tried to move. He dug his broken fingers into the mud of the riverbank and rolled over onto the bones sticking out from his pant legs, wailing. *Have to warn the others. Have to tell them what happened.* Crawling inch by inch as blood fell from his mouth and nose and ears. Far away he could hear a phone ringing, Anna saying she was coming home.

-3-

Juliet called not long after Bea, wanting to make sure the withdrawals hadn't grown worse and to ask if there had been thunder. Bobby told her he'd heard nothing, though he admitted to not listening. His hands still hurt from the scrubbing. Near a whole jug of Gojo had gone through his fingers and under his nails, ridding the last drops of what beer or bourbon may have been spilled on them. It had taken Bobby most of the morning to pour it all down the sink. He'd found he couldn't do it all at once, had to go a few cans at a time and then step into the alley for some fresh air and enough convincing to keep going. But he had, and in the end he had found no real loss. Mr. Jangles had gained another bag of trash to rummage through, and Bobby had gained a brief but sweet sense of freedom. His head still hurt and his bones felt tight to bursting from the flesh that bound them. His vision had gone clouded and blurred. But Bobby had kept on. Had survived, just as he always had and would.

"I'm glad," Juliet told him. "Really, Bobby. I know it must be hard for you."

"Not as hard as what comes next."

"Which is?"

"We'll leave that for now. You on your way to Dorothea's?"

"I am. I confess I'm a little anxious to see what's in her letter. Isn't that ridiculous? I always poked fun at them and never held anything they said as truth. I know it's not God who visits her mailbox, but I'm hoping whoever it is knows something we don't about what's happening."

"I don't think it's ridiculous. Sometimes faith in others is easier to place than faith in high things."

"We could go over there together."

"I gotta do something first," he said. "Won't take long. I'll meet you there."

He heard her breathing and felt his own, a pause that grew from something barely noticed to something larger than either of them could ignore. Him wanting to say the words he felt, hoping she would say them first.

"Bye, Bobby," she said.

He shut his eyes. "Bye."

*  *  *

He didn't know how it worked except for what he'd seen on the TV and heard from others. Some time ago, after Allie Granderson and Zach Barnett had walked out of Happy Hollow and all notions of Bobby's culpability in the matter had been laid as quiet as they'd ever get, Allie's daddy, Hank, had visited the shop to have a word. He said he was taking the Twelve Steps and wanted to make amends, then apologized for throwing Bobby out that window. Bobby hadn't known how to respond and so simply nodded, even shook Hank's hand, and that was the last time the two of them spoke except in passing. Mark had pronounced what Hank did the highest form of courage. Bobby had proceeded to get drunk.

Whether making amends was the first step or the twelfth, Bobby didn't know. The list of those he had wronged felt too long for him to consider. But it felt as good a place as any to begin and much easier than acknowledging a high power. Besides, he had already said good-bye to his sons. He figured he might as well go along with the rest, hoping perhaps it would get him out of heaven sooner.

It was one thing to decide to make amends, another to decide who went first. Those closest should have priority. That meant family. Bobby knew it would hurt his courage too much to go to Junior about the horrible things he'd said when the oaf hadn't been around. There was too much pride in going to Dorothea and Laura Beth and Tommy. Juliet would hurt too bad. That left George, and to George was where Bobby drove.

He recited his affronts, counting off onto shaky fingers how he had never been a good student in George's science class and the one time he and some friends had egged George's house during spring break, the time just after New Orleans and just before Carla took the boys that he'd over-charged George fifty dollars on some vehicle work. Bobby stopped there. Three sorries felt plenty. No sense getting carried away.

Bobby relaxed when he saw George's truck still in the drive. He pulled beside it and got out, practiced what he would say and how. Start off with a thank-you sounded best. Then a confession that George was first because his was the easiest amends to make, the least embarrassing, and that Bobby felt that things would go easier if his sorry came here at George's place rather than Dorothea's, where the walls were thin and the ears were always cocked to listen. He knocked at the wood part of the screen door—no answer. Hollered inside, but George didn't appear. He looked to make sure the little Toyota pickup really was in the drive and that his thirsty mind hadn't conjured it. Then he looked out across the yard to where it dropped to the river and saw the body.

He could feel his legs pumping and the adrenaline shooting through his body, that sense of everything swelling, and yet the world and everything in it slowed to almost a stop. He reached George and fell to his knees. Shaking the old man's shoulders, feeling the cold skin. Touching the spot on his neck where a pulse should be, feeling only the sticky-slick blood that had congealed there. Blood everywhere, staining George's mouth and beard and the front of his shirt, staining George's hands, and what of it his lungs had not coughed up puddled and dried where the bones had punctured through his legs. Bobby crying now, not knowing what to do, slapping at the flies and ants that had been drawn by the smell. Telling George he was sorry for not studying and throwing those eggs, wondering if that apology counted or if it doomed him to the Turn forever.

George's stomach moved. Not out as though in exhale but in, as if collapsing into itself. Bobby shrank back, shouting George's name as George's head turned and his eyes, milky in death, began to shine with a light so white it came as blue and so clear that Bobby shielded his eyes. The body began to loosen itself, every inch of skin and every cell now unbound by what forces had held George Grimm together in life, leaving him nothing but a single light that shimmered into billions, motes of dust, tiny stars that rose from the grass into a blue sky where they winked out one by one. His clothes were all that remained. Two boots and a torn pair of khaki pants, a single bloodied shirt. And something else, poking from the edge of a front pocket. Bobby reached through blurred eyes for the notebook.

He began to read.

## -4-

After everything that had happened and all she had endured, one truth had been made clear to Anna Grimm—that Saturday had been the longest day of her life.

She blinked hard and widened her eyes to chase away sleep. All four windows of her Honda had been down since crossing the Virginia line. The cold air that had kept her awake now made her hunch, thinking of bed and covers and George's soft snores. She turned up the gospel station, sang. Thanked the Lord in loud and flowing sentences for seeing her safely through the valley of the shadow of death and prayed George wouldn't be mad and that her no-account brother-in-law would spend all eternity having his toes nibbled on by the devil's minions.

Things had started off so well that morning: Anna kissing her sister Sadie and her nieces and nephews good-bye and even giving the aforementioned no-account Robert half a hug, waving the slip of paper he'd given her, directions to a shortcut he'd promised would shave almost an hour of driving. She shook her head now, reminded the Lord she should've known better. Those directions had been nonsense at best and a deliberate lie at worst, Robert's way of telling her to think twice in paying another visit. Narrow back roads instead of Kentucky state ones, winding through the hills and lonely places where not a soul dwelled. Anna trying to find a spot to turn around but too afraid that would get her more lost. And worse—no cell service.

Then the car trouble, steam pouring from the hood and a light on the dash she could make no sense of, pulling off the road and wishing George were there. She'd tried calling again, this already well into afternoon. But that part of Kentucky (or had it been West Virginia?) had somehow marooned itself in a time before cell towers and 4G LTE. Thank heaven for that farmer, the one Anna was afraid would rape her but had instead filled her radiator with a jug of water he had in back and given her directions to the interstate. She was half an hour on before she realized she'd left her cell back along the road. By then night had fallen. Every big rig and van that passed looked to be filled with murderers and delinquents. No way could she talk herself into pulling off an exit and finding a pay phone—if such things even existed anymore. She'd kept driving instead, rolled the windows down and turned the radio up and prayed George hadn't called out the National Guard to look for her.

It was twelve minutes after one in the morning on that Sunday when Anna passed the old wooden sign along the road welcoming her to Mattingly. Never had there been a more precious sight. She met the bridge and drove through an empty downtown, across the other bridge and over the railroad tracks. Almost home, praising the Lord through smiling lips, asking forgiveness should she miss church in the morning.

The living room lamp was on and the rest of the house dark. Anna parked and eased her aged body out, grimacing at the kink in her back and her sore legs. She left her bags in the trunk. The front door was open to the screen. She went in calling George's name, saying she was sorry and he should hear the day she'd had: near endless, one thing after another and nothing changing at all.

Silence greeted her.

"George?" No one in bed. Anna walked back to the door and turned on the floodlights outside, stuck her head out and called again. She managed "Geor—" before seeing the body at the edge of the yard.

Anna ran to him as much as her aged body would allow. Shaking him, her head swimming, begging George to wake, saying she was sorry for getting lost, calling to the Lord and to anyone.

All she heard was the river below, and all Anna saw was a stray old tom sitting beneath the maple by the garden, watching.

## -5-

Laura Beth had arrived with the groceries by the time Bobby walked into Dorothea's house. He carried George's notebook in his hand and George's blood on his clothes and for a long while took everyone's questions with a grieving silence. The more Juliet and Laura Beth wanted to know what had happened and if Bobby was hurt, the deeper into himself he tumbled.

He cried as he spoke it, all of them in their places at the table but for the empty spot on the end. Bobby could not remember the last time he had wept. The twins, he guessed. The day Carla had called to say their boys were dead. He shuddered and sobbed and wiped the snot from his nose and faulted no one when they offered no comfort. Dorothea sat in shamed silence as her face grew more and more ashen. Junior and Tommy hunched their shoulders as close to the table as they could manage. Laura Beth's countenance turned peaceful. Only Juliet mourned outwardly and with an appropriate degree. Only she wept as Bobby wept. He would not judge the way of their grieving. He would not reckon them harsh or unfeeling for the simple reason that he had once been called the same, after Katrina and after the boys, when the only comfort he could find had come from the bottom of a bottle and the imaginings of his own heart.

The food Dorothea had intended for dinner and supper lay spoiling on the kitchen counters, the roast thawing and the lettuce already turning brown, both as useless as Bobby's voice from all his talking. He told them of finding George, how he must've gone out to look at the river that morning and slipped, fell to the water and tried crawling back up for help. To Bobby's own wonder, George had made it. He confessed he'd never believed such an old and sick man could be so strong, climbing up that slope an inch at a time while missing so many bones and so much blood.

"He's free," Laura Beth said. The sun shone and the birds chirped through the open window, the one where George always stood to smoke. Bobby saw the smile on her face, as if Laura Beth could see George there still. "He's dead now and he's free."

Juliet wiped her eyes and looked at Dorothea. "That true, Mama? Because you need to tell me how that's so. Tell me how people who are supposed to be dead and in heaven can die once more. I've heard of being born twice, but never that."

"George ain't *dead*," Junior said. He crossed his arms in front of himself, muttering it. "He ain't dead just like Jake ain't dead and Hersey, neither."

"Hersey?" Bobby asked.

Junior said never mind Hersey, his point still held.

"It wasn't like Jake. It was different. Jake laid there gone and bleeding. George *moved*. He broke up."

"Like the stars," Dorothea said. "Yes, Bobby, I heard you the first time. And you expect us to take that on faith?"

"You're the one always told me faith's what sustains us. I bore witness to George's leaving."

"And were you drunk when you bore this witness?"

Bobby held out his hands, trembling as though charged with current. "You tell me. George is gone. Ain't coming back. It was like he'd never been made of flesh and bone at all, like his skin was a shell to hold the light inside."

That silenced them. Junior said nothing more and only sulked along with Tommy, who refused to look at anyone. Bobby shoved his palms to his eyes and rubbed hard, then reached for George's notebook. What came next would be hard for some of them to hear, but Bobby knew it needed saying. For George, his friend.

\* \* \*

"Found this after he . . . left, I guess. In his pocket." Bobby stared at the book. Its brown cover was stained by handling, the binding worn loose. "George once told me he got up each Turn and wrote down everything he could remember of this place and us. All his ideas."

"All his lies," Dorothea muttered. "Damned fool."

Bobby let that be. He opened the book and held it up, flipping through the pages. "Had to get this all down today. This Turn. I think he found a way to get us out of here."

Juliet raised her head. "What?"

Tommy kept his eyes down. "Ain't no way out of here, Daddy. Don't nobody want to leave heaven."

"You ask Laura Beth that, bud. This ain't heaven. Never was."

Laura Beth's grin was all the way now.

"Mind yourself, Bobby," Junior said. "You don't know what you say."

Bobby no longer cared. "Tommy, you go to George's to feed that cat, what happened?"

305

Tommy's cheeks flushed. The rest of him turned as white as Dorothea.

"Go on, son. It's okay. Just tell the truth as we all know it."

"George got the cat and he said he saved it but he *hurt* it and I know 'cause I was there."

"And that was the first time George did that?"

A tentative "Yes."

"I don't know what's happening," Bobby said, "and I don't know what it means, but there weren't no cat there this Turn. I'm thinking George found that out and everything must've clicked inside him. I read through this notebook. He's got all our names written here, things we did before we gave ourselves over to the Turn. He's got you almost getting run over in town, Dorothea. Tommy, your old mama. Juliet and Nolan Reynolds and you, Laura Beth, and Charlie. He's got me, the stuff I did and those I spoke to. All but you, Junior."

Junior's voice shot out, "Don't mean nothin'."

"I think it does. Because underneath it all, George underlined something he wrote. Something I remembered he told me when we first started playing chess, and what I said to him when I finally beat him: 'The beginning makes the end.'"

Dorothea spoke up: "This is no game, Bobby."

"You're right. But the words hold. Everybody's got their own ideas of what this place is, heaven or hell or some part of a river I don't understand or a punishment for lives ill lived. But I think the only one's been right about it all along's Juliet."

The preacher looked at him, stunned.

Bobby nodded. "That's right. The belly of the beast, saving us from a storm. But now that storm's coming, and we all got to make a choice. Only way out is to change our directions. Go back. Choose different. Change the beginning."

"I'll hear none of this, Bobby," Dorothea said. "George talked such. Look how he paid."

"You owe it to George to listen. He died figuring this out."

*"He died because the Lord saw!"* she screamed. Tommy's face twisted into a grimace that ended in a sob. "Because the Lord had grown weary of George's insolence and knew that man would be the end of us all."

Juliet fell grave. "How do you know that, Mama?"

"It was in the letter this morning."

"Let me see it," Bobby said.

"It's burnt." She raised her eyebrows, seizing a point: "I suppose you'll have to take it on faith."

"The Turn's coming apart, Dorothea. Those cracks, they won't stop. What happens when you hear thunder again, and what it strikes isn't a barn or a river but this house?"

"That won't happen."

"You going to take that on faith, too?"

Dorothea stood, slamming her hand on the table. "I will not have you twist my words, Bobby Barnes. You are scared and you are hurt and I'm trying to understand because I am as well. But you have to remember none of us can go against the Lord. His warning is plain. You cannot leave home."

"This ain't home."

"And what is, then? The world you left? The one filled with those who mocked you for the man you became? The world in which you had nothing?"

"No." He broke his gaze, lowering his head and his voice. "That world ain't home, neither. I don't know where home is."

Beneath the table, Juliet reached for Bobby's leg.

"And yet that is the world to which you seek to return," Dorothea said.

He heard a sweet poison to her words, a biting kindness

Bobby did not understand even as a sense of warning flared in his mind.

"What will you propose, Bobby?" Dorothea smiled now. "Go back and rewrite all you did on this day? Fine. I suppose that means you're heading up to the mountain after. Take your ride, like you always have? Kill that person along the road, like you always do?"

Bobby's body went cold as Juliet's hand tightened at his knee. They all stared now, Laura Beth and Dorothea and Tommy. Even Junior looked shocked.

"Who told you that happens?" Bobby said.

"No one needs tell me, dear. You drive up there and you hit that vehicle and you kill that driver and that's the end of your Turn. You live, so far as I know. Can't imagine you not, what with that big ugly truck you drive. That means if such a thing as leaving the Turn were even possible, you would live on as you once did. But what sort of life is that of a murderer? Why, there's not a soul in Mattingly who believes you'd see the grave without killing another first. Turns out that's become prophecy. You would escape the judgment of God, Bobby. That's fortunate, given you would be doomed to hell already had you not been granted heaven. But you would not escape the judgment of man. Such a verdict may not be so lasting but can be just as cruel. You call the Turn a cell. To you, I suppose it is. But leaving will only trade you one cell for another, one much smaller and empty of those who care."

Her smile. Those teeth, so gleaming white they could not be real, as fake as the rest of her.

"I hate you," Bobby said.

"I don't care," she answered. "My job is to keep my family safe. Keep them together. I've failed with George, and that burden is far heavier than you can possibly know. But there has been no thunder. The Turn grinds on as it always has and will, and what we need, Bobby, you and I, is time."

Bobby shook his head. "Why do you keep manipulating me?"

"I'm trying to *fix* you," she said. "Why do you insist on remaining broken?"

Bobby closed the notebook. He wanted to stand from the table but wouldn't, wanting Juliet touching him.

"You forget something, Mama. You forget the man I am. You think that wreck is enough to keep me here, you never knew me at all."

Juliet moved her hand. He stood.

"You and Junior want to stay, I won't say otherwise. But the rest of you need to come with me and figure out the best way to do this."

He did not look behind as he walked to the foyer, only listened for the sounds of chairs sliding back and feet shuffling, neither of which happened. When he turned, he saw Tommy and Juliet still in their seats and Junior's hand hard on Laura Beth's shoulder, keeping her there.

"You can't go, Daddy," Tommy said. "You got to stay with me."

"It isn't safe here anymore, Tom."

Dorothea spoke: "He's safer with us than with you."

"Tommy's right," Juliet said. "You can't go, Bobby. Not yet."

Bobby shot her a glare. "You too? After everything?"

"Please. I'm begging you."

"Begging's done, Juliet. You made your choice, I make mine. I gotta do for me."

He turned again, going for the door. Dorothea offered a final warning: "Don't do this, Bobby. The Lord is watching. He came after George, He'll come after you."

Bobby slammed the door. He turned his voice to the open window and said, "Let Him come."

## -6-

Junior figured Laura Beth was mad but he didn't know why; he'd been nothing but nice that whole Turn. Getting her what she needed, a plate and some tea and what came out to be a whole bottle from Hubie's cabinet. They hadn't gone anywhere that whole day. Bobby had left and Mama had said for everybody else to stay put, what they all needed now was time to mourn George and not upset the balance more. Junior hadn't liked the way Mama had looked at him when she'd said that word—*more*. Like what all had happened was his fault.

So they'd all stayed at the yellow house. Neither Tommy nor Junior had a mind to go elsewhere anyway, and if Junior didn't go, then neither would Laura Beth, and Juliet had already made up her mind not to do like Bobby said. Junior did wonder how that could be so. He'd thought Bobby and Juliet loved each other like he and Laura Beth did. But if that was the case, then Juliet would always back Bobby's play, because that's what loving someone meant, that and sex. Mama seemed confused by Juliet staying behind, too. Them two had sat out back most of that afternoon, talking about the higher things Junior had never much cared to understand.

Maybe it was George that had Laura Beth so bothered. If that was the case, she'd be sad only a few hours more. George would be back then just like Jake and like Hersey because this was heaven and nobody ever left. How could you? And besides, who would ever want such a thing? Junior tried

310

saying all of that and almost said more. Almost said he knew Bobby was drunk when he said George lit up and floated away because George sure didn't do that at all, Junior knew because Junior'd *been there,* all George did was lie along the bank, coughing up blood and showing the bones in his legs. But he couldn't tell Laura Beth that. Junior didn't even think he could come right out and tell it to Mama. Because he'd been on a secret mission from the Lord, and none of them would understand.

Laura Beth remained distant all that afternoon and evening. Junior said maybe they could go upstairs and roll around in the bed. She'd said no, doing it that close to the end of her Turn would only make what Charlie would do hurt more. Not her heart, she'd said, but her body. Laura Beth said she didn't think her heart could hurt any worse, and that had confused Junior all the more given the peaceful voice with which she'd said it.

He took her home that night after saying their good-byes to everyone else. That whole way, neither of them spoke. Junior reached his hand across the seat for Laura Beth to hold. She did, but the touch of her fingers felt cold and dead. He pulled the truck over at the end of her street away from the lampposts so nobody would see and left the engine idling. Laura Beth didn't get out, only stared down the street through her window.

"Wonder what Bobby's doing," she said. "You think he's getting things ready?"

"To what?"

"Leave."

"Ain't no leaving."

"George left."

"He'll be back."

She looked on.

"Bobby wants to upset the balance," he said. "Like George. Maybe the Lord'll go after Bobby, too."

Maybe, he thought, the Lord would send him on another secret mission.

Headlights filled the mirror. Junior looked there and saw Charlie turning onto the street in that fancy car and not even bothering to look or wave, because Charlie Gowdy had no good use for people like Junior unless a bank note come due. Be something, wouldn't it, if Charlie ever knew how his wife had spent a whole lot more time in bed with Junior than with him. Had called out Junior's name in their passion and not his, even if that was because Junior had asked it. That would be something, wouldn't it? Charlie finding out he weren't a real man at all but Junior was.

"I don't want him touching me anymore," she said. "Hurting me like he does."

"Don't want it neither." He squeezed her hand. "Still a blessing. Makes you appreciate the way I treat you."

She said nothing to that and didn't squeeze his hand back. "You know livin' in a house like that was always my biggest wish? Getting all my nice clothes off wood hangers at the fancy stores in Stanley 'stead of the bargain bin at the Walmart. Driving a nice car. Having me a rich husband. Always just wanted things, because I never had any growin' up. Got them, too. All I had to do was trade away my dignity and my soul. And you know what I found out in the end, Junior? Charlie only wanted things, too, and I was one of them. Even now, here and forever, I'll just be his thing."

"You're mine," Junior said. "My thing, too. Right?"

She shook her head and chuckled. "Right."

"Lord give me you, Laur-Beth. I take care of you."

"You do, Junior. As much as I warrant it."

He didn't know what that meant. "He give me you in heaven because He knew you'd have no use for me in the old world. We went back there, you'd never look my way. You'd be fancy again, but I'd still be the same."

"Don't care for fancy anymore. All the fancy in the world don't get me what I need." She turned to him now, that same look of peace now mixed with the water on her cheeks. "I'm leaving."

She opened the door. Junior said, "Tell me you love me."

"I love you," she said, but he thought maybe she didn't and maybe never had. Those were words you should never have to ask to hear.

He watched her walk, head high and that blond hair sparkling like shooting stars in the lamplight. Thinking of all she'd said to him and all he didn't understand. Thinking of her last words—*I'm leaving*—and wondering of the queer feeling in his gut. Halfway to the house, Laura Beth winked and vanished. Far ahead in an upstairs window, a light turned on.

-7-

Juliet had taken Tommy home. She'd tried talking to him, had reasoned and begged and even grown stern, and in the end she still didn't know if Tommy would do as she'd asked. A part of him wanted to. Juliet could see that. Yet in the end the boy's heart lay too broken over George, his fear too great.

"George wasn't supposed to die," he'd said. "The Lord didn't mean that."

"The Lord's not the Lord, Tommy. Not here."

"But He's still watchin'."

She couldn't disagree with that. "Someone is, and that's all the more reason for you to leave this place."

"Will Daddy be there?"

"I don't know."

"Will you?"

She lied: "Yes."

"This is heaven."

"It isn't."

And as he closed the faded and chipped front door of his house, Tommy had said, "I think Junior killed George."

\* \* \*

Bobby wasn't at the shop. The door was unlocked and the lights still on, but his truck wasn't in the bay. Juliet stood in the center of that silence and closed her eyes to pray. This wasn't what she'd wanted. What she had to say should be said in person. But their Turn was nearly up. Time was short. For him, for her, for them all.

She dialed as she drove, the line ringing three times and four, wondering if all her fretting would be for naught. Bobby picked up on the fifth ring.

"Didn't know if you'd call," he said.

"Didn't know if you'd answer."

"Almost didn't. Guess I got tired of riding alone."

"You're not alone, Bobby."

"Really? Lost my boys twice now. Lost you. Why didn't you stand and leave with me, Juliet? All you said about how this place wasn't the end, then you turn right around and choose them over me."

"I didn't choose anybody, Bobby. There's so much you don't know and so much you can't understand."

"Try, then."

"No," she said. "Not over the phone. It has to be face-to-face."

"Over the phone or face-to-face, I'm leaving."

"You *can't leave*, Bobby. Please listen to me. I didn't go with you today because I knew you couldn't convince Dorothea. As long as she stays, Tommy and Junior will. Junior will do everything in his power to keep Laura Beth here with him. Don't you see? I had to stay and try to convince them. I talked to Tommy tonight. I think he might try to change things."

"Change things how?"

"Stop his mom from leaving. Try to talk to her. I don't know. But I think he's going to try, Bobby. If Tommy does, then things will change, the way they did with George's cat. I told him to fix things with Stacey and then come and see you. You'll have to watch over him next Turn."

"Juliet, I can't babysit Tommy. I'm talking to Bea and Carla and I'm going to Timmy's. Tommy wasn't with me that first time. What if him being there screws things up?"

She gripped the phone, cursing under her breath. "You're going to have to figure something out, Bobby. You came to the house with George's notebook because you care about those people. I'm going to Dorothea's and try to talk to her. I don't want Tommy around Junior. I don't know if I even want Dorothea around Junior, but I don't know of a way around that. Dorothea told me today she's afraid of Junior. She *said* that, Bobby. And Tommy told me tonight he thinks Junior killed George."

She could hear the radio in Bobby's truck and the wind gusting through his windows, the thrumming of his tires.

"Bobby?"

"Why would Junior do that?"

315

"I don't know. He and George never got along, but Junior's never really got along with anybody other than Dorothea and Laura Beth. Do you remember what he said about Jake? And something about someone named Hersey?"

"Hersey Childress," Bobby said. "Grows weed. Guess where Junior always gets his share every Turn. Enough for him and Laura Beth both."

"Junior said George wasn't dead just like Jake wasn't and this Hersey, too. Bobby, Junior had a hand in what happened to Jake. Maybe he does something like that to Hersey to get his marijuana. And maybe he figured if those two died and came back, George will, too."

"George isn't coming back," Bobby said.

Juliet said "I know" in such a small voice that she supposed Bobby may not have even heard.

"Why would Junior have even been to George's?" he asked.

"The letter. It had to be the letter, Bobby. Whoever writes them must've found out and told Mama. Mama called Junior."

"And what? Told him to go kill George?"

She shook her head. "No. Dorothea wouldn't do that. But I think she might now. She's lost one member of the family, Bobby. In her own twisted mind, she'll kill us all before she lets us go. She all but told me. Mama is Charlie, Bobby. We're all her Laura Beths."

"Then you can't go back there, Juliet. Okay? You stay away from there. Get Tommy and Laura Beth and—"

"I have to go back there, Bobby."

"You *don't*." He yelled the words, making her wince. "George's notebook had your name and Nolan Reynolds. That time I took you to the diner and I saw you talking to Marjorie Duncan—you said that had been part of your first day and that you went to see Nolan but got lost. I can give you directions, Juliet. I know where Nolan lives."

"It doesn't matter."

"You can go earlier in the day or later. That won't make a difference. Take Tommy and Laura Beth. Just as long as you *see* him."

"It doesn't matter, Bobby. I'm not leaving, and neither can you."

"I'm leaving, next Turn. We can go together."

"We can't go together." Ahead lay the marker, Route 237. A stop sign and a left or a right. Juliet turned left. Always a left. "I can't leave these people, Bobby. I won't."

"Juliet, those people are not your family."

"They are my *flock*. I am their *pastor*. God sent me here because I'd given up. On Him and me and everybody else. That's why we're *all* here, and I'm not going to give up again. I'm not going to run. That's why I can't go. Tommy, yes. Laura Beth. Everyone else, but not you. We have to be last."

"Juliet, I don't—"

"Where are you?" she asked. "Right now, Bobby, where are you driving?"

He didn't say at first. Or wouldn't. "The ridge road. I came up here early, hours ago. Trying to find the curve. I wanted to just . . . I don't know. Sit there, I guess. See if that changes something. But I can't find it, Juliet. The road just keeps going. The curve isn't there."

"It will be," she said. "Soon."

"Everything else I can change," Bobby said. "Bea and Jake and even Carla. But I can't change this. This feels wrong. Even if I change the rest, I won't change this."

"I have to tell you something, Bobby. I should have told you a long time ago but I didn't, and now I'm afraid it might be too late. I'm asking you. Please, don't change anything yet. Stay here with me."

"Why? So Junior can kill us, too, or so the Turn can fall apart? What happens then, Juliet? Either way, I'm going to die. I can't do that."

Her car slowed and moved toward the shoulder, the wheel and pedals working without her touch. Working even now as she pulled on the wheel and pushed on the brake.

"If you leave, I'll die. Bobby? If George was right and changing everything means you'll go back, then everything you do gets reset. Everything happens the way it was *supposed* to happen. That means I die."

The car lurched forward into the middle of the road, the engine sputtering and giving out. A glow coming from around the bend, shining against the far trees.

"I don't understand," Bobby said. "Juliet, I have to go."

"No, don't go. I love you, Bobby."

Silence again, and the echo of the tires. John Fogerty singing of a bad moon.

"Bobby? I'm the one you hit. I told you once that I end my Turn looking out the window. It's the window of my car. I see you. I see—"

Headlights. They shone like stars.

-8-

Tommy lay in bed counting. He'd done that when alive, never in school but often at home. At home, counting had served a purpose.

He would walk from school to the empty house those afternoons, sometimes using the key his old mama safety-pinned to

318

the inside of his jeans pocket but most times not because hardly anybody in Mattingly locked their doors. His supper would have been left out, cereal or a peanut butter and banana sandwich, always with a note telling him to be good and that she would be home soon. He would eat and almost do his homework. Take a shower and maybe pick up his room, put the dirty clothes inside the basket in his old mama's room. Watch TV—cartoons and funny shows about people making dirty jokes and then the news. In his old life, Tommy had always gone to bed after the news. He'd crawl under the covers and see how far he could count before his old mama got home. One time he'd gotten almost to three hundred. He was at forty-seven now.

George filled his thoughts. Mama must have gotten the letter and called Junior. Junior must've gone over there and seen that the cat was gone. Of course Mama would've done that—she wouldn't ever leave the house unless the Lord told her (Tommy frowned at seventy-nine, thinking he hadn't put that part in) and she wouldn't have gone to anyone else for help. And of course STOP GEORGE could mean one thing to Tommy and Mama but another thing entirely to someone like Junior, who threw baseballs through houses and carried at least two guns in his truck.

He had no idea George would die. Tommy saw many things the others didn't but hadn't seen that, and in a way that meant he'd killed George, too, with his words if not his hands. Tommy wasn't sure if a term existed for that, George ending up dead by the very writing he had labored to teach his only student. If there wasn't, there should be.

One hundred twenty-four.

Juliet wanted him to leave. She'd said George wasn't coming back like Junior said and if they all didn't soon leave the Turn, maybe they'd all end up like George. Tommy knew his daddy felt the same. Bobby had stood right there, saying the Turn wasn't heaven and they all had a way out if they wanted one. A way to someplace Bobby didn't call home, but where thunder was just a thing that came after lightning and not a thing that made barns and rivers disappear. He'd wanted Tommy and everybody else to stand up and go off with him, but Tommy hadn't. That had been a hard thing. For Bobby, sure. Tommy was old enough to understand Bobby only wanted to keep him safe. But what had made Tommy mad was Bobby had no idea how hard a thing that had been for *him*, having to pick between his daddy and his mama. So he'd sat there in his seat, as hurtful as it'd been. Not because Tommy had chosen either of them, but so he could hope to choose them both at the end.

Those cracks hadn't come until Bobby had gotten to heaven. That might mean something. Tommy turned that over in his thoughts, hands folded over his thin blankets, passing two hundred. Maybe the Lord should tell Mama that because Mama hadn't mentioned it, no one had. And maybe if there was something big enough to crack the whole Turn, it meant there really was a Lord, and He was warning that if they all didn't stay and start getting along, He was about to whup them all.

That's why at two hundred and thirty-six, when the front door opened and shut and he heard his old mama sobbing, Tommy Purcell grew afraid.

He remembered the day he'd taken all their mail to the yellow house, Dorothea saying Tommy had come to heaven at the right time and George saying later he'd seen that mail, too, and that Tommy's old mama had done what she did not because she hated her son but because something had broken off in her. *She had no hope left, son,* is what George had said. *And when that's gone, people can do some awful things no matter the love they have in them. I know you hurt, but you mustn't hate.*

George had been nice.

Tommy eased out of bed and pressed his ear against the bedroom door, thinking for the first time how alone and small his old mama must have felt. He shut his eyes and thought of the notes she'd left and the cereal she'd set out, tiny fragments of her because the rest could so rarely be there with him. And that, he concluded, was not his old mama's fault. It was simply the hard cost of living in a place not heaven. They had all hurt and been hurt in their own ways. Not only him but Bobby and Juliet and Mama, too. Junior and Laura Beth and George. And even though George was gone and his daddy had vowed to leave, Tommy thought they'd all found a measure of peace in the world after that had never come in the world before. Maybe Tommy's old mama could find that, too, if she were here.

Maybe she could if Tommy were there. If she could talk and he could listen.

He pulled on the knob but the knob wouldn't budge. It never had. Tommy went back to bed and pulled the blankets tight. He plugged his ears and thought of George and morning and how hard it was to be the Lord.

* * *

His eyes opened as the echo of the door shutting rattled the walls. Tommy didn't give himself time to think. He flung open the bedroom door and raced down the hall, past the mail on the table and the closet that hid the Lord's typewriter and

out the front door. Cool air scraped his legs and chest, Tommy
naked but for a skinny pair of briefs. He called to her with the
word that had been someone else's for longer than his old life
had been.

"Mama."

The figure stopped near to the car and turned, showing
him her face. Tommy forgot the cold as he looked upon her
beauty and likeness, so much like his own—the same red
locks and freckles, blue eyes that didn't belong. She stepped
toward him (stumbling drunk, Tommy thought, as he'd so
often seen Bobby) and ran a hand down her face.

"Tommy, what you doin' out here?"

"What are you doin' out here?" he asked. "Sun ain't
even up."

"I . . . need to go to the store."

He took a step forward. "Ain't no store open."

"I didn't mean for you to hear me."

"Yes, you did. You slammed the door and you coulda
closed it quiet." He'd never considered that. "You wanted me
to hear because you wanted me to stop you."

"Stop me from what?"

He couldn't say the words.

She came close but not too close, as though he were a
thing to be avoided. "Why don't you go back inside, Tom?"

"No."

"Tommy—"

He felt the tears and let them come, wanting her to see
them, what she did to her boy. "Why'd you leave me, Mama?"

"Go back inside."

*"No, I won't go back inside."*

She flashed no anger. His old mama always had when
Tommy yelled. Now he spotted only pain there, and he knew

that pain well. It was the pain on Laura Beth's face when she first got to the yellow house each Turn and what was on Bobby's after he'd told his fancied sons good-bye. It was what Tommy had seen in George each time the old man had spoken of Anna, or Dorothea when she talked of Hubert, or in Junior's words every time he told his story of Chipper Jones. It was Juliet when she looked at them all. And none of it should have been. This was heaven, this was home, and there shouldn't ever be sadness at home.

"I hate you," he said.

Her face twisted. "Tommy, please."

"*I hate you.* I hate you and just go."

He spun and ran inside, not only slamming the door but locking it as well, then retreated beneath his blankets. For a long while, Tommy heard nothing. Then came the sound of his old mama pulling away to die and, after, his own soft cries. He lay sobbing until the world began to wake, then rose from bed and pulled the typewriter from the closet.

Tommy would not leave his heaven. There was nothing for him in the old world but pain, and pain would be all the others would find as well. The two letters he typed became the longest ever from the Lord, each a full page. One commanded Dorothea to do all she could to keep everyone inside heaven. (And in case Junior became involved, Tommy stated outright that "all you can" did not mean killing, or else Junior would meet his reckoning.) The other, which Tommy rolled from the machine with faded letters that betrayed his hesitant fingers at the keys, begged Dorothea to let any who wished go.

Which letter to deliver, Bobby would decide. Tommy would go to the shop as Juliet had asked, but only long enough to know if his daddy intended to leave. Then he'd sneak away long enough to visit Mama's mailbox. It would work. It would have to. Tommy would convince his daddy to stay.

And if that failed, the Lord would do the convincing.

## -9-

He heaved deep and sat up, thinking not of stars gone from the jagged sky or Mr. Jangles scurrying back to the shadows, thinking only of the mountain. Hands to his face and then his head, where they formed tight fists around clumps of his hair. Bobby pulled, grimacing not at that pain but at the pain that lay deeper, a heaviness that crushed him.

Juliet. Juliet was at the curve.

It was anger he felt, guilt and despair at this, the final shame piled upon the mountain of others that had become Bobby's idol as much in death as it had in life. Not living in its shadow, not dying, but merely existing and calling that victory. He screamed into the long night at a God who would curse him to love the woman he killed countless times and the woman Bobby must kill finally in order to escape his crumbling heaven. And when his lungs had emptied and his echo had faded down the alley, Bobby found the God he had long shunned now shunned him. Only silence answered. Only that ever had.

She'd said nothing. All those times they'd shared together, confessing their secrets. The day at Boone's Pond and the time Bobby had told her what he did each night on the ridge road, and still Juliet had not told him. And for what reason? For him, to spare Bobby from that hurt? Or was it that Juliet had never considered it mattered that Bobby became the instrument of her death? Until George and his missing cat, none of them had reason to believe there existed a way out of the Turn other than their own deepest wishes. But she should have said something. Bobby yanked at his hair and screamed that Juliet should have *told* him, because if she had, she could have spared him the one thing he had always feared and now suffered—hope gained and then shattered.

Remnants of a rain he had never seen fall soaked through the seat of his jeans. The air fogged at his breath. A single call of a faraway mockingbird ushered in morning. With it, those jumbled thoughts began to fall as oddments until only two remained: Bobby could not go home if doing so meant Juliet's death, and he needed a drink.

"Deserve it." He looked down at his hands. They trembled, though whether from pain or thirst he did not know. Both were seen as one. "Deserve it," again. "If I stay, it'll be with my boys."

He stood and reached for his hat more from habit than need, then pushed on the wood door. The shop's emptiness made the squeaks of his boots louder. Bobby passed the bathroom and the pegboard wall of wipers and belts (without his knowing, he brushed a hand against the very belt he would have used to fix Bea's car) and into the waiting room. He pulled the cell phone from his pocket and dialed Juliet's number, knowing it was too early for her to answer. The message was two words he tried to say without anger: "I'm staying."

What warnings the deeper part of him uttered were shoved away. Bobby moved to the counter and reached under. The bottle felt heavy and smooth and good. He unscrewed the top, let it fall and roll onto the floor. The smell comforted him. He tilted the neck toward his mouth and held it there as his gaze floated to the shadowed figure of a child in the doorway. His heart swelled, thinking Matthew, then snapped at the idea of Mark, returning to beg Bobby to leave him buried.

"Daddy?"

"Tommy?" he asked. "What you doing here?"

"Came by the alley." His voice sounded thick and clogged. "Thought I might catch you out there still. What you doin' with that drink?"

Bobby kept the bottle near his mouth. The coffee maker gurgled to life between them. "Don't know what I'm doing, only that it'll feel good. I need to feel good right now, Tommy. You understand."

"Juliet told me to come by here after I did my thing. With my old mama."

"You saw your mama?" Bobby set the bottle down and came around the corner, leading Tommy to the recliner. "Juliet told me she ain't leaving, Tommy. She won't leave you and the rest, not even for me. Me and her got to be last in the Turn. Don't ask me to explain that, because I can't. And don't ask me to explain why I can't go until she does, because I can't do that either. We just got to get y'all home. The other home. So you tell me, did you fix things with your mama?"

Tommy's top lip disappeared. He chewed on it so hard that Bobby thought it would come back bloodied. "I never talked to her before. I even forgot how she looked. She looks like me."

"Did you talk to her?"

"I called her name. She turned around and seen me. It wasn't so special for her. I guess for her, she'd just seen me a few hours ago."

That tweaked Bobby's heart, but only some. This was no time for sentiment.

"And? What'd you say?"

"We just talked." He stared down at his hands and shrugged. "Guess that's all my old mama ever really needed, just to have someone listen to her. Then she came back inside and fixed me breakfast. When I left, she was in the bed sleepin'."

Bobby exhaled his shock. "You did it. Tommy, you changed everything." He laid his hands to Tommy's bare arms and squeezed. The flesh felt cold. "You did great. That's . . . wait. Why are you still here?"

"Juliet told me to."

"No, why are you still in the Turn? If you changed what you had to, you should be gone."

"Maybe this Turn's gotta end first."

"Maybe." Bobby didn't know. He stood and reached for the remote, turned on the TV. "Sit here and relish your good deed. I'm gonna go wash up, then we're going to Laura Beth's before she leaves for Dorothea's. I don't think it'll take much nudging to get her to leave. You'll need somebody on the other side to help you get adjusted to things, Laura Beth's the perfect one. That sound good?"

Tommy shrugged again.

"What's the matter? You should be happy."

"I am. Just gonna miss you."

"If what George said is right, when we all get back, it'll feel like not even a day's gone by. No matter when you leave or me, we'll all reach tomorrow at the same time."

Bobby patted him on the crown of his cap and left as the morning's news started on the screen. He whistled his way out of the waiting room and into the shop, feeling better than he suspected he had reason to, remembering the bottle still on the counter. No matter. He'd grab it before heading to Laura Beth's. Or maybe he wouldn't grab it at all. If his luck kept, he'd have Tommy freed by the end of this Turn and Laura Beth by the next. By then, maybe Juliet would be more amenable to leaving herself.

His steps slowed and his grin faded at that notion, one that had come so true only to turn to ash. It wouldn't matter when Juliet decided it was time to go, whether next Turn or one in the dim future of a never-ending present. She would still be dead in the world next door, and Bobby would have to live out what years he had left, knowing Juliet had given her life for his own. He almost turned around for the bottle on the counter but pushed on for the bathroom instead, his mind reaching for a solution that refused to appear, so preoccupied that he had turned the knob before spotting the light shining on the tops of his boots.

Bobby wiggled his toes and eased away from the door. He'd never found that light on at the start of his Turn. He remembered that first day, stumbling in from the alley drunk and wincing inside the bathroom because there had been too much light too fast. And all the times since, not so much the recollection of the bulb turning on as the heavy clack of the switch. Now that light was on. And more, the glow that shot from the thin space between the bottom of the door and the concrete didn't shine as light at all.

"Tommy?"

Over the droning of the news came the sound of the recliner's footrest kicked down. Tommy came around the corner with the look of someone far too sad to have just saved his mother from suicide.

"What's wrong?" he asked.

Bobby pointed to the door. Tommy came in slow and with short steps, then stopped when he saw the light. Bobby crept forward, turning the knob again and easing the door open. He gave it a soft push and backed away.

He had heard no thunder, yet the thunder must have come. The crack seemed too large for the room, encompassing most of the toilet and all of the sink and mirror, stretching from somewhere beneath the concrete floor to somewhere above the ceiling, with a heart of light so pure it looked more blue than white and so bright that he and Tommy shielded their eyes. Already, pieces of the ceiling and floor had disappeared where the wound had grown. Erased, as though they had never existed. And the edges, tendrils of black reaching to devour more and all.

"No," Bobby said. "No, not my shop, you can't take my shop." Speaking neither to Tommy nor to the thing that had taken Moser's barn but to that mysterious Other, the Lord of the Turn. "Leave me alone. You let me *be*, You hear?"

And the Lord answered yes.

\* \* \*

To Bobby it must have been as the voice from Moses's burning bush or Job's whirlwind, coming not in words but in sounds that flung him backward. Tommy, too, shrank in fear, his eyes going not to that rushing light but toward the waiting room, where the ring came again.

*The phone*, Bobby thought. *It's not the crack, it's the phone.*

He tipped as he lurched past Tommy, jerking the phone away from the wall and hollering a frantic "Bobby?" that came out a whisper, then tried again—"Bobby's shop."

A voice on the other end: "Bobby? That you?"

"Bea." He turned and slumped against the wall, letting

gravity ease him to the floor. "You liked to scare me to death."

"Maybe you need a good scarin', Bobby Barnes. Whatsa matter with your voice? You tie one on? That what you been doing 'stead a fixin' my car?"

"No. I ain't had nothing to drink in"—*how long?*—"a good bit."

"And I'm the Queen of England. I can hear it in your speakin'. Here ain't even breakfast, and you're sauced."

Tommy stepped inside and shook his head, begging.

"Where's my car, Bobby? I need my *car*. Had to get the sheriff to drive me to the so-curity office in Stanley yesterday. Now I got to get to Camden to pay the cable, else they take Maury off the TV from me."

"I know, Bea, and I'm sorry. I'm gonna fix your car today. Just a belt, like I said, and not even as much as I told you. I'll bring you the difference back."

Tommy said, "*No*, Daddy."

Bobby shushed him with a trembling hand. Not from thirst now. Fear.

Bea went quiet. When she spoke again, it was in a tone Bobby had never heard. "You say I'll be gettin' money back?"

"Just a belt, Bea. Didn't run as much as I thought. I can have your car back by tonight."

"No. No, Bobby, that's fine. Cable office ain't open noways. But if you could bring it tomorrow, after church?"

*Tomorrow.* The word sounded almost foreign.

"I will. I can do that, Bea."

"Plus the difference?"

"Plus the difference."

Tommy glared.

"Well, that's fine then, Bobby. I thank you. I . . ."

330

He had succeeded in the impossible—tying Bea Campbell's tongue.

"They called me a fool of an old woman," she said, "giving you my car. You know that, Bobby? But I felt it in me that I had to for some reason. Like I was *supposed* to. Like it was the Christian thing. A man might not always deserve a second chance, but he should always get one."

Bobby shut his eyes. "I appreciate that, Bea."

The line clicked off. Bobby let the phone hang from the cord and looked at Tommy, who asked, "Why'd you do that, Daddy? You said you was staying."

"Because I had to. Because I won't let that dark out there take me. What happens I stay here, Tommy? Wake up one Turn and I ain't got a shop no more because that thing swallowed it all? Wake up to find it's swallowed *me*? I'll be like George. We gonna all be like George soon if we don't leave. I only ever lived for myself, boy, and that's how I'll die. For me. She's got her reasons for staying, I'll let her stay. But she's gotta know I got my reasons for leaving, and she's gonna have to let me go."

"Who?"

"Juliet. I have to talk to her, but I need to get out to Timmy's first. You'll stay here till I get back. I can't take you with me because I didn't on that first day, and I can't chance Junior finding you, neither. Juliet told me what you said about him and George. That's why we all got to leave, too, Tommy. You keep away from that bathroom, and don't you worry. You done all you're supposed to. You're going home. By the end of this Turn, we'll find tomorrow together."

He didn't give Tommy the opportunity to say no. Bobby found his keys and locked the waiting room door behind him. Junior's Turn had likely started by now. As he left, Bobby heard the recap of the day's news. He was so intent on talking to Jake that he paid no mind to the wars and rumors of wars, and the report of the woman found dead on an old service road near Stanley.

# -10-

Morning came with soft light on warm blankets. One arm wedged under the pillow, the other dangling from the bed. She smelled coffee from downstairs and remembered how that scent had once made her feel quiet and safe but did so no more, and that was when Laura Beth opened her eyes.

She threw the comforter back. It billowed off the foot of the bed and landed at the fireplace, a sail tied not to a boat but to the singular hope that she was not too late. Scrambling out, forgoing the silk robe draped over the far chair or the dresses and skirts in the armoire, running to Charlie's closet instead.

No time to turn on the light. She pushed the door wide to let in the sun and groped with her hands, feeling jeans and pants and T-shirts, boxers streaked with Charlie's excrement. The shirt was somewhere among all those clothes. The polo Charlie called his favorite, his lucky one for golf, and oh, how he needed luck when having to play with men whose voices were soft and genteel but carried a hardness beneath. Alabama men, Kentucky and Georgia and Mississippi men. Looking to *branch out*, Charlie had once told her. Coming into *new territory*.

The shirt, where was the shirt? Laura Beth went to her hands and knees, pushing aside a laundry basket and a set of dumbbells Charlie never used. She had to find it, had to change things, get fr—

"Laur-Beth."

A cry escaped her, nothing more than a peep among the closet's shadows. She reached for something shoved under the basket and freed it, held it to the sunlight, and Laura Beth nearly wept for joy. She brought the shirt to her bare chest and rummaged again, this time through the basket, finding among the clean clothes a single dryer sheet. Charlie's footsteps echoed from the stairs. He said again, "Laur-Beth," as she ran the dryer sheet over the shirt, rubbing it hard into the front and back of the fabric.

At the far end of the closet stood a second door to the bathroom. Laura Beth grabbed a hanger from the rod and turned on the lights over the sink. Wrinkles covered the shirt like veins. The collar had gone bent, curling inward at the edges. He wouldn't like that. Charlie always said the only possession a man truly owned was his appearance.

"Hey," came the voice. "Where's my shirt? Laura Beth?"

"Coming." She slipped the shirt through the hanger and pressed it against her, running her hands over the creases and furrows. "Hung it up here last night in case you needed it right away."

Charlie didn't answer. He'd always answered before. Laura Beth came out through the bathroom door nearest the bed. She tried to smile and held the shirt away, showing him her body. Charlie stared at her through hollow eyes.

"You wash it?"

"'Course I did." Trying to smile.

He held his hand out and took the hanger, sniffing the front of the shirt.

"You iron it?"

She couldn't tell him yes. The dryer sheet may have convinced Charlie that his stupid shirt had been washed, but he had eyes enough to see it hadn't been ironed.

"I was about to," she said. "Won't take me long."

Charlie went dark. "One thing. I ask you one thing, Laura Beth—get my shirt ready. I have to do a million things to keep us going, keep us safe, and you can't do the one thing I ask?"

She saw the flash of his wedding band as it caught the sun. Laura Beth wanted to run but couldn't. Running wouldn't change things, wouldn't save her.

"Go on," she said, and that stopped him. "Hit me. It'll be the last time, Charlie. I swear to God, that'll be the last hand you lay on me and that shirt'll never get clean. Or you can sit on the bed and wait while I get the board from the closet. You don't have to leave for another twenty minutes. Could've ironed it yesterday like you wanted. Then it'd sit on that hanger and just get wrinkled again. You want that stupid shirt to look good today, or last night?"

"Don't you sass me. You know what I think of sassing, Laura Beth."

She knew.

Charlie sat and tossed the shirt onto the floor. Laura Beth reached for it and then her robe.

"Leave that," he said. "You're not the one needs clothes."

She went back to the closet for the board and iron. His eyes were on her. That hungry look. All men looked at her that way, they always had. Junior, Bobby. Even Tommy had upon occasion leered in a way that carried the seeds of the man he might have become had he lived on. All but George. George had treated her as something other than a pretty face.

His heart had been too filled with Anna, and now George was gone.

"What you thinking about?"

"Nothing," she said. "Why are you starin' at me?"

"Maybe I like what I see."

She began ironing the shirt and thought about how having your husband speak such words should bring a warm feeling instead of the cold one that entered her. She'd heard stories from friends (her old friends, ones Charlie had driven away) of how the fires that dwelt inside every man smoldered and burned out over the years. Passion yielded to a sense of tiredness over the world, beauty lessened with familiarity. Not so for Charlie Gowdy. He received what he wanted when and in whatever way he wanted it. Laura Beth's heart had rarely been present. That didn't matter so long as her body had been.

"Hurry up," he said. "Maybe by the time you finish, you'll have a few minutes to take care of something else needs fluffed and folded."

She kept her eyes to the shirt and the spot of carpet by the bed, watching for Charlie's feet to go there. If they did, if he so much as came near, she would mash the iron against his face. Get *those* wrinkles out.

"You don't have the time," she said. "You gotta get there early. Here, I'm done."

She held up the shirt. Charlie actually smiled. He rose from the bed and took the polo from her hand and eased it over his scrawny neck and the paunch of his stomach, then moved behind her. Laura Beth's grip hardened on the iron. She felt him pressing against her and his breaths on her bare shoulder and thought of Junior, all those times he'd done the same. Her decision to leave the Turn had been her own. Laura

Beth had told no one. She had allowed herself no doubts that what Bobby had read from George's notebook had been true. Now, for that moment, Laura Beth wondered not the why of what she was doing, but the how. Juliet had once told her their decisions on this day would have somehow led to a great evil had they not come to the Turn, that if they ever hoped to leave, those choices must somehow be made right. Charlie whispered something she did not hear. His hand went in front and up her stomach, pawing at her breast. She winced at the pressure, the way he always mauled her, and Laura Beth knew all she'd done that morning amounted to a waste. She had changed things, yes, but she had fixed nothing. Charlie was still beating her, just not with his fists.

"I get back tonight," he said, "you be ready for me. And next time you'll have my shirt ironed."

He squeezed hard, bringing a yelp she knew he would take as yearning, then left without further word. Laura Beth remained naked at the ironing board until she heard the Corvette start and Charlie pull away. She went back to the bathroom and stood at the mirror, looking upon a face streaked with tears but not blood. No bruise, no swelling. She saw Charlie's handprint at her chest, the red outline of his fingers, and Laura Beth vowed two things to herself:

There would not be a next time.

And when Charlie returned that night, she would be ready.

## -11-

Away from town, traffic slowed to passing farmers and kids playing chicken on their bikes, men and boys who glanced Bobby's way only long enough to recognize the truck and then find something else of interest. A cloud. A funny-looking tree. No one had looked at Bobby but to sneer or whisper in the old world, and yet that was the world to which he sought his return. The idea of going back seemed a foolish one, something a person would do only to heap upon himself the scorn he knew had always been deserved. Those farmers passed and did not tip their caps. They did not so much as raise a finger off the wheel in acknowledgment. And those boys on their bikes, waiting until Bobby passed before confessing their mamas had warned that's how they would turn out if they didn't keep to their schooling and their Christ-fearing friends. Like that drunk. That Bobby Barnes.

They didn't know how he had changed. None of them ever would. Nor would Juliet, until the end. He had settled on his plan. Its success seemed dim, a fool's hope at best, the only sort afforded to the likes of him.

The Texaco rose in the distance. Bobby stopped the truck at the front pump and let the engine idle. He was supposed to have filled up here on that last day but hadn't, had left after Jake and Timmy said their words and had gone on to the BP and met Junior instead. Of all the people he wished to avoid his last day in the hell of heaven, Junior Hewitt was first. He got out and pumped ten dollars, thinking the amount didn't matter. The storefront windows, glistening in the sun, didn't allow Bobby a look inside. Not that he needed one. He knew Timmy waited. Jake as well.

It was a slow walk to the door, steady and straight. Sheriff Barnett stood where Bobby knew he would be. Bobby took a left for the coolers and grabbed a Coke, careful not to let his eyes wander to the long racks of six-packs and cases beside. He stopped for a bag of peanuts on his way to the register. Timmy started punching buttons.

"Bobby," he said.

"Timmy. Got ten on the pump."

"That all you need?"

"That and breakfast."

He tore the top off the peanuts and dumped them in the Coke, watched the brown fizz bubble near the top.

Jake asked, "Brings you out so early, Bobby?"

Bobby chuckled and took a long sip, crunching down on the nuts. "Now that's quite a story, Jake. Just taking care of some things."

"You don't need no beer?" Timmy asked.

"No. Give it up."

"Since when?"

"Awhile."

Jake fingered his hat. "You serious, Bobby?"

"I am. Thought I might take the steps. Gave enough of my life over to despair. Time I set things right. What I owe you, Timmy?"

Timmy rang up not a thing, too shocked at Bobby's words. Bobby would have chuckled again if he hadn't felt so ashamed. So naked.

"Looks like thirteen and a quarter," Timmy said.

Bobby gave him a twenty from his pocket and nodded at the change, wondering if what had gone so easy could be called fixed. It didn't seem right that the bad course upon which his life had drifted could be righted simply by buying gas and groceries and being civil. But then Jake said, "I'll follow you out, Bobby," and Bobby thought maybe things wouldn't go so easy after all.

Jake waited until the station door closed behind them. He looked back to make sure Timmy couldn't hear, then to the empty lot. "You doing okay, Bobby?"

"Best I can."

"You look good. Different."

Bobby didn't know how to accept that.

"Heard you got Bea's car in your shop."

"Needs a belt is all," Bobby said. "I'll be getting it back to her in the morning."

Jake nodded. "My truck needs some work. Set of tires and plugs. Maybe I'll bring it by."

"I'll do you right."

"Glad to know it."

They reached Bobby's truck. Bobby climbed in and shut the door, laid his elbow in the crack where the window would go had it been rolled up. He didn't start the engine.

"Proud of what you're doing, Bobby. Hard thing to do alone. Kate would call me remiss if I didn't invite you to church. There's always a place for you."

"Maybe I will," Bobby said. "Expect either way, I'll be seein' the Lord soon."

"Well, let's hope it's awhile yet."

Bobby's hand lingered at the ignition. A truck's noise came from the trees down the road. His head turned, as did Jake's, to see Junior rolling by. Slowing at first, as if to turn in, then keeping on, his bug-eyes gawping.

"You sure you're okay?" Jake asked.

Bobby wasn't. Junior had seen him, and even as dim as the man was, he would know the only reason for Bobby to be at the Texaco was if he'd been serious about leaving. Junior's next stop would be Mama's. Juliet.

"You do me a favor, Jake? Check on somebody for me today?"

"Who?"

"The Widow Cash."

"What you want me to call on Dorothea Cash for?"

"No reason. Just seen her about lately. Looked a little confused on things. You go check on her for me, Jake? Soon? No questions?"

The sheriff looked as though he possessed those in abundance. "I will."

Bobby turned the key, bringing the sound of the truck's electronics firing and a dinging noise from inside the dash. The distant sky brought a quiet rumble.

Jake turned his head and looked there. "Didn't think they called for storms today."

"I gotta go, Jake."

"You in a hurry?"

"I am."

Jake patted the side of the door. "You take care, Bobby. We'll be praying for you."

Bobby nodded, too ashamed to say his thanks. "I'm sorry, Jake. For everything I done and all the trouble I caused through the years."

Jake grinned. "I appreciate it, but I don't think that step comes until later."

"Maybe so. Might be the only chance I get, though."

# -12-

Dorothea wouldn't venture from the bathroom that morning until she'd taken time to color her roots. It had been so long that she'd forgotten the process, having to read the back of the box she plucked from beneath the sink before continuing on. The experience was a difficult one. Shameful, in a way that made her feel a charlatan. Old.

She put on her slippers and robe and set the kettle on the stove before going out. Even when Dorothea spotted the flag at the side of the box lowered, she did not hurry. Her fingers hurt and her back. The hinges of her knees were rusted doors trying to swing open. She wondered if time truly was creeping forward, like the bruise on Bobby's face and the way George had coughed near his end. Or perhaps it was something more sinister, that the power she held over heaven and those inside it had begun to wane. Stolen, by George's death and Bobby's insistence upon leaving and Dorothea's own fading faith.

As she descended the paved drive and stepped into the street, she stared at the mailbox and wondered. Not at what lay inside, but if what lay inside would offer comfort at all. The Lord had proven Himself worthy during the long eternity she'd been inside her heaven, had given all of them the praise and love that had gone lacking in their former lives. But now praise and love weren't needed so much as wisdom and guidance, and here Dorothea worried that the God of the Turn might fail her. He had not warned her of George's heart or Bobby's plans, had offered platitudes rather than answers. It was almost as if the Lord had been kept in as much ignorance as she.

The lid squeaked as she tilted it down. The envelope sat not in the center of the box but near the back. Crinkled and worn this time rather than crisp. She slid a finger inside the flap and pulled, then unfolded the sheet of paper inside. The letter was long, by far the longest she'd ever received. Her lips moved in silence, one sentence and then two, head shaking a slow and steady *no* at words that said it was time to let Bobby go if that was what he wanted, that the thunder hadn't come until he had and that was because the Lord wanted Bobby to choose his own path. Telling Dorothea how it was up to her to keep the family together, but it was up to the family to want the blessing that could only be found with one another. Asking her to please not let anybody else get hurt.

Asking her. As if it hadn't been a Lord at all that Dorothea had clung to all this time, but a frightened puppy.

More than anything else, more than the obtuseness with which Dorothea had quietly seen her God and the multitude of ways in which that God had disappointed her, that tone was what shook her—that notion of *begging*. As if by those words, the Lord had bent His knee to Dorothea rather than demand that act from her. Standing there in the empty street, the breeze ruffling her dress and her damp and darkened hair, Dorothea felt a moment of panic mixed with shame. Her mind recalled those times when George and Juliet had questioned her letters and the writer behind them, why God would have need of human implements to offer His will. Bobby sitting at Hubert's old place on Hubert's old sofa and drinking Hubert's bourbon, Dorothea offering the secrets of their heaven, him asking, *Lord writes you a letter every morning. That what you're trying to tell me? I'm in heaven, and God writes you letters?* The anger those words had kindled then and the notion of absurdity they kindled now, the Lord—the true Lord—finding favor with her.

She had been lied to all this while. Made a fool by someone of flesh and blood who mocked from the shadows and played her the puppet, letting Dorothea dangle and dance from the thin strings of faith. And now that someone wanted Bobby freed should Bobby desire it. Wanted Dorothea's family torn asunder.

Dorothea vowed that would not happen. Let the Lord (and for the first time in the world next door, that word made her cringe as it traveled a path across her mind) beg all He wanted. This was her heaven and her people, and already too many had abandoned her, never to return. Hubie first, now George. There would not be another.

The letter shook in her hand. Dorothea placed it inside the envelope and folded the flap down around it, smoothed the front and back with her sore fingers. She held it out from her like a sick thing and ripped the envelope down the middle and ripped it again, grimacing at the ache in her bones. When she could tear no more, she held the pieces aloft in the palm of her hand and let the breeze take them. Freed now at last and beholden to none, the only god herself.

\* \* \*

Laura Beth did not arrive at her appointed time, nor Tommy, and that only served to flame Dorothea's anger more. She embraced it as a garment to shield herself from the cold fear that crept onto the porch overlooking her backyard. Perhaps it was the thunder that had kept them away. She had heard one rumble, far off, some time ago. No matter. So long as it stayed against the mountains and away from the yellow house, Dorothea cared not if the entire world fell away.

A shadow fell across the side of the yard, too small to be Tommy's and too wide for Laura Beth. Dorothea took a sip of her tea as Juliet stepped along the path from the willow to the porch, smiling and offering a good morning as she sat.

"Where is everyone?"

"You're the first, dear." Dorothea set the cup down. "Haven't seen anyone else."

The preacher furrowed her brow. "Junior?"

"Soon, I expect."

Juliet eyed Dorothea's cup and saucer, the brown tea inside. Mama offered her nothing.

"I appreciate the talk we had here yesterday, Mama. What you said. I know we haven't always been as one when it comes to the things that happen here or the reasons behind them. I'd like for us to fix that. I've always liked you very much, Dorothea."

Dorothea smiled, thinking that funny. "I've always seen honesty as the bedrock of all profitable communication, Juliet. Wouldn't you agree?"

"I would."

"Then why don't you dispense with all that blowing of sunshine up my dress and tell my why you're here and how you somehow managed to convince my children to stay away from me?"

Juliet's back stiffened as her mouth fell open. She shook her head before she spoke in words Dorothea could have guessed: "I did no such thing, Mama. I spoke with Tommy last Turn and Bobby, but no one else. I promise you."

"You promise me. As if I can trust your word, Juliet."

"You can."

"Then tell me, what did you say to Tommy and Bobby?"

"The same thing I'm here to say to you. It's time we go, Mama. All of us. That bore no discussing before beyond the realm of argument, but there can be no argument now. George found a way before he died, and that thunder's getting close. Did you hear it a little while ago?"

"Far off," Dorothea said. "Could have been no thunder at all."

"You know otherwise. This place was given to us, on that we both agree. But we were never meant to remain here. Time moves on, and so must we. Together. Let me help you."

"And how would you help me, Preacher?"

Juliet swallowed. Licked her lips. *Thirsty*, Dorothea thought. *Good*.

"It took you years after Hubert died to gather the courage to go out on your own. You used to rely on people to do for you, got Jake to take you to the store and neighbors to tend to your yard. I don't fault you for that, Mama, and I won't judge. Then the one day you decide to get into town on your own, what happens? You almost get run over. It scared you. I know it did. It would have scared anyone. But then you gave up, didn't you? You gave up on living because Hubert wasn't with you anymore, and you came here."

"I came here because I was needed."

"You want to know what I said to Tommy? I told him he has to try and change things with his mother. His *real* mother. And I thought he might when I left him, which is why he might not be here right now."

Dorothea slammed her cup onto the saucer between them, chipping the porcelain. "How dare you do such a thing. That boy has *nothing* apart from us. It's a fool's errand you sent him on, Juliet. One you or anyone else has no idea will even work."

"He's hurting, Dorothea."

"He's mine," she said. "You're all mine. You, Bobby, Junior, Tommy, Laura Beth. You're my family, and all you want to do is leave."

"Together, Mama. We'll leave together, just not Tommy. This place isn't safe for him anymore. It's not stable. I know you love him and so do I, and that's why we have to see him back. But the rest of us will stay. Even Bobby. He left a message on my phone this morning saying such."

At that, Dorothea blinked. "Bobby is staying?"

"Yes. Until we go. Until we all go."

"And why would Bobby decide such a thing?"

Juliet lowered her eyes. "Because he wants us to be together."

Dorothea didn't know if *us* meant Bobby and Juliet or the family. She didn't get the opportunity to ask. From down the street came the rumble of Junior's truck. He pulled into the drive and got out and came walking through the house, out the back door.

"Mama." He bent, kissing Dorothea on the cheek. To Juliet, he said nothing. "Where's everybody?"

"That's what I've been trying to surmise from Juliet's words," Dorothea said. "Strangest thing, I can't seem to get a good read on it."

Junior looked at Juliet. "What's that mean?"

"It means don't worry," Juliet said. "Everything's going to be okay now. But you need to sit a minute, Junior. I need a word."

Junior didn't sit. "Where's Laura Beth?"

"Away," Dorothea said. "Not here with my groceries as she always is. Someplace else. Tell me, Junior, did Laura Beth have the opportunity to talk to our preacher here last Turn?"

"No," he said. "Seen Laura Beth home myself. Why?"

"Because I believe we have a traitor in our midst."

Junior looked to Juliet again, who began backing her chair away from the table too late. He was on her before she could stand, crowding her with his big body, saying, "Where's Laura Beth?" and "What'd you do?" and "Tell me!"

"This why I seen Bobby this morning?" he asked.

"Wait," Dorothea said. Junior whipped his head her way, then took a step back. "What about Bobby?"

"Seen him to Timmy's, talkin' with Jake. Why'd he be at Timmy's, Juliet, 'less it was to fix things?"

Juliet's eyes swelled. "I don't know. Mama, I swear I don't know. Maybe he went to get gas. Or beer. Maybe Bobby's drinking again."

"Or maybe," Dorothea said, "you been lying to me all along."

Junior's cheeks flared. He turned to Juliet once more and laid his hand across her throat, squeezing as he pulled her up. She gagged as slobber ran from the edges of her mouth, pawing and kicking for Junior to let her go, face turning the colors of autumn. Dorothea spoke not a word. The Lord would have her tell Junior to let go, but the Lord was no longer here in the Turn and maybe never had been. Juliet would have to learn. She'd have to let that hard lesson sink in as Junior's wide mouth broke into a grin and Juliet made a sharp coughing sound and a voice boomed across the yard.

*"Turn her loose!"*

\* \* \*

Dorothea stood as Sheriff Barnett came to the porch. He did not run but walked with purpose, long strides as his boots clopped the stone walk, hat tilted low over his eyes. He said it again—"Turn her loose"—and Junior did. Juliet dropped back into her seat, gasping and spilling the last of Dorothea's tea.

Murder clouded Junior's face. He moved toward the steps as Jake climbed them, towering over the sheriff. Jake did not back down.

"What's going on here?"

"Ain't none your business, Jake," Junior said.

"You lay a hand to a woman, it is."

He stepped up, easing Junior back. Juliet's head lay on the table. A bit of her black locks strayed into Dorothea's cup. Dorothea moved it away with her fingertips and offered the preacher no solace.

"Widow Cash," Jake said, "you mind telling me what this is about?"

"A misunderstanding, Sheriff. Nothing more. I told Junior to stop by this morning to price me some trimming in the yard, bushes and trees and whatnot. Juliet had come by first to perform her duties to God and man and ask me to join her failing congregation. Junior fell under the false assumption Juliet was a stranger intent on doing me harm. Nothing more than that."

"Looked like more than that where I stood." He went to Juliet and put his hands on her shoulders. "You okay?"

She couldn't speak, only nodded.

Junior said, "You best get on, Jake. We don't need you here."

"Then you'll get on with me."

He moved, reaching for Junior's hand. Junior smacked it away. "Killed you onced, Sheriff. I'll do it again."

Jake cocked his hat back, showing Junior his eyes. He moved his hand again, luring Junior in, then took it away and replaced it with a knee he drove into the big man's groin. Junior gasped and doubled over, reaching for Jake, the table, calling out a weak "Mama." Jake straightened him with a hand he clamped to Junior's throat.

"Don't know what you meant by that, Junior," he said, "but I don't appreciate the tone." He squeezed harder. "Don't feel too good on the other end of things, does it?"

Juliet's hoarse voice sounded. "Stop."

Jake acted as if he hadn't heard, then relaxed his grip. Enough for Junior to breathe, not enough to let him run off.

"Misunderstanding," Juliet said. She shook her head. "No charges. My fault, Sheriff."

"Juliet—"

"My fault," she said again. "It's fine. Please."

Jake let go of Junior's throat. "Ain't fine," he said.

Dorothea stared at the preacher, wanting to know what was in Juliet's mind. Christian charity, perhaps. She doubted it.

"Get on," Jake told Junior. "I see you around here again, I'll haul you in."

Junior grinned. "Anything you say, Jake."

"And I believe you owe the pastor an apology."

"Sorry," Junior whispered to Juliet.

He looked at Dorothea, who said, "I appreciate you coming by, Junior. And I'm sorry for the misunderstanding. You come on back, take care of them hedges. Meantime, you know what to do."

Junior nodded and eased off the porch. His walk around to the front of the house looked slow and painful. Juliet had regained some of her color but nothing of her peace. Dorothea sat and made her hands shake for Jake's benefit, trying to pick up her cup.

"I appreciate you stopping by when you did, Jake. Must've been the hand of the Lord."

"Something like that. Juliet, let me see you home."

"That won't be necessary," Dorothea said. "Pastor should stay here until she calms."

"Come on." He took Juliet by the arm and helped her up. She cut her eyes to Dorothea as she rose. "Good day to you, Widow Cash," Jake said. "You see Junior again, you give me a call."

She watched the two of them leave, Juliet leaning on Jake's shoulder as they walked, Jake asking again in a soft voice what had happened. Dorothea didn't have to hear to know Juliet wouldn't say. She'd stick to the story that had been presented and would never involve the dead in the affairs of the living. That had happened before with Jake, and to his own end. After they left, Dorothea went inside to prepare another kettle of water. She tossed the broken cup in the trash and considered it no loss. It would be back next Turn. Then she went back to the porch to wait for Junior. He would be back soon, with or without Laura Beth. Then the two of them would talk on how to save their family. Whether it would be through peace or war.

<h1 style="text-align:center">-13-</h1>

Bobby found the shop as he'd left it. He spotted no sign someone had broken in or tried to leave, and the waiting room door was still locked. He turned the key and found Tommy thumbing through the Tom Franklin novel in the recliner, one leg draped over the chair's arm and his head against the cushion as though near dozing.

"You okay?"

The boy nodded.

"Anybody come by? Junior or Juliet?"

"I ain't gone nowhere. Mama'll be wonderin' where I am. I'm late."

"Don't you worry of Mama none," Bobby said. "Your time's short."

Tommy earmarked his page and shut the book, tucking it back inside the crack between the cushion and armrest. "What if it ain't?"

"What if what ain't?"

"What if I'm to do more than save my old mama? What if George didn't know that and I don't either? I'll still be here next Turn and you'll be gone. Won't be nobody here to keep me safe from Junior."

Bobby hadn't considered that. Nor had he stopped to think all he had done that morning could be for naught. George had been a smart man, but even he'd acknowledged that some things inside the Turn lay beyond his reasoning.

"Maybe you should wait, Daddy. Make sure I go first, like Juliet said. I don't want to be alone. 'Sides, if I don't go, it means nobody can, 'less they die for real like George did."

"You'll have Juliet and Dorothea to keep you from Junior. They won't let nothing happen."

"Happened to George," Tommy said. "Please, Daddy? Stay here with me. Don't change nothing else."

Bobby moved from the door closer to the chair. "Tommy, you really fix things with your mama?"

He caught a flicker of something in the boy's eyes, embarrassment or guilt, the same flash Bobby had once seen in his own boys when they'd been caught playing in their mama's flowers or coloring the walls with their crayons.

"She's in bed when I left," Tommy said. "But my heart don't feel no different."

"Ain't supposed to listen to your heart. Supposed to talk to it. I'm leaving, Tommy. 'Nother Turn, shop might not even be here. Might be gone just like that barn, and maybe me with it. You got to believe is all. Believing's got nothing to do with what you feel. Your mama's safe and you'll be safe with her. Now come on, give me a hand."

"What we doin'?"

"Fixing Bea's car. Just gotta make a call first."

He moved behind the counter and put away the bottle

of bourbon, not wanting that temptation, then dialed Juliet's number on his cell. The ring came not on the other end of the line but just outside the shop. Juliet swung the door wide and walked in, phone in her hand. She glanced at it, looked at Bobby with a long stare of defeat. Her mouth twisted into what he thought would be a smile, then her lips turned downward and her eyes narrowed to cry. Tommy bolted from the chair and helped Juliet to his seat. Bobby felt guilty that he hadn't gone to her first. The shock of seeing her like that, he supposed, and yet he also knew it was the memory of the last Turn, her voice saying, *I told you once that I end my Turn looking out the window. It's the window of my car. I see you. I see—*

But he went to her now, taking along a beer from the refrigerator, which he popped and offered, but she refused. Bobby set the can on the table by the chair, wanting it himself. No sense letting something like that go to waste.

"Tommy," she said. "Are you okay? Did you talk to your mama?"

He nodded. "She's just fine, Juliet. Promise."

She smiled then, a bit of brightness that faded like a cloud sliding over the sun. "Junior came after me."

Tommy went a shade whiter. He spoke—"The Lord didn't put that in the letter"—and Bobby didn't care what that meant or how Tommy would know.

He took her hand and said, "Tell me what happened."

"I went to Dorothea's to try talking to her about leaving. Junior came wanting to know where Laura Beth was."

"Laura Beth ain't at Mama's?" Tommy asked.

She shook her head. "I think she's leaving. That or she's scared to go anywhere. Then Dorothea called me a liar and Junior came after me. He started . . . choking me. And

Dorothea didn't do anything, Bobby. She just let it *happen*."
Juliet's shoulders shuddered at the memory. Her words went
soft. "He would have killed me if Jake hadn't shown up."

Bobby took a deep breath. "I told Jake to come by
Dorothea's, check on things. Just had a hunch."

"So it's true, then." Her hand went limp in his. Juliet
swallowed thick. "You were at Timmy's, trying to leave."

Bobby pulled his cap low and looked away. "I got to."

"You lied to me."

"I didn't. I called you soon as I woke and meant that message. Things is changed now."

"What's changed?"

"Shop's got a crack in it," Tommy said. "Like the one in
the barn."

"Where?"

"The bathroom," Bobby said. "Near ran right into it after I
called. Nothing more I can do, Juliet. The black's coming for
me. I got to make my play."

"And what about me?"

Bobby wanted to tell her but knew he couldn't. "We can
figure something out. There's time yet."

Juliet shook her head and rolled her eyes, mocking him. She
stood, brushing Bobby aside and making Tommy step back.

"Where you going?"

"To find Laura Beth before Junior does." She opened the
door, letting in the sun. "Are you coming?"

"Jake let Junior go?"

"I told him to. I wouldn't press charges."

"You what? Juliet, we could have gotten Junior locked
away."

"For a Turn. That's all, Bobby. Then next Turn it all gets

put back, and Junior'd be twice as mad. I can't let that happen. Don't you understand he's as precious to me as anybody else? I have to get him home." She opened the door wider. "Please, come with me. I need your help."

He took his hat off, rubbed his hair. "Can't."

"We gotta fix Bea's car," Tommy said. "Daddy's leavin', Juliet. You need to tell him to stay. What's in that bathroom don't matter."

"Bea's car can wait," Juliet said.

Bobby shook his head. "I can't go, Juliet. I need to stay here awhile."

He wanted to say the words but found he couldn't, they hurt too bad. Juliet didn't move from her place. Sunlight washed her body, crowning the lines on her face and the marks on her neck, making her look frail and frightened and beautiful. She shook her head and chuckled, then said the very words Bobby couldn't.

"Your ex-wife, Carla. She's going to call."

"I have to fix it, Juliet. While there's time."

"You'll save yourself and let us all pay the price. You're the same as everyone told me. Every harsh word true."

"That ain't fair," Bobby said. But it felt to him that it was. People didn't change. He'd told Matthew and Mark that often enough, when the boys had been alive and once they were dead. People didn't change because changing hurt, and there was already enough of that in the world.

"Stay here, Tommy," she said. "Don't go outside. I don't know where Junior went, and the way he is now he's just as apt to come looking for you as Laura Beth. Or come looking for you, Bobby. I suggest you lock that door and call Jake if you need him."

"Juliet," Bobby said. "We can talk this over."

THERE WILL BE STARS

"Sounds to me like the talking's done. You've made up your mind. For the both of us."

With that, Juliet walked out. All that lingered was silence and the sweet smell of her perfume.

\* \* \*

He could get no work done on Bea's car and couldn't decide why, if it was that he had to do the job sober or that he kept watching the clock for Carla and the windows for Junior, or if it was Tommy's insistence on helping. Mostly, Bobby thought, it was Tommy. The boy was afraid. That was understandable. Bobby felt the same, not of leaving, but of all he had done and would do turning to rubbish at midnight's Turn. Yet it seemed to him that it wasn't so much Tommy's nerves that slowed them as much as it was Tommy's intent. Even now he did all he could to ensure failure, dropping tools and handling them wrong, getting in the way with an "I'm sorry" as an excuse. After a while Bobby wished he would have sent the boy with Juliet.

"You can't go," Tommy kept saying, and Bobby kept answering, "We're both going."

Yet as the hours ticked on, Bobby found the work still not progressing, and the simple work he had to do for Bea became a burden he could not shoulder. Carla weighed too much on his mind, and what space she didn't occupy was held by Juliet and Laura Beth. He surrendered not long after and told Tommy they should take a break. Tommy huddled back down with his book. Bobby brought a bucket from the back of the shop and turned it over in front of the phone. He sat, staring, waiting for it to ring.

"I don't know what's going on with you, Tommy. I know

you're scared and I know deep down you don't want to go, but going's best. For all of us. This phone's gonna ring soon. I'm gonna talk. Whatever's in your mind, you keep it there."

From behind him came a weak "Yessir."

* * *

When it did ring, Bobby couldn't answer. He let his hand hover over the receiver but didn't pick up until he began to think it would soon be too late, then lifted it from the hook as if it were a wild thing intent on biting him. Tommy stirred in the chair and laid down the book. He'd said a few minutes ago he couldn't understand the words anyway.

"Bobby's shop."

The voice on the other end sounded like a memory of happier times and so much anguish. It reminded Bobby of treasures put away and the rusty boxes that held them.

"Hello, Bobby."

"Carla. Figured you'd call me."

"Why?"

"I don't know," he said. "The day."

"You remembered?"

"I won't forget."

A long pause, then, "How are you?"

"Been better," Bobby said. "Been worse. I guess that's about as much as a person can hope for. You?"

"Some days are easier than others. Some days I feel almost human again."

He heard Tommy ease from the chair.

"How's Richie?"

"Why do you want to know about Richie?"

"I don't know," he said. "Seemed proper to ask."

"I don't see him. What letters he sends from prison I return refused. We're divorcing, Bobby. There was just no way I could go on."

"I'm sorry to hear that." And, by some miracle, Bobby found he meant it. He felt Tommy's hand at his back, rubbing in small circles.

"This was never the way it should have been," Carla said. "Do you know that, Bobby? We should still be married. Our boys should be growing up and skinning their knees, falling in love and getting their hearts broken. We should be helping them and playing with them and hoping to what God there is they'll be okay, they'll be *safe*, but instead there's me and there's you and if I want to be with my sons, I have to sneak down to Mattingly and visit the cemetery and I'm just so angry, Bobby. I'm so mad that sometimes I think I just can't go on, and I just want to know what happened. To us. To everything."

Bobby stared at the floor. Not listening to his heart. Talking to it. Prying it open as much as he could. "You go on. We all go on as best we can with the wounds we have. We limp and stumble and try to make it to the end, because that's all we can do. You ask me what happened, Carla, I don't know. My head went one way and my heart another, and then me and everything else got pulled apart. You're right, it shouldn't be this way. I'd give anything in the world to have everything I lost, every unpaid bill and every night we spent at the kitchen table wondering if we should put gas in the truck or get the boys new shoes. But those times is gone now, and we can't have them back no matter how much we want them. It's up to us to make a mess of our lives. Up to us to set things as right as we can after."

He heard her sniff, then chuckle. "Haven't heard you talk that way in a long while."

"Guess you could say I've had time to think things over."

Tommy's hand disappeared. Bobby turned his head and watched him walk toward the door and out into the afternoon sun.

"Carla, I need you to do me a favor."

"What?"

"You might hear something about me soon. Something bad. I don't want you to believe it."

"What are you talking about, Bobby?"

"It would take more time to explain than I got. I know you have no cause to trust me ever again, but I'm asking anyway. Just this one last time. Don't you believe what they say. It won't be like that. I think I got a second chance at things, and I'm not going to let it pass. I've wasted so much, Carla. Lost you, lost my boys. I can't get any of that back, but maybe I can give something. Maybe I can give one more thing."

"Give what?"

"Me."

# -14-

Laura Beth silenced her phone after the first six calls. Half of those had come from Charlie, whose messages formed progressive steps from agitated to angry to afraid, blaming Laura Beth for everything from the fit of his shirt to golfing partners who seemed more intent to grill his mismanagement of their ill-gotten gains than shoot under par on the front nine. Charlie had never called before. Laura Beth took that as proof beyond her unmarred face that she had altered things, for better or worse. She also took it as proof that Charlie would return in as much a drunken fury as ever.

Mama, too, had called, wanting to know where Laura Beth had gone and if her tardiness had something to do with the sheriff, whom Dorothea said Laura Beth should avoid at all cost. Laura Beth didn't know why she should. Jake Barnett had never crossed her path inside the Turn other than the day he had died. One clue arrived when Juliet called later, begging Laura Beth to stay away from Mama's and find Jake. Something had happened, and that only made Laura Beth more afraid. She'd kept her plan to leave hidden, but there were no secrets inside heaven. The Lord always watched.

The final call had been the one Laura Beth expected. Junior's message sounded strained, worry and a growing anger that had made his voice come across near as Charlie's, and with the same threats buried underneath: "Laur-Beth, where you at, girl? Been lookin' for you all mornin' long. Mama needs her groceries for dinner. She's worried to where she's mad. Things is happenin'. I need to get you someplace safe. You hear? Call me back."

She hadn't called back and never would. That pained Laura Beth in a way she had not expected. It was as if she'd traveled back to her high school days and broken some poor boy's heart, only this boy had done more than pass her notes filled with song lyrics or offer his letterman's jacket. Junior had in his own way provided safety and comfort far more than Charlie and his money, and yet Junior had been right— there could be no place for them together in the old world. And though Laura Beth had never loved Junior, she mourned him just the same.

He called again after that, and then called every five to ten minutes but left no more messages, and Laura Beth had quieted her phone. In the time that passed, she watched Junior's truck roll slowly by from the crack of light between the living room window and the drawn curtain. He would pass and turn at the end of the cul-de-sac and then roll slowly by again before making another circle through what she thought would be town, then repeat everything again—a Junior's Turn inside the Turn. He never pulled into the drive, didn't knock at the door. Junior had no reason to do so. Laura Beth knew she had chosen the perfect place to hide, the one place everyone knew she had always most avoided.

It was a long wait that morning and afternoon, and lonely. She walked through those big and silent rooms, sitting on leather sofas and running her hands over granite countertops, pondering the emptiness inside the thin shell of her life as it had been. In a way Laura Beth understood this as necessary, bolstering her for what she must do later. Yet her loneliness shouted in all that quiet to the point where being alone here at the end of things felt a harsher punishment than even Charlie's fists. And so when Laura Beth spotted the lingering shadow on the other side of the back door and heard the soft knock and the sound of that quiet voice, she did not hide. She instead opened the door to this visitor who had become more than a friend in the only heaven she had ever known. Who had become, Laura Beth believed, something like an answered prayer.

\* \* \*

"I'd forgotten how pretty you are."

Laura Beth smirked and sipped from her glass. She'd wanted something stronger than water, but it didn't feel right now, partaking in front of a preacher. It'd been bad enough those times she had come to Mama's high from Junior's weed and found Juliet not passing judgment but looking sorrowful, which to Laura Beth felt worse. Juliet looked sorrowful still.

"I'd forgotten what it's like to walk around without feeling like half my face is on fire. How'd you know where to find me?"

"Didn't," Juliet said. "I looked everywhere else and ran out of places. It never occurred to me you'd still be here. I guess I never associated you with this house."

"This is the place where I'd've died." It hurt, saying that. The truth often did. "Sooner or later, Charlie would've done it. He might still. It'd be a bad day at work, or a coffee stain on his suit, or one of the lot he's thrown in with giving him trouble. Or maybe it would be nothing, a good day all around, and he'd just come home and kill me anyway. You always hear people talking about being in a war, saying they never felt so alive as when in the presence of death. Not me. I ain't felt alive in a long time, Juliet. Since way before I got here."

Juliet set her glass on a coaster and leaned in close. "I never knew, Laura Beth. I swear it. None of us did."

"There's a whole other world behind every closed door in this town, Juliet. Sins kept hidden from all. After a while they fester and grow into something you think is bigger than you are. That's why it's up to me to open my own door now. Walk out and face the day."

"You're leaving, then?"

"If such a thing is possible. If George was right. I did what I could this morning, hard as it all was. And things did change. Charlie didn't put his hands on me and he's called since. Both of those have never happened. Junior's been by here looking for me and Mama's called. I know something's happened this morning, and I know that's why I have to see this through. If I stand up to Charlie and leave, this will all be over. If I stand up and stay, at least I'll know I can stand up again. Again and again, Juliet, no matter if it's forever. But if I do nothing, I'm afraid nothing will be left of me at all. There's nothing much left now."

"I went to Dorothea's this morning," Juliet said. "Junior came, asking for you. The two of them got it in their heads I had something to do with you not being there. Tommy, too. I had him go to Bobby's." She pulled down the collar of her shirt, showing the finger marks across her neck. "Junior choked me."

Laura Beth tried to show shock, but all she managed was a turn of her lips. She'd always known the wild animal holed up inside Junior Hewitt, had seen its shadow more than once. Besides, those marks didn't look so bad. Laura Beth had seen worse.

Juliet fixed her collar back. "Bobby had seen Jake early this morning and asked him to come check on Dorothea. I think he knew something would happen. Sheriff got there just in time. Another minute?" She shook her head. "Dorothea didn't lift a finger. She told me last Turn she was scared of Junior, but she wasn't scared on her back porch this morning. Something in her has changed."

"Or been revealed," Laura Beth said. "I'm sorry, Juliet. If there's anything I can do."

"You're doing it. Leave. Find your way back to where we all belong. Tommy's leaving. He fixed things with his mama. Stacey's alive." She dipped her chin. "Bobby's leaving, too."

"And you?"

"I'm here to see everyone away."

"Even Dorothea and Junior?" Laura Beth took her hand. "Listen to me, Juliet. They won't leave. Junior thinks he's a god here. He's got no rules and says all he wants is his to take. Me included. And Dorothea's just too stubborn."

"It's fear more than stubbornness. I can reach them in time."

"I heard the thunder earlier. I don't know how much time's left."

Juliet agreed. "That's why you have to go tonight."

"Junior will try to stop me."

"You let me worry about Junior. I promise he won't get in here."

Laura Beth stared at her glass. "I don't know if I can. What I'm gonna have to do? I don't know if I got that strength, Juliet. Charlie'll kill me."

"You're braver than you think and stronger than you know, Laura Beth. This will work. I know it will. And maybe you'll wake up tomorrow and find me there, too, along with everyone else. Maybe no matter when we leave the Turn, we all find the same tomorrow on the other side."

"Do you believe that?"

Juliet said yes. Something in Laura Beth spoke otherwise, saying the preacher believed only part of that was so. Some would go on to see tomorrow. Some wouldn't.

"I've never been a godly woman, Juliet. Never had use for church. All the things I wanted I could get myself one way or the other. Now I don't think that's so. Would you go to the Lord for me? Ask Him to help me in what comes?"

Juliet smiled and gripped her hands. "We'll go to Him together."

# -15-

Junior tried Laura Beth's house a last time. His stomach rumbled from missing dinner (and, as he checked the clock on the radio, supper, too) and his head hurt. His cell phone lay in pieces on the floorboard, the latest victim of his wrath. Not the last. Nosir. By the end of this Turn, Junior would be breaking more than phones. The only thing left to settle was whose bones it would be.

He'd used a full tank of gas and had not fished at all that Turn, which only added to his frustrations. Andy sold him gas. Junior dared not go to Timmy's and risk meeting the sheriff. He'd wait next Turn to see Jake again, put a bullet in that stupid hat with Jake's stupid head still in it. Maybe do it again the Turn after that. Serve Jake right, kneeing Junior as he'd done.

He'd been to Mama's and over every street in town, had gone back to the trailer and even to George's. George wasn't there. Junior guessed George would never be there again and didn't know what to do with that thought, given the bigger one that crowded his mind. It was as though Laura Beth had vanished.

As if she'd already escaped.

That thought had crossed Junior's mind more than once, a nagging he'd managed to swat away when he'd first gotten to Mama's that morning, but one that had grown too large and heavy to dismiss as the Turn wore on. She would not answer his calls. Laura Beth always answered, if not because she wanted to, then because she knew Junior would keep calling. She wasn't at Bobby's. Junior had gone there as well, found Bobby gone along with his truck. That conniving little whore Juliet had disappeared, too, the two of them likely together. Junior had yet to see even Tommy. His mind flashed back to the old times when he'd first gotten to heaven, the madness and loneliness that gripped him before Mama came along. Junior felt that way again.

Dark fell over Mattingly. By eight that evening, Junior no longer cared about Laura Beth so long as he had someone to talk to. Not a townsperson, one of the dead, but a family member of the living. He took that final pass down Evergreen, hoping to find a light on at the house or Laura Beth waiting at the old bench. What Junior found instead was nothing. The house stood dark, the bench empty, and he began to feel the anger in him turn to something far colder and much more real. Junior felt afraid.

Mama had every light on in the house plus the ones outside when he turned down her street. He pulled into the drive and saw her and Tommy waiting on the porch. Tommy looked to be crying. Mama was flailing her arms and yelling something Junior didn't hear. He got out of the truck and she said, "Why aren't you answering your *phone?*"

"It broke."

"How does your phone *break*, Junior?"

"Broke when I broke it," is what he said. *Just like maybe how I'll break you* is what he didn't. Junior could feel his heart thundering and the tingling of his fingers, things coming apart. "What's wrong?"

"They're leaving is what's wrong," Mama said. "Bobby and Laura Beth."

Junior took the steps and looked at Tommy, who held a handful of Mama's dress. "You tell her that?"

Tommy nodded and wiped his nose.

"Tommy was with Bobby all morning," Mama said. Her eyes had gone baggy and her hair shone too black to be real. Junior guessed she'd gone on and colored it so the gray wouldn't keep showing. "This was Juliet's doing. Tommy told them he talked to Stacey but he didn't. He just wanted to know what they were up to. He finally got away a little while ago and came here. There's a crack in Bobby's shop, Junior. I've been calling you since."

"I can't find Laura Beth. Bobby don't have her. Ain't seen Juliet, neither."

Tommy said, "I don't know nothing about Laura Beth."

But Mama said, "I do. She's leaving. Only reason for her to hide."

Tommy let go of Mama's dress. She laid a hand to the boy's cap and stepped forward to the edge of the porch and looked out over the darkened homes beyond.

"I will not let this family be torn asunder. I will not let the one true gift any of us has ever received go to waste. This. Is. Our. *Home.* And I am the one responsible. The one who has worked and toiled and given of herself to keep all of you happy, and yet you refuse it, all of you. And I have had enough." She looked at Junior now. "You might not know where Laura Beth is, but you know where she'll be. Get out there. Stop her. I don't care what you have to do. Then you come back here and get me. We're going to Bobby's and ending this."

"Can't upset the balance, Mama," Junior said.

"To hell with the balance."

Tommy shook his head. He pulled so hard at the hem of Mama's dress that the white of her bra strap showed. "You can't do that," he said. "Mama, that ain't what the Lord wants."

She jerked Tommy's hand away. "Things change, Tommy. Even in heaven. Only Lord I see here now is me."

\* \* \*

Mama's plan was simple enough that she said even Junior could abide by it. All he had to do was get to Laura Beth's and wait until he saw that shiny Corvette and then stop Charlie, stop him any way Junior could, ram the car with his truck or shoot Charlie in the head and let him die in the street. Anything but let that man inside the house. With Charlie gone, Laura Beth would have nothing to change. With nothing to change, the Turn would still claim her.

Junior would still claim her.

A simple plan, easy enough. Yet as Junior drove, he found one glaring flaw in Mama's reasoning—no Turn could be altered. He knew that well enough, all of them did. They had tried before to save Laura Beth from what must be, had kept her away from the house and had even gone to Stanley once, where Junior had rammed a knife into all four of Charlie's tires to keep him away. It never did. Charlie somehow always made it home in time. Always turned that upstairs light on. Their interference had only made Laura Beth's punishment worse. Junior had wanted to give her his gun, take it to her bedroom and leave it there, blow Charlie away. Mama had forbidden that, saying it would go against both the Lord and the balance to claim a life. But then the Lord changed His mind when Jake died, and now Mama had changed hers about everything, the Lord and killing, too, and Junior minded that not at all. He'd never a heart for the higher things, and he'd kill Charlie forever if it meant keeping Laura Beth with him.

All of that fell away when Junior arrived. Charlie's Corvette was already in the drive. The top was down and the driver's door open. An empty bottle of beer lay in the road. And just as Junior slowed to decide what to do, the upstairs light clicked on.

He came to a stop along the curb and jumped from the truck, flipping the seat forward to grab his shotgun from the rack. Movement from across the street turned his head. He saw nothing but shadow. Laura Beth screamed as he reached the edge of the yard, the sound carrying from behind even the brick and thick windows. Junior racked the shotgun and ran. Up the long slope of grass toward the porch, lungs burning and knees aching, flitting stars clouding his vision as he propelled his big body forward. He reached the first step when the front door flew open. Charlie scrambled out with a look of terror on his blood-soaked face. His hand clutched the space between his jaw and left cheek. A wet stain ran down the right leg of his pants. He registered Junior standing there and lurched down the steps, whimpering. The bloody hand left his face and went to Junior's shoulder. Junior recoiled at the sight, Charlie's cheek hanging by a flap of limp skin, the white bone showing beneath.

"She's crazy," Charlie said. "Help me."

Junior pushed him aside and climbed the steps. At the door he turned to see Charlie running down the street, mad from pain. He did not call Laura Beth's name as he stepped inside and followed another set of stairs to the second floor, to the open door at the first bedroom where the smell of copper and sweat hung in the air.

The shotgun clattered to the floor when Junior saw her. His Laura Beth. She stood motionless at the windows, her dress torn at the neck and the curve of one breast beckoning him. Her blond hair, always so perfectly kept, hung in tangled clumps. And in her right hand the poker from the fireplace, still wet with Charlie's blood. She looked at Junior and gripped the poker harder, her steel look melting into one of peace.

She spoke not through a smile, but through a knowing that her time was done and her Turn now over:

"He won't touch me again."

Junior stepped forward and stretched out his arms. "Laur-Beth?" Wanting to hold her and comfort her, ask her to stay. To please stay. Laura Beth dropped the poker and reached out with a hand that began to glow. Her skin shimmered like a distant point on a summer's day. Her hair shone like gold. From eyes that had once beheld Junior's shy bareness and the mouth from which she had once spoken words of kindness came forth a light so pure and clear it was as if Laura Beth's very heart had been tipped over, poured out, and Junior knew then that he had loved her, but not the most beautiful part of her. He wanted to cry out, say he was sorry, yet those words would not come as her body began to loosen. Laura Beth tilted her head back in a way she never had in the throes of their passion, a way that meant ecstasy and release, slipping from the chains that had bound her in life. The room filled with lights that danced and leapt in hidden music. They encircled Junior and he smelled her, and then those lights winked out one by one.

# -16-

Sunlight kissed her cheek, that warmth marrying the cool breeze and tickling her arms to goose bumps. A sparrow called. Laura Beth opened her eyes to day.

She sat up, curling the comforter about her. The house lay as though paused in midbreath, still and quiet. No smell of coffee wafted up from downstairs.

No one called her name.

In the corner by the window lay the poker. The blood on its curved end had dried, maroon against a black powder coat that had left the carpet stained. Another spatter, thin but with tiny splotches, marked the path where Charlie had fled.

She rose and walked to the far chair for her robe. Her shoulder ached. It never had before. Laura Beth remembered swinging the poker with that shoulder, warning Charlie away. Telling him to stop as rage filled his eyes and his face twisted into that hungry look it always did before he would hit her and throw her down and then throw himself on top of her. Swinging the poker with what strength she could summon, years of hurt and rage and loss. Charlie's scream, the sound of his skin rending. The blood.

And Junior. Junior had been there.

Her phone lay on the nightstand. Laura Beth reached for it, blinking at what the pixels formed on the screen. No messages from Junior or Mama or Juliet. One text from Charlie. Sent from the hospital, he said, telling Laura Beth to get out, they were done, he would take everything she owned. And the date, written in large letters at the top.

Sunday.

There in the quiet house that would have one day become her tomb, Laura Beth wept.

She gathered what clothes could fit into a suitcase and emptied the hidden safe in Charlie's office downstairs, more than enough to get her away. To where, Laura Beth did not know. Yet for the first time she felt as though where didn't matter. Everything felt hers that morning, sun and sky and world. Every place felt like home. She took the stairs down and opened the front door, tilted her face to the wide road beyond. The birds sang of a new day. In the distance, church bells called. To Laura Beth, they sounded like freedom.

## -17-

Juliet had waited at the bench on Evergreen with nothing but her will and what faith she kept to stand in Junior's way. She'd promised Laura Beth to do all she could. Whether that meant lying in the middle of the street or confronting Junior head-on, that was a promise she meant to keep.

But it was Charlie's car rather than Junior's truck that had arrived first, weaving down one side of the road and then the other before whipping into the driveway. Charlie had lumbered out and stumbled inside. The upstairs light had turned on before Junior had even gotten close to the house. It was too late for him.

He'd come out of his truck carrying that shotgun, and Juliet had run. She'd nearly made it to the house when Charlie came out screaming, sparking a few of the neighboring porch lights to life. Juliet had taken to the shadows as Charlie ran past, one hand covering his ruined face as he bellowed into the night. Junior had gone inside. There were no shots, no loud calls. Only light that built from the other side of the window and then burst before fading. Then, minutes later, Junior again, returning to the porch steps where he held his head in his hands and wept. Juliet had wanted to go to him but knew she could not. She'd cut through backyards and gardens to where she'd parked her Volvo and driven to the shop instead, her heart afire with joy and a sadness she could not know.

She pulled the car around to the side street and found the waiting room door open, walked in and turned the lock behind her. Bobby stood in the shop, wiping his hands on a rag. He looked at her and slammed the hood on Bea Campbell's car. As Juliet stepped closer, her eyes caught a

371

glow not unlike what had appeared at the Gowdy home. The crack that had birthed itself inside Bobby's bathroom only a few hours before had now spread, eating away all of the door and half of the wall, its bright heart balanced by black edges that brought a dread she could not stand against.

"It's growing," Bobby said. He whispered the words, as though afraid the timbre of his voice would be enough to rip the world apart. "Shop won't last this Turn."

"Why are you still here?"

He tilted his head at Bea's car. "Had to finish things."

Juliet's heart raced. She backed away from the wall toward Bobby. Her heart raced more. "You can do that tomorrow if tomorrow's what you find."

"No," he said. "Had to be done."

"Laura Beth's gone."

He stopped wiping his hands. "Gone where?"

"Gone," she said again. "I saw it, or at least I think I did. A light like the one you saw from George. Laura Beth stood up to Charlie and now she's gone, Bobby. It worked. Junior tried to stop her, but he couldn't."

"Junior was there?"

"He'll come here next. I locked the door when I came in, but that won't stop him. Mama's put everything on us. You have to go. Now."

But Bobby didn't move. He bent his head and worked the rag through his hands again. "Don't make sense. Laura Beth left as soon as she fixed things."

"Yes."

"But Tommy's still here."

"Where?"

"I don't know. He ran off while I was talking to Carla. I haven't seen him since. You?"

She shook her head. "I was with Laura Beth. You don't think he went to Mama's?"

"Where else'd he go?" He laid the rag on the car. "But that ain't what I mean. If Laura Beth left as soon as she stood up to Charlie, then Tommy should have left as soon as he saved Stacey."

Juliet felt nauseous. "Tommy still has something to fix."

"Or maybe Tommy never talked to Stacey at all."

"Why would he do that?"

"I don't know," Bobby said. "Fear. Or he couldn't find it in himself to care after all this time. That's what got us all here, Juliet. Might be that's what keeps us here, too. Do you have your car?"

"It's around the corner."

"Good. You need to leave. Get to the mountain. Do what you're meant to do."

"I don't . . . Bobby . . ."

"No. Juliet, you can't talk me out of this. It's the only way things can be made right."

"I'm not here to talk you out of this. I'm here to say good-bye."

Bobby's posture loosened. He tilted his head to the side. "You here to tell me good-bye?"

"I'll get everyone out," she said. "Eventually, before it's too late. I have to. I've made my peace with what waits for me at the end. I won't fight it. Faith doesn't mean checking your brain at the door of every church or throwing all you think you know out some stained-glass window. It means trusting. I have to trust now. It's all I have. Going to see Nolan Reynolds is my first test inside the Turn. Letting you go is my last. I won't do the first until it's time, but I'll do the second. Because the truest test for any soul is to be willing to lay down your life for another. I'm going to do that, because I love you and I want to see you safe. I want to see you *well*. Just don't you throw it away, Bobby Barnes. You make me count for some—"

The waiting room door rattled. Bobby stepped in front of her. He opened his mouth to say something when the gun went off, splintering the glass door in a rain of shards that flew inward. He turned, shouting, "Go!" and "Go!" again, pushing Juliet toward the back door. She ran as Junior stepped in, the double barrels of his sawed-off smoking in his hands. Behind him Tommy, looking too frightened to know what was happening, looking like a little boy.

"Get out, Juliet," Bobby shouted.

Junior looked Juliet's way. He caught sight of the wound on the wall and stopped, and in that moment of doubt she slipped away. Juliet pushed at the back door and flung herself into the alley.

There she froze, her escape no escape at all.

# -18-

Bobby shot his hands up and hollered, bringing the shotgun back to him.

"What you doin', Junior?"

Junior came forward, stumbling over what Bobby had left scattered on the floor, wrenches and screwdrivers and a pile of rags, the torn box that had held Bea's new belt. Tommy came as well, tugging at Junior's arm. Junior shrugged it away.

"Come to kill you, Bobby."

"No," Tommy pled. "Mama said you *can't*."

Junior turned and clipped the boy's jaw with the butt of the shotgun, sending Tommy sprawling. Bobby jumped, crying Tommy's name, then stopped when Junior stepped between them. Tommy sat up. Blood oozed from his mouth. Two teeth lay on the floor beside him.

"Where'd she go?" Junior asked. "Juliet?"

"She's gone, Junior. Ain't coming back."

He raised the gun to his cheek. "Reckon you'll have to do for now."

Bobby backed himself against the toolbox and shut his eyes, held his hands in front as if they could stop the buckshot.

The back door opened again, a voice calling, "Junior, you lower that gun this minute."

Bobby opened his eyes. Juliet backed in through the door, her own arms raised. Dorothea trailed behind, holding Junior's pistol.

"You hear what I said, Junior? This isn't how I said for it to go."

Junior swung the shotgun away from Bobby, toward Juliet. She turned and saw the iron aimed at her chest.

"You made Laura Beth go," he said.

"No." Juliet shook her head. "Junior, I didn't. She'd made up her mind already."

He sighted the gun. "You lie. She loved me."

Dorothea put the pistol to Juliet's back, inching her inside. The preacher kept walking even as Dorothea stopped, the gun now heavy in her hand as she beheld the power of the Turn's true God, the splintered wall and the light so beautiful, the black so appalling.

"What have you done, Bobby?" she asked.

"Not me," Bobby said. He watched Juliet come to a stop in the middle of the room, watched Junior and his scattergun.

Sweat dripped down the big man's face, then Bobby realized it wasn't sweat at all. Below them on the floor, Tommy turned toward the clock on the good part of the wall. "Junior, you hear? Juliet didn't have a thing to do with this."

"*Lie.*" Junior gripped the gun harder. "You took her away."

Dorothea tore her eyes from the wall and put Juliet between her and it. She held the pistol out and said, "Junior," in a tone so soft it made him blink. "Not now, son. Now, we talk."

Junior's arm bent.

Dorothea kept the pistol level in her hand until she saw Tommy on the floor. "Tommy? Have mercy, son, what happened to you?"

He said through his hand, "Junior hit me."

"His fault, Mama," Junior said. "Tommy wouldn't stay quiet."

The sight of her boy, Dorothea's youngest, seemed to quell the rage that threatened to explode from within her. Bobby saw that as his only chance.

"Mama," he said. "Let's stop this. There's been enough blood and hurt."

"Yes," she whispered, lips shaking. "Enough. More than enough. No thanks to you. We had heaven here, Bobby. Then you came and turned it to hell. To this." She pointed but would not look at the far wall. "Abomination. And now it's come to this after all. The end of things, or their beginning."

Juliet said, "Mama, please."

Tommy stared at the clock, holding his mouth.

"We're all staying, Bobby. Me and Junior. Tommy, too. He lied when he said he changed things with that drunk of a mother. Why would he go back to Stacey when he has me? Even Juliet says she will remain, assuming Junior doesn't kill her first. The woman you love, choosing us. What does that say about you?"

"Just let me go," Bobby said. "Mama, just let me go then."

"You expect that mercy from me, Bobby Barnes? You have ruined us." She cocked the revolver's trigger and leveled it at Bobby's chest. "'Vengeance is mine, saith the Lord.' I will have mine."

Bobby heard a wet thump over his shoulder. He turned as Junior heaved deep and swayed, the shotgun loose in his hands. His eyes grew round and empty and then disappeared as he fell, thudding against the concrete. Behind him Tommy, a wrench in his hand.

Dorothea's gun moved off target. She shrank back. "Tommy? What did you do?"

"This ain't the way it's supposed to go," he said, the words whistling through the gap in his gums. "This ain't the way any of this is supposed to *go*."

Dorothea raised the pistol. Juliet ran from her place and stood in front of Bobby, who tried pushing her away. In the moment it took for her to move, Dorothea's body shimmered and thinned like the image in an old picture. The pistol clattered to the floor, freed from her gone hand.

"What's happening?" she asked. "Juliet, what's happening to me?"

"It's your Turn," Bobby said. "Time's up, Dorothea."

# -19-

She was there with Bobby and Juliet and Tommy and a tear in heaven she could not explain, Junior lying dead on the ground and the world coming apart. Then came only a moving darkness with neither end nor depth. And after, only Dorothea's reflection in the vanity. She stared at the face, once so strong but now so weak, frightened at how even in heaven there could be loss.

"No," she said. *"NoNoNo."*

Her fist lashed out, shattering the mirror.

And then that great nothing between the worlds, passed through in a blink.

# -20-

"Run," Bobby said, making Juliet pull back from the empty spot on the floor where Dorothea had stood. "Juliet, get out of here. We're running out of time."

"No."

"Go!" he boomed, chasing her away, and Bobby felt his heart shudder at that, what could be their last words. He watched her run. Away from the shop, away from him. She did not look back as she barreled through the back door and into the alley. He kept his eyes to the door as it thundered open and closed, then said, "Come on, Tommy. I have to get you someplace safe. Junior might wake up before his Turn's over, and I don't want you—"

The slow sound of a struggling hand reloading the shotgun stopped him. Bobby turned to see Junior's pockets turned inside out and two barrels pointed at his face, dark moons that jittered in Tommy's hands.

"What are you doing?"

"You cain't leave me, Daddy. I won't let you."

"You put that down." Bobby wouldn't move. One step, one breath, might be enough to scare Tommy into pulling the trigger. Yet the longer they stood there, the more tired Tommy's arms would become, and that might make him pull the trigger faster.

"You know how long I been here, Daddy? How long I waited for you? Longer than you can know. I been here forever. I was here forever before I even found Mama and Junior. They were lost here and didn't even know what was happening until I saved them and made them my family. I had Dorothea for a mama and thought Junior would be my daddy." He looked down at where Junior lay, the man's head seeming to float atop a crimson pool. "But he's too stupid. Junior can't raise no boy to man because he ain't no man. And then George came, but all he ever wanted to do was learn me 'stead of love me. I didn't ever have no daddy till you came, and now you want to *leave*."

Bobby shuffled backward. "What you telling me, you been here forever?" He watched the gun in Tommy's hands, the way it had turned him from frightened boy to frightening other.

*Other.*

"You write those letters," he said. "Tommy? It was you?"

"You got to do what I say, Daddy." Moving closer to where Bobby stood, his eyes narrowed and hard but his hand reaching. "I'm the Lord Almighty and I can hurt you if I want, and I say you ain't leaving. You're supposed to stay here and love me."

"Look over at that wall, Tommy. Them things are going to be everywhere soon. We all got to leave here. This place, whatever it is, it ain't supposed to last."

"So long as I'll be here," Tommy said, "so will my heaven. Because it's *mine*. You and everybody else, you're all *mine*."

"No. Your place ain't here. You got to go back to where you're supposed to be. You got to find a way to live your life."

His mouth twisted to a gory grimace. The gun tilted down. "Ain't nothing for any of us there, Daddy. That's why we come here. To be a family and heal up our wounds."

"You can have family when you get back. You'll get your mama again, Tommy. You'll get her and Dorothea and Juliet and Junior both. You can have them all."

Tommy shook his head. "You as stupid as Junior is? My old mama ain't gonna change. People never do, Daddy. That's what you always say. Dorothea's old. She gets back she'll die, 'cause she won't have heaven no more. Junior ain't got Laura Beth so he'll go shoot Hersey and maybe Sheriff'll shoot *him*. Juliet, she'll be a preacher again. Dorothea's a rich old woman and Juliet's got respect 'cause her job and Junior ain't nothing but a weed smoker and I'm just a poor boy. Won't nobody let us come together like we are here. We all gotta stick to our own kind in the old world. Ain't none a y'all my kind, and I ain't none a yours."

"That ain't true," Bobby said, though he knew it was. "They love you, Tommy."

"Would I have you?" Tommy asked. "If I left, would you be in tomorrow with me?"

Bobby gritted his teeth. In a life full of lies, he settled finally for the truth. "I can't promise that."

Blood trickled from the corner of Tommy's mouth. He winced, chasing the tears, and raised the gun again.

"Go on," Bobby said. "Go on if you got to, but you hurry up before I snatch that scattergun and beat you with it. You want me to be your daddy? Show you how to be a man? Well, it starts right here. You ain't never gonna get all you want. None of us do. We get dreams that turn to dust and work our whole lives only to find nothing at the end but bodies and hearts plumb wore out, and that's the price we pay for the living we do. We're flesh and blood in a world of thorns and teeth, boy. We're *made* to hurt. Point ain't to turn back and run away, point's to keep going. Keep going till you can't go no more. Least then you can lay down to your final rest and do it clean. I love you, Tommy. With all you said and done, I love you. So I guess all that's left is whether you hate me enough to put me down, or you love me enough to let me live."

# -21-

Juliet tried Bobby's cell again. Again, there was no answer. She laid the phone on the seat beside her and ran a hand through her hair. Thinking something was wrong, something else had happened, and when Bobby had needed her most, she had run away. She considered turning back and wondered what good that would do, her being that far into the hills and close to the mountain. Juliet had never turned back before. She had faced the end of her Turn as dutifully as was required and never wavered, seeing it first as a punishment for transgression and then, later, as the final end of her life's choices. Dorothea may have been wrong about a great many things, but she was right about one: there was a balance, and upsetting that balance could bring only hurt.

But she would hurt for Bobby. Even now that felt ridiculous, wanting to save the man who would kill her, yet Juliet had come to accept that life was nothing but a series of contradictions. Bobby would live on. He would face the consequences of his act upon that mountain curve and pay the price of men, and Bobby might in the end find the grace he had so long sought. He would perhaps find a rest, and with that a desire to gather the broken pieces of his life and create something noble and good. Though Juliet believed herself just as broken as any who lived in the world, she also believed herself ready to face her end. She would see the others home and pay her visit to Nolan Reynolds, speak her heart as she would be led. Then she would take her final trip to the curve and kneel before the throne of God, and He would welcome her into His arms.

It was not a good end, she supposed, nor as bad as any other. As foolish as it was to hold to a future she and Bobby could have shared in some other part of time's river, Juliet could not help but embrace a sense of loss, as if something had been stolen from her that she had never possessed. Yet everything she had prayed and worked for would come to naught if something had happened to Bobby back at the shop. If Junior had awakened or Mama come back, if they had killed him, Bobby would be granted no second chance at all.

Juliet braked, hoping there was still time. She threw the gear into reverse when her phone rang. She grabbed it and pushed the button, talking before the phone had even reached her ear.

"Bobby?"

"Where you at?"

"Turning around to find you."

"No," he said. "Keep going. I can't take any more risk of messing this up. This is my only chance."

"What happened? I've been calling and calling. Did Junior—"

"No. Junior'll be fine, I left him on the floor. It was Tommy. He tried to stop me."

"Why?"

"He says we all have to be a family. Juliet, those letters Dorothea gets. They're from him."

"Tommy?" She put a hand to her mouth. "How can that be?"

"He's been here a lot longer than we all thought, even before Dorothea. That's how he knew so much about what people did, how he could know where to put a stupid penny on the sidewalk that would end up killing Jake. And I know why it was Jake. I told Tommy the sheriff always gave me a hard time. He ain't no kid, Juliet. Tommy is *old*. He could've been in the Turn close to always for all we know. Maybe he's grown some or gotten rid of a few freckles, no one would notice him changing. Because he was always Tommy, just a boy."

Juliet leaned back in the seat, stunned. Tommy. All along, the Lord of the Turn had been among them, had sat and played and eaten with them, learning their secrets. Playing Dorothea against George and Junior against herself, sneaking, manipulating them all.

"The letter about Tommy's mother," she said. "He wrote that himself?"

"George told me all that came out when the family was fighting. I guess Tommy found out about Stacey a long time ago and figured that would be a good way to bring everybody together again—comfort a mourning little boy."

"How did you get away?"

"I gave him a choice. Shoot me or let me go. He let me go. I left him crying in the shop." Bobby sniffled and then coughed. "Hardest thing I've ever done. I didn't know he loved me that much. I didn't know I loved him the same. Are you driving?"

"Yes." She put the Volvo in gear and spun the wheel, inching back up the mountain. "I'm almost to the sign."

"Good. I'm a few miles behind. Just keep driving. Next

Turn, you find Tommy. I'm sure he'll be at Dorothea's. It's going to be dangerous for you now, Juliet."

"It won't. I'm all they'll have now, Bobby. They won't harm me. It might take time, but I'll get them away."

She turned left at the stop sign. A few more miles, some hundreds of turns on the tires. All living was a circle.

"I'm not mad," she said. "I was, but not anymore. I know you have to do this. I want you to. But you need to promise me that the man I met here will be the man who returns to the world, no matter what happens. Because that man is good. That man is decent. That man isn't afraid anymore. You didn't change things just to leave. You can say that if you want, I know the truth. You changed because that's who you are now, Bobby."

A long silence. The road fell on, hills and dips and a million trees shadowed in light, the bad moon rising.

"Is it too late for me?" he asked.

"It's never too late."

"I'm drunk, Juliet." His voice sounded a small thing, frail and frightened, the words of one set upon a path to darkness. "I thought I had the courage, but I didn't. I don't know what's going to happen and I can't face it alone. I had to see my boys again. One more time, in case it's the last."

The wheel turned in Juliet's hands. She hung on, tried a final time to keep going. The car moved to the shoulder. She pressed the gas. The car slowed. The U-turn at the end of the curve, right in the blind spot where she never should have been. A mile up or a mile back and maybe none of this would have ever happened, before or again. One mistake that rippled out and out, touching all.

"You can face it, Bobby. You just have to be brave. Live there with what you found here, the good and the bad."

He sniffed again. No laugh followed. Juliet stared into

the darkness at the curve's edge. The car stalled. She pulled on the door handle, beat the windows. Cursed her life and Bobby's and all she would never do.

"I didn't leave," Bobby said. "After Carla. That was the last thing I thought I had to change, but it isn't. There's one more, Juliet."

Her fist banged the window a final time and rested there, her skin cool against the glass. "What do you mean?"

"Fixing things. That's what I'm doing. I got no choice but to be on this curve, Juliet. This curve's all my life comes down to, where all the choices I ever made come to a point I can't run away from. But I can choose *how* I meet it. Do you understand? I never thought I had a choice in anything, but I got a choice in this. That first night in the shop with Tommy, I tried staying away from this mountain. That was wrong, but I learned something from it. I learned I got to be here, but how I come's up to me."

"Bobby, what are you *saying*?"

"I'm keeping you safe."

"No. Bobby, *no*. What did you do?"

"'Greater love hath no man than this, that a man lay down his life for his friends.' I remember that. I remember more, always have. Only difference now's I believe it."

"Bobby?" Her voice louder, almost shouting. "What are you doing, Bobby?"

"I don't know how it will be. I don't know if you'll meet me here again every Turn. But you'll see tomorrow, Juliet. Don't listen to what they tell you of me. Remember who I was here. Who I am. Remember I love you."

Headlights against the trees.

"Save them," he said. "Save them and get home and then save others. Save them like you saved me."

The line cut, the lights brighter, sharpening from wide to narrow against an engine sound. Juliet let the phone drop from her hand as those headlights rounded the turn, aiming at her. She cried for him and loved him back in the seconds before impact, a prayer upon her last breath.

# -22-

Junior arrived that Turn earlier than he'd ever before. Dorothea watched him from the window and stepped out onto the porch as he parked in the drive. She did not wave as he got out. Four plastic bags of groceries crowded his arms. Junior announced he was hungry.

She told him to take them on inside. He placed the bags on the long kitchen counter and then aimed himself toward the gathering room. Halfway to the hall, he turned back and kissed Dorothea's cheek. Junior didn't say he loved her. Dorothea didn't ask if he did. She knew it, just as she knew love had grown a sour thing to him now. She pulled what he'd brought from the bags and balled them up into the trash. Lining the counter were two boxes of cornflakes, a gallon of whole milk, one jar of pickles, three fruit cups, and a bag of potatoes. Of all the despair heaven had given her, that sight cut deepest into Dorothea's heart. She would have to make do now, at least for a time. Laura Beth was gone; Junior would have to be the one to go to the store.

He reappeared in the doorway holding one of Hubert's bottles.

"Can't see a proper breakfast in all this, Junior. I expect I'll have to start calling you for what I need before you leave the trailer. That or we'll junk-food ourselves to death."

He didn't say there was no such thing as death in heaven. Junior didn't say anything at all, only tilted the bottle to his lips and took a long swallow.

The front door opened and shut. Dorothea heard Tommy's feet playing across the wood floor and his voice calling her name in a way that sounded fearful, as if he'd discovered she had left as well. His mouth reversed itself from down to up when he came into the kitchen and saw them. He hugged Dorothea first and then Junior, who took another drink and did not otherwise move as Tommy pressed into the fat of his belly.

* * *

The three of them sat to a breakfast of cereal and mashed potatoes. Dorothea watched as Tommy sank his spoon into the steaming lump on his plate and ate. He hummed as he did, tapping his feet on the floor and moving his head side to side. She'd decided that to him, the previous Turn had never happened. It was like Tommy had washed his memories clean of Bobby and Laura Beth and George and Juliet, as though he had somehow found a Turn inside the Turn to claim as all his own. Junior stared at his bowl. He'd poured milk to the brim. Drops spilled over the side, pooling on the tablecloth. Dorothea watched the cornflakes swell and sink below the surface. She looked out the open window to the sidewalk, wondering where Juliet was and if the preacher would come again, wondering what she would do if Juliet did.

"I kill Hersey," Junior said. "Did this Turn and all the rest. Shoot him in the chest."

Dorothea would not look at him.

"I'm sorry I walloped you in the shop, Junior," said Tommy. "It don't still hurt, does it?"

Junior didn't say either way.

The phone rang. Their heads went toward the sound, each of them knowing who that must be. Dorothea wiped her clean mouth with her napkin and rose.

"You ain't gotta answer, Mama," Tommy told her. "It won't upset the balance."

The machine picked up. No message. Dorothea sat back down and thought maybe the balance had been upset already, not here in the Turn but long before, a fork along time's great river she'd either drifted into or found on purpose. She thought about that far-back day after Hubie's death when she'd ventured from the yellow house alone for the first time and had nearly gotten run over by that truck, how she had passed through its lingering shadow. How awful that had been, knowing that her life could be taken from her in a single careless blink. And then she thought of standing on that corner once more. Daring life as all those in town dared it each day, standing in the shadow of death and yet somehow still finding cause to laugh and dance and love.

Tommy asked, "What's wrong, Mama?"

"Nothing, dear."

"I got your letter from the box," he said. "You didn't go out?"

"No. Thought maybe I'd just let it sit there."

"You can't do that, Mama. Lord wants to talk to you, you got to listen. That's what you always say."

She watched as Tommy leaned forward in the chair and produced the envelope, her name typed across the center. Junior pushed his bowl away, spilling half the milk.

"You should read it," Tommy said. "Bet it's good."

Dorothea felt her chest rise and fall.

Tommy grinned. "Can I?"

"That's fine, Tommy."

He ripped the side of the envelope and pulled the letter out, unfolding it on the table. Speaking slowly, the way George had taught him: "'Do not be afraid. More will come. Heaven is big and your family will be big. There will be others like Bobby and Laura Beth and George. There always have been and always will. Just love each other like I love you.'"

Tommy smiled. "See? You ain't got to be so sad, Mama."

*But I am*, she thought. *Oh, Tommy, I am and so are you. So are all of us.*

"Can you please pass the taters, Mama?"

She did. Tommy thanked her and said they were fine, the best ever. He plunged his spoon in as Junior sat cold and still. Dorothea stared beyond the window again. Outside was sun and birds and the world going by. In the distance, thunder rolled.

## -23-

The call came just after midnight that Sunday morning, dialed by a frightened teenager who along with a dozen others had gone looking for a place to drink. Jake dressed and kissed his wife and called to the rescue squad and fire department, summoning every vehicle and able man. He arrived to a world of shadow and flashing lights at the curve on Ridge Road some miles west of the stop sign.

Everything was just as he'd been told. The teens, all of whom had been herded away from the wreck for Jake to question, looked on in stricken horror. A mass of firemen and squad members worked the opposite side of the road, where the thick trees dropped off toward the valley. Engines and generators whirred the lights set up to brighten the night. Another crew worked the mangled vehicle that had been spun into the trees along the road's left lane. Jake walked there first, stepping through a sea of glass and twisted metal, lowering the brim of his hat to mutter a curse.

One of the men broke off and walked his way. He wore a blue uniform that clashed with his pale face and wiped his mouth as he said, "Bad, Jake. Have to cut the car apart, but we can take our time. Victim's dead."

*Victim.*

"I take a look?" Jake asked.

"Ain't pretty, but come on."

Aside from the tires it was almost impossible to know this had once been a working vehicle, engine and all. The entire front end had folded in upon itself, the windows smashed, the road there slick from gas and oil. The body inside sat motionless, two hands still on the wheel. A stench of blood and death hung in the air. Jake stepped forward and squatted down, tilted his hat back. He stared into the dead eyes of Bobby Barnes.

The passenger seat had been pinned to the dash, a beer can wedged between them. Others lay scattered in the back and along the road.

"Told me today he quit."

"Don't look like it," the man said. "Safe to say he was sauced when it happened. Knew it would someday. We all did."

Jake stood up and breathed deep. He looked across the road. "What about the other? You get an ID, recognize the car?"

"Volvo. Only one I know 'round here belongs to that woman preacher."

"Juliet Creech," Jake said. "She alive?"

"Might be. Car's pretty far down into the trees, and it's steep. We're still trying to get men down there. Don't look near as bad's this one here. Them Volvos, they're right stout."

They looked back to Bobby, though only for a moment. Jake couldn't bear a longer take. The mangled metal that had become Bobby's tomb lay twisted into angles that seemed almost impossible. The impact must have been horrible. The force must have killed him before the steering wheel had even caved in his chest.

"Don't get it," the man said. "You know whose car this is, Jake?"

"Bea Campbell's. Bobby was working on it."

"Why in the world Bobby have Bea's car up here? He'd've been drivin' that truck a his, he'd still be alive." He spat a stream of tobacco juice onto the pavement. "Usually the drunks is what lives and the ones they smash into's dead. Now the world's down one heathen and gained a preacher. What they call that? Karma?"

Jake's phone rang. He pulled it from his pocket and checked the number, said, "This is Jake."

"Sheriff?" came the cry. "This is Anna. Anna Grimm? I just got home and found my George. He's dead."

"Anna? You sure?"

"He's *dead*, Jake. I found him lying outside and he's *dead* and I don't know what to do."

"Okay, Anna." Jake took off his hat, wiped the sweat from his head. "You just hang on now. I'm stuck up here at a wreck but I'm gonna send a squad truck straightaway, all right? I'm gonna call Kate, too, get her out there. Now, you just stay calm. Anna?"

The line clicked off. Jake lowered the phone and said,

"I need a truck down to George Grimm's place. Anna came home and found him dead."

The man winced and lowered his head. "George? Taught me in school. I'll take these men here. Bobby ain't goin' nowhere. Gonna be one of those days, Jake. Sometimes feels like they last forever."

Jake knelt again. He took a final look at what remained and shook his head slowly. It was a final insult, he believed, seeing Bobby like that. Seeing that smile on his dead face, as though Bobby had glimpsed glory in his dying breath.

"Damn you," Jake whispered. "Damn you right to hell."

# -24-

She woke with her head down and Bobby's words echoing in her ears, his voice charged with fear, saying over the sound of the wind that she would see tomorrow and to save the rest as she had saved him. Before she could say no, her eyes had shut and opened again.

The room was quiet, warmed by the morning sun through the window. Juliet lifted her head from the piles of paper on her desk—overdue bills and a tally of worshippers and tithes from a long-forgotten Sunday, an anonymous note decrying the sorry state of the flower beds out front. And her notes, three pages of handwritten scrawl, long paragraphs and underlined phrases, lying next to her Bible, opened to the book of James, chapter 3, verse 1. It may have been a fine sermon, her last. Now she vowed there would be finer ones, and more.

Down the street, the clock tower tolled eight. Juliet called Mama's, listening as the phone rang and rang and the voice said, "No one is available at this time, please leave a message." She hung up and balled her notes, tossing them into the plastic trash can in the corner.

* * *

Bobby's shop was gone. In its place lay a small patch of concrete and weeds. Those who passed were polite but aloof. Juliet asked none of them about Bobby or the place that had once been his home. They would have seen no light and no darkness, no wound, would have only said both the shop and the man had been taken in the tornado years before. Perhaps they never would have heard of Bobby Barnes at all.

She walked on, eyes pointed at a sky of deep blue. He had taken Bea's car. All that time, Juliet had believed Bobby selfish. Now she knew what she had taken as self-love had in fact been a love for them all.

A love for her.

One step and then another, over the bridge and past the spot where Moser's barn had once stood. She wanted to try Dorothea again but decided no. There would be time yet. Time to save them and take them home. Take herself home. Mama was the key. If Mama decided to go, then so would Junior, and Mama finding out just who'd been the Lord she'd served all this while might be enough. She'd get Mama away and then Junior. Tommy would have no family left. She'd say they could leave together, she'd meet him in that bright tomorrow and they'd go to church together, her and him and Stacey.

Juliet would do it for Dorothea and Junior and Tommy, for the Lord she loved, but perhaps she would do it for Bobby more. To honor not the life he lived, but the man he became.

393

# -25-

Darkness.

This void with no end, silent and consuming. A night so thick he feels it crushing him, feels it ooze into his ears and nose and the wide mouth he opens to scream, drowning him in a waterless grave.

The name *Juliet* in his mind and his heart as a sound not far but near trickles through the nothingness. A hungry sound, predatory, made by something or somethings with eyes enough to see and teeth enough to rip and tear and devour.

*Juliet.*

His lungs filling with oil. Choking on this, the end he deserves and the end every life warrants, to dwell in this empty place, wander with the monsters. He reaches with his hands and grasps nothing, kicks against the blackness. Crying to be saved from what he could never save himself from, so much lost and surrendered that he had neither sought nor claimed again, the Turn a mirror and this a mirror as well, showing him the vacuum of his last years. His body goes from rigid to limp. Shapes slither past in blotches darker than dark.

And in these first moments of eternity, a star.

A prick of light in the distance that grows and widens, a light so pure as to shine blue and so bright it illumines the very corners of the void, chasing what dwells there. It enfolds him in its glow like a blanket, like a worn shirt clean and shaped to the contours of his own body. The light breaks over a land drenched in splendor, thick forests and fields of emerald grass and golden wheat, and below him stretches a river wide and crystal that flows to a shining city on a distant hill. And upon that water wooden vessels of every kind, each holding a single person, their hands upon rudders as a great flow carries them on. Some he sees moving swiftly, some slowly. More toward the shallow shores while others keep to the river's center, where the waters run deep. And still others, caught in tiny eddies that turn them in slow circles, holding them there. Their faces blank, bodies still, and yet all keep their eyes to that great city, searching and either finding or searching still.

At the river's bend lies a bridge that leads to the city gates. Multitudes cast their anchors to shore and multitudes sail past, and those whose feet settle upon solid ground are welcomed and embraced. Their worn rags are exchanged for robes of light, and in their nakedness he knows them. He sees the pious and the good and the faithful, their bodies plump and smooth as they are adorned, faces glad and tilted to a sunless light and adoration upon their lips. He sees the scars of those poor and broken and hated, the downcast and castoff, the different and the abandoned. Sees their mangled skin, rough and filthy, and how their steps from river to land are labored and laden. They weep at their welcoming, joy and belonging that come as tears like bits of light that flash and are no more. They take their robes and that wide path upward, racing past the easy procession of the holy, dancing as they go, leaping and shouting, their voices carrying as wind through chimes, and he, too, begins to dance. He leaps and runs and calls out, shedding the rags upon him for raiment that will never wear or dull. The city gates lie wide and welcoming. Trumpets call and voices sing and he knows now this is home, home is a place and was never truly far away. His heart carries him. Above the din and celebration he hears the music of laughter, tiny feet running and the call of two voices.

Shouting his name.

Shouting, "Daddy!"

# DISCUSSION QUESTIONS

1. The reality of time is a primary theme in this story, as well as the idea that time does not always move in a straight line from past to present to future. Do you agree with this notion? Why or why not?

2. Juliet asserts that they have all reached the Turn through various forms of apathy. Whether by means of fear or personal circumstances, each character has in some way "given up" on his or her life. In what ways does the Turn mirror what happens in our own lives when apathy takes hold?

3. Many of the characters have come to decide for themselves what the Turn actually is. For Dorothea and Tommy, it is heaven. For Laura Beth, hell. To Juliet it is a pause in order to right some future wrong, whereas George believes the Turn is nothing so metaphysical at all. Which of these views do you believe most closely describes the truth of their situation?

4. For many of the characters, past events play a large part in why they have reached the Turn. How important are our pasts in shaping our futures? Is there any way to truly escape the things we've done, or are we constantly influenced by them for good or bad?

5. Though proven wrong in the end about the stability of a place she believes eternal, Dorothea takes a great amount of comfort in the fact that the Turn never changes. There are no surprises, no impending tragedies. It's merely a constant stream of the same day. Would there be a value in living such an existence? Would it provide a true sense of peace and safety, or merely the appearance of those things?

6. One aspect of the Turn that Bobby finds most appealing is that things are reset at the stroke of each midnight. What advantages would be found in this? What would be lost?

7. In many ways, this story is Tommy's as much as Bobby's. Tommy was first to the Turn and the author of the letters Dorothea receives in her mailbox. No one works harder than him to keep everyone together, believing they are a family. Do you agree that is what Tommy, Dorothea, Bobby, Juliet, Laura Beth, George, and Junior were? What makes a family, and what doesn't?

8. An argument could be made that regardless of what the Turn truly is, it was created at least in part by the characters themselves and the choices each made or refused to make. Is there a parallel here to our own lives? Do we all in some way create the very monsters we grow to hate?

# ACKNOWLEDGMENTS

I don't know how it works for everyone else, but the characters always come first for me. Not the theme or the plot or "the inciting incident" or any other fancy term you read about in all those books that tell you how to write a story. People. The people always come first. And if I stick with them long enough, get out of the way so they start speaking on their own, those people often become very real to me. So real, in fact, that there have been times when I've turned around at the BP out on Route 340 and sworn I've just caught a glimpse of Junior getting bait out of the cooler. I've seen George down at the post office and passed Bobby in his big red Dodge, talking to people I can't see. I've watched Tommy walking alone on the sidewalk along Main Street.

Such is the novelist's life, I suppose—one lived for much of the time in the cobwebs of our own thoughts. Yet for every imaginary person who sticks by my side, there are at least two (and most times more) very real people who do the same. Daisy Hutton, Amanda Bostic, Jodi Hughes, and Elizabeth Hudson are among the brightest folks in publishing—I think of you all and smile. My agent, Claudia Cross—I see grand things ahead. My thanks to Kathy Richards, who concerns herself with website themes and code so I can keep fountain pen ink on my hands. And most of all, thanks to my wife and children—you guys keep the stories coming.

*The Blue Ridge Mountains*
*Christmas, 2015*

# ABOUT THE AUTHOR

Photograph by Joanne Coffey

BILLY COFFEY'S critically acclaimed books combine rural Southern charm with a vision far beyond the ordinary. He is a regular contributor to several publications, where he writes about faith and life. Billy lives with his wife and two children in Virginia's Blue Ridge Mountains.

\* \* \*

Visit him at www.billycoffey.com.
Facebook: billycoffeywriter
Twitter: @billycoffey